# THE
# BOOST

———

## STEPHEN
## BAKER

**TOR®**

A TOM DOHERTY ASSOCIATES BOOK I NEW YORK

This is a work of fiction. All of the characters, organizations, and events portrayed in this novel are either products of the author's imagination or are used fictitiously.

THE BOOST

Copyright © 2014 by Stephen Baker

All rights reserved.

A Tor Book
Published by Tom Doherty Associates, LLC
175 Fifth Avenue
New York, NY 10010

www.tor-forge.com

Tor® is a registered trademark of Tom Doherty Associates, LLC.

ISBN 978-0-7653-6986-4

Tor books may be purchased for educational, business, or promotional use. For information on bulk purchases, please contact the Macmillan Corporate and Premium Sales Department at 1-800-221-7945, extension 5442, or write to specialmarkets@macmillan.com.

First Edition: May 2014
First Mass Market Edition: May 2015

Printed in the United States of America

0 9 8 7 6 5 4 3 2 1

*To my three sons, Aidan, Jack, and Henry*

# ACKNOWLEDGMENTS

First, a tip of my hat to my lifelong friend Antonio Sanz. After reading *Final Jeopardy,* he came up with the concept for this novel.

The epicenter of this story is the border between El Paso and Ciudad Juárez. On my first visit there, Thaddeus Herrick picked me up at the airport, drove me over to Juárez, and bought me a beer at the Kentucky Club. For that, he has my lasting thanks. It didn't hurt that a bit later he introduced me to my future wife, Jalaire.

My thanks also to IBM's Watson team, headed by David Ferrucci, for the patient one-year tutorial in artificial intelligence and machine learning. And I'll always appreciate the help from Christophe Bisciglia and Eric Schmidt at Google for their help in understanding where cloud computing was heading.

My agent, Jim Levine, helped immensely in the development of the book, with plenty of help from Kerry Sparks, Beth Fisher, and Tim Wojcik. And many thanks to Bob Gleason at Tor Books for buying the book, Kelly Quinn for shepherding it through the editorial process, and Susannah Noel for the copyedit.

Finally, thanks to my friends and family who read and helped edit the manuscript. They include Alexis Romay, Dan Neely, David Rocks, Steve Hamm, Philip and Laurel Schmidt, Claire Schmidt, Jay Greene, Peter Elstrom, and Geoffrey Wright. Rochelle Howe gets a special copyediting badge.

Eventually you'll have the implant, where if you think about a fact, it will just tell you the answer.

—LARRY PAGE, cofounder of Google, 2004

# THE
# BOOST

# INTRODUCTION

**9:02 a.m. Central Standard Time**

"The way you talk, I can tell you're wild," she says.

He has just awoken. From DC to the Mississippi he slept like a corpse. He stirred briefly to glimpse down at the mighty river, and then fell into another long nap. Now he pauses, trying to collect his thoughts. Their burnt orange Sheng-li is driving itself west along a lonely stretch of I-40. Oklahoma scenery flies past their windows at a constant 97 miles per hour.

"How far to El Paso?" he asks.

"You see?"

"See what?"

"Only a wild person would need to ask."

He shakes his head slightly, and tugs at the rim of his red baseball cap, a relic with a stretched-out P on the front. "How far is it?"

"830 miles."

"When do we get there?"

"3:31, if we're going downtown, 3:33 to the Stanton Street Bridge, 3:33 to Cielo Vista Mall, 3:54 to—"

"All right, I get the picture."

With a blink of her blue eyes, she snaps back from her processor, or "boost."

"I know you've gone wild, Ralf, because I'm not getting anything from you at all."

He shrugs. Without subtitles her words make noise and then vanish.

She asks, "Is it gone?"

He looks away from her, out the window to the south, at the rusted remains of oil derricks and the gray hills stretching to the horizon. They'll head west to the Rio Grande, then turn left, following the river to the border, which divides El Paso from Ciudad Juárez, the notorious outpost of the wild in North America. He knows these facts and needs no geotags to guide him. The unlabeled scenery looks blank, like a face without eyes.

He listens to the wind whistling past the car, the hum of the hydrogen engine. That's all he hears. No videos, no soundtrack. He hears himself breathing, as if for the first time. He knows they'll get to El Paso sometime after three. Ellen said so. But he has no idea what time it is and has nothing to tell him. People used to wear wristwatches or look at the screens of their cell phones. But once the processors moved into the heads, clocks slowly disappeared, along with computers and televisions and telephones, and all the other machinery that he remembers piling up in his grandparents' basement. That's all in the head now, he thinks. But not in mine.

He looks at Ellen. With a couple of wardrobe commands, she has turned her pullover to gold and her skin-tight leggings to black, with deep blue highlights. They shine like the feathers of a raven. She's staring straight ahead, living in her boost. He knows she's been spending hours on end in virtual Rome with a college friend of hers, checking out Etruscan art. But by the way she's shifting her weight in the seat and moving her lips, he wonders if she's having sex. If so, is it with him? Ellen has the face of a Greek goddess. It's the Artemis line: a perfect oval surrounded by wavy golden hair, the nose slightly turned up at the end. Her lips move slightly, as if trying out sentences. They look like parentheses drawn by a sharp red pencil. Ellen is his processor now.

"What time is it?" he asks.

# PART I

---

# EL PASO

# ONE

Ralf's memory is shot. His whole life, he has been considered a prodigy of the digital world. But the detailed time-tagged images, the videos, notes, links, they're all gone. All that remains is the wet brain, where memories, if you can call them that, well up in pools of appetites, regrets, and desires. He can fish out only snippets of conversation. The blurry pictures he summons seem to change and fade. They're not distinct images: more like ideas with ghostlike transparencies hovering over them. It's a sorry excuse for a brain, he thinks. There's good reason people like him are called wild.

He tries to dredge up memories from his last full day in Washington. That would be . . . day before yesterday? He isn't sure, and doesn't want to ask Ellen. He remembers sitting at breakfast with Ellen in their second-story apartment in the Mount Pleasant neighborhood, just two blocks up from the zoo. The last specks of snow were melting from the branches across the street, but spring was still a good month away. He was sipping a protein blend and flipping through college basketball highlights in his boost, when a message popped up from Suzy. "Have to talk."

He messaged back. "Talk talk?"

"Face to face."

They agreed to meet for coffee at the Taizhou Tower, near Dupont Circle, and Ralf hurried out to his bike.

Ten minutes later he was sitting across from Suzy, blowing warm air onto his frigid hands. She looked just like Ellen, but a half foot taller. Instead of wavy shoulder-length hair, the standard Artemis style, she kept just a hint of blond fuzz on her skull. Suzy carefully dipped a corner of her scone into her steaming glass of greenish tea. She greeted him with a nod. He messaged her: "What's up?"

She frowned and shook her head. "I meant 'talk,'" she said.

Ralf sat up straight in his chair and coughed. He found face-to-face conversations awkward and he tried, whenever possible, to sidestep them. He nodded, looked at Suzy's eyes, and quickly shifted his focus a few milli-meters down, to the less threatening terrain around the bridge of her exemplary nose.

Over the next few minutes, Suzy whispered across the table to him, the old-fashioned way, laying out the issues. Ever since Suzy's arrival, earlier in the year, they'd been working closely in the chip lab at the Department of Health and Human Services, overseeing the annual pro-cessor updates. Every year, some 430 million Americans wake up one day in the middle of March feeling different, smarter, snappier. Some inevitably complain that they've lost memories or have to concentrate harder to send messages. Some say they notice more ads popping up, or soundtrack music that's hard to mute. But most are satisfied. Their heads work better.

Preparing for the updates is a long process. A few months before the scheduled date, the code comes in from China. A technical panel reviews the changes, and draws up a summary for the Senate subcommittee and the White House. Once the design is approved—largely a formality—the chip is divided into a dozen segments, so that no single person has access to the entire architecture. This is Suzy's first cycle. She's a junior staffer on segment 3, which is mostly data storage, along with other odds and ends. Ralf heads up the all-important segment 4, which runs communications, including six different radio signals and the vital interface to the wet brain.

This year, the country is scheduled to receive the update on March 16. If it goes smoothly, the process will begin with the general population, followed by Congress and the Supreme Court, the vice president and the cabinet, and finally the president. Then, presumably, the country will be on firm cognitive footing for the next year.

Suzy asked Ralf, as he waited for his coffee, to take a look at one of the gates, 318 Blue, in his segment. She had its counterpart in hers, and had found an anomaly. He called it up in his boost, and saw, to his shock, that 318 Blue was wide open.

She didn't have to say another word. Ralf knew. The Chinese were updating the chip with a version of their domestic software. Its surveillance gate was open for both communications and data. What Ralf didn't understand—and still doesn't—is how Suzy Claiborne spotted the anomaly. She was new to the department and often asked him questions that a sophomore comp-sci student could answer. She was perhaps the last person Ralf would have expected to notice an open gate.

As Ralf looks back, the rest of that day is a blur. The details are lost with his boost. But he remembers the general outlines and can bring back fragments of the day, each one wrapped in the animal blend of emotions and physical sensations, chiefly nausea and jangling nerves.

His idea, he recalls, was to upload Suzy's segment into his head, match the two sections, and figure out commands to close the gate. Otherwise, as he saw it, companies would have free run in everyone's boost. They could mine lifetimes of memories. Experts had been declaring privacy dead for decades, but this would obliterate the last vestiges of it.

Ralf was a hacker, had always been one. He knew he could close the gate. He felt he had to. He can still picture Suzy, standing over him as he locked his bike across from the frozen Botanic Pagota on the Mall, whispering that his plan was "reckless."

"If you didn't expect me to do something," he messaged her, "why'd you loop me in?" But even as she complained, she transferred her segment file onto his boost, and he was busy exploring it as they made their way into HHS and climbed the stairs to the lab. In the file he could see the open gates.

While Ralf knew that carrying Suzy's data was risky, he hardly expected to be nabbed the very first day. His messages, like anyone's, could be intercepted, but the surveillance gates in his own boost were locked down, at least as far as he knew.

Minutes after he reached the office, two uniformed security guards hustled him out of the building. Ralf remembers that his colleagues turned their heads from him, as if embarrassed. He felt ashamed. He remembers wondering why one of the guards had grabbed his dirty green gym bag.

Next thing he knew, he was stretched out on a hospital bed in a white room. The sheets on the bed were rumpled. The curtains on the small window high above the bed looked like rags. Smudged on the wall above the sink was a single footprint, far too large to be Ralf's. The sound in his head, if you could call it that, was the solitary hum of consciousness. He had never felt so alone. He summoned his mapping function to see where he was. Nothing came up. Just the same hum. He called up his messaging. Nothing. Ralf felt a surge of panic. He thrashed, and knocked a metal tray from the side of the bed, sending bits of debris falling to the floor. He looked down and saw the tray lying on his gym bag. He felt soreness on the side of his head. He reached up and touched a bandage.

They had ripped out his chip. For Ralf, whose boost had been installed on his first birthday, this amounted to a lobotomy. He was wild. For the first time he could remember, at least with the remaining hunk of brain in his head, he cried.

He remembers hearing explosions, and wondering if it was thundering outside. Then a young Asian man came into his room. The sculpted arms and shoulders of a body builder seemed to burst from his tight white T-shirt. He had a primitive twentieth-century look to him, unenhanced. He didn't say anything, but simply placed his hands on Ralf's shoulders, sat him up, reached down for Ralf's gym bag, zipped it closed and handed it to him. Then, still without a word, he placed a firm grip on Ralf's elbow and led him out of the clinic to the street. He stayed in the doorway and waved good-bye.

Ralf didn't know where he was or what to do. If his boost had been in place and working, dozens of streams of information would be informing him, orienting him, messaging, carrying out thousands of risk scenarios, in short, making him aware. He would have figured things out. But as a brain-surgery patient, recently sequestered and newly wild, he walked in a fog.

He made his way down a tree-lined street and came to an esplanade with an Alexandria Metro stop he recognized. King Street/Old Town. He considered taking the Metro back to the Mall, where he'd left his bike. But he couldn't pay for a ticket without a credit beam from his chip. As a wild man, he was broke.

He would walk. Without geotags, even that was a challenge. He wondered which way to go and got no directions. The only signal coming from his wet brain was the same gentle hum, with no data, no meaning. He was full of questions but powerless to answer them.

He looked at the February sun, low in the southern sky, and took off for the north. In time he felt hungry, but found no signals leading him toward food. He was on his own. He wanted to see Ellen, and to hug her. But he could not message her. He dug into his ancient memory for her whereabouts and came up empty.

He remembers the crunching sound and feel of his footsteps on gravel as he walked north from Alexandria, across the Potomac, and back to his bike. Were they watching him as he walked?

Are they following us now? He turns around and looks out the back window of the car.

"You're not going to see anything back there," Ellen says. "This isn't a movie from 2010."

He peers up, through the windshield. "If any drones are following us," she says, "they're no bigger than bees. They might even look like bees. Kind of useless to look for them." Though Ellen's an artist, she's up to date on spy gadgets. Some of her contract work for the Pentagon includes drone design, which on occasion she incorporates into her leggings and blouses.

Ralf sits back. He's small, dark and wiry, with deep-set violet eyes and black hair that curls around his ears. He's good-looking, to such a degree that his mother convinced him to avoid all of the enhancements they were offering in middle school. He contemplates human beauty, and pictures Ellen without the Artemis package. That reminds him of Suzy, which in turn reminds him once again of the fix he's in. Funny, he thinks, how thoughts meander in the wet brain.

The car speeds ahead, past crumbling clapboard

houses and deserted strip malls, and under rusted and rickety bridges. There was a time, Ralf thinks, when society marked its progress on the physical landscape, building skyscapers, the Golden Gate Bridge, the Eiffel Tower, even stately porched homes, like his mother's place in Montclair. But in the last half century or so, most of the landmark projects have been virtual. What new physical construction there is comes from the Chinese, who have money for such things. For most Americans, he thinks, progress is defined in apps. The physical Oklahoma looks abandoned.

They pass a sign for a Civil War battle at Honey Springs. A Civil War battle in Oklahoma? Ralf wonders if he lugged around that morsel of data, unknown and unread, in his processor for twenty-eight years. He considers the trove of information stored on that chip, entire years of video, every virtual world he's ever entered, every song he has ever heard, every conversation he's ever had, the full database of all his messaging, even much of his sex life. All of it gone.

"Listen," Ellen says, stirring him from his reverie. "How about this? You tell me what you know. I'll do the same."

He pauses for a moment. "It's classified," he says.

In their three years together, she has heard that same phrase a thousand times. "Let me get this straight," she says. "They tie you down, take out your boost, patch you up, and send you as a wild man down to El Paso, and you have to protect their secrets?"

Ralf wants to tell her what he knows. But first he's attempting to run risk-reward calculations in a brain not built for such work. It's painfully slow, and does not deliver answers, only ideas.

"They didn't send me to El Paso," he finally says. "That was my plan."

"Because your brother lives there?"

"My family has roots there, too," he says. "My grandmother grew up there. Her father was a big shot on a newspaper."

"That's quaint," Ellen says, before returning to Ralf's brother. "I thought you two didn't get along. Now, he's the one you run to?"

"I wouldn't call it running, exactly."

"No?"

"I'm taking a trip," Ralf says.

"Semantics," Ellen says flatly. She gestures toward the backseat. "So you usually take trips with no more luggage than that disgusting gym bag of yours?"

"Actually, I wasn't even planning on bringing that."

Ellen pauses and looks at him. He stares straight ahead, as if he were driving the machine. These kinds of conversations, he thinks, would be a lot easier if he had driving to focus on.

"Let me tell you what I worry about," she says.

He glances at her and nods.

"I'm worried that you want to go to Juárez to be at home with all of those wild people. I love you, Ralf, I really do. But that is the single-most . . . It's the scariest place on earth, and if you want to live there, or even visit, we've got a big problem."

"Don't worry," he says. "My destination's El Paso, not Juárez."

Ellen studies his profile and concludes, after a few seconds, that further questions will get her nowhere. So she sits back, and as the car hurtles west through Oklahoma, she tells him her side of the story.

Two days ago, Ellen says, she was working at home, creating herds of dinosaurs for a virtual safari site, when she got a message from her friend Robin. "She said they were rounding up every Artemis they could find. Tall ones, fat ones, every shape and flavor."

"'They'?"

"The government." Then she stops for a moment, replaying the conversation. "Actually, she didn't say that . . . but I assumed it was. I messaged you twenty-three times and couldn't even leave a note."

By messaging friends in her network, and friends of friends, Ellen learned that young men wearing green sweaters had arrested two Artemis women, or Artemi, at a lunch spot on Capitol Hill. Fifteen minutes later, they picked up one near Chinatown, and then one in Farragut Square. "I did the numbers and figured they were eighteen to twenty-three minutes from our house," Ellen says. "So I got in the car."

He asks her where she went.

"I didn't know where to go, so I put it on a shuffle route in Georgetown," she says. "Then Julie messaged me that she saw you on the 14th Street Bridge. She said you were walking and looked terrible."

"Yeah, I love her, too," Ralf says, ransacking his mind to come up with a face for Julie.

"She was worried for you." Ellen goes on to say that she headed over to the HHS building on the Mall, figuring that Ralf would be there. When she arrived, he was bent over his bike, trying to wrench it free without the signal from his boost.

"So why do you think they were picking up Artemi?" Ralf asks.

"Call me naive, but I'm guessing it has something to do with the update, and that hole in your head," she says.

He shrugs. "Then why do you think they didn't stop us from leaving town?"

"Maybe I wasn't the Artemis they were looking for."

This leads the conversation straight to Suzy, a subject that they've agreed tacitly to avoid. Ralf dated another Artemis in grad school. This raises Ellen's suspicion that he might be drawn to her largely for the beauty she shares with Suzy and a few thousand other women in the country, plus others in South America. No words from Ralf could put these doubts to rest.

"Why would they pick up all these people based on what they look like?" Ralf says. "Kind of primitive, wouldn't you say? They have machines that can ID her boost in about two milliseconds."

"Maybe her boost isn't in her head."

The idea, so simple, leaves Ralf stunned. He lowers his head and says nothing.

"What I don't get," Ellen goes on, "is why they rounded up all the normal Artemi and didn't just focus on the one with no hair?" She considers it for a second, and then answers her own question. "I guess she could have bought a wig."

# TWO

"Make it quick," says John Vallinger. The world's most powerful lobbyist, president and founder of Varagon, Inc., is pulling into the driveway of the Walter Reed Army Medical Center in Northwest Washington. For Vallinger, who at age ninety-nine still plays racquetball twice a week, the visit is routine: just a fresh kidney. But it's a busy day. Vallinger has to entertain a Chinese delegation tonight at the Kennedy Center, and then eat the usual pancakes tomorrow at the White House. It's a courtesy he extends every week or two, to keep the president in the loop. He has no time this morning to referee the latest squabbles between his two top aides.

The voice of Tyler Dahl, the younger and more ambitious of the two, echoes in his boost. "Remember the two people who disappeared from the Update Division on Friday?"

"Right," Vallinger says. He entrusted the case to

George Smedley, and he can guarantee, without hearing even another word, that Dahl is about to tell him how badly Smedley screwed it up.

"There was the software genius, Alvare, and then the domed Artemis, Suzy Claiborne."

"Spare me the details," Vallinger says. He climbs out of his black Houyi—a car long enough to feature a full-length bed—and dispatches it to the parking lot. "Just tell me what happened."

"Well, Smedley, for some reason, ordered a roundup of every Artemis in the Washington metropolitan area. It was a huge job for security. I think they got fifty-four of them."

Vallinger steps inside the hospital foyer, for warmth, but continues his boost-to-boost talk. The lobbyist is tall and gaunt, and wears a shiny maroon trench coat. His white hair, parted on both sides, falls onto his forehead in his signature V. "Did he get the one he was looking for?" he asks.

"No," Dahl says.

"Do we know where she is?"

"No idea."

Strange, Vallinger thinks. His company has one of the two machines in the country that can locate and track the movement and behavior of virtually every American by his or her boost. It sits in its own refrigerated room in the company's K Street offices, overlooking Franklin Square. Smedley should have tracked the two employees as soon as he learned they were missing. Suzy Claiborne, Vallinger figures, most likely works for the underground Democracy Movement. Within minutes of sharing the software code with the genius, she was probably rushed to a safe house and shielded from electronic surveillance. If Smedley had harnessed the machine quickly, he might have even exposed an entire cell of the subversive DM network.

He screwed up—all for the pleasure of hauling in scores of dazzling Artemi. Vallinger knows that his young aide would love to speculate with his boss about how Smedley could be so dumb.

But Vallinger will not give him that pleasure. He is aware that Smedley runs a smutty virtual business on the side, and that he was probably scouting the Artemi for talent, or maybe just for kicks. This would be a firing offense in many shops. Vallinger, though, finds a certain value in having such a rogue on call. Smedley is wise to the world in ways that the more intelligent Dahl may never be. To protect himself from Smedley's excesses, Vallinger keeps him off the Varagon staff and pays him as an independent contractor.

"So what happened to the genius?" Vallinger asks his aide.

"Smedley had a contractor pick him up at work. They took him to a clinic in Alexandria to scrub his boost and ended up taking it out. An Asian went into the clinic. I'm told that he killed a couple of people and helped Alvare escape. I can't confirm that. In any case, that's the last anyone saw of him."

"Where is the genius now?"

"We . . . don't know."

"You scanned for him and he's not there?"

Dahl remains silent.

"Are you telling me," Vallinger says, his voice rising, "that even after Smedley screwed up, you neglected to track whatshisname, Alvarez?"

"Alvare."

"Whatever. The wild genius. Didn't you track him?"

"I . . . was focused on Suzy Claiborne," Dahl says softly. "We thought his boost would be scrubbed, or in Alexandria."

"But you didn't bother checking."

"No sir."

Vallinger should be angry. But he enjoys Dahl's come-uppance so thoroughly that the corners of his mouth turn downward into what passes in his world for a smile. In any case, this incident at HHS doesn't concern him.

John Vallinger's nearly eighty years in the technology industry have left him with a rich perspective on set-backs and embarrassments. Those that appear most threatening, he has learned, often recede with time—provided that they're handled smartly, or even ignored. Sometimes there's money to be made from them. Vallinger made his first fortune while working in the mid 1990s as a barista at a Starbucks coffee shop on El Camino Real Boulevard in Sunnyvale, California. He came up with a phony business plan for an e-commerce startup and landed a million dollars in angel funding. He then maneuvered his way into the initial public offering for Netscape, the first Internet stock. Within months, he was rich.

He quit the Starbucks job and rented a small office suite on University Avenue in Palo Alto. Every morning, he lowered his willowy frame into a swiveling Aeron chair with a taut fiber back. He booted up a big fast Dell PC equipped with Windows 95, and scoured for business for his new investment boutique, Varagon, Inc. Vallinger's first move was to short his Netscape stock, which he knew was headed for a dive, and to plow his fortune into high-flying stocks including Enron, World-Com, and SDS Uniphase.

As his fortune climbed, Vallinger became a quiet fixture in Silicon Valley. If you look at pictures from that era, you can often spot his slender form and white sun-starved face, the blond hair already falling onto his forehead in the V. In barbecues in Woodside or champagne brunches in Mountain View, Vallinger is invariably off to one side, usually alone, staring into space. In one photo, taken at a party shortly after Steve Jobs returned to Apple Computer, Vallinger appears to be chatting with Larry Ellison, the voluble founder of Oracle, the business software giant of the time (some of whose database code is still active in the boost). But if you study the photo closely, you'll see that Vallinger is simply reaching around Ellison, probably to turn down the stereo.

You would think that in an era defined by hype and celebration, the antisocial Vallinger would be ignored. Yet Vallinger's silent style created an aura about him, a mystique. People believed he was far richer than he was, that he had more friends than he did, that he must be having love affairs with senators or chief financial officers, or maybe that he was blackmailing them. In short, they thought he was onto something. That was what led a Stanford computer science professor to knock on his door one day and tell him about a project a couple graduate students were working on. It was a search engine called Google.

Vallinger's angel investment in Google drove his fortune into the billions and landed him in *Forbes* magazine as one of the five hundred richest people on earth. His picture, displayed in profile, shows only one half of the V falling across his forehead. The one visible corner of his mouth is turned ever so slightly downward, a sign that Vallinger, in a rare bow to vanity, was attempting to smile for the camera.

It was on a trip to China with top Google investors that Vallinger had his greatest revelation. What he first noticed upon stepping off the plane was a security camera pointed right at his face. From that point on, in the hotels, on the junkets to the factories and universities, he sensed that his movements were being recorded, his gestures noted, his words captured. This was when he glimpsed the future. China was going to control its society, and its Internet. That authority would prevail. It might take a decade or two, or even three, but this command regime would drive China's economy and its technology. With time China's system, embedded on chips, would spread to the rest of the world. When it did, China would need an ally in America. For Vallinger, it was an epiphany. He would become a lobbyist.

All of his labors ever since, sixty-eight years of lobbying, are finally coming to a head. The next update, his crowning triumph, is sailing ahead and only ten days away.

A bit of leaked code isn't likely to interfere.

"Get Smedley on the case," Vallinger says, striding into the hospital. "Tell him to keep me abreast."

# THREE

The car keeps rolling west, past Weatherford and Elk City. It maintains the precise distance, 1.3 meters, between the red Toyota ahead of it and the black Sharpei that's been tailing it since Fort Smith, Arkansas. In a sense, they're no freer than the railroad cars, hitched end-to-end, that used to roll across these prairies on iron rails. Ralf considers making that point to Ellen. But he sees she's busy in her head, probably on a design contract. Not so long ago, Ralf thinks, when his mother was a girl, people had the freedom to steer these machines wherever they wanted. They'd make phone calls, turn around to yell at their kids, even get drunk or fall asleep—all while driving a three-ton machine that was getting instructions from no one but them. It wasn't only the people who were wild. Cars were, too.

He thinks about his mother, Stella. She went through a transformation like his, but in the other direction: from wild to enhanced. Stella played a role in the diplomatic drama with the Chinese that led to the enhancement in 2044/45 of 400 million Americans. The Senate committee she worked for needed someone on staff to have a beta version of the boost, so that they could understand the technology and have at least one person to match wits with the enhanced Chinese team. Stella was the guinea pig. She later grew to regret her role, to the point of resenting the machinery in her own head. Ralf's father, Francisco, vanished before he was born, apparently a victim of the chip wars in South America between the U.S. and China.

Early in the century, when the Internet was still new, theorists predicted that by the 2030s, machines would blow past human intelligence. The next step of human intelligence, and evolution, would be led by these machines. This vision of the future was known as the Singularity. It was the rage early in the century.

The future came, and those big questions seemed to fade away. In 2032, when Stella Kellogg, a small dark-haired gymnast with a knack for foreign languages, graduated from Montclair High School, in New Jersey, wild humans still ran the world. Stella's life didn't look so different from those of her parents. Yes, cars ran by themselves, which still stirred controversy, and tiny machines that would have caused a sensation a generation earlier were stitched into clothing, embedded in jewelry and dog collars. Chip implants slowed the course of Parkinson's disease and helped stroke victims regain body controls. But these microchips were not in the cognition business. So Stella went about her life pretty much as her parents had. She got tutoring for her SATs, improved her scores by ninety points, and was accepted as a freshman at Middlebury College, in Vermont, where she would major in Spanish and French.

It was at a Halloween party that she met Francisco Alvare, a fellow freshman who was dressed in pantaloons, a silk white shirt, and a blue jacket with epaulets. He said he was Simón Bolivar. "¡El Libertador!" he yelled in Spanish, when she asked him. "¿Y vos, quien sos?" Francisco was Paraguayan, and on his sixth Cuba Libre. She pointed to her cardigan sweater and knee-length skirt. "Sylvia Plath!" The music was loud, and he couldn't hear her. Finally they sat on a couch and she shouted the name into his ear. It meant nothing to him. He understood her better when she spoke to him in Spanish. They spent the entire evening on that couch, the South American *generalisimo* and the suicidal poet, drinking rum and Cokes and talking politics. After midnight, Stella invited him back to her dorm. They made love. It was the first time for Stella, and about a month later she learned she was pregnant. That would turn out to be Simon, Ralf's older brother, named—naturally—for *El Libertador*.

In spring of Stella's freshman year, mud season at Middlebury, startling news arrived from Asia. It appeared that the Chinese, harnessing nanotechnology originally developed in San Diego, had placed microprocessors into the heads of two dozen workers at an air-conditioning factory in Shanghai. This wasn't anything close to the Singularity, experts insisted. Instead of the merging of the wet and dry brains, this was simply putting them both into the same box, the head, and then joining them with billions of optical signals. It just moved the computer from its normal perches, on the wrist or behind the ear, to inside the head. It was just a change in geography.

The chips were minuscule, about the size and weight of a single fly's wing. But the casing around them produced a protrusion above the left temple. To cover these bulges, the workers wore blue caps. They became known as "capped," and the word caught on. There were unconfirmed rumors that within days two of the capped workers had committed suicide. But the others appeared to thrive. They had the equivalent of supercomputers in their heads and the software performed much better than expected. After training each individual's processor for several weeks, it could convert thoughts into streams of words, and commands. For many users—and especially the younger ones—it became easy to toggle between the two brains, the wet and the dry. Communication at the plant appeared seamless as the capped workers, according to their managers, operated as one, like a hive of bees.

Back at Middlebury, a very pregnant Stella walked across campus with Francisco to a panel discussion featuring the college's reigning experts in China, business, history, and computer science. The auditorium was packed. The professors, speaking at great length, seemed to agree that the Chinese would abandon the experiment. There were those two suicides, and even if the technology worked, creating millions of enhanced Chinese would threaten the aged leadership.

Francisco jumped to his feet and shouted: "But what if they all get smarter? What happens then? Doesn't it start an arms race, just like *Esputnik*?"

The professors laughed uneasily, but Francisco insisted. "Won't we be like—" He stopped and grasped for the English word, and failed to find it. "*¿Los Neanderthales?*" This drew more laughter from the crowd, and Francisco turned red. But the professors weren't smiling anymore.

Stella wasn't either. She was thinking about the baby who was busy kicking her kidneys, and wondering what kind of world she was bringing him into.

Francisco went on. The Chinese, he said, were carrying out experiments in their "ecosystem." They could do this, he said, because they were "run by dictators." This provoked hissing from a few globalists and China sympathizers in the crowd. Francisco turned around to confront them, and was soon making comparisons in his less-than-fluent English between the government of China and that of his native country, Paraguay. This led to groaning and more yelling in the audience.

Professor Johnson leaned into his microphone and shouted, "What's your point?"

That quieted the crowd. Francisco, still on his feet, pursued his argument—one that Stella recognized from an anthropology paper she had edited for him over the weekend. The Chinese were willing to carry out experiments in their ecosystem, he said, and they were ready to accept failures and death. He paused for a moment, and looked down at Stella. "*¿Como se dice 'supervivencia del mas apto'?*"

"Survival of the fittest," she whispered.

"Because the Chinese are willing to experiment and suffer the costs of dangers, they have an ecosystem that will generate the survival of the fittest," he said. Americans, by contrast, dwelt too much on the risks. "By the end of five years," he predicted, "every Chinese will carry a . . . one of those things in his head. They will achieve the jump to Cro-Magnon. Dictators will use these tools to control them. And Americans . . ." He slumped his shoulders and hung his head forward, imitating a caveman. "You may be freer, but you will be *Neanderthales*."

Some in the audience laughed, and one voice cried out: "What about the Paraguayans?"

But the professors on stage appeared to take Francisco's argument seriously. If the Chinese took this leap, they would no doubt use their superior cognition to move the technology ahead even faster. This could lead to the same exponential growth of intelligence that the Singularity people had been predicting for decades. But it wasn't happening in America.

It was then that the expert in computer science delivered perhaps the most sobering news. The United States had no competing chip, and to come up with one would take at least five years. "By the time we get around to it, assuming we do," he said, "the Chinese will be on their third or fourth generation."

One Christmas Eve, it must have been ten years ago, when Ralf was in high school, Stella opened a bottle of champagne and shared it with him. It was just the two of them that Christmas in her mother's big old house, the replica of an antebellum Southern mansion, complete with a portico and four white columns, in Montclair, New Jersey. Simon was working in St. Louis, and didn't have the vacation days to fly home. Stella's mother had died the previous year. And that evening, feeling sentimental and a little drunk, she told Ralf about the afternoon at Middlebury all those years before when his father stood up and predicted the future. Ralf had video of Stella's story stored in his boost.

All those memories are gone, he thinks, looking out the window. Aside from that one night, Stella avoided the subject of what became known as the "chip wars," and her role in them. Ralf kept files on them in his boost, always figuring he'd get to them later. Now, as he and Ellen cross from Oklahoma into New Mexico, he tries to assemble the pieces.

For seven years, the Chinese appeared to shelve the experiment with the original capped workers. In fact, the government shut down the plant and the workers vanished from public view. Gradually the story settled, in the popular mind, into the realm of historical curiosity. Looking at it from Francisco's Darwinian perspective, China's capped workers appeared to be an evolutionary dead end, like most of the hominids from the Cenozoic Era that anthropologists dug up in Africa.

After college, Stella and Francisco moved with little Simon to Washington. She landed a job on Capitol Hill. Francisco freelanced as a journalist. He said she worked too much. She complained he didn't help enough with the baby. After a couple of months, he moved into an apartment in Adams Morgan with six other South Americans. More than once, police had to break up their raucous parties, known as the *"pachangas"* of Columbia Road. Stella soldiered on as a single mother—though Francisco continued to sleep over from time to time.

It was in the fall of 2041, at the opening session of the General Assembly of the United Nations, that the Chinese dropped their bombshell. The premier disclosed that in the previous month, the government had implanted a more advanced chip into the heads of 200,000 workers in Shanghai. The productivity gains were "staggering." He declared that the Chinese would soon produce enough chips to augment the thinking of all humanity.

Within two years, the Chinese extended their enhancement to the entire population, including the political leadership. The whole country was capped. At global summits, U.S. and European diplomats fumbled with their laptops and phones—technology from the early part of the century—while the Chinese zapped messages back and forth just by thinking. They could model and simulate every conversation, mapping out the most likely course it would take, and choosing the optimal path. It was as if each person alone was a high-performance staff working with a supercomputer.

Meanwhile, the United States, from its leaders in business and technology to the president himself, remained utterly wild. They compensated only by picking a handful of junior government staffers, including Stella, to test the boost. It seems astounding to Ralf that thirty-five years ago, only six years before his birth, the country was run by people as handicapped as he is now. How did they get anything done?

From a historical perspective, they didn't, at least during this crucial period when the Chinese carried out their cognitive colonization of the world. The Chinese extended heavily subsidized chips throughout Asia, capping in the first wave the populations of Vietnam, Malaysia, Singapore. Negotiations commenced with Japan, Russia, Mexico, and Brazil.

The Americans responded with a beta version of their own chip, launching it in a pilot program for fifty thousand people in Paraguay. This was perhaps the most important test for American technology since the Apollo program eighty years earlier.

It was at this point that Francisco traveled down to Asunción. He said he was going just to visit his family. But Stella was convinced that it had something to do with the chip project, which was a growing obsession of his.

The Paraguay project ended in tragedy. Thousands died, either from defective chips or Chinese viruses. The South American chip wars followed, and China emerged on top. Stella never heard again from Francisco.

Within two years, the United States accepted Chinese chips. The only concession the U.S. negotiators won from the Chinese was the proviso that the chips implanted in Americans, unlike the Chinese version, would not permit governments and companies to snoop on U.S. citizens. Those privacy gates were to remain closed.

# FOUR

They're driving through White Sands, near an old missile-testing grounds, when Ellen pulls herself away from her work and looks around. The entire landscape is blinding white, not a sign of life anywhere.

"Tell me again why your brother moved to El Paso," she says.

"I guess he likes the food," Ralf says. "Like I said, we have roots there. He probably likes the weather, too. It's sunny three hundred days of the year."

"The average is three hundred and ten," Ellen says, after consulting her boost. "Kind of weird, though, being so close to Juárez, wouldn't you say?"

"We'll see soon enough."

"I mean, surrounded by all those wild people . . ." She pauses a moment, and then adds, "No offense."

Following the chip wars, the United States and Mexico both capped their populations. But authorities from both countries were powerless to impose the new technology in the border region of northern Chihuahua, long run by drug lords. As a result, Juárez and its environs were left as the largest concentration of the wild west of Mogadishu. Its ranks grew, as wild refugees from the rest of Mexico and beyond migrated to the city. If the wild were a separate breed of animal—and many felt they were—Juárez amounted to the hemisphere's largest wilderness preserve.

There are rumors, Ralf knows, that a small neighborhood in Juárez houses a population of wild Americans. He finds this hard to believe. Juárez, by all accounts, remains primitive and violent. Wouldn't it be easier for Americans, and far safer, to move in with the largest extant wild population in the United States, the Amish cluster around Lancaster, Pennsylvania? He supposes that certain religious issues might discourage some would-be wild immigrants—but enough to send them into the inferno of Ciudad Juárez?

He looks at Ellen, still immersed in her work, moving her perfect lips. So far on this trip, she's spent more time inside her boost than out of it, at least during his waking hours. She stores endless archives in there, decades of news stories, libraries of literature, reference databases in multiple languages—way more than she needs when all of it is easily found on the network. Ralf tells her this on a regular basis. But she likes to rummage around in her own cluttered space. When she emerges from her boost, he thinks, she's confronted by what has to be an unsettling fact: I'm driving to the border with an animal.

Ralf nods off. The car drives on. He's roused as it crosses El Paso's city limit and slows down to 55 miles per hour. Its speaker announces that they're in El Paso and asks where it should go. He doesn't answer. Ellen will provide his brother's address. The orange Sheng-li exits the highway and falls into a slower caravan. The trail of cars, each one separated from the next by about a foot, winds its way past Mexican restaurants, cut-rate dentists, hydrogen stations. It climbs a road called Mesa and skirts the west side of the Franklin Mountains.

Ralf is in no hurry. He has to come up with an agenda, a list. But how do you make a list when you're wild? He touches Ellen's hand and leads her back into the world. "Hey."

She looks at him, smiles, and then looks out the windows. "We're here?"

"Yeah. I need you to take down a list for me."

She nods. "I'll have to do all kinds of stuff for you until you get something back in your head."


Like most couples, Ralf and Ellen first met as avatars. It was on a dating site where couples could meet, talk, stroll or have drinks, and then share adventures and intimate moments anywhere: they could visit Picasso's Paris, Costa Rican rain forests, Egypt in the time of the Pharaohs, even outer space. Each world, no matter how remote, was equipped with bedrooms, many of them decked out in the fashion of the time. In the biblical Bethlehem site, avatar couples could relax on beds of hay in modest barns, like the one Jesus was born in, surrounded by goats, cows, and lambs.

Ralf and Ellen's first date was to the Amalthea, Jupiter's largest moon. They climbed red hills together, dug for Amalthean ice and minerals, and when they tired of that, they sat on the edge of a crater and talked. Ellen found it strange that they had to stay in space suits the whole time, with clear bubbles over their heads. Ralf, though, found it easier to talk on a first date through a couple layers of thick plastic. "It's more realistic," he pointed out. They ended the date chastely, exchanging pats on the shoulder of each other's space suit. But they agreed to meet again the next day.

Ellen's avatar looked nothing like the woman who would eventually be traveling to El Paso with Ralf in the burnt orange Sheng-li. Her avatar had dark hair, wide blue eyes, and a gap between her front teeth. On her forehead were the traces of childhood acne. Her body, while not fat, was thick around the waist and shoulders. In a world of idealized avatars, Ellen's appeared surprisingly real, to the point of including what most would consider defects.

There was a reason for this. Ellen, whose mother pushed her to accept the Artemis package at age twelve, always wondered what she would have looked like if she had kept her original genes. So using the skills she developed as an artist, she took an image of her childhood self and morphed it into a twenty-five-year-old adult. Then, eager to see how the "real" Ellen would fare, she circulated in virtual worlds.

Ralf was among the first to pay attention to her. He found it easier to approach a woman who looked like something less than a goddess. Also, she attracted fewer suitors, which statistically—as Ralf tended to view life—gave him a greater chance of success. Ralf's avatar looked exactly like himself, the same deep violet eyes and curly hair, the same lithe body and shy smile. His avatar wasn't quite as shy as the real Ralf, but it still carried his personality. It was impossible for Ralf Alvare, no matter what world he was in, to be outgoing or talkative.

They continued to date, and eventually they became lovers in their virtual worlds. They first slept together in a tree house, modeled after the Swiss Family Robinson. Later they had sex in a bungalow on the coast of South India, Greenwich Village in the time of Bob Dylan, the Chateau of Versailles (which Ralf found tacky), and for old time's sake, on the lip of the same crater in Amalthea—but this time without space suits. Once, following Ralf's suggestion, they even visited a rustic ranch in Paraguay.

As they dated, they talked about their lives in the real world. Ralf told Ellen about his work in the Update Division. He singled out applications in their virtual love life that he had fine-tuned. Once he kissed Ellen's lips so lightly that it caused her whole body to tingle. That, he said, was his own "feathery" variation in the kiss package, which was introduced in the previous year's update. Before that, he said, even the gentlest virtual kisses were more forceful.

Ellen nodded and kissed him, this time forcefully. She

was far more interested in the kisses than the software behind them.

She told him about her own life, growing up in Paterson and going to art school down the road, in Hoboken.

"Paterson?" he said. "That's right near my mother's place, in Montclair."

"Yes," she said slowly. "I think that's right."

This reference to the physical world gave them both pause. It introduced the idea that neither had dared to bring up: a meeting of their physical selves. These encounters, often so awkward, were known as "reckonings." Many avoided them altogether. But for young men and women who wanted one day to have families, there was no getting around it. If they were to have children, molecules would have to meet and mingle. The reckoning signaled a major commitment for Ralf and Ellen. It was close to a declaration that they wanted to have babies together.

On one Saturday morning in October of that year, Ralf caught an air taxi from Washington to Montclair. He looked down at the trees below, glimmering in shades of red, yellow, and orange, and he thought about his life. What he had with Ellen seemed ideal in the virtual world. Wasn't the reckoning bound to disappoint? He pictured the scars of pimples on her forehead, and those extra pounds around her middle. Those had to be warnings, he thought, about the reality he would soon encounter.

As the taxi landed at the strip near Watchung Plaza, Ralf kicked himself for coming. Why did he need to meet her, anyway? Was he so sure that he wanted to have a family? A baby created a staggering responsibility—a body to care for. Its needs could not be shifted in time or place, much less into virtual realms. Babies chained their parents to the here and now, which was precisely the world Ralf spent most of his life avoiding.

As he walked down Christopher Street, he saw a blond-haired woman making her way in his direction on the opposite sidewalk. She wore a glimmering blue dress that clung to her body. The color matched the eyes on her radiant face. Ralf couldn't help but stare. He felt he'd seen women like her before, but none so beautiful. What was he doing hunting down the physical version of Ellen, with her pimples, split teeth, and extra pounds, when virtual worlds teemed with avatars created in the image of the woman walking toward him? The woman stopped and looked across the street, right at him. She smiled timidly and asked, "Is that you, Ralf?"

Ralf's heart leapt. But as he crossed the street toward Ellen, he felt a mixture of emotions. There was happiness, blended with a huge dose of relief. But he also felt embarrassed that he so clearly found Ellen more beautiful than her avatar. His shyness—which never strayed far—also weighed in. Would a woman this beautiful find him worthy? It seemed that in a matter of seconds, the entire balance of the relationship had shifted. In the virtual world, Ralf was by far the more attractive of the two, and Ellen, in a sense, was in his debt. Now their roles had flipped.

He walked up to her, tried looking into her eyes, but quickly took refuge—as he often did—by focusing on a point just below her eyes. He put his face up to hers and tried to kiss her with the physical version of his feathery app. But Ellen pulled his head toward hers and kissed him deeply. Then, both of them eager to escape each other's eyes, and the awkward questions sure to follow, they hugged.

Ellen also came to the meeting with apprehensions. She had gotten to know Ralf in the virtual worlds as the "real" Ellen. If he was put off at first by her less-than-perfect skin or body, he had overcome that, she believed, and had come to love her as a person unlike any other in the world, real or virtual. She was unique. Now, though, she was unveiling herself as an Artemis, a genetic package she shared with thousands. She and her parents had rejected her real self, and settled for a type. This filled her with shame. Worse, she feared that Ralf would prefer her mail-order looks to the "real" avatar she had created in such faithful detail. It was almost a no-win proposition: If Ralf adored her as an Artemis, Ellen would feel scorned.

Ralf adored her. He couldn't help himself. Ellen, while loving the flesh-and-blood Ralf, with all of his shyness and awkward glances, couldn't forgive him for preferring the Artemis. She often wanted to escape with Ralf into virtual worlds, where she could be her original self. He resisted. "Let me just love you as you are, in real life," he said as they lay together one evening on his couch in Adams Morgan.

"You don't want me for who I really am," she said, pulling away from him.

"I do," he said. "The only you that exists in this world

is the one I'm touching right now." With that he reached a hand up the back of her blouse.

Ellen wrestled free. She argued angrily that the real Ellen was the avatar. But this line, with its inherent contradiction, was tough to defend.

Nonetheless, that winter they moved in together in the apartment on Irving Street, in the Mount Pleasant section of Washington. Yet as their physical lives converged, they found themselves straying from each other. Ralf began avoiding love with the flesh-and-blood Ellen, and all the sensitivities it stirred. It was far easier, he found, to make love in virtual worlds to women who looked just like her. He convinced himself that by loving avatars that looked like his girlfriend, he was remaining, at least to a small degree, faithful.

Sometimes in his virtual ramblings, Ralf would see Ellen's avatar circulating nearby, looking ever more ungainly. She was still hunting for people who might love her for who she "really" was. But he was sure she would never put herself through another reckoning. She had already endured one. Why would the next be any different? Ralf found this sad. To avoid Ellen on dating sites, he disguised his avatar, replacing his round western eyes with Asian ones, and pulling his hair back into a ponytail.

The Mount Pleasant apartment grew largely into a "shelter"—a place for couples to park their bodies and carry out other physical upkeep. Inertia kept them together, along with the improved economics of shared living. When asked, they told friends and relatives that one day they might have a child. But nothing in their relationship pointed in that direction.

### 3/6/72 3:47 p.m. Mountain Standard Time

As they make their way through El Paso, Ellen finally gets through to Ralf's brother, Simon. He gives her an address on Mesa Street, which she passes on to the car. It promptly turns south, skirts the downtown, with its bank towers and hotels, and plunges into a section of the city that looks like Mexico.

"Weird," Ralf says, looking around. Much of the traffic is on horseback, with men, women, and even children clip-clopping along the street and up onto the sidewalks. The Sheng-li settles into a trotting speed. The brick buildings look at least a couple centuries old, their sagging porches held up by rusting iron struts.

Ralf points out the porches, but Ellen is busy in her boost, learning about Juárez. "Get this," she says. "The strongman over there, Don Paquito, has a harem and pet tigers that roam through his mansion. He has a glass eye that he likes to take out and put in people's cocktails, for a joke."

Ralf nods absently. "Are you sure Simon lives around here?" he says. "Doesn't look like his kind of neighborhood."

"My geotags are fading and blinking," Ellen says, shaking her head.

"It's probably all that crap you carry around in your boost," Ralf says. "You don't need all those archives when you can get stuff off the network."

"They don't take up any space at all, compared to video, " Ellen says. "In any case, the network's feeling a little iffy around here."

They pass a beet-shaped woman wearing red boots and short pants three or four sizes too small. "Do you think they still have . . . streetwalkers down here?" Ralf asks.

"Looks that way," Ellen says.

"But why advertise physically, when you can do it in the boost?"

"I bet most of her clients are old," Ellen says, "and maybe they're wild. I mean we're only"—she checks for a second—"about 297 meters from the border." She opens the window and wrinkles her perfect nose. "Smells weird," she says.

"Horse shit," Ralf says.

"No. It's more industrial."

"Probably pollution from Juárez. I think they drive old gasoline cars over there."

"Drive them? With steering wheels?"

"That's what I've heard."

The car continues into an area of smaller houses with tiny fenced-in yards. Then, right where they're expecting to find Simon's house, they come across a market. Ellen has never seen such colors. She snaps images of oranges, mangos, carrots, peppers that look impossibly red, and enormous bunches of spices she doesn't recognize. In one stall, a woman is selling a pile of weavings, most of them in shades of red and blue. "Cool neighborhood," she says.

"I just can't believe he would live here," Ralf murmurs. He asks her to recheck the address.

Ellen tries, but gets no signal. "Maybe we're too close to the dead zone," she says, pointing toward Juárez.

A series of powerful explosions echo in the distance, rattling the tin roofs around them. It startles Ellen, who grabs Ralf's arm. He looks up at the sky. "It isn't thunder," he says. He surveys the horizon, east to west, looking at the shanties of the wild city. "Looks miserable over there."

Ellen finally locates the address and sees that they're on South Mesa instead of North Mesa. She gives the Sheng-li new directions. As it swings around, she looks back longingly at the market. "I'm going to have to come back," she says.

# FIVE

The address leads them to the Cavalry Club. It sits on the east side of North Mesa Street, just a few blocks from the university. The parking lot is nearly deserted. But standing by the wooden door, bareback and un-hitched, stands a single white stallion, its snout buried in a creosote bush. "We should get one of these things," Ralf says. He walks up to the animal and pats its neck.

"Stay back," Ellen says, "they kick."

"Not with their front legs."

"Up front they bite." She walks in an exaggerated arc, distancing herself from the animal and her wild boy-friend, and pulls open the door. Ralf gives the horse one more pat and follows her in.

The inside of the Cavalry Club feels like an old barn. Bridles, saddles, spurs, and other horse paraphernalia hang from the rafters. The floor, made of wide wooden planks, is sprinkled with sawdust. Country music is playing, but not loud enough to drown out the beeps coming from a couple of vintage game machines by the bar. Ralf recognizes one of them—Pong—from a throwback app he ran years ago in his boost. At one end of the bar sits an antique black telephone, probably from the 1920s or '30s, with the handset in a raised cradle and a circular dial on its face. Chairs are mounted upside down on the long wooden tables. A young man with a broom nods at the visitors and finishes sweeping under the last table. Then he deliberately returns the broom to a closet before taking his place behind the bar.

"That your horse out there?" Ralf asks.

The bartender, who looks barely old enough to drink, doesn't bother to answer the question. "Your brother should be here in about ten minutes," he says.

Ralf is taken aback. "You knew I was coming?"

"I have eyes," the bartender says. "You're practically identical." He stands silent, studying Ralf, and then says, "You know, I'm not getting anything from you."

"Long story," Ralf says. Without elaborating, he orders a beer for himself and a chlorophyll drink for Ellen. Then he watches quietly as Ellen engages the young bartender. She learns that his name is Chui, a Mexican nickname for Jesus. He studies philosophy at UTEP. When Ellen asks why the bar is so empty, he says that "no one" comes there, even though it's only two blocks from campus, maybe because the drinks cost twice as much as anywhere else. It's a lucky thing, he tells her, that he's paid by the hour, and not from tips.

"Why would they charge twice as much for drinks?" she asks, looking around. "Not enough sawdust?"

"You'd have to ask his brother," Chui says, gesturing with his head toward Ralf.

Ralf, who has drained his beer, signals for another. This is the first real drink he's had in years. Some people still come to real bars for the wet-brain experience. But judging from the crowd, the retro boom hasn't extended to the Cavalry Club. He wonders how his brother makes a living with this joint.

Ralf's first (remaining) memory of Simon features an angry thirteen-year-old standing at the top of a staircase in their Chevy Chase home, screaming at their mother. The boy is pudgy. He looks slightly feminine. Ralf wonders, as he pictures this scene, if that gender analysis intruded years later into the memory, as a revision. The wet brain is susceptible to such mischief, he knows. In the memory, Simon is yelling, "You killed him!" Crying and balling his fists, he repeats those three words again and again until he's hoarse. Not a great memory to kick off the relationship, Ralf thinks.

It only got worse. At the center of the issue was the boost. Simon didn't get his until he was twelve years old. Like many in his generation, he struggled with it. Puberty was hard enough, and now he had to deal with another tool in his head. He had trouble controlling it. The software commands, which came instinctively to Ralf, confused him. He blamed the boost for practically every problem in his life, for his pimples and his clumsiness. He even blamed it for the powerful new desires coursing through his body which made him want to hug and kiss other boys. Those tormented him and interfered with his sleep. It was true that the boost helped Simon with his schoolwork. Even as he struggled with commands, he managed to call up historical facts fairly easily, and run quadratic equations. But other classmates adjusted far more quickly. So in comparison to them, the boost made him dumber. That angered him. The saddest part, though, was that the boost led to the chip wars in South America, into which his father and his father's entire family had disappeared, never to be heard from again. Meanwhile, it was his mother, serving in government, who helped cap the entire country. From Simon's perspective, she was solely responsible for the globe's technological leap, and all of its repercussions—or at least the negative ones. As he repeated loudly that one night, and again in later years, he blamed her for his father's death. It gave him little comfort that his baby brother, capped before he could walk, shifted effortlessly between his two brains, and appeared to be developing into a more advanced line of human. It was also clear, at least to Simon, that Stella adored the baby boy—and loved him far more than she did the angry pimply-faced and boost-challenged adolescent screaming at her from the top of the stairs.

Stella was struggling, too. Barely thirty years old, she found herself alone with a rebellious boy and a precocious infant. What's more, China's growing dominance fueled the growth of America First!, which quickly grew into the nation's leading political force. It marked the rise of Rev. Tommy Q. Foley. In barely three years, he rose from leading the country's largest megachurch, in the suburbs of Dallas, to Speaker of the House. Foley, it was well known, answered to the nation's preeminent lobbyist, John Vallinger.

With the America First! takeover, Stella lost her job in the Senate and moved with her two boys back to New Jersey. Simon grew only angrier. Stella ended up sending him to a progressive boarding school near New Hope, in the Philadelphia suburbs. Her mother was all too happy to bankroll this chapter of Simon's education, if only to remove the rebellious boy from the household.

Ralf takes a sip from his beer and looks at Ellen. She and Chui have stopped talking, and are messaging instead. She's smiling, and looking happier than she has since they left DC. Her glass of green liquid looks untouched.

"Excuse me," Ralf says, clinking his glass with his finger.

Chui and Ellen both look at him.

"You said Simon would be here in ten minutes?" he says.

"Ten, twenty minutes, a half hour," Chui says. "When it comes to numbers, he's not always real precise."

"Can't you message him?"

Chui leans forward on his elbows and looks at Ralf. "How well do you know your brother?" he says. He flashes a quick smile to Ellen. This has probably been the theme of their messaging.

"We haven't seen a lot of each other," Ralf admits.

"Well, I don't think he messages with anybody," Chui

says. "He's a throwback kind of guy. He actually writes notes by hand."

Ellen laughs. "How does he send them? Carrier pigeon?"

"Sometimes, yes," Chui says gravely.

**3/6/72 5:52 p.m. Mountain Standard Time**

The sun sets over the Franklins in streaks of purple and orange as hulking Oscar Espinoza directs his KIFF Wrangler across the east side of El Paso and turns up Trans Mountain Road. In the middle of Espinoza's broad face sits a nose that has been compacted and bent to the left. Its value—and a questionable one at that—is largely ornamental. Espinoza breathes mostly through his mouth.

His mission on this Sunday evening, which popped in as a message from George Smedley, is to stop by the Cavalry Club, on Mesa, and keep an eye on Ralf Alvare, who appears to be in the parking lot. "Don't interfere with him," Smedley messaged. "Whatever you do, don't zap him."

This is a reference to Espinoza's last assignment. Under the orders of Tyler Dahl, he was tracking a geneticist who had surprised people in Washington by traveling from his labs in Bethesda directly to El Paso. The fear was that the scientist, like others before him, would cross into Juárez, carrying his secrets into the so-called dead zone. Espinoza prevented this from happening, by zapping him with the llegal boost-scrubbing tool Dahl had provided. He must have pushed the button too hard, because the scientist fell dead at the border. It took all of Vallinger's connections in El Paso, and a fortune in fees, to keep the case out of court.

During this ordeal, Espinoza suffered a series of debilitating headaches. Out of nowhere, it seemed, searing pain would shoot from a molar to the back of his head. The pain brought tears to his eyes. At first, he went to a dentist, thinking that one of his teeth was rotting, or impacted. The dentist found nothing, and the headaches continued. It was only later that Espinoza figured out that Vallinger—or Tyler Dahl—had the controls to his boost, and could produce and call off the headaches with simple commands. An app instructed the nerves to create pain, just the way others told them to simulate the taste of a Tecate beer or produce orgasms.

Espinoza now understands, and even accepts, that Vallinger has access to his boost, as well as the tools to manipulate it. The man is powerful, and he pays well. What torments Oscar Espinoza is the idea that someone on Vallinger's staff might one day administer a killer headache and then, perhaps, receive a message, or maybe a lunch invitation, and simply forget about the employee in El Paso, doubled up in pain. In that circumstance, Espinoza thinks, he will hold the zapper right to his temple and push the button. The last victim of his tool, he suspects, will be himself.

Espinoza crosses the mountain and sees the valley of Juárez stretched out in the distance. Its sparkling lights are dimmed by a cloud of smog hanging over the city and stretching into South El Paso. He looks at the tiny dots circulating on the roads. Ancient cars. He gets a pang of nostalgia for his driving years. Those distant memories, lodged only in his wet brain, seem almost like a dream now. The mountain on the horizon carries the same message it has for more than a century. The big white letters read: *La Biblia Es La Verdad. Leela,* or THE BIBLE IS THE TRUTH. READ IT. As Espinoza's KIFF turns south on I-10 and heads toward Mesa, he wonders about religion in the wild world. Would those people actually page through the physical book—and believe the words? Espinoza ransacks his boost and finds a copy of the Bible, an audio version, and a few old movies with biblical themes: *The Robe, The Ten Commandments,* and a vintage HBO documentary on a twentieth-century athlete, Moses Malone. Maybe one day he'll take a look, he tells himself.

When Espinoza pulls into the Cavalry Club, he parks next to an orange Sheng-li. Keeping a safe distance from a white stallion standing near the door, he walks into the tavern. Two people are seated at the bar, a dark-haired man with a couple days of beard growth and a stunning blond-haired woman who looks his way. Espinoza recognizes her look. It's one of the genetic packages, but he can't come up with the name. Juno? Diana? He searches her image in his boost and comes up with it: Artemis.

He sits at the far end of the bar and orders a seltzer. The bartender serves him his drink and returns to the other two. Nobody pays much attention to Espinoza, at least once they take in his nose. He looks casually around the tavern. Piled high near the bathroom is a mountain of paper, probably for packaging. He looks toward the trio to his right. Funny, he thinks. He's picking up only two signals. They wouldn't hire wild barmen at places like this, would they? Sipping his drink, he ponders the potential benefits. They probably work for cheap, the poor losers. It would be easy enough to cheat them out of money, since the wild can't count to save their lives. . . . But how do you go about paying a wild man? Espinoza ponders this question. They can't receive credit beams. He wonders if they deal in pieces of paper—old-fashioned checks or currency—and whether banks actually employ people to handle such chores. Probably not. The whole world is built for the boost.

It might be easier for a wild man just to go over to Juárez, where the whole system is based on old-fashioned living, at least as far as he's heard. People probably carry some sort of money in their pockets, and wear wrist-watches. Maybe they still carry phones. Espinoza likes the idea of a world full of gadgets, physical toys, and briefly warms to the idea of Juárez. Then he snaps out of it. If you go to Juárez and some mafioso dumps you in a vat and turns you into *pozole,* or one of the American drones roaming the streets mows you down, the wild life loses its charm.

The man and the woman at the bar stand up. They look ready to leave. Espinoza prepares to follow. He messages the bartender for the check and beams the payment with a 1% tip. Clearly, the bartender has a boost—which means one of the other two is wild, or at least cloaked.

Outside, the sound of trotting hoofs signals the

approach of another horse. A moment later, the door bangs open and an older version of the guy at the bar strolls in. Maybe it is a package, Espinoza thinks, though he's never seen this one before. His hair recedes in two deep troughs from his forehead, and he wears it longer than usual in back, tying it into a small ponytail. He shakes the younger one's hand, and then tries awkwardly to turn it into an embrace. This doesn't quite work. The young one pats his back and introduces him to the Artemis.

**3/6/72 6:28 p.m. Mountain Standard Time**

"I had a feeling I'd be seeing you," Simon whispers to Ralf.

"How so?"

"Just an inkling." He smiles, taking in his little brother, a younger, thinner image of himself. "So," he says, "you lost your boost?"

Ralf nods. He can't remember seeing Simon ever looking so content.

"You were always one with your boost," Simon says, still whispering. He has an eager look, as if he has rediscovered his brother. "I was the one born to be wild, not you!" He shakes his head and says, "My brother, the prodigy."

Simon's words stir a sense of panic within Ralf, and an awakening of his childhood anxieties. He is eager to escape into a more manageable virtual conversation—an option he may never have again. Avoiding Simon, he looks toward Chui, who's standing discreetly down the bar, still messaging with Ellen. At the other end stands a behemoth who carries on his face the wreckage of what was once a large nose. He's looking in their direction. Ralf turns his back to the man, collects himself, and looks into his brother's eyes. "I need your help," he whispers.

"What kind of help?"

Ralf speaks the words quietly but clearly. "I need to get a new one." The shift from personal to logistical issues brings a sense of calm. Conversations are easier when they come with a to-do list.

"That's what you came down here for?" Simon asks, looking crestfallen.

Ralf nods.

"And you think I can help?"

"That's the idea."

### 3/6/72 7:48 p.m. Mountain Standard Time

The brothers stroll out of the Cavalry Club, still talking, Ellen a couple paces behind. "Is this yours?" Simon asks, walking up to a massive coffee-colored KIFF Wrangler.

"No," Ralf says. He points to the Sheng-li coated with desert grit. The two brothers talk some more before Simon beams directions to Ellen and swings onto his horse.

Oscar Espinoza lingers by the bar, pretending not to follow them. He reaches into his pocket as he bides his time, and fingers the smooth contours of the zapper. Meanwhile, he sends a message to Smedley: "Leaving the bar." He includes an image of the two brothers talking. The Artemis stands to one side of them, looking directly at Espinoza.

**3/6/72 9:52 p.m. Eastern Standard Time**

The dashing avatar of George Smedley is curled up on a bearskin with the avatar of an Inuit woman when the message from El Paso arrives. Smedley's avatar is an idealized caricature of himself. It has the same sharp nose and sardonic smile. Like Smedley, it wears thick graying hair combed straight back. When dressed— which is the exception on these sites—the avatar even wears Smedley's trademark falcon feather. The only difference in the avatar is its age. The physical Smedley has grown grayer and heavier with the years.

This evening Smedley is busy testing a prototype for a new sex site, Arctic Love. It needs more work. Customers on other sites can have their trysts on tropical beaches, Buckingham Palace, even villas in ancient Pompeii. His developers, he thinks, have to give them a better reason to opt for an igloo.

When he sees the message from Espinoza, he pops out of the virtual igloo and back into his physical world, a two-story apartment in Washington's Kalorama district. He has just had it refurnished with antiques from the middle of the twentieth century. Sitting on a red "womb" chair signed by Eero Saarinen, Smedley opens the image from Espinoza and looks at the two brothers. He sees the Artemis behind them and gasps. Suzy Claiborne, he thinks. The domed Artemis is wearing a standard-issue blond wig. She must have traveled to the border with her coworker. Unlike Ralf Alvare, she carries the update code in her boost, and her boost in her head. She must not, under any circumstances, cross into Juárez.

He sends a message to Espinoza: "Follow the Artemis."

Espinoza hurries outside and climbs into his KIFF. He sees the dirty Sheng-li turning south on Mesa. The other brother follows on a trail to the side of the road, trotting on a white-hoofed sorrel.

# SIX

**3/7/72 6:43 a.m. Mountain Standard Time**

Ellen blinks her eyes open. She's stretched out on the dark blue sofa, wrapped in a knitted serape. Desert sunlight pours in from the patio window. The sturdy palm tree outside is leaning in the wind, which whistles past the window. Simon sleeps in the Murphy bed across the room, snoring gently. She looks down from the sofa and studies Ralf. He's lying on a thin strip of foam rubber and wound up in a blanket. His face is buried in a pillow he improvised by bundling his shirt and jeans and wrapping them with a towel. He looks dead to the world. She wonders if the wild sleep better, and concludes that they probably do. Less interference.

Ellen heard the brothers whispering late into the night. She must have been falling in and out of sleep, because she can only recall snippets. But she knows Ralf is counting on his brother to help him find a new boost.

They talked about a "processing center" near Fort Bliss, and said something about dead people's boosts.

She thinks about putting someone else's boost, a dead person's, inside her head, then flipping through that person's memories and photos, and receiving messages from his friends. She'd have to come up with a standard response. "No, I'm sorry," it would say. "He's dead. Could you please remove him from your list?" Or maybe simply, "He or she is no longer operating this boost." Then Ellen contemplates her own boost. Will petabytes of her memories carry on, as clutter, in someone else's head? She shudders at the thought.

Stepping over Ralf, she makes her way into the bathroom and pulls on her only leggings. In a little closet, she finds a neatly stacked pile of Simon's T-shirts. She tries on one with horizontal blue stripes, and adjusts the leggings to a navy blue. She looks at the unkempt Artemis in the mirror. Her hair's a mess. Her face could use a micro-scrub. The grit in the desert seems to dig into the skin. Still, an Artemis could wake up in the gutter and manage, somehow, to look fabulous. It's the nature of the package.

Ellen walks to the kitchenette and finds a tea bag and a mug. Next to the sink, she sees an antique stove. She turns a knob and a flame leaps up. She waves her finger through the flame, quickly at first, and then more slowly, watching the fire wrap around it. The experience of fire is one area where simulations in the boost just don't cut it, she thinks.

She places a kettle on the flame and turns to consider Simon's apartment by the morning light. The kitchen is lined with Mexican ceramic tiles, each one embossed with a hand-painted butterfly. She wonders about a man who would buy a stove like this and decorate the kitchen with such lovely tiles.

Ellen studies the delicate butterfly tiles. They're unlike anything Ralf would ever buy, or even notice. This reminds her that Simon is supposed to be gay, according to Ralf. She knew that, but then forgot. Of course, lots of people act out their sex lives in their boosts, and leave it there. That's no secret.

The apartment's bowed wooden floors look at least a century old, as does the Murphy bed. Ellen checks in her boost for the history of the building, the Palmore, and finds that it was built in 1913 as a refuge for rich Mexican children during the Mexican Revolution. Beyond the palm tree out the window she can see the expanse of Mexico. The wind stirs up dust devils among the shanties of Juárez, which extend to the brown mountains in the distance. One of the mountains carries white lettering, something about *la Biblia*. She wonders if wild people are more religious than everyone else. That would make sense, since they carry around more mystery in their lives—or at least fewer answers. They don't know what diseases they're most likely to get, or what food and medicine to take to avoid them. It's like a crap shoot. They don't know much more about their lives and their bodies than the cavemen did. Then again, even with all the advances from the boost, people still die with chips in their heads. Death just comes a couple decades later, barely a blink in eternity. So religion shouldn't be that much less relevant, she thinks. The wild people just have more empty time to consider it. The subject of death reminds her of Ralf's mission to get a used boost, which seems creepy.

The water boils. As she pours the tea she catches the reflection of her striped shirt on the glass cabinets. It occurs to her that she could walk down to that market on South Mesa to take a closer look at those weavings. Why not? They might fit into a vintage design she's doing for the Ritz Cracker app. For today, at least, she's a tourist—and she suspects that she doesn't fit into Ralf's plans. She checks in her boost. It's 1.5 miles, twenty-nine minutes on foot, to the far end of South Mesa. She just has to walk down Prospect Street, cross I-10, and make her way south from there.

She leaves her tea steeping and is about to head out when Ralf sits up on the floor, bleary-eyed, and asks her what she's up to.

"About to take a walk," she says.

"You don't want breakfast?"

"I'll pick up something in that funky part of town we went through yesterday," she says. "You weren't planning on my company. . . ."

"No, not really."

"'Cause it sounded like you and Simon were going to go shopping for something. . . ."

"Yeah, sort of."

"Involving recycled chips?"

"It's just something I wanted to look into," Ralf says. "Probably won't lead to anything."

Simon groans in the Murphy bed and rolls over, holding the pillow to his head.

With a hand signal, Ellen asks Ralf to join her in the kitchenette. He climbs to his feet. He's wearing only the same pair of red plaid boxers that he's had on since they left Washington.

Ellen whispers, "Why don't you borrow some clothes from Simon?"

Ralf nods impatiently. "We didn't get around to discussing clothes last night," he says.

"But you told him about your boost."

"Well, he could tell. Anyone who gets within ten feet of me can."

"But you drove all the way down here with me, and barely talked to me about it."

They're standing face to face in the kitchen, Ellen looking earnestly into Ralf's eyes, Ralf inspecting the shelves, the pots and pans hanging on the wall, the hand-painted tiles, and then glancing into the living room, where Simon is snoring again.

"Look at me," she whispers.

He looks at her and immediately leans forward and kisses her lips.

"Stop that!" She pushes him away. "So why don't you open up with me?"

"I guess I'm only getting used to the idea now," Ralf says. "Plus, I worried that if I told you too much, you could get in trouble if they found it on your boost."

"Give me a break."

"I'm serious."

"I'd get in trouble for something I know, and not for riding two thousand miles in my car with a guy who for some reason has had his chip surgically removed from his head, presumably by—" She's about to say "authorities," but the word sounds wrong somehow, as if she accepts that whoever took out Ralf's boost had the right to do it.

"By force?" Ralf offers.

"No, I'm talking about who did it."

"Oh," he says. "That."

Ellen says nothing, asking him with her eyes to open up, and tell her the story she's now caught up in. He gives in, and recounts the story from the beginning. He tells her about finding the open gates on the Chinese update, uploading Suzy's file, the guards who intercepted him, the dirty clinic he woke up in, and the strange wordless man who guided him to the door. He talks. She listens. Simon sleeps, or pretends to. These people are probably not following him, Ralf says, because he no longer has the chip with the update code.

His hope, he tells her, is to get in touch with one of Simon's friends who has a friend at the "reprocessing center" at Fort Bliss. A machine there uploads the data from used boosts, and adds them to a national archive. "They can't read our boosts while we're alive," he says. "Or at least they're not supposed to. But once we're dead, they put all the data together. They analyze our shopping patterns, diseases, whatever."

"And you want to get your hands on a dead person's boost?"

"That's the idea."

"Okay," Ellen says, sounding unimpressed. Then she adds one more question: "Where's Suzy?"

Ralf shrugs. "I don't have a clue."

# SEVEN

Ellen first sees him as she peers out the window from Telas del Rio Bravo, a Mexican boutique in South El Paso, where she's buying a new set of clothes. He sits in the café across the street. His mountainous body is perched on a tiny bar stool, the nose flattened against his face like a crushed carnation. She glances up and down the street and sees a coffee-colored KIFF Wrangler parked a block to the north. The same one from the parking lot last night. It's so wide that it juts into traffic, forcing cars and horses alike to bend their paths.

The sales lady comes back with a pile of flowered blouses. "This is all we have in six," she says. Ellen tries to concentrate on the shopping, picking up the blouses and beaming them onto a model of herself in her boost, and turning it around to see the fit. But she can't concentrate. Across the street, the big man on the stool is drinking a cup of coffee. He stares in her direction.

Ellen pays for two blouses with a credit beam and asks the woman if the store has a back exit. "I think someone is following me," she whispers.

The woman nods, as if this happens regularly. She hands Ellen the blouses in a bag and leads her through a storeroom piled high with boxes. They brush past colorful garments hanging from rails. Pushing open a door, she guides Ellen into an alley. "That's north," she says, gesturing to the right. "West is behind us, out the front door."

"And?" Ellen asks, puzzled.

"The border's right over there," she says, pointing across the alley. "You'll want to stay away from there."

Despite this warning, Ellen takes off for the south. That's where the market is. From the shaded alley she passes into the blinding sunlight of a parking lot, then turns to the left and peers around the corner of South El Paso Street. No sign of the man with the nose. Where the big KIFF was parked stands a single horse hitched to a street sign. Its head is disappeared deep into a trash can.

"Why are they chasing me?" she instinctively messages Ralf. It bounces straight back. She finds Simon's link from last night and sends a message to him: "A man is following me in South El Paso. What to do?"

**3/7/72 10:15 a.m. Mountain Standard Time**
"Do you think I'll get the boost today?" Ralf asks when Simon finally climbs out of bed.

"I'm not sure you'll get it, period," Simon says. He makes his way to the kitchen and drinks a glass of water. "If you do, it won't come easy, or cheap." As Simon walks through a series of morning rituals, from brushing his teeth to watering a lonely grape ivy in the kitchen window, Ralf follows him, asking questions.

Simon explains that the reprocessing center, from what people say, is under tightened scrutiny. There are reports that agents from Juárez are getting their hands on chips, probably by bribing officials, and taking them back into their wild zone. It's as if they're appropriating American lives—or at least lifetimes of Americans' experiences. The goal, some say, is to hack the chips and introduce some sort of virus that will crash the boosts in 430 million Americans—or even the whole world. Or maybe they want simply to control the enhanced population, or to steal billions.

"Of course, I think this is all a lot of paranoid crap," Simon says. "But I want you to understand the climate of fear around here. It's going to make getting a chip a lot harder."

Ralf asks if the Mexicans have machinery to download and read the chips.

"Nobody knows," Simon says. "But I doubt it."

"The guy you're trying to get in touch with, he's a friend of yours?"

"A friend of a friend, sort of."

"How are we going to get the boost from him?"

"Probably bribe him," Simon says, walking into the bathroom. "If we're lucky." He shuts the door.

Even after talking into the early morning hours, Ralf's

brother remains largely a mystery to him. Ralf has little idea, for example, how Simon makes a living by running the empty Cavalry Club. When he asked him about it, Simon answered cryptically, saying something about "alternate revenue streams." Then late in the evening, when Ralf revealed his discovery of the open Chinese gate, 318 Blue, in the software update, Simon nodded and said, "I know."

"You know about 318 Blue?"

"Well, the name is new to me," Simon admitted.

When Ralf pressed him on what he knew about the chip update, and how he learned about it, Simon skirted the question. "Ralf," he said, reprising his old role as the know-it-all brother, "not everything about the chip runs through the chip—or the 'boost,' if you insist on calling it that."

Ralf shook his head, puzzled.

"What I mean is that if you want to learn about the chip, you have to do your thinking off of it. Because the people who control it also control the information about it. It's a walled garden. Using the chip to learn about the chip," he added, "is like trying to chew your own teeth."

"Oh, I see," Ralf said angrily. "It's a conspiracy." He assumed that this evil cabal, as his brother saw it, was enabled by a crew of talented but incurious technicians, including himself.

"Call it what you will," said Simon. He pointed to the bandage peeling off Ralf's temple. "I don't think that hole in your head came from a random act."

Ralf argued that Simon was confusing two issues.

One was the effort in the update to eavesdrop on an entire nation's cognitive processes through Gate 318 Blue. But that did not necessarily mean that people who "controlled" the chips created an alternate version of events, or even that they could. "Do you think they have people putting together phony stories that all of us accept as gospel?" he asked.

"Not all of us accept them." Simon sniffed.

It had been three years since Ralf had last seen Simon, and exactly the same amount of time, he realized, since he had wanted to punch someone square in the face. Simon was two feet away, leaning against the kitchen counter. Instead of punching him, Ralf launched a verbal attack. He asked him, point blank, if he lived out his sex life in the boost.

"I do," Simon said calmly. "I have gay sex in a few worlds. In another one, I'm a straight woman named Simone."

"Is that as false as the news in the boost?"

"It is."

"So you tell me to get off the boost, but you carry out your entire emotional life on it."

"Not my entire emotional life," Simon quibbled. "My sex life. Look," he added. "I'm not holding myself up as a model. Virtual sex is shallow. You could call it a lie. It's probably not as fulfilling. There's no trace of love. But it's easier and neater. They've given me a tool— forced it on me—and I use it occasionally. Guilty as charged."

"If they open that gate, they'll be able to spy on your sex life," Ralf said. He wanted Simon to appreciate the battle he was waging for privacy, and the sacrifice he had made.

"True enough," Simon answered. "But if people find out about the surveillance, maybe they'll start to distrust the chip. That wouldn't be a bad thing."

"And we'd all go back to do all of our thinking with this thing?" Ralf pointed in the direction of his wet brain. "I don't think that will fly."

### 3/7/72 10:47 a.m. Mountain Standard Time

Simon rushes out of the bathroom. "A message from Ellen," he says. "Someone is following her in South El Paso. The guy from the bar last night."

"The bartender?" Ralf asks. He pictures Chui standing behind the bar, messaging with Ellen.

"No, a guy with a funny nose and a big brown KIFF."

Ralf's heart races. "Should we head down there?"

Simon doesn't answer. He's staring blankly, consulting his boost. "Oh my God," he says.

"What!"

Simon snaps back from the boost. "She has to hide," he says.

Ralf waits for him to continue.

Simon walks into the kitchenette and gulps another glass of water. "There was this incident a couple months ago," he says, rinsing out the glass, "where this guy used some kind of a Chinese tool to zap a scientist they said was heading into Juárez. It was supposed to wipe his chip clean. It might have done that, but it also killed him."

"What's this have to do with Ellen?"

"There's almost nothing about this story on the chip," his brother says. "I remember hearing it from a friend."

"What's your point?" Ralf is growing exasperated. Simon clearly still struggles to carry on a conversation when he's dealing with his boost—just as he did as a child.

"It's just, like I was saying last night, if they don't want you to find the story on the chip, it won't be there."

"Or maybe it's just that you can't find it," Ralf snaps. "What about the guy who killed the scientist? And what does it have to do with Ellen?"

"Oh. I remember hearing about the guy who did it, or allegedly did it, and they said he had a boxer's nose. It made me wonder if it's the same guy who's following you—or her."

"I remember him from the bar. What's his name?"

"I don't know."

"You have his image in your chip. Run a match against a database."

"No can do, Mr. Chip." Simon allows himself a smile, and Ralf, once again, feels a strong impulse to hit him.

"Wait a minute," Simon says, fetching new information. "She says she's going down . . ." He waits a moment and looks back at Ralf. "Lost it."

"Holy God," Ralf says.

Simon resumes. "Down Kansas . . . No, no." He's talking to himself. "If she's walking south and he's in the KIFF, she should follow a one-way road going north, like South Campbell, unless maybe he's south of her and coming back in her direction. . . ."

"Tell her!"

"Okay, okay."

"Or you could just go shotgun," Ralf says, wondering why the idea didn't occur to him earlier. This way, Simon can climb into her boost, see through her eyes, and steer her toward safety.

"I wouldn't know how to start," Simon says.

When Simon first got his boost, at age twelve, it came with demonstration software. Using it, he had the sensation that he was walking into a different room. This was the boost chamber. He could shut the door and find himself facing a large touch screen. By controlling his thoughts he could form messages, enter virtual worlds, carry out calculations. The training room offered all kinds of safeguards. After Simon composed a message, a note would pop up asking if he really intended to send out this thought. Simon would click in his mind on Okay.

The boost chamber was training wheels for the dry brain. It was an apprenticeship that his friends blew past in a matter of days, or even hours. For them, boost commands quickly became second nature. But Simon continued going into that virtual room, year after year, closing the door and following its explicit instructions. Well into his twenties, he found it comforting. Then one morning, following a national cognitive update, he awoke to discover that it was gone. Vanished. Once all of the new users were infants, authorities apparently concluded, no one needed an old training program from the '40s. This was a rude shock for Simon, but he kept quiet about it. He was so embarrassed to still rely on training software that he never dared ask anyone— especially Ralf—why it was gone.

He looks up to see his brother talking to him. "You run your sex life in your boost and you don't know how to run shotgun?"

"When it comes to the chip, I pick and choose," Simon says glumly. He then returns to his boost and instructs Ellen to walk south on Campbell, and to send him a stream of images. "I think she's okay," he says moments later, as the images start to arrive. "She's walking east on Fourth, or maybe it's Father Rahm . . ."

"These names mean nothing to me," Ralf says. In his three days in the wild, he has never felt so powerless.

"Okay," Simon says, "she's turning right on Campbell, and . . . oh my God, the guy's on foot, right across the street!"

"Tell her!"

### 3/7/72 10:50 a.m. Mountain Standard Time

Ellen hurries down South Kansas Street, the package of blouses clenched in her right fist. She darts from the doorway of one store to the next, ready to take refuge if the big man with the nose appears. She's sweating, but the dry desert heat promptly turns it into salt.

She stops briefly and captures the image of the brick wall behind her. The dark bricks look old and worn, and probably date from the early twentieth century, or even before. Then she transmits the image to her wardrobe and calls for her leggings and shirt to switch to the same color pattern. The leggings transform immediately, camouflaging the lower half of her body with bricks. But the shirt she borrowed from Simon stubbornly retains its blue stripes. Ralf's brother, she sees, buys old-fashioned, immutable clothing. She's disappointed, but not surprised. Looking at her reflection in a shop window, she sees that the bricks clash with the striped shirt. She takes a flowered blouse from her bag and puts it on over Simon's shirt. That's better, she thinks, regarding herself. Not perfect, but Artemi don't need to be.

She is receiving only fragments of information from Simon. Single words come her way: "God, one-way, Kansas, scientist." Then comes a map of South El Paso, with its grid of one-way streets. With her geotags flickering, this could prove useful. But she doesn't see herself on a map. There's no dot. She turns it off to look at the image that pops in. It's Ralf sitting on the couch, looking uneasy. This is followed by more words about one-way streets. She hears Ralf's voice for a moment, saying something about "the guy who killed the scien-tist." Sounds like he's frustrated with Simon, too. Ellen wishes she could turn Simon off. When it comes to the boost, he has the skill of a toddler.

She gets the message to head south on Campbell. The wind picks up and blows her hair into her eyes. She holds it back with a free hand, thinking maybe she should stop and buy a hat. Simon asks for images, and she obediently sends him a stream. She reaches Campbell and takes a right. By her count, she's four blocks north of the market when she hears Ralf's voice yelling, "Tell her!"

A moment later comes the message from Simon. "Duck into the shoe store!"

Ellen pivots to her right and is hit by a blast of air-conditioning as she steps into Zapateria Ramon.

### 3/7/72 10:18 a.m. Mountain Standard Time

As Espinoza drains his coffee, his eyes on the magnificent Artemis in the boutique across the street, he picks up the scent of churros frying nearby. He sees the Artemis at the counter now, holding up flowered blouses. She looks his way, and he lowers his gaze.

She doesn't look anything like a desperado headed to Juárez, of all places. He almost feels like crossing the street, facing his quarry head on, and directing her north, to Cielo Vista Mall. That's her kind of place, he tells himself. It's the last brick-and-mortar mall in West Texas, a place where people actually walk from store to store and touch things. It's a throwback, but that's its charm. They even have a skating rink. Espinoza considers offering to drive her there in his KIFF—once he has eaten.

She pays for the clothes and disappears into the back of the store. Espinoza waits. Then he pays for the coffee and crosses the street to the boutique and peers in the window. She's gone.

Espinoza is walking in the direction of the churro stand when a message from George Smedley pops up.

"Well?"

"Following her in South El Paso," he responds.

"Are you certain she's the domed Artemis?"

"Has hair."

"Likely to be a wig," Smedley answers.

"Could be," Espinoza admits. He's aware that Smedley has access to Vallinger's tracking machine, which could tell him if the Artemis currently shopping in South El Paso is the one he's looking for. "Why not confirm with a data track?" he asks.

"Not in the office," Smedley replies. Then he asks, "Coordinates?"

"South El Paso Street and East Paisano Drive."

There's a pause, and then Smedley messages: "That's five hundred meters from the border!"

"You're telling me?"

"Is she in sight?"

Espinoza lies: "Across the street."

"Send image."

Espinoza pulls out an image from Ellen's visit to the boutique and sends it.

"That image was from a half hour ago," a new message says. "Where is she now?"

"Close by," Espinoza fibs again.

"Let me run shotgun." The last thing Espinoza wants at this point is to run a surveillance and interdiction job with his boss inside his head.

"I'm on top of it," he responds. "There she goes. Gotta move."

Espinoza has to get her back in sight—as soon as he eats. He stops at the churro stand and is transfixed by sweet strips of dough frying in an inch of bubbling oil. He orders a half dozen. He watches avidly as the teenaged boy fishes them out with a metal spatula and sprinkles them with confectioner's sugar. Espinoza tells him to add just a bit more sugar, and then asks, as casually as possible, if the young man has seen an Artemis lately. "She's carrying a small bag," he adds, helpfully.

"Is she very beautiful?" the boy asks. Espinoza sees that he's staring at his nose, which angers him.

"Asking if an Artemis is beautiful is like asking if a dog has four legs," he snaps.

"Most do," the boy notes as he strings more dough into the oil.

"Do what?"

"Most have four legs."

"Right. Have you seen the beautiful Artemis?"

The boy points toward Kansas Street. "About five minutes ago," he says. "If I see her," he adds, "should I tell her you're looking for her?"

Espinoza takes off in the same direction without answering.

Why is it, he wonders, as he eats his first churro, that the old-world flavors of the physical world still hold sway south of Paisano Avenue? Could it be that the dead zone stretches north from Juárez and numbs the boosts in South El Paso?

A message pops in from Smedley: "Update please."

"Following. Nothing new," he responds.

"You're carrying the new tool I sent?" Smedley is referring to an updated zapper that John Vallinger brought back from China. It features a modulated charge, which wipes the boost more gently and poses less risk of collateral damage. It could have saved a life on Espinoza's last assignment.

"Got it," Espinoza responds. Technically, this is true. He received it, but he left it at home in his top bureau drawer. It had a plastic molded case that felt cheap to him, and he didn't like the action on the button. He could picture it jamming in a crucial situation. Better to err on the side of too much force than too little. What if he zaps a dangerous enemy and nothing happens? For all he knows, the person might zap him back, or shoot him.

"Image please."

Espinoza waits a full minute and then responds, "Good, huh?"

"What?" Smedley answers.

"The image I sent."

"Didn't receive."

"Shit," Espinoza answers. "Transmission . . . dead . . . border . . . more later. Bye."

He turns the corner and a gust of wind almost knocks the paper cone of churros from his hand. He looks across the street and spots the Artemis. She has a hand on her head, holding back her hair. He captures the image just as she looks up to see him. Then she dives into a shoe store. Espinoza takes a moment to study the image in his boost. The colors are a bit faded, which makes her look even more sublime. He sends the image to Smedley while wondering, as he nibbles on a churro, if ugly Artemi are as rare as three-legged dogs, or if ugliness is even possible for such creatures.

Smedley immediately messages back. "That's her. Holding on to her wig with her hand! Interdict."

Standing on the corner, Espinoza reaches for another churro and mulls the possibility of an ugly Artemis. It's probably something philosophers write about, he thinks, flattering himself. Then he hurries across the street.

**3/7/72 11:11 a.m. Mountain Standard Time**

Ellen watches him come toward her. She snaps an image. A passing horse obscures most of Espinoza's face and body. All that can be seen of him is a greasy paper cone lifted high and the right side of his face. She sends it to Simon all the same and snaps another one as Espinoza runs between two horses, sidesteps a taco cart, and enters the store. Breathing hard, he walks straight up to her and says, "Señorita, I think you dropped this." He presents her the paper cone with one remaining churro. The grease has made the gray paper transparent.

"That's not mine!" Ellen says as she captures another image, this one full face.

Espinoza tries to exchange introductory packets with her, but Ellen blocks him from her boost. She sits down in one of the blue chairs and asks a young saleswoman wearing a white smock if she can see the line of Catspaws in size 7.

"It comes in black, gray, white, and a mixture of orange and white that we call popcorn," the woman says.

Ellen asks to see them all. As the saleswoman disappears into the stock room, Espinoza lowers himself into the chair next to Ellen. He's eating a churro. "Do I know you?" she asks.

"From the bar last night," he says, with his mouth full. "Oscar Espinoza." He smiles and extends a large dirty hand, which she ignores.

"I have the feeling you're following me."

"Listen," Espinoza says. "A woman like you shouldn't be shopping down here, not so close to the border. I'm supposed to make sure that you stay north of here." He gestures up Kansas Street. "You should go to Cielo Vista Mall. They have nice places on the west side, too."

Ellen has been sending a stream of images to Simon, and is now getting back fragments of responses, which distract her from what this man is saying.

Espinoza swivels in his chair and pulls a black plastic object from his pocket. "See this?" he says, holding it close to Ellen's nose. He lowers his voice to a raspy whisper. "It's called a zapper. If I pull this part right here"—he runs his thumb across a black button—"it sends out a charge that will wipe your boost clean. Everything on it. That's what a zapper does."

Ellen stares at him, speechless. She sends an image of the zapper toward Simon. It seems to take forever.

"Now I'm told you have some very valuable data on your boost," Espinoza continues. "I say, 'Good for you.' But the authorities want to make sure that you take your valuable data far from here, maybe, as I say, up to Cielo Vista Mall. Up north of I-10. Down here it's a security hazard."

Ellen nods blankly and says nothing. The saleswoman returns with boxes of the shoes. She asks Espinoza what he's looking for. He wonders if they have the same lines of Catspaws in size 14. She says they might and goes back to look for them.

A coherent message from Simon finally arrives. "Ask him who he works for." Ellen transmits the question, and he answers: "Don't you worry your pretty head." He's staring at the parting of her silky blond hair, where the individual strands are rooted to the skull.

She opens a box of black Catspaws and tries to fit them on the models of her feet in her boost. It's not working.

The saleswoman returns, her arms piled high with five enormous boxes, which she plops at Espinoza's feet. He opens a box of "popcorn" Catspaws. They look more like something a lion would wear. He tries to engage his boost, and seems to fail. "Something's funny about the signals down here," he says. Resigned to trying on the shoes the old-fashioned way, he unlaces one of his black army boots and pulls it off, exposing a dirty white sock with a big toe poking through.

At that moment, Ellen dashes out of the refrigerated store and onto the hot and crowded sidewalk.

"Hey, hold up!" Espinoza shouts. He runs out the door with his one socked foot, and hobbles after her south on Kansas.

Ellen darts among the pedestrians and vendors on the sidewalk. She looks over her shoulder. Espinoza's head towers above the crowd, moving crookedly. He's losing ground to the younger and faster Artemis. She races across the street, right in front of three horses and a bus, to the opposite sidewalk.

Her goal is to reach the market on South Mesa. Lots of people will be there. She calls up the street map. It appears with blurry edges. Still, she sees her dot inching along Kansas Street. But the map is twisted—as if there's a glitch in the transmission, and it's hard to tell whether she's moving north or south. The dot blinks erratically. She passes East Seventh and looks back. No sign of Espinoza. She reaches East Ninth and turns right. This is where the market should be. But she sees only a row of abandoned warehouses. She keeps running. She sends images to Simon, but most of them bounce back. She reaches Stanton Street. Is the market on the other side?

She starts to cross the street, only to see a huge coffee-colored KIFF bearing down on her. She turns back and retreats down an empty alley. At the end of it stands a large shade tree, a mesquite—an unusual sight in the sun-scorched barrio. It seems to beckon to her, offering shelter. She imagines herself climbing to safety. She heads toward it.

Running down the alley, she looks over her shoulder. Espinoza is on foot, sprinting in her direction, wearing one boot and carrying another in his hand. "Stop!" he yells. "Let me talk to you!"

She keeps running and reaches the tree. The branches are far too high for climbing.

Espinoza is getting closer. He has the zapper in his other hand and is pointing it toward her.

Ellen steps to the other side of the tree. She sees a chain-link fence with a child-sized hole in it. It's too small for Espinoza. She captures an image and attempts to send it. A single wooden plank extends away from her on the other side. She wriggles through the fence and scampers along the plank, over a dirty creek. As she runs, she instinctively raises her hands and her shopping bag to the back of her head, to protect herself from Oscar Espinoza's zap. It doesn't come. Reaching the end of the plank, she steps down into a marshy thicket of salt cedars and desert willow, and tromps into a very different world.

# PART II

———

## JUÁREZ

# EIGHT

Oscar Espinoza stands by the mesquite tree, staring at the hole the lovely Artemis slipped through. He was close enough to zap her. He probably should have. But he couldn't bring himself to kill or maim such a gorgeous creature. They might meet again one day, he tells himself, as he returns the zapper to his pocket. When that happens, he will let her know that he chose to save her life—at great risk to himself.

He turns around and walks north toward his double-parked KIFF. A message pops into his boost: "Status?"

Espinoza wonders how to respond. He climbs into his KIFF, tells it to carry out an illegal U-turn and head north, toward I-10. The vehicle tells him that a U-turn is not feasible, and proceeds instead to circle the block and drive north.

"Where are you?" Espinoza messages Smedley,

avoiding, if only for a minute or two, the bad news he must deliver.

"Now I'm at Vallinger's HQ," Smedley tells him. "I have the machine on. I see you driving north on Stanton Street. Where's the Artemis?"

"You don't see her on the map?"

"No."

"The reception's miserable close to the border."

"She's close to the border?"

"Very."

"Then why are you driving away from it?"

Espinoza comes up with a new idea. "She is not the domed Artemis," he messages.

"How do you know?"

"Her hair is connected to her skull. I saw the roots."

Smedley ignores the issue and returns to the unanswered question. "Where is she?"

"She isn't wearing a wig."

"Where is she?"

Espinoza gives up and responds with a single word: "Juárez."

A moment later, waves of pain surge through his skull. He lies back and moans as the KIFF drives north toward the mountains.

### 3/7/72 11:35 a.m. Juárez Standard Time

Ellen emerges from the muddy grove of salt ashes into the sunlight. The bag of blouses dangling from her hand. Her shoes glisten with mud, and drops of it dot the bottom of her leggings, which are still camouflaged in the colors of a South El Paso brick wall. But she's not in South El Paso anymore. That much she knows. She calls up a map in her boost and gets only the archived grid of El Paso. The network connection is dead. She walks onto a shadeless dirt street lined by rows of houses painted brown, pink, and a light shade of blue. A small boy dashes across, glancing at her for a moment before reaching a door. He pounds on it, yelling *"¡Abre!"* It opens, and he disappears inside, taking one more look at her as he pulls it closed behind him. Now the street is deserted. Ellen looks at a street sign and reads *Calle Lerdo.*

She was hoping at first that she had simply crossed a creek in El Paso into a slightly more Mexican neighborhood. But this is a different country. She walks down the middle of the street, like a gunfighter in an old movie. The stores, she sees, are all closed. She looks at the *zapateria,* with only two pairs of identical black shoes in the window, the *peluqueria,* with the old-fashioned red-and-white barber pole, the *bufete de abogados* Sanchez y Quintanilla. She tries looking up *"abogados"* in the boost, and is relieved to see that the translation app is stored in her archives. *Abogado* means lawyer. It cheers her a bit to think that this city of the wild, reputedly one of the most dangerous places on earth, keeps lawyers employed. Doesn't that mean there's rule of law?

Ellen's idea is to parallel the border for a block or two, and then cross at another point, hopefully hidden from the man with the brain zapper. She'll then take refuge inside a store and send an urgent message to Simon, something along the lines of, "Save me!" She might be in an alien world, she tells herself. But civilization, and home, is only a couple hundred yards to the north.

She takes a right on Avenida Malecón. Three boys are playing with a tennis ball in the street. When they see her, they run away, yelling something in Spanish, and vanish around the corner. Ellen can see people peering at her out their windows.

In the distance, church bells ring. Then she hears the whir of a motor and the sound of tires on the road. She reaches the deserted Calle Francisco Villa and takes a right. The vehicle is getting louder. Ahead, she can see the vegetation along the river. It's only a few yards away.

A door opens and a young woman with long black hair and a red blouse runs directly toward Ellen, saying, "*Venga, venga.*" She's followed by a young man. Before Ellen can run away, the woman wraps her arms around her. She and the man drag the struggling Ellen onto the sidewalk, up three steps, and into a house. Then they slam shut the door.

### 3/7/72 12:17 p.m. Mountain Standard Time

Simon cannot think of anything in the physical world to lighten his little brother's mood. Ralf has been shuffling around the apartment most of the morning, mumbling to himself. He worries about Ellen, naturally enough, and is powerless to communicate with her. Simon knows his brother is fed up with him for being such a klutzy go-between. The last image Simon got from Ellen was more than an hour ago. The grainy image featured a meaty male hand cradling a piece of black plastic with a button on it. Simon had no idea what it was. He made the mistake of telling Ralf about it, and was then unable to tell him what it was, or even what it looked like.

A few minutes later, Simon finally heard from his source about getting a used chip for Ralf. In a message, he told Simon that stealing chips was a violation of national security laws. "They're scared folks in Juárez are going to get their hands on a few and send them back with viruses." He counseled Simon to forget about it.

When Simon passed on this intelligence, Ralf looked skeptical. "The encryption's pretty sophisticated," he said. "I don't think a few wild people can—" He stopped mid-sentence. Even the mention of wild people filled him with gloom. He fell back on the couch and stared blankly at the ceiling.

Simon can understand his pain. Ralf has dedicated his career to the technology in chips. In all likelihood, he'll live the rest of his life without one. Ralf without a boost, he thinks, is like Van Gogh without hands. Or maybe without eyes.

And because of the mess Ralf's in, a man known to be a killer is stalking his girlfriend in South El Paso. Simon again calls up the last image Ellen sent. He attempts an image match in his boost, but comes up with far too many results: snuff bottles, scarabs, water pistols, diaphragm cases, old gas-fed cars called Bugs. Other people manage to call up precise results for their image searches, but Simon always falls short. His search this time seems to bring every possible black object with a curved surface. He doesn't mention this to Ralf. It will only frustrate him.

"You know," he says to Ralf, "I think it would have made you feel weird to carry around a lifetime of someone else's experiences in your head."

"I'd just delete them and use the processing power," Ralf answers.

"Do you have any idea how long it would take to erase years and years of video?"

"Maybe I'd just cordon off all the other person's shit," Ralf says, sitting up on the couch. "There'd be plenty of room for mine."

"You know," says Simon, "there are still some computers around. You don't necessarily need to have it in your head." He tells him about a technology museum at UTEP that has one of the first data centers from Googun.

"That would be Google," Ralf says. "That was a company that actually provided a lot of the search for the original boost, at least the American version."

"Whatever. So I was thinking you might be able to go over there and use it. You know. To do your work."

This brought a high whinnying laugh from Ralf. "That would be a crack-up," he says. "Me at the controls of a seventy-year-old machine that uses about as much electricity as this whole valley. I would bet," he continues, "that that machine hasn't been turned on since the '30s, or maybe even earlier. Functionally, I'd say, it's slightly less useful than an abacus."

Simon doesn't hear him. He's immersed in his boost, inspecting an image that just arrived from Ellen. He sees some mesquite branches with a bit of chain-link fencing behind them, and what looks like a wooden plank.

The image is grainy. It comes with no message, and is time-stamped 11:30 a.m.—or almost an hour ago. He doesn't know where it is. But the fact that it's grainy and took an hour to make its way to his boost tells him that it was sent from an area with spotty coverage. And that plank. He scrutinizes it. It appears to be crossing something, leading somewhere. He decides to keep worrisome thoughts from his brother, at least for now.

He glances down at Ralf. "Come on," he says. "Let's ride the horses over to the tavern." He doesn't mention that he has a phone call to make.

# NINE

Coming in from the blazing sunlight, the windowless Cavalry Club at first looks pitch black. As Ralf's eyes adjust to the darkness, he sees a solitary figure lying face-up on a long table. That would be Chui. Ralf can see that he has his eyes open. He's tensing and relaxing his fists, but his mind is clearly occupied in a virtual world far from the El Paso tavern.

Simon grabs Chui's arm and gives it a shake. "We could have been draining your beer," he says, as Chui sits up blinking, regaining his bearings.

Ralf walks over to the bar and studies the old-fashioned telephone. "Do you think I could call Ellen on this thing?" he asks, reaching for the receiver.

"Don't touch that!" Simon yells.

Ralf pulls his hand back, startled. "I was just—"

"Sorry," says Simon. "It's just connected to a business

associate of mine in a different . . . time zone. It could wake him up."

"You mean this thing actually works?"

Simon ignores the question and tells Chui to serve drinks. "Want a beer?"

"Well, it might make me a little sleepy in the middle of the day," Ralf says, "but sure." He's still thinking about the telephone. The only people who might get woken up from an El Paso phone in early afternoon would have to be on the other side of the earth, maybe China. Unless, he thinks, the associate is a Mexican who takes siestas. But that wouldn't be a different time zone, would it?

He gulps down half of his beer. He was thirsty, he realizes, and didn't have the boost to monitor his body and alert him to add fluids. The beer washes away the dust caked in his mouth and down his throat. He drinks more and wonders if the growling in his stomach is also trying to tell him, the old-fashioned way, that he's hungry. If he doesn't get a new chip, Ralf is going to have to learn to read new signals.

As Chui draws another beer, Ralf asks him if there's anything to eat. Chui nods, reaches below the counter, and promptly deposits a plate of blue lunch pellets on the bar, protein 150. Ralf eats a couple of them and finds them utterly tasteless. He has eaten the same lunch hundreds of times, turning the experience into *moules frites,* Cobb salads, peanut butter and jelly sandwiches. In the last month, he'd been enjoying a new app for couscous with merguez sausages and a spicy harissa sauce. "Do you have any normal food, with taste?" he asks Chui.

"We don't usually serve people like you," Chui says, adding a sympathetic shrug. He tells Ralf about a downtown restaurant called Chancho's that serves real food. Lawyers and bankers eat there, he says. "Normal people can't afford it."

Behind them, at the end of the bar, Simon is hunched over the telephone, talking to someone in low tones. Ralf wonders if it might have to do with Ellen.

"You ever use that thing?" Ralf asks, gesturing with his head toward the phone.

"Nope," Chui answers, making it clear with his eyes that further questions will get nowhere.

As Ralf piles the tasteless pellets into his mouth, it occurs to him that Simon's troubles in messaging Ellen might have more to do with Simon's boost mismanagement than with Ellen. He asks Chui if he remembers the woman from last night.

"The Artemis?"

"Yes, Ellen. You were messaging with her, right?"

Chui, apprehensive about the direction of the discussion, nods slowly.

"Could you do me a big favor and message her? Just tell her I'm here and wondering where she is."

Chui tries. He pauses for a second and concentrates, and then shakes his head. "It bounced back," he says.

"It was a long-shot," Ralf says, and he downs half his glass of beer. It works a lot better than the *euphoria* option on the beer apps in the boost. The lightness in his head is offset by a grounding in his gut, which somehow feels just right. He wonders if this is how it feels to be an animal. That gets him to thinking about how special it is to ride on an animal like Clover, the beast his brother lent him. He burps loudly. This produces a new and different beer sensation for which, he's sure, there's no app. When Ellen comes back, Ralf thinks, they'll make love, the old-fashioned way. They hardly ever do that.

Ralf feels bad about Ellen. She knows that he's attracted to every Artemis he sees. She's not blind, or dumb. Ralf wonders how many of the people with genetic packages end up like Ellen, regretting the face they lost, and the individuality. Given a choice, he imagines, most of them would still choose collective beauty over the risk of being uniquely ugly. Still, plenty of Artemi go to great lengths to distinguish themselves from the beautiful crowd. They often fail. Suzy, for example, shaved her head, only to find that she was in a large subgroup, the domed Artemi.

Ellen spends her life making artwork of unique beauty. Maybe it's because her beauty is off the shelf. This is the first time that idea has occurred to Ralf. He wonders if it might be profound. Or maybe he's just getting drunk. He thinks about the man following Ellen. What's happening to her?

Simon winds up his business in the corner and joins his brother at the bar. He orders a beer, and another one for Ralf.

"Got another job for you," Ralf says to Chui. "Remember the big guy who was sitting at the end of the bar last night?"

"Guy with the nose," Chui says, nodding. "Gave me a one percent tip."

"Did you know him?"

"No," Chui says. "And I'd remember."

"You have an image of him that you could do a search on?"

"Yeah, let me see." He puts down the beer and concentrates, matching the image from the quiet drinker at the end of the bar with tens of millions of faces. "Nothing," he says.

"I couldn't find one either," Simon says, relieved that the problem had to do with the database, and not his woeful technical skills.

"Try this," Ralf says. "Take his nose out of the image and match the rest of his face."

Chui immediately starts the hunt. Simon first needs some pointers on how to clip the nose out of the image. Ralf tries to give him instructions, but it's hard, because the beer has clouded his thinking. Plus, everyone has a different way to organize the boost, and different commands. Early on, each user tries out commands and the machine responds. Usually it's wrong. But when it works and the user registers a satisfied thought, the boost interprets it as a success, and it learns. That's how each machine evolves with the brain hosting it, and it's one of the challenges he'll face, Ralf knows, with a reconditioned boost, if he ever gets one.

Simon is still hard at work clipping the nose from the photo when Chui comes back with a result. "Got it," he says. "It's an old news story about a boxer named Oscar Espinoza, from Las Cruces. This picture's from

'41, when he was a twenty-five-year-old heavyweight. Get this," he adds, laughing. "They refer to him as 'hard-nosed.'"

Ralf tries to do the numbers. "So the guy's . . . fifty now, and sometime in the last . . . twenty years he's gained a chip and lost a nose, presumably without winning a championship."

"He's fifty-six, and it was thirty-one years ago," Chui says, adding precision to the foggy figures issuing from Ralf's wet and addled brain.

"Whatever," Ralf says, with a dismissive wave that almost knocks over his glass. Who needs such details? In the last few minutes, he has gained a new respect for estimates and broader concepts. As he takes another gulp of beer, he finds himself believing fervently, at least for the moment, that being wild will steer him toward the big picture. "Any data on where he lives?" he asks.

Chui takes a second. "Nope," he says. "It's like the guy got scrubbed from the boost-sphere."

# TEN

The back door opens and quickly shuts. Stella Kellogg, sitting in her dining room, hears scuffling feet, feels a ripple of winter air, and catches a glimpse of a bald-headed figure dashing up the back stairs. "Hey!" she yells.

"Sorry," comes the response from upstairs. "I just can't moss out 24/7. Only did two laps in Brookdale."

It's no use belaboring the point, Stella thinks. For three days Suzy Claiborne has been sheltered at her colonial home on Christopher Street, in Montclair. Outfitted with illegal jammers by the underground Democracy Movement, or DM, the house is an electronic refuge, like the White House or the Pentagon, its inhabitants untraceable—at least by their boosts.

She has two guests in the house, Suzy and the Chinese activist Bao-Zhi, who came to Montclair a day after Suzy, immediately after liberating Ralf from the clinic in Alexandria. Bao-Zhi is an expert in martial arts, and wild. If he speaks English, Stella has never heard it. On the few occasions that she has seen him, he has merely nodded his head and kept walking, invariably to the bathroom or kitchen. He spends almost all of his time in his third-floor bedroom. He chants and beats on a drum. Using a portable gas stove he brought with him, he cooks pungent soups. Like Suzy, he awaits his next assignment.

The idea was that Suzy would stay put here, off the grid, for a day or two, until technicians working for the DM outfitted her boost with a revamped electronic profile and ID number. Then she could put on a wig or grow her hair, develop a new wardrobe, and prepare herself for her next assignment. Artemi are easy to insert into government and industry. Their beauty, no doubt, plays a part. But due to a technical glitch, and the confusion surrounding Ralf's disappearance, Suzy's transition is delayed. The new profile isn't ready yet, and Suzy's growing impatient.

With no virtual worlds to explore in her boost, Suzy kills time feeding logs into the old fireplace and staring at the flames. Bao-Zhi's chanting from the third floor provides a meditative soundtrack. "What are the chances they'll be looking for me in Brookdale Park in Montclair, New Jersey, at three p.m. on a Sunday afternoon?" she asked the evening before, as the two of them sat by the roaring fire. Stella was astounded that someone with the technical smarts to work in the cognitive update department could say something so dumb.

"They put in a search for you, and when your boost

pops up, anywhere in the world, it gets ID'ed, mapped, and time-stamped."

"They don't see Bao-Zhi when he slips out to Watchung Avenue to pick up whatever powders and potions he uses," Suzy objected.

"That's because he's wild. But you, it's as if you're carrying a beacon. Didn't you know that?"

Suzy, her eyes on the flames, nodded slowly. "Yeah, I guess," she said. But this afternoon she ignored the warning, for the third time—and she doesn't seem too concerned. Stella hears her upstairs, singing in the shower.

Stella, now in her late fifties, has been living in this New Jersey suburb since she lost her job in Washington, twenty-eight years ago, following the America First! takeover of the government. Her hair has turned from auburn to silver, and her back has curved slightly, as if bearing the weight of a lifetime of disappointments. As the years passed, Stella's boys left home, Simon first to boarding school and then to college in St. Louis, Ralf to college in Pittsburgh. Stella nursed her mother to her death, and always figured she would sell the place and move back to Washington. But the government, in this age of Chinese ascendancy, was really just a one-party state run by business interests. The only job offer she received, a decade ago, was to work as a lobbyist in Varagon Inc., the K Street firm of John Vallinger. The money was good, and she convinced herself, briefly, that she could add a valuable moderate voice at Varagon, that it might work.

She met Vallinger at the job interview. It wasn't in the

usual virtual meeting, but face to face. Even remembering the meeting makes Stella's skin crawl. Vallinger, his gray skin and angular face crowned by wispy white hair falling down in a V, laid out for her his simple vision of the world. The boost represented the greatest advertising and entertainment platform ever invented, and the possibilities for business were endless—no matter who ran the country. This was an information economy. So even as Chinese companies took over what was left of the auto industry and asserted their muscle on Wall Street, there was plenty of money to be made—as long as the government left the boost free and unregulated. "Defend freedom in the boost," he said, echoing America First! slogans, "and keep the government out of our heads." He trusted that Stella, who had experience in the original Chinese negotiations, could bring diplomatic expertise and a veneer of bipartisanship to the firm. Stella left the interview shaken by Vallinger's withering vision. Months later, she signed up with the underground Democracy Movement, a secret organization run from the back of a pizza restaurant in Asbury Park, New Jersey.

Stella's diplomatic work to help push through the chip agreement in the '40s still fills her with shame and regret. Early on, it drove a wedge between her and Francisco, who took up the fight against the chip in Latin America, and was never heard from again. As an adolescent, Simon loathed the chip in his own head. He blamed her for screwing up his thinking, and he grew ever more devoted to memories of his father. Simon is in

El Paso, lost to her. Aside from formal greetings on birthdays and New Year's, she rarely communicates with him.

Ralf has found another way to disappoint her. He dedicates his genius to maintaining the chip—upholding the order she is busy trying to bring down. He spends much of his life in virtual worlds. She remembers visiting his Mount Pleasant apartment one time and seeing him and his Artemis girlfriend, Ellen, sitting in a near catatonic state, both in their own orbits, Ralf probably at some sporting event, Ellen no doubt touring galleries in Europe. Yet three months ago, when her group got unconfirmed reports about the open blue gates on the next update, Stella and her organization looked to Ralf, hoping that once he saw the Chinese plans he would lend his unique talents to hacking the chip and closing the gates. This could bring her son back into her life. The plan seemed to work almost too neatly. Suzy landed a job in the Update Department, befriended Ralf, and managed—despite her bare-bones knowledge of the technology—to find what appeared to be the open gates. She showed them to Ralf and he seemed ready to take action, at least according to Suzy. But he was picked up and taken to a clinic in Alexandria. Bao-Zhi freed him. That much she knows. Ralf hasn't been heard from since. Messages to him bounce back, and his bike, according to DM reports, remains locked to a post across the street from his office in the Department of Health and Human Services. Stella wonders if her son is imprisoned, or even dead.

Such concerns don't seem to weigh upon Suzy. There's something rough about her, and heedless, Stella thinks.

She has heard rumors about violence in Suzy's life, including one story that she stabbed her abusive father. Stella has trouble picturing this cheerful Artemis wielding a deadly weapon. Whatever ordeals Suzy's been through, she has the personality to put them behind her. It's not clear whether this comes from innate optimism or dreaminess. In either case, the woman seems to glide through life free of worry and fear. She regards sensible precautions as silly rules for fearful people—like Stella.

Suzy comes thumping downstairs, through the kitchen and into the dining room, still humming and hungry for her first meal of the day, which she eats in the midafternoon. Stella sees that she's shaved her head again. The soft down that was forming is gone, and the smooth Artemis skull glows with the opaque light of an egg. "I thought you were growing your hair," Stella says. After all, Suzy was supposed to be preparing for another assignment, blending in somewhere as a traditional Artemis.

"Oh yeah," Suzy says as she sits down. "Forgot." She takes a bagel, dips it into her green tea, and lifts it, dripping, to the opening parentheses of her perfect mouth.

Stella says nothing. She reaches with her napkin and blots the drops of tea on the old walnut table to keep it from spotting. She wonders how the Democracy Movement settled on this woman, who seems just as cavalier about security protocols as she is about table manners.

Even with the signals to her boost stymied by electronic jammers, Suzy appears to sense Stella's judgment. "I can always wear a wig," she says.

# ELEVEN

**3/7/72 1:16 p.m. Juárez Standard Time**

The boy, the only one in the family who speaks English, shows Ellen how to wrap the tortilla around the beans and then use it to mop up the brown sauce on the chicken. *"Mole poblano,"* he says, smiling broadly, as he stuffs half of a bean-filled sauce-drenched tortilla into his mouth. Ellen runs *"mole poblano"* through the archived translation app in her boost and gets back *"poblano mole."* Big help, she thinks, as she dabs at the sauce with a tortilla.

Four of them sit around a square folding table in a tiny dining room. The grandmother sits across from her. Ellen still doesn't know her name, since the other two simply call her Abuelita. She's short and squat, wears a blue apron, and keeps her graying hair tied up on her head in a bun. She seems friendly. In fact, she startled Ellen by kneeling down, as soon as she saw her, and embracing the Artemis's mud-spattered legs, saying something about *"Santisima Virgen."* The daughter, Juana, had to pry her arms away from Ellen, saying, "Abuelita, *no seas tonta!"* (Ellen quickly fed that to her boost. She got back, "Granny, do not be an idiot!") Juana, who must be about twenty, seems friendly enough, but doesn't speak a word of English. Then there's the boy, Alfredo, who looks about sixteen. He speaks good English and stares at Ellen with even more passion than his grandmother.

*"¿Te gusta el mole?"* The grandmother is looking across the table at her, and pointing with a stubby finger at the brown sauce. Ellen doesn't need translation to understand the question, but she has trouble responding. In the capped world, people simply speak their own languages and rely on the boosts to translate. But here she has to make the noises in another language, something she's never done. She can either read the boost's translation, and struggle with the pronunciation, or listen to the translated sentence in the boost and try to repeat it. Some of the sentences are too long for this. She listens to one and picks out a single word she recognizes: *"Delicioso."*

The old woman claps her hands and says, *"¡Bravo!"*

Ellen tries another sentence, asking where she can cross the border: *"¿Donde se puede . . ."* She forgets the rest. They wait quietly as she listens again to the phrase in her head. She finishes it: *"cruzar la frontera?"*

All three shake their heads grimly, and the grandmother wags a finger, saying, "No, no."

"They shoot people who cross the border," Alfredo says.

"Who's they?"

"Who do you think? The Americans."

"That's ridiculous," Ellen says. "I'm an American." She goes on to explain to Alfredo that the border patrol will be happy and relieved to see a fellow citizen emerge safe and unscathed from her detour into Juárez.

Alfredo laughs. He leans forward and asks, "Why do you think they have the drones patrolling our streets?"

Ellen considers the question for a moment. "To stop the drug traffic?" she asks.

"No," Alfredo says. "It's to keep us from crossing into your country—and to hunt and to kill any Americans who come over here. That one you saw," he points toward the window looking out on the street. "It was coming after you."

The boy must be brainwashed, Ellen thinks.

# TWELVE

The coffee-colored KIFF Wrangler climbs from El Paso's downtown. It crosses a bridge over I-10 and cruises up Prospect Street in the historic Sunset Heights neighborhood. To the left of the tree-lined street lies a gulch, which leads down to the river and, beyond it, the dusty expanse of Juárez. There, some two million wild people, the largest congregation of them on the continent, are busy doing whatever occupies unibrained folks on a sunny afternoon in March. The street he's climbing is lined with apartment buildings, including the Palmore, the home of Simon Alvare. Oscar Espinoza, looking from left to right, knows nothing about Simon. But the person riding shotgun in his boost, George Smedley, finds plenty to tell him.

"Look to the right," Smedley's voice says. "That mustard-colored place with the courtyard. He's been up in that apartment for the last sixteen hours. Doesn't even look like he's moving around. Must be asleep."

Espinoza instructs the car to park around the corner, on Corto Street. He hates hosting Smedley. But it was the price for having him call off the headache. So physical pain was replaced in the very same location by a carping presence. On days like this, Espinoza loathes his job.

"Where should I go?" he asks.

"Your voice hurts my ears," Smedley says. "Just message me!"

"I'll message you when you start messaging me," Espinoza says, raising his voice and wishing he could evict this squatter from his boost.

A message promptly pops up: "Okay, okay."

As Espinoza climbs down from the KIFF, he sees two men on horseback trotting into the small lot. One wearing a leather hat rides a white-hoofed sorrel. The other, his face burnt by the sun, sways uneasily on a paint. Espinoza recognizes them both from the tavern. "The two brothers," he messages Smedley.

"Can't be," his boss responds. "Ralf is in the apartment."

Espinoza is digesting that apparent contradiction when Ralf rushes up to him on the paint, pulls the horse to a halt in a cloud of dust, and says, "Where's Ellen?"

"Ellen?" Espinoza says.

"Don't tell him," Smedley instructs him, and then asks: "Who is he?"

"You were following her," Ralf says to Espinoza. "Where'd she go?"

"It's Ralf," Espinoza says. He means to message it to Smedley, but the words come out of his mouth.

"Who are you talking to?" Ralf dismounts from the horse and confronts Espinoza, his eyes at the level of the man's thick neck. Behind them, Simon climbs off his horse and also makes his way to the KIFF.

"Can't be Ralf," Smedley messages.

The information is overwhelming him, inside and outside of his head, and Espinoza simply stops talking. In a stream of messages, Smedley keeps insisting that the man cannot be Ralf, because Ralf is upstairs, immobile, in the apartment, and probably asleep, if not dead. He orders Espinoza to clarify: Is the woman he was following in Juárez named Suzy or Ellen? Ralf, meanwhile, keeps asking what Espinoza did with Ellen. His breath smells of beer.

Espinoza simply keeps his mouth shut and tries to think. He attempts to lock in to the two brothers, and comes up half empty. "I'm not getting anything from this younger one," he messages Smedley.

"Tell them that government authorities are investigating stolen data from the Update Division of Health and Human Services, and that Ralf Alvare and Suzy Claiborne must report immediately to Washington." Smedley's message reads more like a memo, and it delivers way too much information for Espinoza.

Ralf and Simon can see that Espinoza is receiving messages. His eyes are blank, his bushy eyebrows knitted in thought, and his lips, like those of a struggling reader, appear to mouth words. They wait.

Espinoza attempts in his confused mind to synthesize

Smedley's information. But it's too much. Smedley resends the message, which doesn't help one bit.

Finally, Espinoza blurts out: "Ralf Alvare is upstairs. He may be asleep, or even dead. He and . . . the Artemis have stolen data, and if they don't go back to Washington I'm going to have to use this." He pulls the black plastic zapper from his pocket and points it at their heads.

Smedley's voice rings inside Espinoza's head: "Idiot!"

Ralf stands speechless, his thoughts confused by the beer still sloshing in his stomach. But Simon is scrutinizing the tool in Espinoza's hand. "What is that thing?" he asks.

"A powerful weapon," Espinoza says, "from China."

"What's it do?"

"Scrubs data from your boost."

"All of it?" Simon asks.

Espinoza nods gravely, pleased to have the conversation focused on something he understands.

"Did you use that on our friend this morning in South El Paso?"

"The Artemis?"

Simon nods, and Ralf looks on with a stricken expression.

"Keep your trap shut!" Smedley tells Espinoza.

"No," Espinoza says, after a pause. "But I will not hesitate to unless—"

"Unless what?!" Smedley shouts. "Just keep your mouth shut!" He has abandoned the niceties of messages and is yelling at Espinoza.

"Unless Ralf Alvare and the Artemis meet me

here"—Espinoza refers to the time in his boost, 3:22—
"at five this afternoon." He then turns and starts to walk
away, before realizing that he was standing right next
to his KIFF. He returns to the vehicle, nods good-bye
to the brothers, climbs in, and rides away while the voice
of George Smedley berates him. Espinoza finds himself
longing for solitude, even if it comes with a splitting
headache. He wonders, as the car climbs toward Trans
Mountain Road, if he could exchange Smedley for the
migraine. Then he comes up with a question for his boss.
"If Ralf Alvare is sleeping, or dead, in the apartment,"
he asks, "who is that guy we were talking to?"

Smedley considers the question for a moment and
responds in a quiet voice that Espinoza hardly recognizes.
"Beats me," he says.

# THIRTEEN

**3/7/72 3:58 p.m. Juárez Standard Time**

The rapping on the door wakes the grandmother from her nap, startling her. She makes her way from the easy chair to the front door and peeks through the window. Without removing the chain guard, she opens the door and speaks to a young man outside. Ellen looks at him through the living-room window. He wears a buttoned-down white shirt and khaki pants and keeps his dark hair neatly parted. He could be a Mormon missionary, Ellen thinks, except that they usually travel in pairs. Ellen picks up only words from the conversation. *Peligro, seguridad, Kentucky Club, Don Paquito.* Where has she heard that name before?

The grandmother calls the children to the door, and the three of them huddle briefly with the visitor. Then Alfredo looks toward Ellen and, with the wave of his hand, asks her to join them. He explains that the visitor,

Enrique, will take her to see Don Paquito. "It's for your safety," he says.

"I'm not going," she says, returning to her chair. "I just want to go back to El Paso."

But over the next several minutes, they convince her to go. It's for her own safety, and theirs, too. She might get shot if she returns to El Paso, unless they're expecting her. If she stays put, a drone could come back and pulverize the entire house. It has happened before. "They know where you are," Alfredo says. He adds that Don Paquito is hardly a drug lord. "He's a . . . businessman," he says.

Ellen is frightened. She doesn't want to go alone with Enrique, even though he has a nice smile and looks like a missionary. "Come with me," she says to Alfredo. He looks first to his grandmother and his sister, and then back to Ellen, and nods.

Ten minutes later, Ellen and Alfredo walk along Avenida David Herrera with Enrique. The atmosphere is transformed. The virtual ghost town that she experienced on her first walk is now alive with sounds and smells, and above all, people. Old gas-burning cars roar by, sending plumes of black smoke into the air and honking at the children riding bikes in the street. Drivers leer at her through open windows. Ellen, still holding the bag with the blouse, feels embarrassed by the brick camouflage on her leggings. She wonders briefly if she could buy another pair of pants here. Foolish thought, she tells herself. She has no money for the wild world and anyway, she'll be heading back to El Paso in no time.

They come to a busy commercial thoroughfare, Avenida Juárez. Stores and restaurants line the street, and streams of pedestrians circulate on the sidewalks. Vendors have big blankets stretched out, covered with statues and trinkets. Boys pushing wheeled carts sell fruit popsicles and tamales. Ellen sees Africans and Chinese. A family with two small children in tow looks American. A group of Indian women pass by, each dressed in bright saris of red and yellow. They're laughing and speaking a language Ellen has never heard. She records a snippet and feeds it to her boost, and learns a moment later that it's Tamil.

"This doesn't feel like Mexico," Ellen says to Alfredo.

"People come here from everywhere," he says.

They walk across the street and into a dark saloon called the Kentucky Club. Six or seven people sit at stools along the parquet bar. Chandeliers hang from a ceiling lined with thick wooden beams. In the song echoing through the tavern, a man sings, "Tear drops, rolling down my face, trying to forget my . . . feelings of love . . ." The idea that groupings of wild people in this bar are all condemned to listen to the same song at the same time intrigues her. How much of their lives, she thinks, do they spend seeing and listening to things they don't like? Or do they learn to like things, because other people do?

Alfredo touches her elbow and points to the end of the bar. Enrique is holding the receiver of an old-fashioned telephone to his ear. He beckons with his hand, and she walks to the phone. He hands her the receiver. It's heavy. A tinny voice comes into her ear. "Hello, is that you, Ellen?"

It's a man's voice, and it sounds vaguely familiar. Ellen says nothing. She worries that even by making the simple statement that yes, it is she holding this phone to her face in this dark club in Juárez, she will certify her presence here, making it harder to wish away her detour through the fence and go home. Some sort of organization is clearly at work, folding her into this city. Enrique is a part of it. So is this telephone and, perhaps, Alfredo and the grandmother, the fearsome drones and Don Paquito. Ellen wants no part of it. As the man on the other end says, "Ellen? Ellen?" she keeps quiet.

Alfredo appears at her elbow. "Say something," he says. "It won't hurt you."

Ellen shakes her head. She listens to the voice. She knows it, but can't assign a face to it. She holds the mouthpiece to her eyes. It's circular and has dozens of small round holes.

"Speak into it," Alfredo urges her.

Finally, Ellen puts it to her face, covers her mouth with the other hand, and whispers: "Who are you?"

"Chui," he says. "It's me, Chui, from the Cavalry Club."

"Why are you talking on this machine?"

"They called me."

"Who?"

"The man you're with, in Juárez. Your guide."

"My guide?"

"You can trust him," Chui says.

Alfredo is on his tiptoes, leaning toward Ellen's face, trying to hear the conversation. She shoos him away, pointing to the far end of the bar. He walks about halfway down, where Enrique is sitting on a stool, and looks back at her.

"Chui," she says. "They want to take me to see Don Paquito. I just want to come home."

"Do what they say," he answers. "Stay away from those drones, and don't try crossing the border."

Ellen nods solemnly and asks, "Where's Ralf?"

"Simon's brother?"

"Yes."

"He was in here drinking beers a while ago. He's probably asleep now, I'd guess."

"Is he going to come here?"

"Why would he do that?"

Tears spring into Ellen's eyes. "To . . . rescue me," she manages to say.

"Hey, listen," Chui says. "You'll be okay. Just stick to your guide. If you want to talk to me, just come back to this phone in the Kentucky Club. I'm on the other end."

Ellen nods. She dries her eyes with the crook of her elbow, mumbles a good-bye into the receiver, and places it in its cradle. She joins Alfredo and Enrique. The three of them step out of the dark Kentucky Club onto Avenida Juárez. They turn right and make their way through the international throng toward Avenida 16 de Septiembre and the headquarters of Don Paquito.

# FOURTEEN

Oscar Espinoza's words echoed in Ralf's wild mind. "Ralf Alvare is upstairs, probably sleeping or dead." This had to mean that his boost lay somewhere in Simon's apartment. It was the only piece of him they could trace. Ralf ran up the stairs. He rifled through his gym bag and inspected every inch of the floor by the sofa, where he had slept. He ran his finger along shelves in the bathroom, and even the toilet. On his hands and knees, he inspected the kitchen floor. Then he carefully wiped the table where Ellen's undrunk cup of tea still sat. It was only when he went back to the green bag and unloaded it on the living-room floor that he saw a shiny speck. It was obscured by the lint at the bottom of his bag. But when he moistened a finger and lifted it to his eye, he could see a gleaming bit of ceramic the approximate size and weight of a bee's wing.

The chip now lies on a butter plate on the living-room

coffee table. Simon has covered it with the dome of a blue ceramic coffee cup, so that a breeze from the patio or the opening of a door won't blow it away. They've concluded that the chip must have fallen into his bag from the tray by his bed in the Alexandria Clinic. Or perhaps the quiet Asian man who led Ralf out to the street placed it there. In any case, some twenty-eight years of memories and videos lie under that cup, along with Ralf's entertainment and communications complex and a couple zettaflops of processing power. That's as powerful as supercomputers from the '20s, and fast enough to count each grain of sand on every beach on earth in a half second, though Ralf certainly has more practical applications in mind. One of them has to do with hacking the software update, which is also on the chip.

"The thing is," Simon is telling him, "as soon as you get this into your head—assuming you can—they'll know where to find you."

Ralf is growing impatient. It's as if half of his brain is lying under that cup. He just wants to get it back where it always was, to be himself again—and to put an end to this wild chapter of his life. Once he's himself again, he tells Simon, he'll figure out a way to stay safe.

"Imagine this," Simon says. "We find someone to implant it, and next thing you know, that guy with the nose comes back with that black tool and zaps you. What then?"

Ralf thinks about it. "Maybe we can use it," he says, "to flush them out."

"Flush them out? We've already seen them! It's the big guy in his KIFF, and he's got someone else running shotgun in his head."

"But we don't know who's sending them."

"Okay," says Simon, warming to the subject. "We flush them out. Let's just imagine that we put the chip out in the desert someplace. We set up a trap, and his KIFF falls into a big ditch. Once we have the man there, at our mercy for food and water, is he going to be able to give us details on who hired him?" He shakes his head. "Whoever is doing this, I don't think he gives privileged information to his goons."

"So what do we do?"

"I have an idea," Simon says.

### 3/7/72 5:09 p.m. Mountain Standard Time

At the end of a dirt path, the orange car parks and the purring engine goes silent. The two brothers climb out. "Santa Teresa International Golf Club," Simon says, extending his arms toward an expanse of scrub country, backed by a cinder block wall and bathed in the soft late-afternoon light. As they start walking toward the wall, Ralf can still make out the contours of the old golf course. The fairways, overgrown with sagebrush and creosote bushes, are bordered by cypress trees and flow down to what used to be putting greens. The weeds there, now tall enough to camouflage a white-tailed deer, still have a touch of green to them. Their ancestors, a half century ago, were tiny nubs of grass that were doused in chemicals, mowed, and coiffed. They were as foreign to this desert as orchids or daffodils, he thinks. Now they're expressing their wild side—a bit like him.

The golf course lies fifteen miles west of El Paso, in the abandoned border town of Santa Teresa, New Mexico. Simon came up with the idea of coming here. Ralf resisted at first. They argued. Simon's plan was to draw Espinoza to the border, where his boost wouldn't work so well. For this, they would leave the package containing the chip in a deep ditch, and Espinoza would crash his KIFF while approaching it.

"Killing him?" Ralf asked.

"Probably not." Simon shrugged, as though issues of life and death bored him.

Ralf wanted to know what they accomplished by crashing their pursuer in the desert. "We buy ourselves time," Simon answered.

They set off an hour ago. First they packed water and protein pellets into Ralf's green gym bag, along with a tiny ceramic snuff bottle, imported from China in the 1800s by one of their ancestors. Simon had wrapped Ralf's chip in packing gauze and stuffed it into the blue bottle. Ralf didn't see the sense of dwelling at such length on the container, a delicate oval decorated with hand-painted water birds. "Indulge me," Simon said as he found a niche for the bottle in the cruddy gym bag. "One family heirloom inside another."

Santa Teresa, Simon explained as they rode west, was the brainchild of a border entrepreneur. "He was either a visionary or a crook, depending on whether you'd lent him money, I guess." The development sprouted during a brief spell of euphoria in the late twentieth century as the United States and Mexico negotiated a free trade agreement. "The border was going to disappear," he said, "at least at Santa Teresa." The idea was that Mexican workers and American managers would live in the same industrial village straddling the land between New Mexico and Chihuahua. Companies would build factories there, where everyone—laborers and their bosses alike—could walk to work. Maybe they'd ride bikes. The golf course epitomized the Utopian vision. The front nine were in the U.S., the back nine across the border, as was the club house, the 19th Hole. It was famous for its large and elaborately constructed margaritas.

Santa Teresa soon fell on rocky times, Simon said. By the time it opened, companies were finding cheaper laborers in China. This stretch of New Mexico became a crossing point for northbound drugs. Weapons headed in the other direction, arming the warring mafia that trafficked the drugs. Juárez turned into a battle zone. At the same time, America's economic decline, brought on by debt, greed, and an education system that didn't produce enough brainy types for the information economy, gave birth to growing waves of xenophobia. Mexicans were the prime target. Mexicans were taking American jobs, living on welfare, sending their children to school for free. Given the grim horrors of Mexico's drug war and the anti-Mexican pressure growing in Washington, the government had little choice but to bolster border security. Early in the process it erected a big wall, bristling with sensors, right through Santa Teresa's golf course.

The wall still stands there, Ralf sees. About ten feet

high, it's built of cinder blocks, lined by a deep ditch and topped with iron spikes. On the far side, the cratered roof of the 19th Hole bakes in the desert sun.

He takes a step in that direction when Simon catches him by the shoulder. "Look out," he says.

Ralf looks down and sees that they're standing at the edge of a cliff, about twenty feet up. "You barely see it," Simon says to him. He explains that they're standing at a tee for one of the holes, either nine or ten. "I think they hit from this bluff with their drivers, and the green was on the other side of the wall. There's a little path here," he says, leading the way, "where they'd drive their golf carts down to the fairway."

Ralf slowly follows him down the hill. When they get to the bottom, Simon grabs Ralf's green bag and pulls out the Chinese snuff bottle. He walks along the desert floor, looking for something. After a few seconds, he stops and reaches down. With two hands he lifts a chunk of brown sandstone the size of a house cat. A snake underneath it darts away, within inches of Ralf's right foot, leaving the sound of its rattle.

"Forgot about them," Simon says. Lowering himself to his knees, he inspects the moist dirt uncovered by the rock. Then, with his right hand, he digs a hole a couple of inches deep, lays the blue bottle into it like a miniature mummy, and covers it with the rock.

"We just leave it there?" Ralf asks.

"Where else?"

"He drives off the cliff, probably kills himself. We leave him in the car, dead or dying, pick up the rock, put the bottle back into my gym bag, and drive home—

knowing nothing about his organization, and who sent him here. That's your scenario?"

"Don't bother with the details," Simon says. "We just don't know. But if we meet him where he's planning for us, in my apartment, he's in a position of strength. Out here, he's weaker."

"His car isn't dumb enough to drive off a cliff," Ralf says.

"We'll see," Simon says.

They walk from the site of the buried chip toward the cinder block wall. "It doesn't look so high tech," Ralf says to Simon. "More like something King Arthur would order up."

"They moved to low tech as the budgets shrank," Simon says.

Wandering away from Simon, Ralf comes up to a pit, an old sand trap. He looks into it and is surprised to see a patch of glittering white sand. It stands out on the deserted golf course like a gold tooth on a corpse picked clean by crows. He points to it and shouts to Simon, "Who tends that sand trap?"

"You noticed," Simon says, smiling as he walks toward his brother. "That's why we're here." He explains to Ralf that the sand covers a trap door leading to a tunnel first dug by the drug mafia early in the century, and used for the last decade or so as a secret conduit between the wild world of Juárez and its supporters, suppliers, migrants, and refugees. "This is the lifeline to the wild world," he says.

"And what does this lifeline have to do with *you*?" Ralf asks.

He doesn't have time to answer. They hear the sound of a vehicle above, tearing through the desert plants and bumping over rocks. "Sounds like he's coming fast," Simon says.

## 3/7/72 5:15 p.m. Mountain Standard Time

Oscar Espinoza is half expecting the two brothers to skip the follow-up meeting. He also knows that the Artemis—at least the one he saw—won't be there. She is in Juárez, as he knows firsthand, and will not likely be available for a boost-scrubbing encounter with his zapper. There might be another Artemis around—the true domed one. But he doubts it. So after knocking on their door at the Palmore and waiting a few moments, Espinoza turns around and lumbers down the steps. But Smedley, still riding shotgun in his boost, orders him to climb back to the landing. "Break into the apartment!" he yells.

"What for?"

"To get information, for starters. Like where they might be."

Espinoza, weary of hosting his meddling boss in his boost, tries to collect his thoughts. He has spent the entire afternoon with Smedley, most of the time processing barked orders and finding ways to sidestep them. But this time he comes up with an idea for Smedley. "Just do a search for Ralf Alvare's boost," he says. "That's what we're looking for, right?"

"I guess that's right," Smedley concedes.

Some ten minutes later, Espinoza is in the KIFF, heading north on I-10 toward Santa Teresa. When the vehicle misses the turn at Sunland Park, Smedley starts barking orders.

"Left here!" Smedley commands as they reach a dirt road. Seconds later, he tells Espinoza to follow a right curve up a hill. Espinoza dutifully transmits the order to the vehicle. It would be easier if Vallinger's command center, which has the details on Ralf's boost, could simply provide the map coordinates to the KIFF and let it hunt for itself. But Smedley keeps that information to himself and provides Espinoza only with turn-by-turn instructions.

At one point, Espinoza asks Smedley about the nature of the mission. "Do we want the boost as it is or do we want it erased?" he asks.

"As it is," Smedley answers. "But zap him if you see he's crossing into Mexico. He's only about a hundred yards away from the border."

The ride up the rocky path makes Espinoza's head hurt even more. He presses his palms to his eyes and sees the colors of the desert, the browns and yellows, swirl in a tightening vortex. He orders the KIFF to halt, and the vehicle promptly skids to a stop. "Take off the headache," he tells Smedley.

"Oh, I hit that by mistake," Smedley says.

"Don't joke."

"I'm not kidding," Smedley says. "The interface on this machine is a bad joke." He tells Espinoza that he'll turn it off, but struggles to find the right command. Espinoza hears him grumbling about the "stupid app" and its "god-awful interface." He finally gives up. "I'll do it later," he says. "I promise."

Espinoza sits in the KIFF, waiting. The vehicle is half-way up a steep hill, probably the remains of a tee on the front nine. Espinoza breathes heavily as the pain throbs through his head.

"Go get them," says Smedley's voice.

Oscar Espinoza, wracked by pain, orders the vehicle forward. It climbs to the top of the hill, rolls forward, slows down, and stops.

When Espinoza looks down, both he and Smedley can see that the KIFF is perched at the edge of a cliff. Below they see the two brothers, both faces pointed right toward them.

Espinoza climbs out of the car and begins to jog down the side of the hill. He would like to yell to the brothers, telling them to wait, that he doesn't want to hurt them, but the pain in his head is too great.

He hurries down the hill, looking at the scene unfolding below. The brothers appear to be arguing. The older one with the hat has the younger one, Ralf, by the elbow. He is tugging him away from the advancing Espinoza, toward a pit with unusually white sand.

As he gets closer to the border, his connection with Smedley dims. The phrases turn into simple words. "Run! Catch them!" The pain from the head and the tooth seems to ease.

He sees the two brothers jump into the pit of white sand. The older one, looking back at him, starts digging in the sand. Then he hoists open a sheet metal door, and the two of them climb inside and disappear.

"Catch!" Smedley orders.

"They're gone. Can't you see?"

"Go!" Espinoza, all 260 pounds of him, sprints toward the pit and hurls himself into the white sand. He locates the door, opens it, and crawls inside. He finds himself in a tunnel. It's dark and cool. He sees the brothers ahead of him, two forms silhouetted against the light at the end. Espinoza, still panting, lies in the darkness and quietly rejoices. Smedley's voice is gone, and the pain has vanished from his head. In this tunnel, he has found a measure of peace.

# FIFTEEN

Don Paquito does something strange with his eyes, Ellen notices. When he hears something that surprises him, or maybe something that makes him mad, he bats them heavily, as if trying to push out a dust mote, or maybe a tear, and then pauses for a second or two, before returning to the conversation. The first time he did it was when Ellen mentioned, early in their conversation, that she supposed he was in the drug business.

He batted his eyes, gazed for two or three seconds toward the twenty people in the next room typing on prehistoric computers, and then looked back at the Artemis sitting before him. "What makes you say that?" he asked, speaking with a soft Spanish accent.

"Well," Ellen said, not expecting to be pressed on such a simple point, "You're the . . . leader of Juárez, from what I've heard, and the business of Juárez is drugs. Everybody knows that."

That was when Don Paquito did the second strange thing with his eyes. He arced one brow impossibly high, into a peak that seemed to stretch halfway up his forehead. He just left it that way for a second or two, by way of response, before slowly lowering it to its place. There was something about the green eye under that acrobatic brow that looked familiar to her.

"I'll bet you can wiggle your ears," Ellen said.

"What's that?"

"I was just saying that if you can move your eyebrow like that, you can probably do tricks with your ears," Ellen said.

That was when she saw Don Paquito smile for the first time.

She likes his looks. He's small, probably not much more than five-seven, with wrinkles that dance across his face when he smiles. He has short-cropped black hair that's turning gray on the sides. His teeth are straight and true, though a bit darker than the sparkling norm in the United States. Ellen wonders if he smokes cigars.

When Ellen arrived at his offices, escorted by Alfredo and her "guide," Enrique, she caused a stir. The three entered through a crowded waiting room, where several dozen people were gathered on wooden benches and folding chairs. There were mothers with children, adults with their elderly parents, all of them dressed as if for church. A couple of the men wore neckties, something Ellen had seen only in old movies. When they saw Ellen, the crowd rose to its feet, and it seemed that everyone offered her a seat at the same time. She looked about, confused. Standing in one corner of the room, a pastry vendor reached into his glass case, pulled out a chocolate donut, ceremoniously shooed the flies from it, and lifted it to her on a white napkin. She walked past him, flashing a confused smile.

Enrique pulled Ellen by the elbow, leading her past the crowd and into the next room. This was the one where two dozen people typed on the old computers. Some of them talked on telephones, like the one Ellen had used at the Kentucky Club.

"What's this?" Ellen asked Enrique.

"The newsroom," he said.

They moved into the next room, a hall with potted palm trees and café tables embossed with the blue and white label of Corona beer. "This room is called the *playa,*" Enrique said. "It means 'beach.'"

Ellen nodded. She drummed her fingers on the table. She looked down and was embarrassed to see the ridiculous brick pattern on her leggings. Then she wondered why she should care about her appearance for an interview with a drug lord, if that's what Don Paquito was.

A young woman wearing blue jeans and sandals walked up to the table and announced that Don Paquito was waiting for her. Ellen felt frightened. Alfredo patted her shoulder, and said he had to leave. "But when will I see you again?" she asked, feeling lonely and abandoned.

He shrugged and walked backward toward the waiting room, with a wistful smile.

"It'll be all right," said Enrique, all business. "We know how to find him."

With a lump in her throat, Ellen followed the young woman into a small dark office. On three sides stood shelves piled high with books, in English and Spanish. On the wall to her left hung a large poster featuring a somber-faced Mexican, clad in white, with a pointed moustache and penetrating eyes. Under it were the words: *¡Tierra y Libertad!*

"That's Emiliano Zapata," came a voice from across the room. Don Paquito was sitting at a shiny walnut desk with brass fixtures. Ellen recognized it from her art studies as a Louis XV. She looked at Don Paquito. What struck her was the eyes. They smiled more than his mouth, and she felt she knew him.

Ellen instinctively fed Zapata's name into the archives of her boost and learned that he was a leader of the Mexican Revolution, gunned down in a town called Chinameca in 1919.

Don Paquito gestured toward the only other seat in the office, a metallic desk chair on wheels, and Ellen sat down. He asked her if she wanted something to drink, "Some lemonade, perhaps?" She nodded, and he called toward the door. *"¡Elenita, agüita de limón para la señorita!"* Moments later, the young woman came into the office carrying a tray with a tall glass of lemonade and a chocolate donut that looked suspiciously like the fly-covered specimen from the waiting room. Ellen ignored the pastry and drank down the cold, sweet lemonade, emptying the glass. *"Tráele más,"* Don Paquito said. The woman darted out the door and returned with a pitcher, and filled Ellen's glass.

Leaning back in his desk chair, the Mexican went on

to grill Ellen about what she knew about Juárez. That drew her comment about the drug economy, sparking the first batting of Don Paquito's eyes.

"And what do you know about me?"

"Nothing," she said, taking a sip of lemonade. She remembered the story about the tigers in his house, and the harem, and the glass eye that he popped out from time to time. But she kept that intelligence to herself.

"Surely you must have something about me on your chip. Your boost. Petabytes or zettabytes of data, and nothing about me?" He acted hurt.

"There's no network coverage here," Ellen said. "But I do have some archives." She promptly carried out a search and unearthed an old news report about a man named Don Paquito who had wrested political and military control of Juárez from a previous generation of drug lords who ran the Juárez cartel. "It says you're ruthless," she said.

"'Ruthless,'" he said, trying out the word in his mouth. "After the Boston Red Sox made their very foolish trade with the Yankees, they were 'ruthless,' too." He laughed at his own joke, which made no sense to Ellen. She focused on his pronunciation of "Yankees," which sounded almost like "junkies."

He went on to ask her about her family in Paterson, New Jersey, her education at Rutgers, where she majored in graphic design. He told her that he also did some studying in the United States. "American Studies," he said dismissively. "Should have done econ."

She looked at him quizzically.

"I could have used more mathematics, and statistics," he said. "Everybody could."

Ellen nodded slowly. That was one of Ralf's talking points, which she found tiresome.

"You think that you can do all your math in your chip," Don Paquito said, "and that we wild people might as well give up in those areas. But you have to know which questions to ask." He pointed to his head. "You get the questions from the wild brain." He lifted his eyebrow in a modified arc, as if to punctuate the point.

That led to more discussion about language and art. Ellen contributed a few tidbits, but it was mostly Don Paquito who did the talking. He mentioned Montaigne and Emerson and José Ortega y Gasset, paintings by Caravaggio and José Siqueiros. Ellen, suddenly weary, stopped paying attention. Looking down, she traced her finger along the orange pattern of the bricks on her leggings. Either he was trying to impress her, she figured, or Don Paquito was a lonely man.

Then he stopped talking. The room was silent, until other noises began to intrude. Ellen could hear a fly batting against the screen in the window. She could hear the voices in the newsroom next door. She could hear Don Paquito's rhythmic breathing. They sat.

Now Ellen, no longer frightened of this drug lord—if he is one—is thinking about what she can get from him. He appears to be reading a document on his desk.

"So," she says, breaking the silence, "can you help me get back to El Paso this afternoon?"

Don Paquito looks up. "I thought you'd never ask," he says. "But I don't think that's such a good idea."

"Why?"

"Why did you come here?"

"Well, I . . . I got into a bit of a jam, and—"

"Someone was chasing you, wasn't he?"

How does he know? She wonders how much to tell him. "Well," she says, "sort of."

"He won't chase you over here."

She takes a moment to digest that thought. From the logic of it, she should stay in Juárez forever, or at least for a long time. That, she says to herself, is not going to happen.

"Why did you come down to El Paso?" Don Paquito goes on. "From your home in Adams Morgan?"

"Mount Pleasant," she says.

"Mount Pleasant then."

"My boyfriend has family down here."

"Ralf," he says, "has Simon." He pronounces the second name in Spanish.

"You know about Ralf, and Simon?"

"I know about a lot of things," Don Paquito says. He gestures toward the newsroom. "I don't know if you noticed, but I'm in the information business."

"I just want to get back to Ralf," Ellen says.

"From what I'm hearing," Don Paquito says, "you'll be seeing him over here."

# SIXTEEN

"Let me get this straight," says John Vallinger. "I give you instructions to stop Ralf Alvare and his chip from crossing into Mexico. So first you chase his girlfriend over there. Then, just minutes ago, you chase Alvare and his brother, and they both wind up in Juárez. The man you've hired to apprehend them follows them and is now off the grid. Do I have that right?"

They're sitting around a gleaming mahogany table in Vallinger's K Street office. Outside the thick soundproof windows, each dressed with a cats-eye shade, Washington, two swallows chase each other, dipping and soaring in the evening sky. A Renaissance oil portrait of a prince, barely one-foot square, surveys the proceedings from its perch on an olive green wall. The prince has a bowl cut, with black bangs nearly down to his eyes, and he wears a leather beret tilted to the right, almost in the fashion of China's original "capped" workers.

George Smedley sits across from Vallinger. He struggles to maintain eye contact with his boss. Wearing a three-piece suit with his emblematic feather in his lapel, he slouches slightly in his chair.

"Do I have the story straight?" Vallinger asks.

Smedley nods his head ever so slightly.

"That's a yes?" Vallinger asks.

"Yes, essentially," Smedley says in a low voice.

Sitting with them is Tyler Dahl, often mentioned as a possible successor to the aged Vallinger. Smedley cannot abide him. Dahl studied humanities at Williams but fancies himself a tech specialist. Smedley is aware that the younger man views him as an enemy and spreads poisonous rumors about him. Smedley's lucky, he knows, that they come from such a self-interested source. Vallinger tends to discount the rumors—even though a number of them are true.

Sitting next to Dahl are a sprightly legislative assistant Smedley once tried to date, and three other people he has never seen. Two of them wear military uniforms.

"Essentially?" Vallinger asks. "Am I missing something?"

"Excuse me?"

"You said I had the story essentially straight."

"Right," Smedley says. He coughs to give himself time and then weighs his words carefully. "First, there's no indication that our man, Espinoza, is in Juárez. He went into the tunnel. He may be back. Then you make it sound like we drove these people into Juárez. That wasn't our intent. They escaped into Juárez, and there's every indication that that was their design from the beginning."

"Precisely why I gave you instructions to keep them from there," Vallinger says.

"But we can and should assume that our operative on the ground, Mr. Espinoza, will eventually apprehend them and bring them back."

"I won't hold my breath," Vallinger says. He turns to Dahl and asks for a technical report on the value of the data on Ralf Alvare's chip, and the prospects that it can be engineered, or hacked, to interfere with the upcoming national update, which is nine days away.

Dahl happily proceeds to deliver a detailed report into the boosts of everyone sitting around the table. The report shows the diagram of the software, including the altered Gate 318, which is highlighted in blue. This change, his document asserts, will "modernize" the American base, bringing it into "harmony" with the world standards coming out of China. Speed will increase by a factor of three, and the increased "transparency" through 318 Blue will allow businesses to study and "optimize" the buying, working, and health patterns of the American population, leading to greater efficiency, energy savings, and economic growth. In addition, the update will provide a new service, already popular in China, called "Teamwork." It will for the first time allow people not just to exchange messages with their friends, but also to share feelings and sensations. An army platoon leader, for example, will have an awareness of the location of his soldiers and an inkling of what they're experiencing. "This is just a prototype," Dahl says. "A fuller version should come in the next update. But this will be enough for early adapters to tinker around with it." Once they get used to the software, according to the document, human teams should operate with the "synchronized efficiency of army ants." These changes, the document states, have the support of the U.S. Chamber of Commerce, the Department of Homeland Security, and, naturally, the White House.

"There's one other feature on this chip," he adds. "It's something called R function, but I'm still looking for the details on it. I've sent messages to—"

"You can leave that one alone," Vallinger interrupts. "I've been briefed on it."

Smedley listens as Dahl details the threats to update. Global terrorist organizations are expected to launch network attacks in the coming week to disrupt the deployment and, perhaps, compromise the software. Domestic extremists, such as the Democracy Movement, are working to agitate against it, and they can expect strong support from Luddite sectors. To date, though, he says, the DM has struggled to get their message out. "Luckily," Dahl says, engaging his voice for the first time, "they can't get their message in the boost. And that's the only place people go to for their news."

"The biggest danger," he says, reverting to messaging, "is this." Two photos pop up. He explains that Ralf Alvare and Suzy Claiborne, both employees of the Update Department, disappeared on Friday after an unauthorized transfer of the software update code. Claiborne vanished almost immediately, never even showing up for work following the transfer. Alvare was apprehended "by private security," but later escaped from an Alexandria location "with the information apparently still on his chip, but . . ." He pauses, searching for the right words. "But not lodged internally."

"Lodged internally?" one of the military officers messages.

"The chip wasn't in his head."

"Your private security forces removed a man's chip?" The officer looks alarmed.

Vallinger, never comfortable with messaging, raises his voice. "We thought it the most prudent course—or at least Mr. Smedley did."

"Now that man, Alvare, has taken refuge in Juárez with his chip?" This information clearly wasn't in the documents Vallinger's team prepared for the Pentagon.

"Right," Vallinger says. "As of twelve minutes ago."

"Where's the woman?"

"She seems to be off the grid, probably in a safe house. But she has popped up a couple times in a New Jersey town, near New York," Vallinger says. "I think we can locate her."

"She's not the important one," Dahl says. "From what we see, she was a DM plant. Her mission was to engage Alvare. He's the one who can disrupt the whole program."

"Is he really so special?" Smedley asks.

"A master hacker," Dahl responds. "One time, at college, he hacked the chips so that the custodial staff at Carnegie Mellon spoke for two days in Urdu. Or maybe it was Pashto." He stops briefly and consults his boost.

"Actually, it was Tamil," he says. "Funny the tricks the memory plays. . . . Another time," he continues, "as a prank, he tweaked the spatial orientation of the University of Pittsburgh basketball team. In one game, they missed every shot, and were shut out, I think, 68-0."

"That's impossible!" Vallinger says. He lived far into middle age with only his wild brain, and the idea that basketball players would rely on their boosts to such a degree disturbs him. "If they use their chips to calculate the arc on their shots, they deserve to lose, for chrissakes," he says. He goes on to speculate that a reasonable coach would call a quick time-out and tell them to use their wet brains, "which run the body a whole lot better than the chip."

"True," Dahl says. "And wet brains are also good for spatial orientation." He gestures out the window toward the traffic below. "But turn off the boosts of these people and the controls on their cars, and see how many of them can find their way home."

While the discussion veers into a debate about the wet brain versus the dry, Smedley hunts in his boost for items on Ralf Alvare, pranks, Carnegie Mellon, even Tamil. He finds nothing. He scans the records of the Pitt Panther basketball team, and finds one loss to Villanova, 63-0, in the Sweet Sixteen round of the 2063 NCAA Tournament.

"Not much about Alvare's pranks on the network," he says in a message, "except for that one basketball game."

"You won't find any of that stuff in the boost," Dahl responds. "They don't want to give people ideas."

"Let's get back to the matter at hand," Vallinger says, once again with spoken words. "Could Alvare disrupt the update from Mexico, without a boost in his own head?"

"If he has access to computing, he conceivably could. We have to assume they have advanced machinery in Juárez, but we don't know what it is," Dahl says.

Vallinger nods grimly toward the military men at the table and sends them a private message. Minutes later, the military contingent departs, along with the legislative aide. This leaves Vallinger, Smedley, and Dahl around the large table.

"There's a bigger issue, and I think it concerns you," Vallinger says, looking directly at Smedley. Then he nods grimly to Dahl, who begins another prepared presentation.

"Word appears to be spreading quickly on certain networks about the nature of the coming update," he says.

"There's always chatter about those things," Smedley says. He leans back in his chair, yawning.

"This isn't exactly chatter," Dahl says. "It includes information about the surveillance gate."

"There have been rumors about one coming forever," Smedley says. "I've been hearing them for years."

"But these reports," Dahl goes on, "mention an update worker who just had his boost removed."

Smedley twists in his chair. "My God," he says. "Someone at that damn clinic must be talking. First they let him escape, with the boost, then they talk." He pounds on the table, a bit too theatrically. "I'm finished with them."

"It's not just that," Dahl says, smiling as he comes in for the kill: "The reports mention that he's in El Paso."

Vallinger leans across the table toward Smedley. "Who in the clinic would possibly know that?" he asks.

Smedley looks at Vallinger's hands, pressed hard against the table, and studies the liver spots. They remind him of maps of Minnesota and northern Wisconsin, each one dotted with thousands of lakes. He wishes he were swimming in one of them now, or maybe ice fishing. He wants no part of this discussion. If only he were on the other side of the window, looking for a restaurant or walking back home. But he's stuck in this office, and Vallinger is staring at him. The dark bags under his eyes seem to sag more than usual. He must be up for another face stretch soon.

Smedley pushes himself to concentrate on the matter at hand. "Where are these rumors surfacing?" he finally asks. "I'm not seeing any of them in my circles."

"The network analysis shows that it broke Sunday evening on a sex site, Hard to Miss an Artemis. It's been spreading, more or less virally, through the whole virtual sex world since then," Dahl says.

Silence. Smedley leans forward and places his elbows on the table, and then rests his chin in his hands, trying to affect an air of indignation mixed with concern. "Alvare's talking," he says.

He doubts that Vallinger believes him. While Smedley's ownership of virtual sex worlds, including Hard to Miss an Artemis, is obscured by a dense fabric of false names and meticulously encrypted software, his involvement in them is hardly a mystery. Only a few days ago he used the Alvare affair to drag in practically every Artemis in Washington—with the notable exception of Suzy Claiborne. All of them were offered employment in the very sex site in question.

It was a day or two later that he found himself cavorting with a very pretty avatar in a virtual resort overlooking the Bosporus, and telling her that every act they were committing, along with all the other information coursing through their boosts, would soon be monitored through an open surveillance gate. That led him to tell her the story about the newly wild man in El Paso. He recounted it as a comedy, a computer science genius who from one day to the next finds himself reduced to the thinking apparatus of a caveman. It was so funny that he tried it out on two or three other women that very night. Smedley was aware even as he spoke that he shouldn't be telling them so much. But they seemed so interested, and so warm, and they all vowed they wouldn't tell. He wonders who those Artemis avatars might be in real life. They could be anyone, he realizes, man or woman. Practically the only people he can rule out are the wild—the Amish, the elderly holdouts, a smattering of rural Luddites, and Ralf Alvare himself.

He lifts his head from his hands and sighs. "I guess it's academic at this point, but Alvare himself must be the leak."

"On a virtual sex site, without a boost?" Vallinger dismisses the idea with a wave of a spotted hand.

"Maybe Espinoza then," Smedley says.

Vallinger says nothing. He stares at Smedley, perhaps

awaiting a confession, or at least a more plausible story. Smedley hears his labored breathing and finds himself wishing that the old man would simply keel over. He glances at Dahl, who is turned away from the uncomfortable scene and studying the portrait of the Renaissance prince.

Vallinger breaks the silence by pounding the table with his right fist. For such a thin fist on a sturdy table it makes a resounding bang. "I think it was you," he says, still breathing heavily. "I want to know what you're going to do to make it right."

Smedley, feeling vanquished, answers meekly with a question: "What do you propose?"

# SEVENTEEN

**3/7/72 7:36 p.m. Juárez Standard Time**

Could it get any worse than this? Ralf thinks about it. Pushed by his brother, he has crawled through a tunnel into what is reputedly the most dangerous city in America. He has no money, no Spanish, no map, and, most importantly, no boost. His girlfriend is at large somewhere in the same city. And his brother, who sits across the table from him in this grubby convenience store, is eagerly describing to him, in far more detail than Ralf would choose, the particulars of his sex life in virtual worlds. If Ralf had his boost, he would no doubt escape into a virtual world of his own. But today he's stuck with his brother, in his wet brain and in Juárez.

They sit on folding chairs at a metal table decorated with the ancient blue and white emblem for Carta Blanca beer. Simon is happily piling through a bag of Sabritas potato chips and taking regular sips from a jumbo bottle of lukewarm grapefruit soda.

It was only about an hour ago, Ralf estimates, that they emerged from the sand trap tunnel onto the dirt roads of greater Juárez. Simon took one last look down the tunnel. If Espinoza was following them, he was far behind. The risk on the Mexican side came, he knew, came from drones. He grabbed Ralf by the hand and pulled him toward the road, saying only, "Hurry!" They trotted through a section that seemed almost rural. It was scattered with cinder block huts topped by corrugated plastic in orange or green. Women hunched over dry fields, planting. They called to their children, telling them not to run after the outsiders. Ralf and Simon moved east, Simon looking back every few steps. The sun set behind them.

When they reached a crossroads, he grabbed Ralf by the elbow and tugged him to the right. They ducked into a small grocery store with a hand-painted sign over the door, Trastos. The woman behind the counter smiled and said, "*¡Ay que sorpresa, Simon!*"

"They know you here?" Ralf asked, still panting.

"A little bit."

"*Y este debe ser tu hermanito,*" the woman said, sizing up Ralf. "*Son casi idénticos.*"

Simon nodded with a smile and translated for Ralf. "She can tell we're brothers."

"Right," Ralf said. "Listen, we should think about getting back. It's late."

"I think we should probably spend the night here," Simon said, looking uneasy.

"Here?" Ralf said, pointing to the floor.

"They know me. They have cots in the next room.

Late as it is, I just don't think it's smart to crawl through that tunnel again. We really don't know who might be waiting for us."

"Why can't we just cross a bridge, like normal people?"

"'Normal people' don't cross bridges from Juárez into El Paso. It's one of the most highly defended borders in the world."

"So are we going to cross through the tunnel tomorrow?"

"We'll talk about that."

"Let's talk now."

The woman came to the table and plunked down two bottles of yellow soda pop and a big bag of potato chips.

"Okay," Simon said to his brother. "The people chasing you—or us—are over there, right?"

Ralf nodded.

"Now do you understand what this drama's about?"

"The open gate in the update," Ralf said impatiently. He found Simon's questions patronizing.

"Do you have any thoughts about who arranged to have that gate left open?"

"Industrialists, I guess," Ralf said. "I don't know."

"Powerful people, though. Right?"

"Obviously."

"And who gets in the way of what they want? Who are their enemies?"

Ralf fidgeted in his chair and looked toward the door. "I don't know," he said, anxious to end this cross-examination. "Who?"

"That Asian guy who led you out of the clinic,"

Simon said. "You heard some explosions, right? What were they from?"

"Listen," Ralf said. "Why don't you just tell me what the hell you want to tell me. We don't have to drag this on. You know stuff you're not telling me."

"I don't know who's chasing you," Simon said. "But I don't think it makes sense to hurry back across the river until we have some sort of plan."

Ralf can tell that Simon was planning this excursion into Juárez, at least since the lunchtime meeting with the guy with the nose. When they reached Trastos, he saw that his brother just happened to have loads of Juárez currency in his pocket. The money looks like plastic poker chips, in green, red, and yellow, each one stamped with 1, 5, or 20 "*dolares.*" It's odd, Ralf thinks, that while the U.S. capitulated twenty years ago, switching to Renminbi—while still calling them "dollars"—the Mexicans appear to be holding true to the greenback, albeit in plastic. Could it have something to do with drug revenues? Ralf noted that one of Simon's dollars bought two grapefruit sodas and the large bag of chips. The woman gave Simon four pieces of candy for change. Simon distributed them to the barefooted children who stood by the table gawking at them. Either a Juárez dollar is worth a lot, Ralf thinks, or junk food is cheap in the land of the wild.

Perhaps to distract Ralf from questions about returning to El Paso, Simon launches into a philosophical discussion about perception and reality, in traditional body life and virtual worlds. He tries to use his own sex life as an example, but Ralf refuses to engage. He stares at his brother in stony silence, not even breaking it to eat a potato chip.

Simon evidently gets the message, because he is now retreating into the broader theme of the virtual. "You have to understand," he says, "how primitive these virtual apps were when we were kids. They had this Swiss Alps app, and it just felt like you were climbing stairs and looking at a slide show. They had food apps, and I swear the only flavors they had were sweet, sour, and salty."

This breaks Ralf from his silence. "There were two problems," he says. "First, they only had a basic read on the brain. So they couldn't get very specific, distinguishing between different sweet sensations, like between vanilla and chocolate. The other problem was that people are different. You might experience a potato chip through a different combination of neural connections than I would. So each person had to have patience and train the app to deliver the experience like real life. Even now, the apps still rely on tricks. One of them might give you salty, but dresses it in the shape or texture of anchovies or olives, and you provide the customized detail with your own knowledge. A lot of it works through suggestion—teaching the brain what to expect."

"But what about sex when you haven't had any?" Simon asks. "That was my problem."

"Not sex again."

"I'm just saying . . ." Simon goes on to describe the generation gap that he still feels with his little brother. He and his friends grew up with their experiences grounded in the wild brain. Each one, whether it was the taste of strawberries or the feeling of diving into a cold pool, was highly nuanced—a staggering combination of colors, sensations, thoughts, and memories, all of them processed by a brain that had evolved over billions of years. "Then they come along and give us virtual apps that were just the crudest version of reality," he says. "When we were disappointed, they called us Luddites." He stops to shovel more Sabritas into his mouth, and washes them down with a gulp of the soda. "But your generation was different," he says. "You accepted the virtual as real."

"Not really," Ralf objects.

"Well, close to it. It was part of your life. Here's what really bugged me. Everybody started accepting the virtual as real, just because enough of you believed it. It was as if you had a quorum."

Ralf rolls his eyes. He reaches for the soda, lifts the bottle, and puts it down. "I'll tell you one thing: I'd take an ice-cold virtual soda over this warm crap," he says.

"But would the app have all the same tastes?"

"It'd probably have some better ones, if anybody bothered making it."

"Okay," Simon says. "Maybe artificially flavored grapefruit soda wasn't the best starting point. How about this. When I was a kid, they had this cherry flavor. They put it into sodas and candy and gum. It really didn't taste like cherries at all. Not at all! But people began to accept it as cherry. That's what happens with apps."

"Only in the beginning," Ralf says. "Let's say that in the beginning they had a crude cherry app. It tasted like sugar and it was red. That was it. But then in the next round of research, they began to dig deeper in the realm of sweet, and they began to find different combinations that gave the experience of cherries versus peaches and mangoes. They got better. At the same time, they did research on haptic technology, re-creating the physical sensation, like how far the teeth sink into the skin of a cherry before it breaks, and then creating that physical sensation in your brain. It's still not anywhere close to perfect. But for a lot of people it's close enough—especially if they haven't experienced the real thing."

"That's the way it is for me with sex," Simon says.

"Oh, come on!"

"No, I just want to make this point," Simon says. "I'll try not to embarrass you."

Ralf, now resigned, sighs and waits.

"Look, I won't go into details." Simon glances toward the counter, to see if the woman is eavesdropping. Then he leans forward and whispers, "My whole sex life is in these worlds, like I told you. In one of them, I'm a woman. I meet people, or people's avatars, and we talk and what not, and we have sex. Now in the beginning, the avatars weren't really much like people. They were more like cartoons. The sex didn't feel real, or what I imagine to be real. But it was good enough, like the fruit you're talking about. But now it's getting more real. There are all kinds of physical complications I won't go into, things that happen to you when you have a real body. It's stuff I don't want. I think that when it comes to certain things, I want a simulation that feels like a simulation."

"It sounds like you're scared of reality."

"No, reality's fine," Simon says. "But I don't like confusing it with the virtual stuff. If I do, I might lose track of who I am." He leans across the table, lowers his whisper by a notch, and adds: "Or even *what* I am."

"But you're acting like that virtual world isn't real," Ralf says. "It is. Those are real people. You're talking to them, interacting with them. You're part of their lives, and they're part of yours, even if you don't know who they are."

Simon appears to have lost interest in the conversation. He is looking toward the door opening, which is covered by a curtain of dangling strips of green plastic.

"In any case," Ralf says, yawning, "these questions about virtual worlds aren't something I have to worry about, at least for now. Nobody does around here."

Simon pays no attention. "Hear that?" he says. A buzzing noise comes from outside. It grows louder as they listen, second by second, turning into a low roar. Children who were playing in the street hurry into the store. They huddle behind the counter. No one says a word. Then come a series of explosions that shake the ground, knocking Ralf's bottle of soda to the floor, where it shatters.

"A drone," Simon says darkly. "It's probably after us."

# EIGHTEEN

Oscar Espinoza leaned against the rounded wall in the darkness of the tunnel for fifteen minutes or so, enjoying the pain-free head he no longer shared with George Smedley. He saw the two figures ahead of him scurrying toward Mexico. He couldn't catch them, he thought, even if he wanted to. So which way should he crawl? It was a thorny question. By following the brothers into Juárez, he could escape his boss and the excruciating headaches. But crawling to Juárez would land him in a dangerous city of the wild. What's more, Espinoza, despite his name, had only a school boy's knowledge of Spanish in his wet brain. He would be a foreigner. He would be without his KIFF.

Espinoza lay back on the dirt floor of the tunnel and considered the options. His stomach growled. He hadn't had a bite since those churros in South El Paso, almost seven hours earlier. Pressed by hunger and fear, he came up with a solution. He would escape into Juárez, get something to eat there, maybe drink a few beers. Then he would return to the tunnel, crawl back to Santa Teresa, and reclaim his KIFF and the rest of his life, hopefully without further Smedley intrusions. With that, he set off on his knees.

An hour later, as the sun sets, Oscar Espinoza basks in the sensual pleasures of old Mexico. After finding a tiny restaurant, El Mezcal, he convinced the owner, an old man wearing a black Colorado Rockies baseball cap, to buy Espinoza's Bowie High School ring, a big chunk of silver and copper, encrusted with low-grade gems, for a pocketful of plastic currency. He learned, to his delight, that one single red chip would underwrite a feast, including a plate of fire-roasted goat, a mountain of refried beans, a basket of corn tortillas, and an avocado salad. An entire family gathers around his solitary table and watches him eat. The children whisper to each other and laugh, probably joking about his nose. But they seem friendly. When Espinoza fishes into his pocket, pulls out a yellow chip, and asks for *"cerveza,"* one of the children grabs it, races into the kitchen, and returns with a full six-pack of Bohemia. Espinoza downs one of the beers in a single gulp. It's warm. Only slightly disappointed, he opens a second and wonders how much of this plastic currency it might cost to rent a bed for the night, preferably with a woman. He figures he might as well spend every chip before he returns to the tunnel. Plastic Juárez money won't buy anything back home.

He's into his fourth beer and second plate of goat when he hears a buzzing noise outside. The family hears it, too, and the mother quickly gathers the children into the kitchen. She says something to Espinoza. He doesn't understand a word. She looks worried and motions for him to follow her. He picks up his plate of food with one hand and the two remaining beers with the other and walks into the kitchen. The buzz grows louder, turning into a roar. The family moves out through the back door of the kitchen. Espinoza follows them, still holding goat and beer. He finds himself in a warren of hovels, and among a stream of Mexicans hurrying away from the street.

He hears a deafening bang, and then another and a third. His ears ring, but within seconds he can hear babies crying and mothers calling out their children's names. He has lost sight of the family from the restaurant. The goat meat has fallen off his plate, which he drops to the ground. With the two beers dangling from his hand, he walks back toward El Mezcal and finds only its smoldering husk. The drone has disappeared. He hears its distant buzz to the east.

Either they sent the drone to kill him, he knows, or someone mistook him for Ralf Alvare. In either case, he'll likely bring death and destruction to anyone foolish enough to offer him shelter this evening in Juárez. Espinoza spots a wooden roof beam in the wreckage of El Mezcal. He sits on it, opens a beer, and mulls his options.

**3/7/72 10:41 p.m. Juárez Standard Time**

I'm a prisoner, Ellen thinks. Not an uncomfortable one, by any stretch. She had a long and delicious dinner with

Don Paquito, and afterward he poured her a tiny glass of premium tequila, which tasted like nectar. When she said that he laughed, and promptly refilled her glass. It occurred to her that he might be trying to seduce her. Warmed by the tequila, she wasn't certain how fiercely she would resist. But he kept his distance, shook her hand chastely at the end of the evening, and directed one of his assistants to show the señorita her bedroom.

Now Ellen is stretched out in a colonial-style bed with a checked blue canopy and overstuffed pillows. The paintings on the wall feature action portraits of Dallas Cowboys painted on black velvet. Initially, she decided to find some entertainment stored in her boost, maybe music. But instead she lies back and thinks about her three hours with Don Paquito, and all of the questions left unanswered. What was this news business he kept referring to? After an evening with him, she had no idea. And how did he know about Ralf and Simon? He gave her only the vaguest of responses, but he indicated that she probably would be seeing them tomorrow.

"We'll go back to El Paso together?" Ellen asked.

Don Paquito shrugged and downed a full glass of tequila, his fourth or fifth by Ellen's count. "If it seems safe," he said. "The decision will be yours."

Ellen thinks about the man with the flattened nose who followed her through Juárez, who sat next to her in the shoe store and begged her to accompany him to the mall, and then hobbled after her while putting on his shoe. She thinks about the lunch with that family, and the friendly boy, Alfredo. Will she ever see them again?

In the distance, she hears explosions, three in a row. Was it thunder? That brings to mind the summer storms over Paterson that kept her awake as a child. This time, though, she sleeps.

### 3/7/72 11:06 p.m. Juárez Standard Time

"You knew we were coming over here, didn't you?" Ralf's voice wakes up Simon, who was already asleep.

"Huh?" They're lying side by side on thin folding cots jammed into a windowless pantry.

"You knew we were coming over here. You put money into your pocket. You led us to the tunnel. Why didn't you tell me?"

"Because you wouldn't have come."

"I might have."

"Well, I didn't think so. Sorry if I was wrong."

"Why don't you tell me about what you do over here, and how it fits in with your tavern? All you've told me is about 'alternative revenue streams.' While you're at it, maybe you could tell me what we're going to be doing over here. You must have some kind of plan."

"We're safer over here."

"With those drones after us?"

"Yes, even with the drones. They're fairly primitive, and you can hear them coming. Over in El Paso, you'll have people hunting you. The next wave is sure to be smarter than that first guy they sent."

"The guy with the nose?"

"Yeah, him. We were lucky."

"So tell me about what you do over here."

"Tomorrow. I'm sleepy."

"What do we do tomorrow?"

"There's this guy I want you to meet."

Ralf, feeling sleepy, too, halts the questioning. "Okay," he says. He turns over and wraps his arms around the pillow. Then he thinks of one more thing to tell his brother. "You know," he whispers, "I go on those sex sites, too—or at least I used to." Simon doesn't respond. Ralf listens to his brother's shallow breathing and concludes that he's still awake. "Just didn't want you to think you're the only one," he adds.

# NINETEEN

**3/8/72 8:12 a.m. Eastern Standard Time**

Early on a crisp Tuesday morning, a young man wearing a green backpack leans his bike against a tree on Christopher Street in Montclair, New Jersey. He slips to the back of the white colonial house and knocks on the kitchen door.

Suzy Claiborne opens the door for him. She's dressed in her running clothes and has the crown of her bald head covered with a tiny red knit cap. She has in mind once again to sidestep Stella's restrictions and take a trot around Brookdale Park.

"Just the usual supplies and one message," the courier says, shrugging out of the backpack. He unzips it and unloads three packages of commodity food, carbohydrates, greens, and protein. "Does the Chinese guy eat any of this stuff?" he asks, gesturing with his face toward Bao-Zhi's third-floor quarters.

"He's wild," Suzy says. "It would taste like animal feed to him. He cooks his own stuff up in his room."

"Then there's this," the courier says. He draws a tiny rolled-up piece of paper from the bottom of his backpack and lays it carefully on the kitchen table. "Arrived this morning on a pigeon."

They hear footsteps coming down the hall, and Stella appears in the kitchen. She's wearing her housecoat, a black Japanese kimono, and has her hair tied up in a plaid handkerchief.

"You just lean your bike against a tree in the front yard?" she says to the courier. "The instructions were to leave the bike in the park, walk up Montclair Avenue, and cut through Hinck's Alley to the backyard."

"Sorry. Forgot about that," the courier says.

"We're under surveillance here," she says.

Suzy, defending the courier, says, "Bao-Zhi just walks out all the time."

"He is going out too much," Stella admits. "But at least he uses the back door and cuts through the alley. I've watched him. And he doesn't leave a bike leaning against a tree." Stella pauses and studies Suzy, dressed in her track gear. "Planning to take another run this morning?"

"Just doing some sit-ups and things in the basement," Suzy says.

"With that hat on?"

"Yeah, well . . ."

Stella, muttering to herself, picks up the tiny message from the table. "This just came in?" She unfolds it, reads the message, and gasps.

"What is it?" Suzy asks.

Stella shakes her head, refusing to answer, and sits down on a kitchen stool. With the hand holding the message, she waves toward the courier, telling him to leave. Once he's gone, she says to Suzy: "The paper says that Ralf's in El Paso, and that he's wild."

"What paper?"

"Long story. It's one with special information. Some of our people get it, and they send around bits of it by couriers and pigeons."

"It says that Ralf is out in El Paso?"

Stella nods.

"That's just across the river from Juárez."

"I know." A shadow of a smile crosses Stella's face. Ralf got in trouble, she's thinking, and he went to Simon. It gratifies her that her sons, who seem so different and barely saw each other after they moved to Montclair, are now finally together. At least she assumes they're together. It doesn't bother her much that Ralf is said to be wild. They must have pulled out his boost in that Alexandria clinic, she thinks. It has to be hard on him, she knows. But in her years with the DM, Stella has grown ever angrier about the boost, and what she views as its political and economic mind control. She is often tempted to have her own removed, as several DM members have done. The trouble is that wild people, for all their courage and sacrifice, are virtually useless in the movement. Their thoughts are hazy and they can't communicate them with the others, except for occasional paper scribblings. Going wild is like retiring. Still, Ralf lived too much in the boost, she thinks.

By nature, Stella's mind searches for things to worry about. She's always been a worrier, even back in college. But now, in the Democracy Movement, worrying is central to her job description. To worry is to be on the lookout for potential danger. It's omnipresent. Every week, it seems, another cell is uncovered and destroyed. Her worrying, Stella is convinced, has saved lives, including her own. With this new tidbit of news about Ralf, new worries bubble up. If word of Ralf's arrival in El Paso has spread all the way to her house on Christopher Street, his enemies must also be in the know. They might kill him. If he's with his brother, they might kill them both. She wonders if she should travel to El Paso herself. It's where her grandparents met and her mother was born. Is there anything she could accomplish there?

Later in the morning, Suzy has her long legs stretched out on the living-room couch. She's still in her running clothes, but without the hat. A small plate of protein sits on her stomach, and she savors it in small bites as eggs with chorizo, one of her favorite apps. The fire burns slowly. The drum upstairs seems to pound in time with the winter rain beating against the windows. "Ugly out there," she says as Stella walks in.

Stella nods absently and sits in a rocking chair by the fireplace. The weather is the furthest thing from her mind.

Suzy proceeds to describe, in great detail, a scheme

she has to mobilize opposition to the coming update. "Everyone hates the boost," she says.

Stella tries to be diplomatic. "I think you might not be circulating with a broad enough range of people," she says.

Suzy takes another bite of her breakfast. "No offense," she says. "But I'm kind of stuck here."

Stella nods and goes on. "The biggest concern most people have with the chip isn't that it's too powerful, but that it might not . . ." She hunts for the right word. "Might not be powerful enough."

"Huh?"

Stella explains that if Americans fail to keep their chips up to the Chinese level, the population will grow relatively dumber, and the Chinese will place their investments elsewhere, costing jobs. What's more, smarter and faster chips, along with a host of new apps, promise to make life more fun. With updated boosts, games will be more captivating. Food will taste better. The virtual worlds will work better, with richer colors and faster action—zero latency. Sex will be fabulous.

"That's what they were saying in the update division," Suzy says. "Even Ralf talked about it."

It's a hard line to oppose, Stella thinks. Those who dare to face crippling headaches. They find relief by seeking shelter in safe houses equipped with electronic jammers, like Stella's own. It amounts to self-incarceration. The only other remedy is to rip out the chip. Stella herself doesn't know how she'd handle life in the wild.

### 3/8/72 8:16 a.m. Eastern Standard Time

George Smedley wakes up to the sound of rain pounding the glass sunroof of his Kalorama condo. His feet are tangled in his black silk sheets and his forehead drips with sweat. His head is killing him. Smedley had a nightmare that even by the pale morning light seems vivid and real. He was walking down the main street in an old Western town, a place lined with saloons, wooden banks, and feed stores. From second-floor balconies, women in various stages of undress—all of them Artemi—shouted at him, taunting him, daring him to stop. He wanted to so badly, but he couldn't. He had to keep walking, and cross a river. Those were his orders, and everyone knew it. Smedley was someone else's puppet. His legs drew him forward toward a terrifying place he wanted to avoid. Every second, he moved closer.

The sun in this dream shone down relentlessly, like a punishment. Smedley could not avoid it. He saw no shadows, no sign of relief. He didn't know his mission, only that he must continue.

His head hurt, and he had this idea that when he crossed the river he would find relief. Yet as he started to cross, people warned him to stay put. A bearded beggar told him to beware. Behind him, Artemi shouted at him, their warnings blended with ridicule and cruel laughter.

Smedley had an idea. He would escape into his boost, into a safe and welcoming virtual world. Yet as he tried to toggle from his wet brain into his dry, pain shot through his head. It seemed to start in a lower molar and burn up into his temple. He cried, and the laughter from the balconies grew louder. Smedley began his solitary walk across the bridge. The pain only grew as he approached the other side.

It was then that he realized, to his great relief, that he was dreaming. He could end the pain simply by waking up. Sure enough, when he awoke, sweaty and tangled, the world seemed to return to normal. Gone was the dusty Western town, replaced by his modern bedroom, with its tones of white, black, and gray, and highlights of pink. The searing sun was but a memory. Cool rain-scented air streamed in through his cracked-open windows. Everything from the dream was changed except for the punishing headache, which continues to hammer his right temple.

Smedley holds his hand to his head and tries, as he battles the pain, to formulate a plan.

# TWENTY

They both hear the sputtering and the roar coming from around the corner. Ralf dives from the dirt road into a pile of garbage by a shack. He assumes it's a drone. But Simon, who has spent time in Juárez, identifies it. "A gasoline engine," he says. "A truck."

Ralf climbs to his feet, and moments later a square-shaped truck painted red and green hurtles down a side road and turns right in front of them. It stops with a screech of the brakes. He sees a General Motors truck, at least sixty years old. The metal grill, only inches from their faces, looks like the grimace of a large animal, perhaps a bear. The truck belches a cloud of smoke from the rear. Simon looks to see who's driving, but the early-morning sun reflects off the windshield. Still, he can guess who's inside from the purple and yellow flag dangling from a pole soldered to the cab.

"Revolutionary Militia," he says.

The driver turns off the ignition. The truck shudders for a couple of seconds, and then is quiet. Three young men climb down from the cab. They look to be in their early twenties. One is tall and skinny, and wears a black Boston Red Sox baseball hat. The other two are short and square. One of them looks at them through round-rimmed glasses; his friend wears a red knit cap and holds his hands in his pockets, as though he's freezing. All three are in blue jeans and blue jean jackets, each one embroidered with the same purple and yellow banner. The skinny one carries in his right hand a metal pipe about two feet long. The men walk up to Ralf and Simon, looking grumpy. They say nothing. They stop, all in a row, looking the brothers in the eyes. This appears to be a routine they've practiced.

"*Hola,*" Simon says.

They don't answer.

The shorter man wearing glasses finally says, "*Cabezudos.*"

"*Yo sí,*" Simon says and adds, pointing to his brother, "*Pero no él.*" He says to Ralf, "I told these guys that I'm capped, but that you're not."

"That's what '*cabezudo*' means?" Ralf asks.

"Uh-huh."

"Why do they care?"

"*¡Cállense!*" says the man with glasses, who appears to be the leader.

"That means 'shut up,'" Simon whispers.

In the following minutes, the man with the glasses interrogates Simon, while Ralf and the two others look on. He asks him what they're doing in Juárez, how long they plan to stay, and if they plan to meet anyone. Simon, speaking Spanish like a native, explains that they ran away from some "bad people" in El Paso who work for the "dictatorship." When asked where they crossed, he points toward the west and says "Santa Teresa." He explains that his brother, after living his entire life as a *cabezudo*, was captured in Washington and had his chip removed.

That seems to interest the three, who look back and forth at each other and nod.

Simon shows them the bandage, now dirty, above Ralf's right ear. The tall man carrying the pipe steps forward, reaches for the bandage, and tears it off.

"Ow!" Ralf says, shielding the wound from the others. But the tall man pries Ralf's hand from his head and exposes a small patch of skull, recently shaven. It has a puffy red line a half inch long.

The man steps back, and Ralf puts his hand to the wound to make sure it's not bleeding.

When asked to explain their presence in Juárez, Simon explains that they're planning to see Don Paquito, and hoping that he can help them recross the border far from the "bad people" who are chasing them.

The three Mexicans huddle briefly. Then the short one with the red cap grabs Simon by the elbow. The tall one reaches for Ralf. They load them into the truck and attempt to blindfold them with red-checked bandannas. Their knots are slipshod, and the bandannas keep falling. The man with the glasses shouts at his colleagues, calling them *"pendejos."* He finally grabs two large brown paper bags and stuffs them over Ralf and Simon's heads. Then the truck roars to a start and takes off toward the west.

Several minutes later Ralf and Simon are prisoners in a garage, the bags off their heads. Their hands are bound behind them to their metal stools with the same bandannas. They sit at opposites sides of a table. It has old jars and cans of paints and coatings and is covered by a stained brown blanket. The two short men have departed, leaving the tall one to guard them. The door of the garage doesn't close, and through the opening Simon can see a bit of the scene outside. It looks like a war zone. Across the dirt road is a burnt-out building he's never encountered before.

Ralf's wrists hurt from the bandanna. The way his hands are bound to the stool forces him to twist in a way that he knows is going to be unbearable within minutes. He looks at his brother. Simon's gray T-shirt is riding up his belly, exposing a white patch of flab. But he sits straight up, his feet tucked neatly under the stool's metal rung, his hands behind him like a soldier who has shifted from attention to "at ease." Ralf watches his brother looking out the crack in the door, back at the guard, than outside again. He looks fully engaged, and almost happy. He must love Juárez, Ralf thinks.

"Could you ask the guy to redo my wrists so I can sit up straight?" Ralf whispers.

"Shhhhh." Simon purses his lips and shakes his head. Then he leans forward, steps off his stool, with his hands still tied behind him, and climbs back on again. It's a demonstration. Ralf tries to step down. He stumbles, almost bringing the stool down on top of him.

"Eh!" the guard yells.

But Ralf quickly climbs back onto the stool, as Simon did, with his torso straight and his feet behind the rung. It feels much better, even though the wrists still hurt.

Simon asks the guard in Spanish if he can talk to his brother, "just to pass the time."

"Okay," the guard says in accented English. "But I listen."

"Good. Maybe you'll learn something," Simon says. Then he launches into the history of Juárez, starting with the U.S. manufacturing operations that moved from the U.S. Rust Belt to the Mexican border in the 1980s.

"Just tell me who these guys are," Ralf says, "and what they want."

"I'm getting to that," Simon says. "Once Juárez turned into an export capital," he explains, "it became a capital for illegal exports, too. Like drugs."

"I know that," Ralf says.

"That's when Mother's grandfather, our great-grandfather, got famous. He was working at a newspaper in El Paso, and he wrote articles about how the *maquiladora* captains were exporting drugs. His girlfriend at the time, who was later his wife, used information he had to make investments. It was probably illegal, or at least unethical, because it hadn't been published yet. She made a shitload of money. That's what they used to buy that big house in Montclair."

Ralf knows nothing about financial markets. "So what does that have to do with these guys?" he asks.

"Not much. I'm just telling you that we have roots down here." Simon takes a breath and considers how to abridge his historical narrative for an impatient audience. The Mexican guard, he sees, is sitting on the floor with his back against the wall. He has his head tilted to one side. His eyes are shaded by the rim of his red baseball cap. He might be asleep.

"These guys," he says, gesturing toward the slumped-over guard, "are from the militia of the Revolutionary Brigade, or *Brigada Revolucionaria*. Their goal is to keep Juárez wild." He goes on to explain, in more detail than Ralf would have chosen, how Juárez, starting in the 2040s, developed into the capital of the wild world. The early years were a period of great optimism. Immigrants streamed in from all over the world. Writers, artists, film directors, even a few billionaires came in from Paris, New York, and Silicon Valley, and built mansions up by the mountains. The rest of the world was heading into a techno-world developed by software engineers in the employ of multinational companies and dictators. Ciudad Juárez—long known as the murder capital of the world—was suddenly the capital of native human intelligence, the same genius that produced Shakespeare, Newton, Einstein, Jesus Christ. If the rest of the world was going digital, Juárez would build a franchise on knowledge, ideas, and the potential of the analog world.

Ralf snorts. "That's a bit much, wouldn't you say?"

"Maybe," Simon admits. "But the key was freedom. The boost-sphere was controlled. Juárez was free, all things being relative. At least not all the information was tied to commercial messages and political propaganda."

"It is in the boost?"

"You tell me."

Ralf considers the question for a few seconds and then says, "Go on."

"It was a glorious vision," Simon says. "But of course it came up short. This was a poor, corrupt city, after all. A hellhole. It couldn't turn overnight into Athens in the age of Pericles. The drug business dried up in the U.S., as people turned to virtual drugs. The narco lords, at least the ones that stuck around, had to stay alive. They went back to the old lines of business. Prostitution, gambling, drugs for the market over here. It was small-time stuff. They weren't billionaires anymore. But they had enough to buy off the police departments. Same old, same old . . .

"But what really threatened it was economics," he says. He explains that both Washington and Mexico City viewed Juárez as a threat. If their populations saw that the wild could run a thriving and free city, people might push to go wild. It would be a viable alternative, and governments might lose control.

"Of course, they could have just bombed Juárez and destroyed it," Simon says. "I wouldn't be surprised if they considered it at some point. But instead, they demonized it. They blockaded it, starved it economically, and then held it up as a model for the failures and backwardness of the wild world. If the public complained about the boost, and all the surveillance and control that comes with it, the governments could just say, 'Look at Juárez.' And that's exactly what they do. What's more," he adds, "the Juárez they describe is much worse than this!" With a sweeping motion of his face, he surveys the garage, as if its grimy walls and the used tires piled in puddles of grease represented the city itself. "With their control of the boost, they've turned it into a caricature," he says. "They tell people that Juárez makes its money from drugs—even though the export market has been dead since the '40s."

Ralf is eager for Simon to tell him about the "militia" that has them trussed to stools in this dingy garage. But there's no hurrying him, he sees.

"So the people in Juárez look across the river to El Paso, and what do they see? It's a richer place. It's modern. It has new cars that don't stink. People over here," he adds, "can't understand why any of us would ride around on horses. We tell them about the surveillance over there, the mind control. But they see that we can go anywhere we want. It's a different kind of freedom. We're freer to move our bodies, to travel. They have privacy in their heads. But some of them long for the boost. It provides a whole world of entertainment. We can go to the movies in our head. We can participate in them. That's still a radical concept in Juárez. They also think the boost makes us smarter."

"It does!" Ralf says.

"That's a whole other discussion," Simon says. "But the point is this. They look at their kids, and they see them growing up wild and without a future outside of Juárez. It's like a small island. So people have started to sneak down into Mexico, with their kids. They're getting capped, becoming *cabezudos*. It's a big mess, of course. Unlicensed doctors and vets are giving them chips from dead people—the same thing you were after. People die in the operation. Some go crazy with the new chips. Some rip them out. But for some people, it works. Now there's this entire *cabezudo* minority. They have all kinds of advantages. Even without a network, they can do all the math, they can store data, images, memories. They get better jobs, and their kids clean up at school.

"So," Simon goes on, "how do you think that makes the locals here feel? They're still wild. They maintain this vision of Juárez and the glorious analog economy, the modern-day Athens I was telling you about. But they're getting infiltrated. If things keep going the way they're going, Juárez is going to turn into a two-tiered city, with the wild on the bottom. That's why these militias are growing. They're defending the status quo."

"What are they going to do to us?" Ralf whispers.

"Puh," Simon says dismissively, shaking his head. "They'll take us downtown and report us and feel like they've accomplished something."

"And then?"

"We'll go talk to Don Paquito, and see what we can do about our problem in El Paso."

Ralf starts to ask Simon about Don Paquito when a familiar roar drowns out his voice. Next comes the sound of screeching brakes. The spindly guard springs to life as his two buddies push open the door, flooding the garage with the sunlight and racket of a raucous neighborhood.

# TWENTY-ONE

Ellen lies in her bed and gazes out the window at a busy pigeon nest on the ledge. She's been awake for more than an hour, lying in bed and surfing archived music and videos in her boost, when she hears a knock on the door. The same young woman comes in carrying a silver tray with a glass of orange juice, a cup of coffee, and a bowl of what looks like creamy yogurt. "Breakfast?" she says.

Ellen nods and thanks her. The woman opens up space on the bedside table by moving a framed photograph. It features a young Don Paquito, his hair black, his face crinkled into a broad smile, posing with a stern-faced woman. She deposits the tray, nods solemnly at Ellen, and departs, closing the door gently behind her.

Ellen takes a small spoonful of the yogurt. The bitterness surprises her, and she quickly cloaks the taste with

a maple-syrup app from her boost. Even without network coverage, she's relieved to see, the food apps still
work. She wonders what her boost would feel like after a few years in Juárez. It would be like bookshelves
in her grandparents' days, she thinks: Lots of stories and
history, but with no connection to what's happening
today.

Finishing her yogurt, she wonders if she'll see Ralf
today. If not, will she be free to go home? She'd be
happy to skip El Paso altogether, and fly straight to
Washington, or maybe New York. This brings to her
mind the idea of "wild" airplanes from Juárez. She pictures airplanes with no computation on board, no messaging or ground-scans, just humans in a bare cockpit
using their ears and eyes to steer clear of mountains
and skyscrapers and other traffic, humans peering
through clouds to spot landing strips. No, she thinks,
they would never let wild planes into U.S. airspace.

She thinks about Don Paquito, and those tricks he
does with his eyebrows. He's so foreign, and yet at the
same time, there's something playful about him, and
familiar. Last night at dinner, he suddenly started inter-
rogating Ellen about her looks, about the Artemis line,
and why her family made the investment. "What did you
look like before?" he asked.

"Oh, I don't know," Ellen said, confused by the question. "I was only like, thirteen."

"Do you have a photo?"

"Not on me," she said, laughing. She resumed her
dinner, which featured some sort of meat—she couldn't
tell which—in green sauce. It was so delicious, both

spicy and just a bit sweet, that she didn't even consider using her boost to tinker with the taste.

"You must have a photo on your chip," Don Paquito said.

She finished chewing the food in her mouth and swallowed it before saying, "Yes, I suppose I do."

"Send it to me."

She wondered if he was a sexual deviant. People like that back home had sites to go to. But maybe over here, they needed physical photos, or even real people. "I can't send you a photo from my boost," she said.

"Yes you can." He told her that he had a laptop computer with an e-mail account. "So do the reporters," he added. "That's how they do a lot of their reporting. By e-mail."

"And you have a network?"

"Oh yes."

"But I can't send anything over here. There's no boost network."

"There is," he said. "Right here." He explained that the Chinese built wireless local area networks, or LANs, for the boosts when they first came out, in the '40s. The idea was to let the early adapters trade messages with their uncapped friends and colleagues, who were still on the Internet. "I got one of them a few years ago," Don Paquito says. "Never got a chance to use it, until now."

"I'm not getting anything, though," Ellen said. She looked up her friends in Washington, and then Simon. All the connections were dead.

"No, you'll only get what's on this LAN," Don Paquito

said. "All you'll see is my computer, once I turn it on. And the newsroom."

He went on to explain how to send him e-mails. It involved digging into the archives of her boost and unearthing an old e-mail. "Just search for @hotmail.com or @gmail.com," he said.

Ellen did, and hundreds of historical e-mails popped up. Most of them were from the '20s and teens. The earliest one, from May 1995, caught her eye. It was from Bill Gates, the chairman of a company called Microsoft Corporation. It had to do with jumping on "the Internet Tidal Wave."

"Now what?" she asked.

Don Paquito told her to erase the message from the e-mail, and to cut and paste the photo from her boost into the message space, then to place PacoCorazon@ Juárez.mx into the address line, and send. Ellen was convinced it wouldn't work. Instead of picking out an image of herself, she browsed a collection of old movie photos and selected one of an actress named Julia Roberts. She attached it to the Bill Gates e-mail, added the address, and sent it.

Don Paquito, visibly excited, hurried out of the dining room to check his computer. "Not yet!" he shouted every minute or two, while Ellen finished her dinner. Finally he returned, looking crestfallen. He asked her what year her e-mail came from.

"1995," she said.

"Oh that's why! It's too old," he said. "Find a newer e-mail, preferably from the '40s." It was back then that they added an e-mail "bridge" into the boost.

Ellen obediently harvested an e-mail from 2042. It was from the White House, and it concerned the news of the Chinese boosts. She pasted in the image of Julia Roberts, addressed it, and sent again, confident that it would never reach Don Paquito's Mac.

But two minutes later he returned with a printed photograph. He waved it back and forth to dry the ink, and then laid it down on the table. Julia Roberts looked up from the paper, her broad toothy smile, her nose tilted ever so slightly to the left, her shiny almond eyes. "You look older than thirteen," Don Paquito said, shaking his head. He leaned down and inspected Julia Roberts's face for several seconds, and then lifted his eyes to Ellen, studying her perfect Artemis eyes, her straight nose, the closed parentheses of her mouth, which were turned, for the moment, into a slight frown. "Yes," he said finally. "I can see why you had the procedure done."

Ellen felt offended. "Why?" she asked.

"You were a bit . . ." He struggled for the right word. "Do you say 'horsey'?"

She washes, dresses in yesterday's clothes, and ventures out of the bedroom. The same people are back in the newsroom, typing again on their machines. She wonders if she could send them e-mails, or receive messages from them. A door opens on the far side of the room. A young boy, probably only twelve or thirteen, hurries past the computers. He's saying something in Spanish. Ellen can't hear enough of it to replay it for her translation app. But it interests the people in the newsroom, and almost all of them are now looking at her.

"What is it?" Ellen asks.

The workers look back and forth at each other, as if to nominate a spokesperson. But no one speaks. The boy rushes to Don Paquito's office and pounds on the door. When the door opens, Ellen catches a single phrase— *Han secuestrado a los americanos*—and runs it through her translator. A moment later a tinny voice inside her head says, "They've kidnapped the Americans."

# TWENTY-TWO

**3/8/72 10:49 a.m. Juárez Standard Time**

From the moment the two shorter militia members burst into the garage, Ralf can tell something has changed. They're jumpy and excited. They shout to each other. They laugh hysterically. Their balance seems off. The one with the glasses comes over to Ralf, still bound to his stool, and squeezes his cheek between his thumb and forefinger. It hurts. Still squeezing, he shouts something, and Ralf feels bits of spit on his face. The young man leans over until his eyes, on the other side of the thick glasses, are only an inch or two from Ralf's. Ralf can smell onions on his breath. He braces himself, wondering if the guy is going to kiss him. Then the man laughs again, releases him, and says, *"¡Cabezudo!"*

Simon tries to tell them that he's the *cabezudo,* not Ralf. But the kidnappers are not in a listening mood. They continue yelling. Then one of them leaves with the tall one, and the truck roars away.

Silence returns. They're alone with the young man with the glasses, who now appears to regard them with an air of sadness. He sits at a makeshift desk in the corner, a board supported by two steel trash barrels. He picks up a pen, writes something on a piece of paper, and then slams it to the desk, as if the words he wrote offend him. He stands up and starts to sing hideously out of tune:

"*Acuerdate de Acapulco, de aquella noche, Maria Bonita, Maria del alma . . .*"

"He's totally amped up on something," Simon whispers. Ralf nods.

When the man stops singing, Simon asks him his name. At first he refuses to answer. Then he shouts, "*¡Comandante Zeta!*"

The garage is silent again. Ralf hears heavy congested breathing. "You stuffed up?" he whispers.

"*¡Cállense!*" Comandante Zeta hisses. He walks over to Ralf and runs his finger along the red line of Ralf's wound. "*¿De verdad te arrancaron la máquina?*" he asks.

Simon answers for Ralf, saying that yes, they pulled out Ralf's chip. Ralf remembers that he still carries the blue Chinese snuff bottle with his chip in his front pocket. He worries that this drug-addled Comandante Zeta will steal it from him.

Zeta goes back to the desk and returns with a long silvery blade, an old letter opener. He waves it in front of Ralf's eyes. The blade has rust on it, Ralf sees, and the edges are dull. Zeta is smiling. "*Vamos a echar un vistazo, ahi dentro,*" he says, telling them that he plans to look inside Ralf's wound. He wipes the blade on his pants. Then he reaches into his pocket and pulls out a cigarette lighter. He runs the flame up and down the blade.

Ralf hears the congested breathing again, and looks over at his brother. Simon's eyes are bugged out, and Ralf can see that he's working his hands on the knotted bandannas, trying to free himself. He's not making any progress that Ralf can see.

Zeta brings the blade close to Ralf's head. He giggles. Ralf can feel the heat on the blade. "Don't do this!" he shouts.

Zeta giggles again, and then is silent as he moves the blade closer to the wound. His lips are pursed. Ralf swings his head away.

"*Quieto*," Zeta says under his breath.

He grabs Ralf by the hair and brings his head closer to the blade. He starts giggling again, but this is cut short by an eruption from under the table between Ralf and Simon. The table falls and jars of paint crash to the ground as a giant emerges between the two men and swings a potent right fist into the startled face of Comandante Zeta. His glasses shatter and his nose makes a splintering noise as he falls backward onto the garage floor, out cold.

Oscar Espinoza, breathing loudly through his own flattened nose, smiles broadly. "I haven't had that much fun in years," he says to the two brothers. He bends down and unties the bandannas.

"Are you going to . . . arrest us?" Ralf asks.

"Over here?" Espinoza says. He laughs. "I was just

doing hourly work in El Paso," he says. "But I think that gig is over."

The three of them hurry out into the busy street. Simon recognizes the neighborhood and guides them toward Trastos, where his friends are. As they walk, Espinoza tells them about his adventures, about eating goat at the restaurant that was destroyed by the drone, not knowing how to get back to the tunnel—with his geolocation service gone kaput—and finally finding a place to sleep under the table in the garage across the street.

When they reach Trastos, Ralf and Simon order grapefruit soda and Espinoza asks for two beers. He asks Simon how to say "goat" in Spanish.

"*Cabra*," Simon says.

"Could you ask them if they have any *cabra* here?"

It turns out they don't, and Espinoza ends up settling for a ham and cheese sandwich with a family-sized bag of potato chips. As he eats, he tells them about the assignments he handles for George Smedley, who works for a rich man named Vallinger.

Simon nods knowingly. "Does George Smedley spend a lot of time on sex sites?" he asks.

Startled by the question, Espinoza says, "Not with me, he doesn't."

"Just curious," Simon says.

Espinoza goes on to tell them about the headaches that Vallinger's machines can deliver, and how he almost went mad chasing them around El Paso with Smedley running shotgun.

Ralf asks him what happened to Ellen.

"The Artemis?" Espinoza asks.

Ralf nods.

"She walked across a board to Juárez," Espinoza says. "She was scared of me. I told her I just wanted her to get away from the border, that she could even come with me, in my KIFF, to Cielo Vista Mall—which is much more her type of place than these stores in South El Paso. She's very classy," he explains. "There are some things you just see."

Outside, they hear the roar of a truck. Ralf and Simon freeze, but Espinoza keeps eating. "That's not the same one," he says, reaching for another handful of chips. "Different engine. I wouldn't worry about those three that had you tied up. The two that are still standing don't want to end up like their friend."

The truck engine turns off. A young man pokes his head into the store. He sees Simon and breaks into a broad smile. Simon waves at him and tells the others, "Don Paquito sent a truck to pick us up." The three of them thank their innkeepers and pile onto the back of the old pickup truck. It first stops at the Juárez side of the tunnel, where Oscar Espinoza climbs down. He makes off for the tunnel, and his KIFF, while the truck turns around and heads eastward, toward downtown Juárez.

# PART III

―――――

# FAMILY

# TWENTY-THREE

The driver drops Ralf and Simon a few blocks from Don Paquito's headquarters. In the streets surrounding it, anti-drone barriers crafted from steel and cinder obstruct all but pedestrian traffic. Ralf and Simon wind their way through what feels like a war zone. But when they reach headquarters, the lobby is bustling. Women clutching purses occupy the benches and the scattered chairs. Men, looking uncomfortable, mill about in ill-fitting jackets. Small boys circulate, selling chewing gum and coconut candies. The pastry vendor stands to one side, offering discounts on bear claws and sugared *palmeras*.

On the way downtown, Simon tried to prepare Ralf with background. "There's some stuff I haven't told you," he said as the truck bumped along dirt roads.

"Well, duh," Ralf grumbled. "You might start with who the hell is Don Paquito?"

"I told you. He's in the information business."

"And you're an informer?"

Simon laughed. "No, no. I don't know that much."

"But you work for him, right?"

"Sort of."

"In drugs?"

"How many times do I have to tell you that there's no more export business for drugs? That's just American propaganda."

Ralf glowered at Simon and then turned away and stared out the truck window. Every time Simon mentioned propaganda, Ralf felt that his brother was implicating the boost and, by association, him. It angered him. What did Simon expect the United States to do? Remain wild? Revert to dirt roads like Juárez, where kids, from what he was seeing, spent their days playing in mud puddles? The brothers didn't exchange another word until the truck turned left off Avenida 16 de Septiembre and dropped them off.

As they make their way through the waiting room, Simon grabs Ralf's arm and whisks him past the pastry vendor. "I've got something to show you," he says. He pushes open a door and leads Ralf into the newsroom. "Just like I told you," he says. "The information business."

About half of the people in the room look up from their computers. A few of them recognize Simon and wave. One of them yells, *"¡Siiiiiiiiiiiiiiimón!"*

On the far side of the newsroom is a hall with a skylight, potted palm trees, and tables set up like an outdoor café. Ralf sees Ellen walking his way past the tables. She's the loveliest sight he's seen in weeks. His heart skips and he takes two running steps toward her and wraps her in his arms. He feels his chest heaving and his cheeks are wet. He buries his head into her hair, to hide it from his brother and the people at the computers.

"You missed me," Ellen whispers.

He grunts that he did, but feels embarrassed that his emotions are on such vivid display. He wonders if it has something to do with being wild.

He pulls her back, studies her face, and kisses her on the mouth.

Simon, who has been standing next to Ralf, touches his brother's shoulder and points to a man standing behind Ellen. Brushing Ellen's hair from his eyes, Ralf looks up. The man is shorter than he is and trim for his age. He seems to be standing at a slight angle.

Simon starts to make the introduction. As Ralf steps back from Ellen, he looks at Simon and the man, who he assumes is Don Paquito. They're both smiling at him. Still self-conscious about his tears, he looks from one to the other, and back again. It's the same smile, the same broad cheeks, the same eyes.

"Oh my God," he says.

Ellen, standing next to him, is seeing the same thing. But for her, the show is in triplicate, a father and his two sons. She stands speechless.

Ralf, at a loss for words, finally says: "You didn't die in Paraguay."

Don Paquito, once known as Francisco, steps forward, favoring his left leg, and tries to embrace the son he never met. Ralf, still stunned, stands tall and motionless as the shorter man awkwardly wraps his arms around him and whispers something Ralf doesn't understand in Spanish. Then he releases him.

Ralf turns away from his father. He's confused, and now even more embarrassed. He doesn't know what to call the man, or whether he speaks English. Speaking to no one in particular, he asks, "Does Mother know he's alive?"

**3/8/72 12:33 p.m. Juárez Standard Time**

Minutes later, sitting at one of the café tables with Simon, Ralf repeats the same question. No, Simon says, their mother does not know that the father of her children is alive, much less that he is Don Paquito, the legendary power broker and reputed drug lord of Ciudad Juárez.

"That makes me almost ill," Ralf says.

"He wanted to protect her," Simon explains. "And you."

Ralf ignores the point. "What do you call him?" he asks. "When I first heard the name, I thought 'Don Paquito' was a bit ridiculous. But now that I know he's my father—at least biologically—it sounds almost obscene."

"I call him 'Papá,'" Simon says, pronouncing it in Spanish.

"Well, I won't do that."

"How about Paco?"

"Where's that come from?"

"It's short for Francisco. I think it comes from Saint Francis of Assisi. They called him Pater Comunitas, or father of the community. That turned into Paco."

"Maybe I'll just call him Don," Ralf says, getting up and walking away from Simon.

Spotting Ellen walking through the newsroom, he hurries to catch up to her. "You might be the only one who hasn't been lying to me, one way or another, for my whole life," he says.

She smiles and touches him on the cheek. "Feeling a little sorry for yourself?" she asks. When he nods vaguely, she guides him toward her bedroom. A maid, who is fluffing the pillows on the bed, leaves as soon the two step in, saying, "*Con permiso.*"

Ralf strips off his clothes, walks into the bathroom, and takes a shower. When he comes out, he finds Ellen lying on the bed, naked. He lies down next to her and softly traces with his finger the outline of her face. As he begins to kiss her cheek and eyes and her neck, she tells him how Don Paquito went to such great trouble to see a photo of her as a child. "I just figured out why," she says.

"Why?" he asks, pulling back from her.

"He wanted to see the genes that might—" She pauses for a second, searching for the right word.

"He was looking at you as the mother of his future grandchildren," Ralf says.

She nods.

"God," he groans, rolling over on his face. "What a way to kill the mood."

**3/8/72 2:37 p.m. Juárez Standard Time**

Don Paquito ordered up a feast. He dispatched four assistants from the newsroom to the Mercado Central, and they came back an hour later with a side of lamb and baskets brimming with fruit, cheeses, avocados, big bunches of cilantro, and chilies of all shapes and colors.

As they sit down for lunch, Ralf avoids the place next to his father, and instead slides in between Simon and Ellen. He's determined to steer clear of all personal issues, especially any that might concern his mother.

Ralf has never known life with a father and has no idea how to deal with this one, or even whether to accept him. He misses his boost. If he had a networked boost, he could read up on this man, study maps of Juárez, calculate the time it would take him to walk from this drab dining room, decorated with what looks like framed documents, to El Paso. With his boost in place and functioning, he could slip off into a virtual world. He could escape. The wet brain, he thinks, provides no relief. It's just me and my life. I'm stuck with myself.

An elderly waiter wearing a pleated white shirt and a clip-on black bow tie carries large plates of food from the kitchen and arranges them carefully on the table. As Paquito—or Francisco, as Ralf has decided to call him—passes around the plates, he pronounces each item slowly in Spanish. He hands the stuffed peppers to Ellen, and says, "*Los chiles rellenos,*" with an extravagant rolling of the R. He lowers his nose toward a steaming basket, and says, "*Tortillas.*" He closes his eyes, inhales, and shakes his head slowly in appreciation. He pulls out a yellow corn tortilla, spoons a slice of avocado onto it, and adds a small mountain of chunky salsa, with tomato and onions and cilantro. *"Aguacate con pico de gallo,"* he says, rolling the tortilla and taking a small bite.

"God," Ralf thinks, "he's trying to teach me how to talk." To cut short the lesson, he blurts out a question: "All those people in the newsroom. What exactly do they do?"

"Those are my reporters and editors," Francisco says. "They put out a newspaper. *La Tribuna,* or *The Tribune.* That's my business. I'm a publisher."

"A newspaper?"

"We have 290,000 subscribers," Francisco says proudly, taking another bite from his rolled-up tortilla.

"Three hundred thousand now, Papá," Simon says. The word "Papá," coming from his brother's mouth, makes Ralf cringe.

"Three hundred thousand?" Francisco smiles and calls to the elderly waiter. *"¡Pepe! Que nos traiga una botella de tequila, de los buenos,"* he says. "We're going to have to celebrate three hundred thousand with excellent tequila."

Ralf, who has rolled some refried beans and *pico de gallo* into a tortilla, had no idea that newspapers still existed. It still makes sense for the wild world, he supposes. But he finds the idea pathetic to the point of sad. All of those people work in that room, he thinks, to create a product that dies on paper. Their words go nowhere. They cannot get their work onto the boost. No one can forward their stories to anyone. Their words just feed the wild brain, where they're stuck until they're forgotten, which is probably about the same time that the next paper shows up.

He watches Francisco, who beams as he pours golden liquid from an old dust-covered bottle into four small glasses. For him to be so proud to have a measly three hundred thousand subscribers, Ralf thinks, makes it even more pathetic. More than 10 billion people have boosts, he knows, maybe 11 billion by now. Certain games and virtual worlds reach billions of them. For big time publishers, an audience of three hundred thousand people amounts to a rounding error. What's more, the tiny readership that waits for a physical paper to arrive at their door must be from the most backward and ignorant segment of the wild population. He wonders how much they can afford to pay. As Ralf takes his first sip of the fiery tequila, he experiences a shift in sentiments toward the publisher who's busy raising toasts at the head of the table. Gone, at least for the moment, are his anger and resentment, his sense of betrayal and distrust. Now he finds himself feeling sorry for the man.

Ralf ends up drinking four shots of tequila and wolfs down a mountain of food. His emotions during the meal careen wildly, but he keeps quiet for the most part, preferring to engage his mouth for food and drink, not words. He barely listens as Francisco regales the group with old stories from the South American chip wars.

It's not until after lunch, feeling groggy and a bit dim-witted, that Ralf makes his way through the newsroom and the sunlit café room, or *playa*, and knocks with his knuckles on Francisco's open office door. He steps in and plunks himself down in a wooden chair under the poster of Emiliano Zapata. Francisco, misinterpreting the visit, starts talking about family. Ralf interrupts him, saying he wants to talk "business."

"Look," he says, "I don't know how much you know about me. But they're going to be updating the boost in the U.S. next week. I need to put a fix into the software. For that I need to find someone, either here or somewhere else, who can put my boost back into my head."

Francisco looks at him gravely. "You have the chip with you?"

Ralf nods and points to his pocket.

"There are people around here who do that kind of work. It doesn't always . . . turn out well."

"I know," Ralf says. "Simon told me. Think we can get it done tomorrow?"

"Probably not until later in the week."

Ralf squirms in his chair. "Listen, it's kind of a long story, but I'm in a hurry. We have a deadline coming, and I . . ."

Francisco looks at him with a sly smile. Then he raises one eyebrow into a tall arch, and slowly brings it down. He reaches into a desk drawer and pulls what looks like a packet of folded paper from his drawer. He tosses it into Ralf's lap. The banner of the paper, written in Gothic lettering, is simply THE TRIBUNE. The headline on the lead story reads: SURVEILLANCE GATE OPEN IN COMING UPDATE.

Ralf starts to read the story. Then he notices another article at the bottom of page one: LEADING GOVERN-

MENT CHIP DEVELOPER ON THE RUN IN EL PASO. The article, which, for Ralf's "own security," avoids naming him, mentions that the software engineer was nabbed at work at the Department of Health and Human Services, rushed to a clinic in Alexandria, from which he was later "liberated," and is now "reputed to be newly wild."

Ralf looks up at his father. "How did you learn this?" he asks.

Francisco gestures toward the people working in the newsroom. "Those people are professionals," he says dryly. "The best in the world."

# TWENTY-FOUR

**3/9/72 8:09 a.m. Eastern Standard Time**

Stella, still in her black kimono housecoat, sits quietly in the living room in Montclair, sipping a cup of coffee. She looks out the window at the birds jostling for places at the next-door neighbor's front-yard feeder. Suzy is still upstairs. Bao-Zhi has not yet begun his drumming or chanting. In another month, Stella thinks, the early spring flowers will start to bloom, the daffodils along the front walk and the forsythia out back. She wonders what will be happening to her son Ralf by then, and whether she and Suzy and Bao-Zhi will still be holed up in their electronic refuge.

A massive black Houyi pulls up at the curb, scaring the birds away. Stella has never seen the Houyi before. It sits there for minutes on end. Finally a door opens on the curbside. Out steps an elderly gentleman wearing a shiny maroon trench coat and carrying a leather briefcase. He walks out to the sidewalk and then turns left up Stella's walk. He moves with a slight stoop and carries a worried expression on his haggard face. He has white hair, which falls onto his forehead in a V.

Stella gasps. She rushes to open the door before he rings, and she greets John Vallinger with a simple "Hello."

"Been a while," he says with only the chilliest trace of a smile. He steps inside the Montclair house. "I understand that my communications go kaput at the door," he says.

Stella forces herself to smile, but without acknowledging his point. "Would you like a cup of coffee?" she asks.

Vallinger shakes his head and makes his way, uninvited, into the living room and drops down on the blue satin couch. He places the coat to one side and lays the briefcase on the carpeted floor.

Stella pauses in the hallway to assemble her thoughts. Her operation is exposed. That much is clear. Vallinger's organization must have learned about Suzy from her runs in the park. Then it was easy to trace her signal back to the place where it went dead, which led them straight to this house. Now Stella, so careful for a decade to cover her tracks, is in the open. She wonders if the old man knows about the wild Chinese activist on the third floor, who for some reason is not yet making his typical noises. What else does Vallinger know? She sits across from him in her mother's old rocking chair. The floor is cold on her bare feet. She shifts her weight to one side and pulls her legs up under herself.

"I know what you're up to," Vallinger says, looking straight at her.

"That makes one of us," Stella says, forcing a smile.

"I've come here . . ." Vallinger pauses for a moment to deliver a line he has prepared for the occasion. ". . . to ask for your help. I think you'll find that we share common interests." Stella says nothing, and he continues. He tells her that she probably "misconstrues" the nature of the coming chip update. Stella remains quiet as he recites the virtues of the enhanced chip. The theme appears to excite him. He leans forward, plants his elbows on his knees, and clasps a pair of hands dotted with liver spots. The update, he says, will nearly double the processing power, raising it above the current Chinese level. This is "strategically vital" for the United States. New security features will make it nearly impossible for hackers to get access to the boosts. "You wouldn't believe how exposed we all are right now," he says.

Stella concentrates on looking directly into his watery blue eyes. She refrains from any sort of nod or other affirmative gesture that could be interpreted as agreement. She is listening carefully to other noises in the house, and worrying that Bao-Zhi will wander down, as he often does, looking in the pantry for his herbs or potions. She hears nothing.

"You're probably wondering about the so-called surveillance gate," Vallinger says, with another attempt at a smile.

Stella, still avoiding nodding, says: "What about it?"

"I probably shouldn't be telling you this," he says, as if they're old confidants. "It has to do with counterterrorism. Frankly, police have asked for this adjustment. They will be looking at certain anonymized data in the boosts. This doesn't represent a threat to normal citizens. But if they see certain patterns in the data, which are proven to be tied to terrorism, then they can get a warrant to intervene. It's really just to make us safer."

"What was it that I misconstrued?" Stella asks. "And how can you claim to know what I'm thinking in the first place?"

"My point is that you're describing this surveillance gate as a fundamental shift," Vallinger says. "Where actually it's just part of an evolution. There's been a certain type of anonymous surveillance on the chips for years. Decades."

"You say I'm describing something?" Stella asks, lifting her voice for the first time. "Excuse me, but how in the world do you know what I'm describing?"

Vallinger leans down and digs for something in his briefcase.

At that moment, Stella sees a movement in the window. The messenger has leaned his bike against the same tree in the front yard, about ten feet from Vallinger's Houyi. On his way to the back door, no doubt he has noticed the meeting taking place in the living room. He is ducked behind the rhododendron, probably wondering if he should figure out some way to deliver the message before attempting to sneak away unseen. Stella can see the top of his red bike helmet reflecting the morning sun.

Duck lower, she thinks. Lower!

Vallinger finally pulls a packet of paper from his case and tosses it onto the coffee table. It's a newspaper, *The Tribune*, with the headline about the open surveillance gate in the next update. Below it is the news about the unnamed Ralf in El Paso. Stella got the gist of the news yesterday in the pigeon-carried message she received. But it startles her to see the paper, faceup on the coffee table, with its bold headline about her son. In all her years of hearing about *The Tribune*, Stella has never seen the newspaper before. Someone in her movement—she doesn't know who—has access to it and spreads its news through pigeon and courier networks.

She reaches down and picks up the newspaper, the first one she's held in her hands since she was a child. It's only sixteen pages, four large pieces of folded paper. But it has a heft to it that she doesn't associate with information. Its smell is musty. She touches the headline, and her finger leaves a small black smudge. She reads the story and is taken aback to see the detail about Ralf's extracted boost. Who did the reporting for that? This reminds her of her grandfather, who lived into the '40s. He had been a newspaper reporter in El Paso, and she remembers hearing journalism stories from him. She wonders if there might be old copies of his newspapers packed in boxes in the attic. That reminds her of the current inhabitant of the third floor, Bao-Zhi, who remains oddly silent. No noise from Suzy, either. Stella steals a glance out the window. The messenger's helmet is no longer in the rhododendron, but his bike still leans against the tree.

She looks back at Vallinger. He appears weary, she thinks, or ill.

She holds up the paper. "What does this have to do with me?"

"Let's not be naive."

It occurs to Stella that Vallinger is mistaking her for the source of the stories in the paper. Nothing could be further from the truth. In fact, she's on the opposite end of the chain, receiving only tidbits of news small enough to wrap around a bird's leg. Yet somehow he believes that she sits at the nexus of a potent intelligence network—that she's powerful. Stella says nothing and wonders what she can gain by appearing to know more than she does.

"Now tell me," she says. "You said we had shared interests. What are they?"

"The U.S. of A.," he says.

She says nothing and resists the impulse to roll her eyes.

Vallinger launches into a lengthy monologue about the makeup of the Democracy Movement. As he describes it, some of the activists are loyal opponents of government policy. He places Stella in this category. "You worry about personal freedoms," he says, "about Chinese control of the chip. Sometimes you think we get carried away. But you want what's best for this country." On the other side of the movement, he says, are "revolutionaries." He says they're affiliated with "Chinese terrorists and Mexican drug lords pursuing a radical global agenda." Stella's thoughts turn to Bao-Zhi. Would Vallinger consider him a terrorist? Most likely, she thinks, glancing again out the window. She hears a rattle at the kitchen door, and then a moment later sees a red helmeted figure dart past the living-room window, jump onto a bike, and pedal down Christopher Street.

Vallinger, caught up in his narrative, misses the drama outdoors. He sits forward on the couch and gestures with his bony hands as he describes a vast Luddite conspiracy. He says it's committed to reversing evolution, turning humans back into Stone Age farmers, even hunter-gatherers. "Last time we tried the Stone Age, there were a couple hundred million people on earth, max. Most of them keeled over by the time they were thirty. Now," he goes on, "we have 10 billion. This planet cannot sustain us in our primitive state. These people—your colleagues, with all due respect—are pushing us toward starvation on a scale never seen, and global war."

"So you think I'm working with people whose goal is to destroy humanity," she says.

"With all due respect," Vallinger says. "Many of them. But not all."

"Why would I do that?"

"I would imagine there's a bit of 'the enemy of my enemy is my friend,'" Vallinger says. "Plus, I would argue that you might not know the views of all your colleagues that well."

"As well as you?"

"I know some things." He purses his lips and, for the first time in the meeting, looks pleased with himself.

"So," Stella says. "If you and I have shared interests and my colleagues, at least a certain number of them, are out to destroy humanity, how would you propose that we work together?"

"We could talk about that. But I think I'll need to accept your offer of a cup of coffee."

Stella unfolds herself from her chair. She pads on bare feet toward the kitchen. Deep in thought as she makes her way down the broad shadowed hallway, she doesn't notice the coiled figure of Bao-Zhi crouched behind a bookcase.

### 3/8/72 8:43 a.m. Eastern Standard Time

In her decade as a Democracy Movement activist, it's one question Stella never considered, even as a hypothetical: What kind of coffee would John Vallinger like? Ever since the afternoon she walked out of the job interview with him on K Street, dismayed by the man's vision of their country as an obscenely profitable networked subsidiary of China Inc., she had reclassified Vallinger as a reptile, albeit a diabolically intelligent one—not someone who would be sitting in her ancestral living room in Montclair awaiting a cup of coffee. She reaches for the worst ground beans she has, a house-blend decaf that's been moldering on a shelf for a year or two, and drops a few tablespoons of it into the pot.

Childish behavior, she thinks. But who invited him? Stella decides to take her time. She puts a kettle on the flame—the old-fashioned way—sets it to low, and wipes the kitchen counters as she waits.

She wonders why Vallinger would assume that she was a source for *The Tribune*. She doesn't receive the paper and wouldn't even know how to buy it. She lives hiding—at least until today—in an electronically jammed refuge from which she can communicate only by a messenger on bicycle. Would she be sending reports by means of cyclists and pigeons to the editor of a newspaper she never sees? Unlikely.

Still, Vallinger thinks it's her. She was aware, of course, that Ralf was preparing to hack the update, that he was nabbed, and that Bao-Zhi liberated him from a clinic in Alexandria. So it would be reasonable to consider her as a source on Ralf. And Simon lives in El Paso. In most families, when two brothers get together after years apart, the mother might be expected to be in the know. It isn't normal for such news to come from a messenger who has unwound a piece of paper from a pigeon's leg. How was John Vallinger to know that her family, if you could call it that, was different from most, that the Kellogg-Alvares, as Ralf liked to say, "took the fun out of dysfunctional"?

She wonders what Francisco would think if he could see what the family has come to. He was angry when he left Washington for Paraguay, all those years ago, sure of himself and certain that the boost would lead to tyranny. He was contemptuous of her, and her junior role in the negotiations. One night, after he'd been drinking, he called her a "lackey," and Stella, already pregnant with Ralf, hurled a half full bottle of Bohemia beer at his face. It was a week or two later that he left, never to be seen again. Stella considers her work in the DM a silent tribute to Francisco, an admission on her part that he was right.

She hears steps in the living room and imagines that Vallinger, weary of waiting, has gotten to his feet to check out the artwork on the walls.

He seemed so smug in saying that her colleagues were out to destroy the world, as if he had an inside line on the DM. What he doesn't understand is that insiders themselves, even ten-year veterans like Stella, are kept largely in the dark. The DM is organized in a cell structure. Each person communicates only with a small team and has no knowledge outside of that circle. Stella knows that it extends throughout the country and into Europe and China.

It was a Chinese affiliate that lined up Stella with Bao-Zhi. A stern rapping on the door announced his arrival. He stood at the entrance, mute and grim-faced, his eyes fastened onto Stella's. Even through his spring coat, she could see the sharp definition of his shoulders and upper arms. He reached into his pocket and pulled out a crumpled piece of paper, which he flattened and handed to her. "Please house this man indefinitely," it said. "He's wild and speaks no English. Follows different chain of command. Thanks."

Since then she has not exchanged a single word with the man, and wouldn't know how to begin. He's a mystery. She's heard from Suzy that Bao-Zhi's mission to free Ralf was violent. Suzy, though, has a fertile imagination. This leads Stella to wonder if Vallinger might possibly be speaking the truth. Could the DM be teeming with violent Luddite revolutionaries and Mexican drug lords? The vision seems paranoid to her. But she has no way of knowing.

She pours coffee into her least favorite cup, a lime green mug with a picture of a cow. She's tempted to pour one for herself until the odor of the coffee reaches her nostrils. It smells like wet cardboard. She carries the mug down the long hall and almost drops it when she steps into the living room.

Bound on the floor like a trussed hog lies John Vallinger. His hands are tied behind him. His feet are stretched back and lassoed to his belt, and his mouth is bound with four or five layers of brown duct tape. Above him, with shoulders squared and a face expressing clear-eyed defiance, stands Bao-Zhi. He's wearing a blue Montclair High Lacrosse sweatshirt that he must have pilfered from Ralf's bureau.

Upon seeing Stella, Vallinger writhes and groans. Boa-Zhi silences him by pushing his foot on the small of the lobbyist's back.

Stella stands speechless. Then she says, "You have to let him go, Bao-Zhi."

Bao-Zhi responds with a flurry of loud Chinese. He shouts like a warrior, Stella thinks. "Let him go," she repeats, for lack of anything else to say. She hears more Chinese.

"Suzy!" Stella shouts upstairs. "Get down here!" She doesn't know what Suzy can accomplish, but she needs someone to talk to, and the only other English speaker on site is indisposed.

Suzy hurries down from her room and gasps, halfway down the stairs, when she sees the scene. She's wearing her red running outfit, but without the hat. Her skull, recently shaven, gleams.

"I'm trying to tell him to let him go," Stella says. "But he just answers in Chinese."

"That's . . . John Vallinger," Suzy says, pointing at the prisoner.

"I'm telling him to let him go," Stella repeats.

But Suzy is paying no attention. She walks down the rest of the steps and slowly approaches Vallinger. She keeps her distance, the way she might from a thrashing swordfish. She leans down to get a good look. Then she reaches up with a hand and gently pats Bao-Zhi on the shoulder. Turning her head around, she asks, "Where did he catch him?"

It occurs to Stella that Vallinger might be right. Maybe she is surrounded by fanatics and violent revolutionaries.

"Where did he catch him?" Suzy repeats.

"He came here and knocked on the door, and I was just making him coffee," Stella says, waving the green mug. She's agitated, and some of the swill splashes onto the carpeted floor. "He followed the electronic trail of a certain jogger, who went out into Brookdale Park every morning and then came back to this house. It wasn't really that hard."

"Oh," Suzy says.

"So I need Bao-Zhi to understand that he has to untie this man," Stella continues. "But I can't understand a word he says."

"Translate in your boost," Suzy says. "That's how I talk to him. You don't need the network for that." She points her lovely face toward the warrior and says, "Bao-Zhi?"

He points at Vallinger and unleashes a torrent of Chinese. Suzy, Stella, and, no doubt, his captive, all translate it in unison. "He is the number-one enemy, the most wanted man, the foe of the people. I rejoice that he is captured and will be proud to conduct him to be tried for his crimes." Bao-Zhi taps his chest three times and gives the supine Vallinger a soft kick with his right foot.

Vallinger looks up toward Stella and arches his eyebrows, as if to say, "I told you so."

While the three capped English speakers in the house can translate the Chinese, the wild Bao-Zhi makes no sense of Stella's commands to untie the prisoner. Finally, Suzy locates a charcoal pencil and a drawing pad—relics from an art course Stella took long ago at the Bronx Botanical Garden. She calls up the written Chinese in her boost, and laboriously copies the phrase for "Release him." 他释放。

She shows the pad to Bao-Zhi. He shakes his head defiantly and shouts again that Vallinger is the "number-one enemy."

"I've got an idea," Stella says, grabbing the pad. She turns to a fresh page and takes ten full minutes to write a sentence. While she works on it, Suzy reaches for the cup of coffee and takes a sip. She grimaces and then offers the cup to Bao-Zhi. He takes a sniff and shakes his head sternly.

Stella finally finishes her work and shows it to Bao-Zhi: 你是在这个家中做客。

He places his hand on his forehead for a second, reflecting, and then nods respectfully to Stella and begins to untie his foe.

Suzy whispers, "What did you write?"

"You are a guest in this house," Stella answers.

After Bao-Zhi finishes unbinding John Vallinger, he stands up and makes the slightest bow in the direction of Stella, and then walks slowly up the stairs toward his chamber. Vallinger climbs to his feet only to make the transition from the floor to the blue sofa, where he lands with a groan. He covers himself with his crumpled trench coat. His forehead is red from the binding, and streaks of gray stick'em adhere to his skin. His white hair, drenched with sweat, is plastered sideways. He leans back, his eyes closed and, from the motion under the cape, appears to be rubbing his raw wrists.

A thumping noise comes from the third floor and Stella groans. She imagines Bao-Zhi carrying out days or weeks of ritual lamentations. But the noise grows as it descends the stairway. She looks up to see Bao-Zhi coming down. He carries his duffle bag over one shoulder. His big leather drum dangles from his other hand, bumping the banister with every step. He makes his way past the recumbent Vallinger to the front door. With a half turn, he bows again in the direction of Suzy, then turns and inclines his head toward Stella. He then maneuvers his way out door, down the walk, and onto Christopher Street, where he heads in the direction of Watchung Plaza.

"I feel sorry for him," Suzy says.

That brings a sigh from Stella and a burst of laughter from the blue sofa. "I mean being so foreign and wild and all," Suzy says. No one responds, and Suzy disappears down the hall toward the kitchen.

That leaves Vallinger and Stella alone. "So," Stella says, "you were saying something about working together?"

Vallinger sits up and rubs his eyes with the tips of his fingers. He looks ten years older than he did when he first walked in the door. He asks for a glass of water. Stella hands him the green mug of coffee, now cold. He takes a sip, considers it, and then takes another. "You could start," he says, speaking in a strangled voice, "by refraining from feeding news to that Juárez paper." He gestures toward *The Tribune,* which is lying next to the coffee table.

"Juárez paper?" Stella says. "Ciudad Juárez?"

"Let's don't act dumb, please."

She mutters under her breath. With Ralf in El Paso, and Simon, too, she can now see why Vallinger links her to the news stories. "What difference does it make?" she says. "Nobody reads it."

"People do," he says.

"What do I gain by shutting up?"

"Peace." He takes another sip of the cold coffee and stifles his grimace.

"This after you take my son to a clinic and rip out his boost?"

"That was a rogue operation," Vallinger says. "It was never supposed to happen that way." She waits, expecting him to say he's sorry, but he changes tack. "I think you got even by sending that Chinaman over there. He killed three people, and a fourth is still in critical condition."

He could be lying, Stella thinks. She presses on with

the meager leverage she has. If she holds back from talking to *The Tribune,* she asks, can Vallinger have the surveillance gate closed on the chip?

He shakes his head, as if he were on her side. "The Chinese finally have that, after thirty years of trying. They're not going to give it up."

"So I don't talk to *The Tribune,* and what I get in return is peace," she says, "meaning that you refrain from bombing my house or blowing up my car? Is that what I get?"

"Listen," he says, rising to his feet, "the update is an issue of national security." He tosses his coat over one shoulder, and he starts to pace. "If you get in its way," he says, "if you organize resistance to it, or manufacture outrage, we are going to rain down on your operation with a force that you'd be hard-pressed to imagine. The focus of this attack, the epicenter, will be that thriving family news business of yours in Juárez."

Stella nods dumbly and stays seated on the rocker, lost in her thoughts, as a rejuvenated John Vallinger grabs his briefcase and strides out the front door, shutting it with a bang.

# TWENTY-FIVE

**3/9/72 12:33 p.m. Juárez Standard Time**

A cold front has swept into the Rio Grande Valley, ringing the puddles of Ciudad Juárez with frost and whipping the city with icy north winds. In the paved downtown, the sidewalk vendors have taken the day off, and except for a few idle traffic cops, the streets look deserted. In retrospect, Ralf thinks, wrapping himself in a borrowed sheepskin overcoat, it's not a great day for a stroll. But Francisco insisted. Dressed in a thick blue overcoat with a black beret perched at a tilt on his head, he's leading the way past the last anti-drone barricade and down Avenida 16 de Septiembre. Ellen walks at his side. She's wearing a red ski jacket over a long blue dress that she borrowed from the chambermaid at Francisco's house. This allowed her finally to shed her brick-patterned leggings. Ralf watches Francisco gesture with both hands as he talks, probably describing the benefits of wild-grown vegetables or gas-fueled engines. Ralf has been with his father only one day, and he's already growing tired of hearing him.

"Talks a lot," Simon says, as though reading Ralf's mind. He's walking next to his brother, gripping the lapels of a thin cotton sport coat to his chest. His pudgy fingers look blue. "Whichever restaurant he takes us to, I hope it has a fireplace," he says.

Ralf takes in the ragged downtown of Juárez for the first time. Across an empty square he sees a big church, perhaps a cathedral, made of cinder blocks. Northward, to his left, is El Paso's downtown, its glass towers less than a mile away. The brown Franklins loom behind them, their peaks dusted with snow.

Lining the avenue in Juárez are tiny stores, each one no bigger than a walk-in closet. Ralf stops at the window of an electronics store. Its shelves are piled with relics that no one with a functioning boost would ever need. He looks at colorful cell phones and laptop computers dating from the 2030s. They have a shiny panel under the keyboard. People move their fingers there, he knows, to tell the machine what to do. How primitive it is, he thinks, to communicate information with fingers. It's not that far removed from the dots and dashes of Morse code, or even smoke signals. One shelf of the store displays wristwatches, all of them synchronized to the same time: 1:19 p.m. His grandparents strapped these machines on their wrists.

"Hurry up," Simon calls to him. Ralf trots to catch up. He's feeling a bit better today. Right after breakfast, Francisco informed him of an appointment the next morning with a prominent doctor in town—a neurologist—to see about putting the boost back into his head. So by this time tomorrow, Ralf is thinking, he might be his old self. He plans to get to work immediately on hacking the update software and shutting the gaping surveillance Gate 318 Blue. Slotting his fixes into the approved and meticulously vetted update won't be easy, especially without a network connection. But tomorrow, if all goes well, he can start working on it.

Francisco leads them down a few steps into a short passageway, and from there to a tiny elevator. The four of them squeeze in. When the doors open, they step into blinding sunlight. It's a circular restaurant covered by a windowed dome. "It revolves," Francisco tells them as a black-suited waiter leads them to a table.

"Drug lords built this place in the '20s," Simon whispers to Ralf. "It hasn't revolved for years, maybe decades. No spare parts."

Francisco, meanwhile, leads Ellen by the elbow and is pointing out the towers of El Paso, the winding path of the Rio Grande—"or, as we call it here, El Rio Bravo del Norte"—and, to the south, the Juárez Mountains. He shows her the mountain bearing words in Spanish: "*La Biblia es la Verdad. Leela.*"

"Do you understand that?" he asks.

Ellen feeds it to her boost and nods. "The Bible is the Truth. Read it," she says.

"Very good," he says, bringing the others into the conversation. "She's learning Spanish!"

"Papá," Simon says. "It's not so hard if you have a boost."

"Oh," Francisco says, looking embarrassed. "Forgot."

They sit down to a feast featuring chicken *al pipián,* a spicy sauce with a pumpkin seed base, steaming pork tamales wrapped in corn husks, and a salad made of cactus, or *nopal,* which Ralf finds a bit gooey. He looks across the table and sees that Ellen hasn't even touched hers.

While the others continue to wash down the food with glasses of bitter *Juarense* beer, Ellen sticks to mineral water. Ralf imagines that she's turning it into a pink champagne experience with her boost. He wonders if she's matching it with a euphoria app. She alone seems to find Francisco's stories amusing.

It's not until the waiter places the dessert—a big bowl of golden flan—onto the table that Francisco brings up the purpose of this outing. "You're my family—or close to it," he says, smiling at Ellen. Turning to Ralf, he says, "I left your mother all those years ago. I'm not proud of that. Now I'm a newspaper publisher in this very strange place. You deserve to know what happened in the years between."

That said, he spoons heaping portions of flan onto four plates, distributes them, and instructs the waiter to bring a big pot of coffee. Then he tells his story.

"Things weren't going so well with your mother back then," he says. "Or if you asked her, I'm sure she'd say things weren't going well with me. Or maybe that I was a jerk, or worse. In any case, we fought all the time. Some of it was personal. I wasn't . . . entirely faithful to her, and she knew it.

"But some of our problems had to do with what was happening in Washington at the time. The long and short of it is that the empire was crashing. The Chinese had the new chips and the software to run them, and the feeling in Washington was like, checkmate." He looks around the table to make sure that the three understand the chess analogy. They nod.

"The Chinese understood quicker than you—the United States—that the coming war would be cognitive. Now the U.S. had some of the best technology companies in the world. Apple, Google, Microsoft, IBM, which they used to call 'Big Blue.' They made a lot of stuff for businesses and consumers. Of course the Chinese were active in these fields, too. But they were spending more of their research money on the technology that would help them win the cognitive war. They developed spy software and defended themselves with the best cryptography. And they worked on the boost."

"Papá," Simon interrupts. "We know this stuff."

"Okay, okay," Francisco says. "Anyway, the Chinese start implanting their chips widely in the early '40s, and then right away, the Americans throw up their hands and think they've lost. They start moaning and groaning. 'Oh, we're wild. Our president's wild, we're so stupid and they're so smart.' I'll tell you, at that point, the Chinese didn't need to have chips in their heads to win the war. The perception that they were superior was enough. The Americans rolled over, gave them Hawaii, sacrificed the dollar, and surrendered."

"That's what Mother was doing?" Simon asks.

"Well, she wouldn't call it that, but, yes," Francisco says. "She had one of the first chips. She was the test case for her Senate committee. I had never been around a person with a chip, of course, and having one in her head was a real adjustment for her. It added to stress, for both of us. Then, using the chip she figured out some things about me, which I resented." He pauses and shrugs. "To be fair, I suppose she did, too. In any case, we argued about these things. Sometimes it got loud. We were in a little apartment in Adams Morgan, and the neighbors would pound on the walls and say, 'Shut up!' Then you," he says, pointing at Simon, "would wake up and start asking all sorts of questions, and your mother would blame me, and I'd drink a big glass of rum and get even louder. It was terrible. I ended up spending a lot of nights with my friends in a place down Columbia Road.

"Anyway, one of my points in those arguments was that the chip was just a computer. The Chinese could impress everybody by calculating big numbers in their heads at meetings, or sending messages to each other. But the real thinking came from the biological part. The brain—the wet brain—was still the crucial cognitive engine. Everybody had one. Now it's true, the Americans needed good computers. But they didn't necessarily need them inside their heads. They certainly didn't need Chinese computers there. What was the rush?

"They were scared," he says. "It was like a—" He pauses, looking for the right word. He turns to Simon. *"¿Como se dice 'una estampida'?"*

"A stampede," Simon says.

"Oh, that's easy. It was like a stampede." He pronounces it *"estampede."* "Your mother was part of the team. I blamed her for it. I was thinking, 'The Americans are surrendering. The country's going to turn into a client state of a dictatorship.' You didn't need a boost to see that coming. In any case, my marriage was falling apart, and the Chinese and the Americans, who by now had their own chip, were heading down to South America to battle for market share. That's where the cognitive war was going to get hot."

Francisco takes a sip of coffee. Then he calls over the waiter and orders a pitcher of tequila. "So one day I tell Stella that I'm going down to Asunción to see my folks and do some work. What I don't tell her is that my ticket is one-way. I'm not proud of this, but it's the truth. I kiss her good-bye. She's four or five months pregnant, and frankly, I think she's happy to see me go. I kissed you good-bye," he says to Simon. "That one hurt." He pauses to pour four small glasses of tequila. He distributes them and then downs his with a single gulp.

"Now Paraguay," he says, "was the test market for the American chips. We were the . . . Indian rabbits."

"Guinea pigs," Simon says, correcting him.

"Precisely, the guinea pigs. When I get down there, it's pretty easy to see what's going to happen. The Americans are going to roll out their chips, and the Chinese are going to do everything they can to disrupt it. Now the Chinese have been researching for decades into all sorts of cognitive weaponry. They have viruses and worms and trojans and all sorts of programs to interfere with computer systems. We all know that. So it makes perfect sense that they will try to sabotage the American chips in Paraguay. At least it's a possibility. A successful sabotage might kill people. Perhaps thousands of them. The only way to protect the Paraguayans, the way we see it, is to keep the Americans from implanting the chips in the first place."

"We?" Ralf asks. "You were with some group?"

"We called ourselves the Nuevos Bolivarianos. They called us revolutionaries, and said we were anti-American. But the only revolution we wanted was to maintain the cognitive status quo—the human brain without a chip. Though yes, some of us were anti-American, others were against the project mostly because we knew, or at least suspected, that the Chinese were going to sabotage them. The battle between those two countries was about to start and it was going to take place inside our heads!

"It was in September of 2044 that we made our big move. We blew up a warehouse across the Rio Paraguay from Concepción. We had intelligence that the first load of chips was there. Everything about the operation was a success. We moved in with great secrecy. The plastic explosives, which came from Venezuela, worked impeccably. They left nothing but . . . *escombros*."

"Rubble," Simon says.

"There was only one problem," Francisco continues, "and it was a big one. The chips were not in that warehouse. The Chinese or the Americans—we still don't know which—fed us false intelligence. There were three watchmen in the warehouse. They all died.

"So suddenly, we were murderers. The army launched a massive counterattack against us. They had informants in our group—the same ones who gave us the wrong warehouse. They led the soldiers right to our doors.

Within a week of that attack, almost all of my friends were in jail or killed."

"How did you survive?" Ralf asks.

Francisco downs another shot of tequila and slowly scratches the side of his nose. "I was an informant for the Americans," he says quietly. "Now I did not tell them about our attack, and I didn't rat on my *compañeros*. But I told them about members of our group who seemed to be pro-Chinese. I felt that by working against the deployment I was helping the United States. That was the side I chose." He stares down at the white tablecloth.

No one speaks. Simon rolls back his head and looks up through the dome at the wintry sky. This is one piece of information he didn't know. Ralf takes a spoonful of flan, swallows it, and follows it with a sip of tequila.

"I don't get it," Ellen says. "Did the Chinese plant spies in your group?"

"Of course," Francisco says. "They wanted to know what we were up to. They wanted us to fail, so that the Americans could roll out the chips and they could sabotage them. That's what I always believed, and I believe it to this day. That's what happened. We failed. We were dismantled. The Americans went ahead with the chips."

"What did you do?" Ellen asks.

"I left Paraguay the next day. I was lucky that the Americans did not kill me right away. They knew that I knew about the warehouse bombing. They had to know that. They knew that I didn't tell them. So I was aware that my days were numbered. The survivors in our group—and there weren't many—were likely to be suspicious of anyone who didn't get killed. Of course, people were suspicious of them, too. Everyone was suspicious of everyone else, and the way to settle things, all of a sudden, was to kill people. So it didn't make sense for me to stick around. I found a truck driver who was going to Santa Cruz, in Bolivia, carrying a refrigerated load of Argentine beef. I went along. When we crossed the border into Bolivia, I hid among carcasses of cows. I almost froze.

"So I get to Santa Cruz. I have no money, and only the clothes on my back—which stink of beef. My only asset is my education, and my English. Santa Cruz, at that point, is the capital of Bolivia's coca industry. I start out as a laborer, a *peón,* working like a mule and living in a little shack with eight bunk beds. Sixteen of us in this little space! It smelled worse than the meat truck. Eventually they see that I'm not a *peón,* that I speak English and know about economics. So I work my way up in the business. Pretty soon, I'm flying around and making deals. I'm going down to Lima, to the port of Callao, up to Santa Marta in Colombia, to Belem and Recife in Brazil. I make a couple of trips to Mexico, one to Culiacán, another one right here to Juárez. At this point, the chip wars are exploding all over the continent. But that's not my fight anymore."

"So what happened in Paraguay?" Ellen asks.

"Just what I feared. The Americans rolled it out. The chips worked wonderfully—*una maravilla*. Really," he adds, "despite everything people said, the Americans were ahead of the Chinese in this technology. Much smoother software interface. But within a week or two, a virus started spreading in the chip. I wasn't there, of course, but friends who were told me about it. People started going crazy. They got horrible headaches and went suicidal. People were jumping off bridges. One guy set himself on fire in the Plaza Uruguaya, right across from the train station. I think my whole family died, though I never got official word. In the end, the government and the Americans had to take the chips out. It was over in Paraguay.

"Before long, the two countries moved on to different markets, to Chile, to Argentina, finally the big one in Brazil. There was violence and all kinds of intrigue. But as far as I was concerned, the die was cast in Paraguay. The rest of the chip wars were an aftermath. The Chinese won. As I say, that was no longer my war. I was into a different business.

"That new business was also in crisis—because of the chips. The drug business could not thrive in a surveillance state, and that's what was coming in every country. As the chips rolled out in Bolivia, Peru, Colombia, the governments finally had a way to monitor their populations. They could watch the narcos, step by step. If the narcos tried to stay wild, as they did here in Juárez, they could arrest them. It was illegal not to have a chip. If the narcos made deals with police or army officers, as they always had, the government could see that, too. Everything was visible.

"It's hard to understand now what a dramatic change this was. These countries had always been so free— much freer than the rich countries, the U.S. and Europe. You could lose yourself in the mountains or stretches of jungle bigger than some European countries. The law wasn't a problem. It was really just a starting point for negotiations, and if you had money—as we did—you almost always got your way.

"Well, with the chips, that freedom just evaporated. Gone. Everything was visible, traceable, documented. What's more, the chip started to eat into our market. People didn't need expensive cocaine anymore when they could buy a cheap euphoria app."

"So did you get a boost?" Ellen asks.

"I considered it," Francisco says. "I like electronics. I like toys. I like the idea of having entertainment available all the time, and being able to communicate with my friends. I could see that the things we had—the money, telephones, computers, movies—they were all going to move into the head. The wild world was going to be a lonely place without much opportunity. I saw that. So, yes, I considered getting a boost."

"You never told me this!" Simon says.

"You never asked," Francisco says. "So anyway," he says, turning back toward Ellen, "I considered it. But I was an illegal alien in Bolivia with a work history that was sure to raise questions. To be honest, I wasn't sure if I'd rather be a citizen in a surveillance state or an outlaw on its fringes. In the end, I chose the fringe.

"Back then we knew that Juárez was wild. Everyone knew this. So four of us got a plane, loaded it with product, and took off for San Andres Island. That's a part of Colombia that's up in the Caribbean. We flew all night. It was just like a normal drug run. But instead of selling the cargo and flying back, we sold half of it there and flew north. We figured we'd sell the other half in Juárez.

"There were three of us in the plane who knew each other pretty well. Me, my friend Sapo, and his cousin, Raul. The fourth was the pilot, a man named Javier. I had a funny feeling about him from the beginning. He was a big fat Argentine, and new to the trade. Why would anyone jump into a dying business at this point? I couldn't understand that. Also, he was capped. It seemed strange to me that someone with a chip in his head would take a great risk to fly to the capital of the wild world.

"So I was suspicious of Javier. Sapo vouched for him. He said he used to date Javier's sister in Buenos Aires. Of course that led to lots of jokes, about whether Javier's sister looked like him. The usual stuff. I guess I forgot about my suspicions, or suppressed them, because we flew north with him. It wasn't until we were going over the Tehuantepec isthmus of Mexico, the skinniest part, that I began to wonder. I'd been over Tehuantepec before, and the army always shot at small planes like ours with surface to air missiles. SAMs. They always missed, but SAMs were part of the normal experience around there. This time, it was silent.

"Javier was listening to the radio, constantly. That wasn't so unusual. But when he heard the Gringo voices, he would do this thing with his little finger." Francisco holds his tequila glass and gently beats his finger against it. "At first I thought it was just nerves, or that he was keeping beat to a song in his head. But his finger would go quiet. Then the Gringo voice came on, and the finger came back to life. We assumed that the Gringos he was listening to were the anti-drug and anti-terrorism people. He was tapping his finger against this little metal ring on the side of the control panel. I pointed it out to Sapo and Raul, and we watched it for ten or fifteen minutes, all the time our suspicions rising. We figured it had to be some sort of signal he was sending."

"What did you think he was?" Ellen asks.

"DEA," Francisco says. "Bringing us in to jail, and squeezing us for our sources, delivery routes, couriers, bank information, the usual stuff.

"So we're flying north over the Pacific, and we go over land again near Culiacán, in Sinaloa. This is where guns fire pretty much nonstop. Javier knows this. He's sending out flares left and right. Those are things you fire off to divert missiles. He's ducking, and he's saying, 'Whoa, that was a close call.' We know that no one's shooting at us. This isn't our first plane ride.

"This is where it would have been really convenient to have chips in our heads. We could have sent messages back and forth. But all we could do in that plane was send signals with our eyes and our fingers. It was hard to come up with a strategy. If the guy hadn't been the pilot, it would have been easy. But you can't take out the only person who knows how to fly when you're at fifteen thousand feet. This is what I wanted to say to Sapo. But I couldn't get the point across.

"Next thing I know, Sapo has . . . what's the white rope you use for clotheslines?"

"I think it's just 'clothesline rope,'" Ellen says.

"Well he has some clothesline rope around Javier's

neck, and he's pulling hard. I can tell because it digs into the fat, and you can't even see the rope. Of course, Javier can't talk. His eyes are bugging out and his face turns bright red. He lets go of the control stick, and the airplane starts to dive.

"Raul and I are screaming for Sapo to let him go. But Sapo, since he was the one who brought Javier on board, is feeling betrayed. Or *more* betrayed, I should say. He's yelling: 'Tell us who you work for, *hijo de puta!*'"

Francisco's voice is rising as he tells the story, and the only other people in the restaurant, three heavyset men who look like off-duty cops, are looking in his direction. He lowers his voice to a hoarse whisper and continues.

"Sapo's a strong man, and I guess he pulls too hard, because Javier collapses to one side, and his head falls in a tilt, like he's been hanged. The airplane is diving and we're all screaming. I start to push Javier's body from the seat. First I have to unbuckle him, which isn't easy when you're panicking. Then I have to shove his big heavy body off to the side. But these planes are tiny, and there's nowhere to shove it. So I manage to pull it toward me, and I climb over it into the pilot's seat. Now I've never piloted before, but I've been on lots of runs, and I've watched them. I know how the control stick works. I grab it and pull it back, and the plane levels off."

Francisco takes another sip of his tequila and looks at his three guests, trying to gauge how much detail to pack into his story. "Two problems," he says. "First, we think that Javier was sending some kind of code with his finger, and that as soon as that code stops, they'll realize that something has changed and start shooting at us. We can't do much about that. The second problem: We don't know where we are, and we can't ask the people on the radio for instructions, because they'll know we're amateurs. So we turn off the radio. Sapo has a road atlas for Mexico. We start looking at it, the various states, Sinaloa, Durango, Zacatecas, and matching what we see below us to the maps. We don't have a clue!

"Then we see these big mountains. 'These have to be the Tarahumara,' I say. I push down the control and we climb over them, barely. Then I see Copper Canyon, which, by the way, is spectacular. That puts us into the state of Chihuahua. Long story short, we find Chihuahua City, and then we drop down to about an altitude of fifteen feet. We're not much higher than a truck. We can see every pebble. Flying like that, we follow Highway 45 all the way to Juárez. When we get to a landing strip near the border, I try to land the plane, not with great success. I think you call it a 'crash landing.' The three of us climb out before it explodes into flames. I barely noticed until later," he adds, "that my leg was broken. I never really got it fixed.

"Still the crash turned out to be a good thing. First, if we had tried to sell our drugs in Juárez, we would probably have been killed within a day or two. Newcomers weren't appreciated in the business around here. Second, it destroyed Javier's body. If you kill a DEA agent, it's best not to leave a lot of evidence. Of course," he adds, "we never found out if he was DEA or not. For all we know, he was tapping tangos with his baby finger and the gunners in Tehuantepec and Sinaloa were taking the day off. We'll never know."

Francisco gestures out the window beyond a long stretch of shanties. "It was just over there that we landed," he says. "So we're thinking this is the promised land. Ciudad Juárez. No boosts, no surveillance, everyone's a narco. It sounds like a dream, except for one thing. The city had way too many narcos facing a dramatically shrinking market. Now Juárez had a very long history of dealing with such problems. Early in the century, it was known as the murder capital of the world."

"It still is," Ralf says.

"Yes. But that's propaganda. They also say we sell drugs here, and we haven't done that for twenty years. Anyway," Francisco continues, "they had a heritage of drug wars. When we arrived here it looked like a new one, even more vicious, was about to break out. Anyone who could count—and you didn't need a chip for that—could see that we had a surplus of narcos. It was unsustainable.

"So there we are, the three of us, trying to figure out how to make a living for ourselves in Juárez. For Sapo and Raul, it was just a question of picking sides. There were two cartels, the Juárez and the Chihuahua. They were run by these two cousins: El Greñas, or the Mop Head. He had very curly hair and was famous for playing the banjo. Or maybe it was the mandolin. . . . What's that tiny guitar?"

"The ukulele?" Ellen says.

"*Exacto*. The ukulele. The other was Santiago. They

called him El Mortífero, which means 'deadly.' They both said that since they were cousins, they'd cooperate and there would be peace. But of course everybody knew that they'd end up slaughtering each other. I said this to Raul and Sapo, but they couldn't see any other future for themselves outside of *el negocio,* and they both went to work for Greñas. Within a year, they were both dead."

Francisco, who with minimal help has emptied more than half of the tequila, dabs at his eyes with his napkin and takes a couple of breaths.

"So," he says, "I have to figure out a new career for myself. Even with their market shrinking, the narcos still have most of the business in town. You absolutely want them as customers. But to stay alive, you want to work for both of them. Now, what do they need? They're shipping into an American market that is changing, day by day. As the new chips are spreading throughout the population, it's becoming harder to send wild people across the border. The U.S. is starting large-scale electronic surveillance. Everyone knows that, but no one knows the details. Where can the drug runners go unnoticed? That information is worth gold. Providing that information, I decide, will be my new business.

"I was sharing a room in a boarding house just down the street from here with a guy named Silvestre. I called him Sibo. He was from Mexico City, a *chilango.* He called me Pancho, which is a Mexican nickname for Francisco. I hated it. It sounded to me like someone wearing a big *sombrero* and dressed in a blanket. So I asked him to call me Paco. That turned into Paquito, which I hate more than Pancho. But what can you do?

"Anyway, we started printing this newsletter together. In the beginning we were just informing the local people here in Juárez about what was going on if they crossed the border. We did interviews on the street, looking for people who had just crossed, or who knew others who had. In the early days, there was a lot more traffic crossing the border. That was before Washington and Mexico City locked us out. We'd ask people, 'What's happening in Santa Teresa? What's going on around Fabens?' Then we'd write it up. It was pretty much a trade publication for the drug industry. Then we found people who had contacts in Washington, and in Chicago, and in Mexico City, and we started writing about how the whole continent was changing. Everybody wanted to know. The first weeks, we printed up only about two hundred copies. By the end of the second month, we were selling ten times that many. Then I started thinking: If we know this about the U.S., what is going on in China and in Europe and Africa? We had people here, a whole new exile community of wild people. These were very curious people, and intelligent. I mean, think about it: They moved to a faraway city in a different continent because they wanted to keep their heads working the same way. How many people would do that?" He looks around the table for an answer, but gets only shrugs.

He continues. "Even though they didn't have boosts, they still had contacts back home. So I set them up.

There was still e-mail back then, and they could communicate with their friends back home. Pretty soon, we were publishing news that people couldn't find anywhere else. We were sending the papers all over the world, using some of the old drug-smuggling routes to ship them. We were hiring correspondents on every continent."

"Wait a minute," Ralf says. "If these people had e-mail, then they also had the Internet. Couldn't they just read the news there?"

"News on the Internet was drying up," Francisco says. "Everything was going to the boost. Almost none of it was news. There was no business model for news reporting. The companies and governments that ran the boost weren't the least bit interested in publishing the kind of news that we were running."

"Oh, give me a break!" Ralf says.

"You don't believe me?"

"There's still news in the boost," Ralf says. He looks for support to Simon, who's staring blankly out the window, like someone who's heard this same discussion more than once.

"Okay," Francisco says. "Tell me this. You live in Washington. There's lots of news to cover there. Do you know any journalists?"

Ralf thinks about it. "Not exactly. Maybe they just don't use that word anymore. A lot of the news," he adds, "is put together automatically, with machines finding information, focusing on certain subjects or memes, and then organizing it."

"Are the machines doing the reporting?" Francisco asks.

"I'm sure they're doing some kind of reporting," Ralf says, "though the process is different. More efficient, I'm sure."

"That story about the open surveillance gate in the chip," Francisco says. "The one that was on the front page of our paper. Did machines report on that? Can you find that news in the boost?"

"Well, I don't have my boost right now. . . ."

"But do you think the story's there?"

"Probably not," Ralf admits.

"In time," Francisco says, continuing his story, "e-mail disappeared. The companies that used to run it started to unplug their big old computers. Electronic communications moved entirely to the boost. That meant that we had to set up an analog information network. We started using couriers. We actually found a few telegraphs that still worked. One of them in China is functioning to this day. In some places, we used pigeons. You'd laugh. It's technology Hernán Cortés would recognize. And some of our news is very old. But even old news has value when its only competition is no news.

"I have this theory," Francisco says, as he signals to the waiter for the bill. "Whenever a new technology is introduced, it kills one market and creates a new one, or maybe more than one. When I was young, people were willing to pay just about anything and even risk their lives for an hour or two away from themselves.

They wanted to escape. Millions of them took drugs. This was a mammoth escape market.

"Then came the boost. That provided a cheaper and safer way to escape. You could escape into virtual worlds or load a euphoria application without breaking the law. That basically killed drugs, at least as a mass market.

"Now in the boost, practically everything can be fun. You don't have to read a dry article about a war in Syria or Cameroon. You can go there in your boost, and shoot guns, and learn something about the place in the process. It's the spread of the entertainment economy. That's where most of the money is. But even so, a certain number of people—three hundred thousand of them, at the very least—are willing to pay a lot to learn what's really happening. If in the past, people paid a premium for escape, now there's a surplus of it. It's cheap. And there's a shortage of reality, or news. That creates a booming news market. I have it practically all to myself!"

"So what happened to the two cousins, the drug lords?" Ellen asks. Ralf leans forward, eager to hear. Simon leans back and rolls his eyes.

Francisco, glancing at Simon, places a handful of red chips on the restaurant bill and closes the leather cover. He smiles at Ellen and lifts his right eyebrow in the highest of arcs, and then gently lowers it. "I've talked enough for today," he says, pushing back his chair and standing up. "I have to leave something for tomorrow."

# TWENTY-SIX

Oscar Espinoza stands ankle-deep in the white sand trap at the abandoned Santa Teresa Country Club. He has the trap door held open with one meaty hand and is calling to a man standing on the other side of his parked KIFF. George Smedley comes trotting in his direction. He's wearing a tight-fitting white exercise suit, with running pants and a matching golf shirt. He'll freeze, Espinoza thinks. Smedley holds on to his Panama hat as he makes his way toward the sand trap. His signature peregrine falcon feather pokes out from the hat's charcoal band. Espinoza, while far from an expert on men's fashion, dreads guiding this person through Ciudad Juárez.

"Just sending a couple of last-minute messages before entering the dead zone," Smedley says. He ducks into the tunnel, and Espinoza follows him, shutting the door behind them.

"My headache's gone!" Smedley says. Then, looking

down the tunnel, his mood darkens. He complains about the cold and adds, "You didn't say we'd have to crawl."

"A little brown might help your look," Espinoza says as he pads along on all fours. "Your knees will match your feather."

The plan, as Smedley outlined it at dinner the night before, is to make contact with Ralf Alvare and, if possible, with Suzy Claiborne, and to offer them both a small fortune, or maybe even a large one, to return with Smedley to Washington, where a team of the nation's best surgeons will replace the boost in Ralf's head—after first removing the stolen update code. That's assuming that Ralf still has the chip, as Espinoza has led Smedley to believe.

They were eating in a Mexican restaurant on Kansas Street, G&R's, as Smedley laid out the plan. Espinoza was working his way through a mountain of chiles rellenos, half of them stuffed with cheese, the others with hamburger. Espinoza wadded his mouthful into one cheek to talk. "I told you that the Artemis over there isn't the domed one you're looking for."

"I know what you said," Smedley snapped. "You were close enough to see the roots of her hair, but not close enough to catch her. Just humor me on this one."

"What do we do if Alvare says no?" Espinoza asked.

"Offer him more money."

"Whose money is it?"

"We'll give the bill to Vallinger. He can decide whether he wants to pay it." Smedley winced from the unrelenting pain in his head. He had pushed for Espinoza to rush straight from the airport to the Santa Teresa tunnel. But

Espinoza urged patience. "It's dangerous there at night," he said. "I don't want to leave my KIFF all night at that golf course."

For Espinoza, it was a strange and novel experience to spend time in El Paso with Smedley. No longer in their usual roles—supervisor and lackey—they were now closer to suffering colleagues, both of them answering to a higher power, John Vallinger and his top aide, Tyler Dahl. Smedley had the headache, and this time Espinoza had been spared. Probably an oversight, he thought.

At certain moments over dinner, it seemed to Espinoza, it almost felt like they were friends. Smedley told him about a handful of media properties he owned, including some popular virtual worlds. "You never know. There might be a place for you there," he said to Espinoza as they finished up dinner. "Some of the sites are pretty kinky."

Crawling through the tunnel the next day, Espinoza is still wondering about that comment. Did it have something to do with his nose? He shifts his thinking to the current assignment and details for Smedley some of the dangers they'll likely face in Juárez. He tells him about the revolutionaries who briefly arrested the Alvare brothers. "They want Juárez to stay wild. They're kind of fanatical, but not really that strong. Kind of weak, actually."

When Smedley asks him how the Alvare brothers freed themselves, Espinoza realizes that he's talking too much. "Oh, I don't know," he says. "Maybe they're still prisoners there."

"But you said they were at Don Paquito's headquarters."

"Oh, that's right. I think Don Paquito's people freed them. But I'm not sure. When people talk in Spanish, I don't always catch everything."

When they step out into Juárez, a group of boys wrapped in old quilted coats is waiting for them. They try to sell plastic coins to the Americans, but Smedley and Espinoza push past them. "Those look like tiddlywinks," Smedley says.

"They can buy some good stuff," Espinoza says. He retraces his steps from the two days before, winding his way along the dirt roads, past the chicken coops and the pigsties.

Smedley tags along behind, gripping his bare arms in the cold. "Do they have any buildings with heat over here?" he asks.

"Move faster and you'll warm up," Espinoza says.

Then he hears a familiar rumbling noise. "Come on," he says, breaking into a jog. "Run." The noise grows louder, and he sees the Revolutionary Brigade truck turning around a corner and coming their way. The truck skids to a stop in front of them, and the same three young men climb out. One of them wears a bandage across his nose. The two others carry baseball bats.

The gangly one says something, but his words are drowned out by another roaring engine much louder than their truck. The men turn around and see a drone hurtling toward them. It's as big as an elephant and it moves forward on hexagonal wheels that behave more like feet. The revolutionaries race to one side of the street. Espinoza grabs Smedley and hurls him to the other side. He dives in the same direction just as the drone fires a screaming missile. It slams into the truck and destroys it, sending scraps of metal and plastic high into the air. Espinoza and Smedley, both lying on the ground, cover their heads as the debris rains down.

"That was the call I made," Smedley says, smiling.

"You called for a drone escort?"

"Protection."

"I don't think it's going to make us a lot of friends over here," Espinoza says, as the three revolutionaries scamper away.

"Who gives a shit?"

Espinoza climbs to his feet. "Come on," he says. "There are some people around here who make good goat, if they can find a stove to cook it on."

They take off walking toward the city with the drone following a block behind.

# TWENTY-SEVEN

Simon tells the bartender at the Kentucky Club that his brother, Ralf, has never had a margarita in his life. "Make him a good one," he tells him in Spanish, with Herradura. He orders club sodas for himself and Ellen. Then he walks down to the end of the bar and picks up the old-fashioned phone.

"That's like the one he has over at his tavern," Ralf says to Ellen.

"That's where he's calling. He's talking to Chui." She tells him about her visit to the same bar, two days earlier, with Enrique, her "guide," and Alfredo, the boy whose family she met. As the bartender pours Ralf's margarita into a large glass with a salted rim, Ellen describes the lunch she had that first day, and how she thought she'd be able to cross back to El Paso that same afternoon. It was just a couple hundred yards away, she says. It still is, but it now seems so distant, almost unapproachable. "When are we ever going to go back?" she asks.

"As soon as I get my boost," Ralf says, trying to cheer her up. "I know where the tunnel is. Our car's waiting for us on the other side of it." He casually takes a gulp of the margarita and promptly coughs it out, spraying the polished mahogany bar. "Wow," he says, wiping the bar with a napkin. "I think that drink's made for smaller sips."

Ellen takes a tiny sip herself, and winces. "The margarita app is a lot smoother," she says.

Simon joins them. As he settles on a bar stool he pats his brother on the back.

"Business call?" Ralf says.

"Sort of."

"Now that we've heard all about Francisco's history, how about you tell us what your business is over there at the tavern," Ralf says.

"All right," Simon says with a sigh. "I knew I'd have to sooner or later." He tells his brother about the handwritten message he got from Don Paquito three years ago, when Simon was working at a brokerage in St. Louis. "I didn't have any idea who he was," Simon says. "He offered me a lot of money." They met at the deserted Santa Teresa Golf Club. Simon recognized his father immediately. It was just a grayer version of the face that appeared over his bed when he was a child, waking him up to kiss him good night, talking to him in Spanish and smelling of rum. "Same guy," he says, taking a sip of his club soda. "He even did the same trick with his eyebrow. Have you noticed that?"

Ralf nods.

Francisco convinced him, Simon continues, that he wasn't the monster he was made out to be, that he didn't have a harem and tigers and a full stable of killers on call. "He gave me the same talk he gave you about journalism and truth in the boost. He told me he had a problem. He had a business that was growing too fast for him to handle. He had to figure out how to deal with all the revenue pouring in."

"It couldn't be that much," Ralf says. "Three hundred thousand people times, what?" He quickly gives up pushing any arithmetic through his wild brain, already addled by tequila. He takes another sip of the margarita.

"You have no idea," Simon says. "How much are you making in your job in Washington?"

"Four million a year," Ralf says, shrugging. "Government work." He takes another sip of the drink.

"Well, if you wanted to subscribe to *The Tribune*, five days a week, fifty weeks a year, it would cost you three months' wages, before taxes."

"Get off it!"

"A million a year," Simon says, nodding. "He has about a hundred journalists on payroll and sizable distribution costs. But compared to the revenue, it's nothing. Of course he spends almost nothing on technology. About ninety percent of the money that comes in is pure profit."

Simon goes on to describe in great detail how he and Chui run what amounts to a brokerage out of the tavern, and how they juggle Francisco's billions in accounts all over the world. He mentions exotic financial instruments and associates he works with in Shanghai, Montevideo, and Zurich.

"Do the Americans know about this? Does the government?" Ralf asks.

"Oh, yeah," Simon says. "They're big subscribers. If you need to know things, you can't ignore it. That's why we can charge so much."

"And Mom?"

"Something tells me she's going to figure it out pretty soon."

# TWENTY-EIGHT

**9:07 a.m. Eastern Standard Time**
*"Your family news business."*

Vallinger's words have been echoing in Stella's ears for a full day. It's hard for her to believe that Simon, who's running a tavern in El Paso, would be operating secretly as a newspaper publisher across the border. And Ralf, who lost his boost just a week ago, would not likely hurry down to Ciudad Juárez, of all places, and launch a new career in journalism. She sprinkles protein onto a little mound of green on a plate, the fixings for her usual lunch, a *salade niçoise*. A full day after John Vallinger's visit, Stella is still mulling his line about her family. Could her cousin, Ted, a musician in Red Bank, New Jersey, be playing some role in Juárez? The idea's too crazy even to consider.

Suzy walks into the kitchen, still in her striped pajamas, and pours herself a cold cup of coffee. Then she joins Stella in the living room. She sits on a corner of the blue satin couch last occupied by John Vallinger.

"I'm still thinking about the 'family news business,'" Stella says

Suzy points to the copy of *The Tribune* still lying on the coffee table. "He just meant that Ralf and Simon are talking to reporters from that paper," she says. "Or at least he thinks they are."

"I think it's more than that," Stella says. "But I can't do any research about it in this house. I've been looking through the documents I have in my boost, and there isn't anything about *The Tribune*."

"Go outside!" Suzy says. "They already know we're here."

She's right, of course. Stella hurries to the closet, pulls on a black overcoat that Ralf bought at a vintage store, and for the first time in more than a week, she steps outside. Startled birds fly away from the neighbor's feeder as hundreds of messages and updates cascade into Stella's boost. She'll read them later.

She searches for the publisher of *The Tribune*, in Ciudad Juárez, and comes up with nothing. It's not even mentioned. Maybe, she thinks, Vallinger had it wrong. She looks for *Tribune* references in Tijuana, Laredo, Nogales, and Brownsville. Nothing. She looks for facts about Juárez and finds a full dossier: *The Tragedy of Ciudad Juárez: City Gone Wild*. She downloads it and walks back into the warmth of the house. Reading while she eats lunch, she learns that the city of three million people has the highest murder rate in the world. Its economy is based almost entirely on the shipment of drugs and other contraband. Diseases long eradicated in the rest of the world, including HIV/AIDS, multiple sclerosis, rabies and even bubonic plague, all flourish in Juárez, where the average life expectancy is a mere thirty-six years old. Horrified, Stella reads on. The de facto leader of Juárez is a drug lord known only as Don Paquito, an Argentine who rose to the top by eliminating his competitors through a series of gangland executions. Stella tries opening a photo of Don Paquito, but nothing comes up. She reads that he has a harem in his Juárez palace, and that he has tigers as house pets. He lost an eye during some battle decades ago, and he likes to pop out his glass eye as a gag. Sometimes he drops it into other people's cocktails. He is rumored to be a drug addict.

Stella hurries to an ancient bookshelf that stands in the dark corridor between the living room and the kitchen. Just yesterday, Bao-Zhi was crouched behind the same shelves before launching his attack on John Vallinger. The books are caked with dust, their bindings dried and cracking. Stella quickly finds the one she's looking for. It's called *Donkey Show,* and it's written by her grandfather, Tom Harley. It tells the story of a journalist in El Paso—a thinly veiled Harley—who is on the track of a notorious drug lord in Juárez, Gustavo Jiménez. Stella, who read the book as a girl, flips through the early pages looking for a passage she remembers. She finds it on page fifteen:

Everyone had a story or two about the local drug lord. One man claimed that Jiménez had pet tigers roaming through his mansion on the east side of Juárez. He had a harem, too, he said, and threw all-night parties. The cop added that Jiménez sometimes popped out his glass eye and dropped it in people's drinks, for a laugh.

"Suzy!" Stella runs with the living room, where Suzy is stretched out on the floor, still in her pajamas. She has one leg up in the air and is pulling her knee toward her face. "Take a look at this," Stella says, putting her finger on the passage about Jiménez. "A story in the boost says exactly the same thing about a drug lord in Juárez, Don Paquito."

Suzy lowers her leg and reads the passage. "You mean there are two drug lords in Juárez, this guy and the one you read about in your boost, and they both have tigers?"

"And a harem," Stella says. "And a glass eye."

"I can't imagine that every drug lord over there has . . . all those things," Suzy says.

"I think they copied it from the book," Stella says.

"Why would they do that?"

Stella stands up and walks toward the kitchen. "Because they'd rather tell us stories than the truth."

"Who's 'they'?" Suzy calls from behind her.

Stella starts to answer, but is startled by the form of a man in the window of the back door. The messenger. He wears his helmet on the back of his head and arches his eyebrows as if to smile. She opens the door and he comes in, blowing on his cold hands. "What was going on with that creepy-looking guy you had in here yesterday?"

Stella doesn't answer. It occurs to her that she failed to draw up a report on Vallinger's visit to the DM, and has yet to pass along the very significant fact that their cover has been blown. She was so wound up about the "family news business" that she forgot about the entire movement. She should have a detailed report ready for the messenger, but has nothing.

"I mean, no offense, if he's your father or something," the messenger says. "You'd probably think my grand-father looks creepy. . . . Hey," he says, picking something up off the floor, "You didn't see what I delivered yes-terday. I slipped it under the door." He deposits a small packet on the kitchen counter. Then he reaches into his pants pocket and pulls out a much thicker wad of papers. "They sent over a big one today," he says. "I think it's from something the Chinese guy told them. Is he coming back?"

"Wait a second," Stella says. She hurries into the living room and retrieves the sketch pad and charcoal pencil that she and Suzy used for Bao-Zhi's Chinese calligraphy. She scrawls a short message on a clean sheet of paper: "Cover blown. Vallinger visited house, issued threats. Bao-Zhi attacked him before leaving. Send no more messages." She folds it into quarters and hands it to the messenger. "Take this to them," she said. "Never come back here again."

# TWENTY-NINE

Ralf lies belly-down on the bed he shares in Francisco's headquarters with Ellen. He's fully dressed in clothing his father bought for him: new blue jeans, a gray woolen sweater, and tall leather cowboy boots with elevated heels and pointed toes. The boots, freshly shined, leave brown spots on the white bed cover. But Ralf can't be bothered. He lifts his head from the pillow. "Let's go to the Kentucky Club," he says.

Ellen sits on the side of the bed and strokes the back of his head. "We can't go drink margaritas every time you're feeling down," she says softly.

"Maybe just this once," he says.

It was just an hour earlier that Ralf received the diagnosis he'd been dreading. The neurologist in Juárez, an affable young doctor named Ocampo, had opened an incision over Ralf's temple and concluded, after a painful five minutes of poking around, that Ralf's connection, or "jack," had suffered too much damage for the boost to be reinserted. "Who operated on you?" he asked Ralf in fluent English.

"I don't know," Ralf groaned.

"An animal could have done this," Ocampo said, peering into the wound. "It looks like he pulled it straight out with his teeth, or maybe his talons."

Ralf asked if the jack could be fixed. "Perhaps," the doctor said. "But it would require brain surgery."

"Not the kind of thing I could have done today?"

The doctor, thinking Ralf was joking, just laughed.

After the doctor stitched up his despondent patient, he removed Ralf's boost from the blue snuff bottle and inspected it through a microscope. "The chip actually looks okay," he said. "All of the damage seems to have been inflicted on the jack."

"That means it could go in someone else's head?" Ralf asked.

"In theory, yes. But it's not something I'd want to do."

"You mean to host my boost in your head?"

"Well, now that you mention it, I wouldn't want that. But I wouldn't want to put my boost in someone else's head. It would be like letting someone into my life."

"But you don't have a boost. . . ."

The doctor assured him that he did. "Not all of us are wild over here," he said. He told Ralf that a couple years back, during a brief diplomatic thaw between Juárez and Mexico, he had traveled in a government-authorized van to Durango and had a reconditioned chip fitted into his head. His new chip provided math and translation, lots of music and video, and "basically the world's entire medical knowledge base." Chips in Juárez aren't as useful or fun as elsewhere, he said, because they aren't on a network. "We can't visit virtual worlds, which makes a lot of people unhappy. Then again, unlike you, we're free of surveillance."

Ocampo said he was hoping for a chance at some point to cross the bridge into El Paso, or even to Chihuahua City, and refresh the content on his chip. "What I have up there is getting kind of stale," he said. Then, remembering that he was talking to a person likely to remain wild the rest of his days, he tried to steer the conversation away from technology. "Food's better in the wild world," he said. "Have you tasted the *chilaquiles verdes* around here?"

Ralf walked the several blocks back to Francisco's headquarters. He didn't bother delivering the bad news to Simon or his father. Instead he marched straight to his bedroom, shut the door behind him, jumped on the bed without saying a word to Ellen, and buried his head in the pillow. Ellen could guess right away what he had learned. But it took her ten minutes of cajoling to get him to provide details.

A half hour later, Ralf still shakes his head. "He kept repeating, 'An animal could have done this,'" he says to Ellen. She's sitting on a corner of the bed and holds a hand on his cheek. "When he was saying that," Ralf recalls, "I was actually feeling offended—on behalf of the animals." He smiles for the first time. "I mean, we're all animals, when we get right down to it. We just allow ourselves to forget it sometimes. The chip makes it easier."

Ellen manufactures a supportive smile and nods, even though she's not sure where Ralf is going with the argument.

Ralf, now serious, reaches across and touches Ellen's face. "You're like *chilaquiles verdes,* or whatever they're called," he whispers.

"Huh?"

"I was just remembering what the doctor said, when he was trying to make me feel better. He said the food tasted better in the wild world. It's true. Then, just looking at you, I was thinking that the same thing might be true about people, and relationships."

"You mean," Ellen says slowly, "that you and I might do better paying attention to each other than to all of the . . . virtual stuff?"

"I know, it sounds like a cliché," Ralf says.

Ellen nods. This is hardly new terrain for them, and she worries that soon they'll be making the same old and painful comparisons between her "real" but blemished avatar and the exquisite but "false" Artemis she has become.

"Even when I'm being faithful to you, in my boost," Ralf says, "I do mash-ups of our good times. It's just easier to manage . . . memories of you—which are all good. Great, actually. Than to manage the relationship in . . . real time."

Ellen takes a few moments to digest Ralf's semi-coherent words. He has admitted that he's not faithful to her in his boost. That's not exactly news, but still, it's the first time he has said so. She notes that twice he used the word "manage" to describe their relationship—or more specifically, what he does to her. It's not an especially warm word, she thinks. Where does "love" fit into what he's trying to manage, or for that matter, what she's managing? She knows she is not blameless. She too avoids the physical Ralf and spends much of her free time with others, or with memories of Ralf, in the boost.

While these thoughts occupy Ellen's mind, Ralf reaches across her back and lifts her blouse.

"Oh no," she murmurs.

"I know what you're thinking," he says. "I'm a wild man looking for sympathy in the form of old-fashioned, molecule-to-molecule love, which is all I can hope for anymore." He raises the blouse over her head and inspects her naked torso. "And," he continues, "that in my efforts to make the best of my new life—I'll immediately describe this real-life experience as 'superior' and 'deeper.' And *that*, you're thinking, could grow to be very tiresome."

He leans over and plants a lingering kiss on her mouth. "You're thinking," he says as he pulls back from her lips and looks at her, "that living with an evangelist for the wild life could be a nightmare. You worry that eventually I might become fanatical about it and push for you to have your own chip taken out—though, hopefully, not by animals." By this point, he is brushing her breasts with the back of his hands. "You might even worry that I'll insist on settling down with you in Juárez."

"Just five minutes ago, I worried you were feeling suicidal," she says. "Next thing I know, you're comparing me to Mexican food and getting turned on. I never thought that you might turn out to be an evangelist for the wild life. But now that you mention it, it does sound . . . unpleasant." She reaches for her blouse and starts to put it back on.

"Bear with me," Ralf says, taking the blouse from her hands, and tossing it back on the bed, beyond her reach. He jumps to his feet and strips off his clothes. It ends up taking a lot of pulling and pushing, and even a helping hand from Ellen, to pry off the new boots. Ellen, resigned by this point, takes off her pants and underwear, and snuggles close to Ralf. She kisses his neck and reaches with a hand down his back.

Like new lovers, they explore each other. They find that the smells and tastes are different from the boost, and they bump into each other with an awkwardness that they had forgotten. Rolling over, Ellen clocks Ralf in the cheek with her elbow. In virtual love, Ralf thinks, as he rubs the spot, the inside of the elbow is engineered to be a mild erogenous zone. But the elbow's bony outside, the weapon he just encountered, simply ceases to exist. Ralf feels a wrenching in his back—something he never experiences in virtual sex. He rolls over and pulls Ellen on top of him. He stares into her radiant eyes. How lucky he is to be with her, he thinks, and how foolish he has been to spend so many days and weeks living away from her in his boost. Yes, she has issues about the face that she gave up all those years ago. But together, without taking the easy refuge of virtual worlds, they can work those things out. He strokes the back of her thigh, marveling at the smoothness of her skin, and then dips his hand between her legs. At that moment, he feels himself losing control.

"Shit," he says.

Ellen laughs and hurries into the bathroom. "It's okay," she calls back. "I wasn't really in the mood."

# THIRTY

"They say here," Stella reads, "that he's called the Viceroy. Did you know that?"

"A viceroy?" Suzy says.

Stella doesn't bother responding. She leans over the thick memo the bicycle messenger delivered. It is spread out on the kitchen table, and she is studying every word. It's a profile of John Vallinger, lifted from the most recent edition of *The Tribune*. It details the career of the ninety-nine-year-old lobbyist, who made a career out of spotting technology trends and tying them to business.

"I didn't know any of this," Stella says, shaking her head. She reads on. Vallinger later became the leading lobbyist in Washington, virtually the only link between the xenophoic America First! party and the power in China.

Vallinger, she reads, has almost single-handedly pushed through the opening of the surveillance Gate 318 Blue, which is due to be released in the coming national cognitive update. The lobbyist, who agitated for the change for fifteen years, managed to include a control on the gate—which his company will operate.

"This can't be true," Stella says. "Get this. It says that he—quote—'will harvest a micropayment every time one of his clients—a who's who of global blue chip companies—burrows into the boosts of 430 million Americans, whether looking for facts, behaviors, desires, social connections, or national security issues.'"

"That's the gate I showed Ralf," Suzy says.

"It's like he controls the whole thing," Stella says. "He's the gatekeeper."

Suzy, with a glass of water in her hand, looks over Stella's shoulder. "But is it really that surprising," she says, "that they're looking at all this stuff? I always assumed people were snooping on my chip."

"I don't think it's ever been quite this bad," Stella says. "He also has investments in a company, Connectomix. Ever hear of that?"

Suzy takes a sip and thinks about it. "I don't think so."

Stella reads: "The Baltimore-based company, with angel financing from Vallinger, specializes in decoding the connections of the human brain, and re-creating people's knowledge and memories." She puts the paper down. "I wonder," she says, "if they can read people's brains without killing them. Seems like something they should mention in the article."

"They're talking about the wet brains, right?" Suzy asks.

"Yes, wet. They get the data from the boost through the surveillance gate, and then the wet brain by studying the connectome, which I guess is each person's map of neural connections. Looks like he has all his bases covered. Reading this," Stella goes on, "I'm not so surprised that Bao-Zhi tied him up."

"Bao-Zhi was up to date on all that stuff," Suzy says knowingly.

"He was?"

"Oh, yeah."

"If I were to study your connectome, what would I learn about Bao-Zhi?"

Suzy giggles as she walks out of the kitchen. "You'd have to kill me first."

Stella digs into her boost and replays her last conversation with Vallinger. She watches him throw the crumpled trench coat over his shoulders, and say: "If you manage to organize resistance to it, or manufacture outrage, we are going to rain down on your operation with a force that you'd be hard-pressed to imagine."

What an ass, she thinks.

Turning her attention from her boost, Stella begins to process her situation in what she imagines are ancient, reptilian nodes of her wet brain—the parts focused on survival. Vallinger, she knows, believes that she is feeding reporting to this newspaper in Juárez. He has warned her against "manufacturing outrage." The next thing he sees—assuming that he subscribes to *The Tribune*—is a story not only designed to stir up outrage, but also casting him as the demon behind it all. Would it be so terribly surprising, Stella wonders, if Vallinger dispatched forces to Montclair to "rain down" on her operation? She thinks it's a safe bet that he will.

## THIRTY-ONE

**3/10/72 4:17 p.m. Eastern Standard Time**

John Vallinger, his feet up on his gun-metal desk in his K Street offices, pages through Thursday's *Tribune*. Vallinger looks much like his old self. He has cleaned the gummy remains of Bao-Zhi's packing tape from his forehead, and has combed his white hair into the familiar V. He wears an old-fashioned gray woolen business suit. One of the last men in Washington who still wears a necktie, Vallinger has adjusted his to a bright shade of scarlet.

It matches his jaunty mood. It's only six days until the national cognitive update, and the investigative piece in *The Tribune*—the one his sources warned him was brewing—has left him largely unscathed. Earlier in the morning, when an El Paso source first messaged the details of the story, Vallinger was exultant. "They took our head fake," he told his aide, Tyler Dahl. He explained that in basketball, a sport popular in his childhood, a player faked with his head, making it look as if he were going to shoot the ball, and drawing the defender into the air. Then, when the defender landed, the shooter would launch his own shot, sometimes being fouled in the process.

"Oh," Dahl responded, not understanding for one moment what his ancient boss was talking about.

"What I mean," Vallinger said, "is that they took the story we wanted them to run with, and not the one we wanted to hide." The news about the open surveillance gate, he explained, wasn't likely to shock anyone. Everyone had assumed for decades that governments and businesses were spying on their boosts, notwithstanding the pious vows from politicians. Powerful commercial interests, including most of Vallinger's clients, had indeed found easy access into the boosts. They had been burrowing in the heads of capped humanity since the very dawn of the technology, in the 2040s. The new open gate, Vallinger said, only "harmonized" the American chip to the Chinese standard, and "removed the friction" from data mining on a global scale.

"So what's the news you didn't want them to know?" Dahl ventured to ask.

"Oh, I shouldn't tell you," Vallinger said, breaking into his peculiar smile, with the lips turned downward. It resembled, in everything but its context, a grimace.

Only later in the afternoon does Vallinger begin to wonder where the reporter got all of his facts. He had assumed that the source was Stella Kellogg. But the details about the way Vallinger carries out business, from his trusted contacts in Beijing to the way he pounds his fist, when angry, on the mahogany table in the conference room . . . How would she know about that?

Vallinger thinks about the Chinese fanatic who attacked him in Kellogg's house in Montclair. Where did he go? Could he be a source? Vallinger doesn't know. He wonders about George Smedley and the secrets that he leaked on the sex site. Maybe the information is coming from him. Yesterday, he and Espinoza disappeared from Vallinger's map, apparently crossing into the dead zone of Juárez from a border town near El Paso.

The relief that Vallinger was feeling when he first read the *Tribune* article has evaporated. "Tyler!" he shouts.

The young man appears in his doorway.

"Get in touch with your sources in El Paso," Vallinger says. "Find out what Smedley and his friend are up to in Juárez."

### 3/10/72 3:11 p.m. Juárez Standard Time

Midafternoon at the Kentucky Club. The winter sun streams through the closed window, lighting up a constellation of dust motes. One customer leans forward on a bar stool, nursing a Bohemia. Another has fallen asleep in one of the leather-upholstered booths. In the back, a noisy game of darts has been going on for nearly an hour.

The telephone sitting on the bar rings, and the bartender answers. "*¿Bueno?* . . . Okay," he says in Spanish. "Right." He listens. "I'll pass it along," he says. "Got it. One man with a feather, another one with the nose." Then he calls back to the *Tribune* reporter who's been playing darts. He hands him the phone. "It's for you," he says.

# THIRTY-TWO

As servants cleared the dinner table, Francisco and Ralf heard a hubbub and hurried off to the newsroom. Simon is nowhere to be seen. Ellen remains alone at the table, her chin resting on her hands, thinking.

How much of the life of a twenty-nine-year-old woman, she wonders, is in her boost? She has all the scenes of her school days. She has her first piano recital in Nutley, where she botched a Beethoven sonata and cried. She has countless scenes featuring the little girl with wide blue eyes and a gap between her front teeth—a face that one day ceased to exist. She has the wrenching ride with her mother to the aesthetic specialist, and all the arguments she and her mother put forth about becoming an Artemis. What would happen, Ellen thinks, if she simply ditched all of those memories? The wild humans in Juárez, these people carrying the dishes into the kitchen, they don't lug around decades of recorded memories in processors in their heads. Do they miss them?

Ellen has been digging through the archives in her boost to research history of memory. In the early years, she's learned, humans had to trust their wild brains for every single recollection. Of course, they didn't always agree on what they remembered, and these conflicting versions often led to quarrels, even wars. Toward the end of the Middle Ages, a German goldsmith named Gutenberg invented the printing press. In the centuries after that, it became more common for people to supplement their memories with books. The shelves were like an annex of the brain. People could look things up.

Then there was this scientist named Gordon Bell, Ellen learned, who in the first years of the Internet tried to record every moment of his life. He recorded his strolls through San Francisco, his conversations, his meals. He wore a movie camera around his neck and covered his body with different types of sensors. He had this idea that each person could carry around a supplementary electronic memory recording the bits of their lives. This would free up the wild mind for more creative jobs than simple data storage. Bell, it seemed, anticipated the boost. But his company, Microsoft, seeing only a small market for this concept, didn't invest in it. Within a few years of Bell's explorations, people could record much of their lives with their cellular phones and networked glasses. These gadgets carried their messaging, images, videos, and they tracked their movements through the world. They seemed at the time to capture people's lives. As the machines morphed into jewelry that clipped to clothing or the ear, they behaved more like the boosts that eventually replaced them.

Ellen reaches across the table and pours herself a small cup of coffee. All of those scenes in her boost, she now understands, are not memories at all. Memories occur only in the wild brain. That's where she experiences life. The archives in the boost are valuable only as prompts for the real memories, in the wild brain. If she called up that piano recital—which she'll never, ever do—it would trigger the feelings first of panic, then anger and shame, a powerful stew of emotional memories that overwhelm the dry stream of data issuing from the boost.

Then she thinks about time. By a certain age, people carry in their boost more recorded memories, both from virtual worlds and flesh-and-blood life, than they have time left to watch them. Like everyone, Ellen has only a limited number of days on earth. It makes more sense, she thinks, to use them to create new memories, and not to spend them watching reruns.

So does she need her boost? When she crosses back to the United States, which she's determined to do, she'll certainly need the processing power and messaging links of the boost, along with such essentials as credit swipes and at least a few apps to make the commodity food palatable. So she will need a boost. But will she need hers?

Ralf strolls into the dining room, clomping loudly in his new cowboy boots. "They've got a big story breaking down there," he says, pointing toward the newsroom.

Ellen, deep in thought, doesn't acknowledge him. She takes another sip of her coffee.

"What's up?" he asks.

"Thinking."

"About what?"

Ellen sighs and looks up at him. "What would you say," she asks, "if I told you that I'd take your boost?"

"You mean put it in your head?" He sits down, wide-eyed, and pulls his chair close to her.

She nods.

Ralf thinks about it and taps his boot nervously against the table leg. "Are you sure?" he asks.

"No, but I wanted to talk about it."

Ralf is tapping his boot so hard that Ellen's coffee is sloshing in its cup. "Will you cool it with the boot?" she asks.

"Okay." He stops. "So, you'd need to do it tomorrow, and we'd have to go over to El Paso, because you'd have to transmit the data to me. Then I'd need a computer of some sort to hack. . . ." He pauses and thinks some more. "I don't think it's a good idea," he says flatly.

"Why?"

"You'd lose all your memories, and you'd gain all of mine. It probably isn't a healthy thing, or fun. Have to say, though, it would be pretty weird."

"Those aren't really memories," Ellen says.

"They're close enough."

Ellen lowers her head. "You're worried that I'd see things you've been hiding from me," she says.

Ralf doesn't rise to her challenge. "There's got to be a different way," he says.

**3/10/72 9:27 p.m. Juárez Standard Time**

"I don't know about you," George Smedley says. "But tomorrow I'm going back. I don't give a hoot about Alvare's boost or Vallinger's update."

Smedley is stretched out on one of the two cots in the Trastos store on the west side of Juárez. It's the second night of sharing these close quarters with Oscar Espinoza, and he's not happy about it. The dirt and grit of Juárez have turned Smedley's white running suit gray. The knees are still brown from Wednesday's crawl. Even his Panama hat, sitting on piled cases of powdered milk, looks defeated. The falcon feather is bent nearly in half.

Worse, Smedley feels sick to his stomach. Oscar Espinoza, using the smattering of Spanish he knows, found some people in the neighborhood to cook large portions of goat, and Smedley and Espinoza have eaten it today for breakfast, lunch, and dinner. Smedley burps, and the oily taste of goat, which to his mind has just a hint of urine to it, coats his mouth.

Espinoza has never looked happier. He hums as he gets ready for bed and pries open a can of peaches. "I'm telling you," he says, popping half peaches into his mouth like peanuts, "if you want to get downtown, you find some way to call off the drone. They're not going to let us march down there with an armed escort. Someone will just shoot us."

Espinoza has talked, in his fashion, with the people at Trastos, who have connections with Don Paquito. They've let him know that as long as the drone is with them, they're stuck. Someone from Don Paquito's operation will be out to see them tomorrow—though probably not the Don himself. No one seems to recognize the name of Ralf Alvare, he says to Smedley as he strips off the clothes he's worn for three days straight.

"If you had just told them how important this is—that we're representing John Vallinger—Don Paquito would have come out today and spared us this," Smedley says. He rolls over on his cot to avoid the spectacle, only inches from his head, of the naked Espinoza crawling between the sheets. "You think they have a shower here?" Smedley asks.

"Most likely," Espinoza says. "Or maybe just a hose."

"You might ask them tomorrow morning if you can use it."

# THIRTY-THREE

**3/11/72 8:12 a.m. Eastern Standard Time**

Even though Stella told the messenger never to return, he's back first thing Friday morning, rapping at the kitchen door as Stella washes dishes. He wears the red bike helmet and an apologetic smile.

"I know, I know," he says as Stella opens the door. "But they woke me up and insisted." He hands her another packet of papers. Then he reaches into his pants pocket and pulls out a tool made of curved black plastic. He explains to her that it's a zapper, made in China. "If they're about to capture you, you're supposed to zap yourself," he says. He adds that it's dangerous, telling her to hold the tool at arm's length—"not right next to the temple."

Stella turns over the device in her hands. It's surprisingly light. She doesn't tell the messenger, but if the zapper is so dangerous, it would make more sense, she thinks, to shoot at their captors—and not direct it against Suzy and herself.

The two women each have a bag packed. They plan to head out to El Paso in Suzy's car tomorrow morning. Stella came up with the idea yesterday. Going through the hundreds of old messages that poured in when she stepped outside of her electronic refuge, she found a few from her sons. One from Ralf especially touched her. "Captured. Working with you after all this time. They're taking me across the Potomac, into Alexandria. I love you." That was followed a day later by more messages from Simon. The first said simply, "Ralf's here, with girlfriend. Wild. Other than that, okay." Another was an image of Ralf on horseback, looking sunburned. (Didn't Simon know to give his brother sunscreen, and a hat?)

It wasn't until after lunch that she spotted a piece of paper on the kitchen counter. It was the message dropped off while Vallinger was holding forth in the living room. The next day, the messenger had picked it up and put it on the counter. But with all the excitement, she had forgotten about it. When she opened it, she learned that both of her sons had crossed from El Paso into Ciudad Juárez. This was no surprise. Her messages to Simon had been bouncing back, leading her to suspect that he had crossed into the dead zone. What's more, if people were chasing him in El Paso, where else could he go?

That afternoon, Stella decided to join her sons on the border. It was the logical move. For the first time ever, all three of them appeared to be working on the same side, and facing the same enemy. This was a chance for Stella to piece together the remains of her broken family. When she announced her plan to Suzy, her housemate was in the living room, kickboxing.

"When?" Suzy asked. She leapt and performed a scissor kick in the direction of an antique Chinese lamp, one of Stella's favorites.

"Maybe Saturday."

"Can I come along?"

"The trip will be dangerous," Stella said.

Suzy managed to shrug while holding a powerful leg straight in the air. "Then it's better if there are two of us," she said. She lowered her leg and bent toward the floor, where she planted her hands and lifted herself into a graceful handstand. "I'll start getting my stuff together," she said as she flipped to her feet and bounded upstairs.

"I don't know . . . ," Stella said.

Suzy paid no attention. "We'll take my car," she shouted from the second floor.

Vallinger has technology on hand, Stella knows, to track their boosts. If he wants to blow up their car or have it pushed over a bridge, he simply has to issue the order. Still, the national cognitive update that obsesses him is only five days away. Nothing Stella and her cohorts are doing seems likely to derail it. She hopes that Vallinger might just relax, leave the two women alone, and celebrate his triumph.

As the messenger leaves, waving good-bye one last time through the kitchen window, Stella considers the road trip to El Paso. Should she and Suzy make their

way west through Pennsylvania and Ohio before turning south? It might be more fun, she thinks, to angle
south through the Alleghenies, seeing West Virginia and
Kentucky.

She casually opens the messenger's packet and takes
a look. When she takes in the hand-copied headline from
*The Tribune,* she gasps. She speed reads the summary
and then calls upstairs. "Suzy! We're leaving. Now!"

"You said tomorrow," comes the reply from upstairs.

"Okay, but first thing."

# THIRTY-FOUR

Papers are strewn across the floor and piled up on desks in the newsroom in Juárez. The electric relic of a coffee pot, left on all night, gives off a fungal aroma. At some point, after the Friday paper went to press, the beverages switched from caffeine to alcohol. Three empty bottles of tequila lie on the floor, in a large puddle of spilled green salsa. *The Tribune* staff, it's clear, broke a big story and then partied.

Ralf, who struggled to sleep with all of the commotion outside his door, emerges from the bedroom with weary eyes. He picks his way in bare feet across the *playa* and into the newsroom. Finding a computer that's on, with a story still displayed on its screen, he sits down in a swivel chair. Simon, coming from another bedroom, walks up behind him. He's wearing a royal blue housecoat and slippers. His long hair, missing its rubber band, hangs down his neck. "The story you're looking for is on this one," he says, pointing to the next computer. Ralf rolls his chair to it. Simon leans over his shoulder, and the two brothers read the article together.

BOOST UPDATE TO COMMAND RESPECT, the headline reads. The subhead, in italics: *Chinese Software Incites Millions to Bow to Authority*.

"Whoa!" Simon says.

"Shh!" Ralf puts his finger to his mouth and continues to read. The article details the "Respect" feature in the coming update. Already in place in China and a number of other Asian markets, the software automatically determines the voices of authority in a society, both government and corporate. Each time a person heeds those voices, the new Respect software sends signals to the brain, which trigger a flow of endorphins from the pituitary gland and the hypothalamus. This produces a wave of euphoria, similar to that associated with opiates. With the new Respect function in their boost, billions of people, according to the article, will not only feel eager to bow to authority, "they could even develop an addiction to it."

Ralf reads to the bottom of the screen and stops. "Isn't there any more?" he asks.

Simon reaches past his brother's shoulder and runs his finger across a rounded piece of plastic. More text moves onto the screen. "It's called a mouse," he explains.

"Very cool," Ralf says, as he continues reading.

The article says that John Vallinger, the renowned lobbyist, pushed the legislation on behalf of his blue-chip clients. Leading companies plan to establish themselves as "authorities." If they succeed, consumers will experience a "rush" when they purchase products or services from market leaders, which should allow these companies to raise prices. "Marketers have been working to associate their brands with pleasure for centuries," says one branding expert. "But this takes the guesswork out of it." He points, however, to economic risks: Small companies and start-ups might find themselves locked out of markets, which could stifle innovation. "Why should the big companies invest in developing new stuff, when everyone is already bowing to them and emptying their pockets?" he asks.

For now, according to the article, developers have refrained from implementing the negative option available in the Respect software. This would punish people, triggering emotions associated with guilt or even physical pain when they bucked authority. "We don't think we need to go negative on it at this point," says one software developer, who asked to remain unnamed. "Positive reinforcement should be sufficient. I mean, we're talking about addiction."

One political scientist, also unnamed, cites the potential complications of the software. If the boost's machine-learning algorithm determines that the American government is taking orders from the Chinese, he says, U.S. citizens may get a rush from bowing to the Chinese. But he says that this would only reinforce an established trend. "When it comes to governments, Chinese dominance is not exactly new."

The crucial link between the Chinese government and multinational corporations, according to the story, is Varagon Inc., the K Street office of John Vallinger, "the centenarian who stands to make a fortune from the Respect software." His firm is reputedly charging companies "platinum prices" to skirt the algorithms and achieve a "pre-loaded" ranking as "authorities." To maintain their dominant positions, they will have to pay hefty annual fees. Rumors circulating in Shanghai, according to Chinese sources, speculate that Vallinger, working with Chinese authorities, might hold monthly or even daily auctions in every industry, granting the prized "authority" ranking to the highest bidder. Conceivably, companies could bid state-by-state, which would create yet more revenue for Vallinger.

The story goes on to say that Vallinger's Chinese partners released news of an open surveillance gate a month ago in hopes that this story would occupy the opposition, including America's Democracy Movement (DM). "They figured that the old-guard opposition would go nuts about the surveillance stuff," says one source close to Vallinger. "But they'd have trouble getting the public excited about it."

The government briefly considered testing the update in a regional market, according to officials. But that proposal has been scrapped. Now, with the exception of top Washington officials, the entire population will be updated the night of March 16, says a source within the Department of Health and Human Services. "There was a perceived risk that people would find out about the Respect function and make a big fuss," he says. "They're far less likely to do it once the update has been achieved."

Ralf pushes his chair back from the desk. He looks at Simon and shakes his head in wonder.

Simon asks if Ralf's chip, still sitting in the blue snuff bottle, carries the code for the Respect function.

"It might be on the code Suzy sent me," Ralf says. "Her segment had social mores, I think. But it won't make much difference unless I get the boost into somebody's head who can find it."

"We'll work on that," Simon says. But he has his mind on something else. He starts searching around the chaotic newsroom. He sticks his head into Francisco's empty office, and then walks down the hall toward the print shop. He returns with two copies of the paper, and tosses one to Ralf.

"You know that guy who was chasing us and then rescued us?" he says.

"Of course. Guy with the nose."

"He's out at Trastos with his boss, and a drone escort." Simon says that a man named George Smedley, who works for Vallinger, apparently wants to negotiate with Ralf and Don Paquito. "I'm going out there to talk to them first," he says, waving the paper as he walks toward the door. "I'll give 'em a look at the news."

# THIRTY-FIVE

Simon recognizes his virtual lover the moment he steps into the Trastos store. George Smedley looks up at him blankly. He sits in a plastic beach chair and has his hand in a bag of Sabritas potato chips. He's wears a dirty white leisure suit of some kind with brown spots on his knees. On his lap he holds a Panama hat with a bent brown feather sticking out of it. He hardly looks like an ambassador from the richest and most powerful lobbyist in the world. He is, however, almost identical to the avatar Simon has hooked up with repeatedly in three different virtual sex sites. His face is the same, if a bit more wrinkled, and his body has almost the same form, though shorter and dumpier in the molecular version. Smedley's avatar even insists on carrying that same brown feather everywhere he goes. At least twice he has introduced it into bedroom activities, with mixed results.

It was during long and languorous afternoons with

Smedley's avatars that Simon heard about the man's life. He learned that Smedley owned the very site they were on, as well as several others. He was very proud of this and bragged about the tens of millions of customers in five continents. In passing, he told *Simone* about the open surveillance gate in the chip, and about the software engineer—a genius, by all accounts—who had lost his boost and was heading down to El Paso.

Simon brought this reporting back to the reporters at *The Tribune*, but never told them how he had coaxed the intelligence from his source. He didn't disclose that his avatar, Simone, was turning into a virtual version of the Mata Hari.

Simon, in fact, has mixed feelings for this lover. He considers him self-centered and a braggart. But they are on intimate terms, and he has to restrain himself as he walks into Trastos from reaching down and stroking his hand softly along the side of Smedley's upturned face and then kissing him deeply.

"You must be . . . ," Smedley says, without getting up.

"Simon," he says. He reaches down, but instead of caressing Smedley's face, he grasps a hand still covered with bits of potato chip and gives it a bone-breaking shake.

It's only then that Simon looks past Smedley and sees a familiar giant figure seated at the same table, devouring meat covered with gravy. He waves at Oscar Espinoza, who smiles and gestures toward his plate. "Goat?"

Simon shakes his head. He sits down with them and smiles broadly. He can hardly contain himself. This is the first time in his life that he has been with a flesh-

and-blood lover—or at least something very close to one. The fact that he is encountering him as a man, as Smedley, and that this man is in the dark, makes it doubly exciting. He wonders if Smedley recognizes his eyes, which are practically the same as Simone's. He remembers thinking years ago as he designed his avatar that if Simon and Simone dressed as Muslim women, with a *hijab,* the two would be indistinguishable. Part of him longs to share the secret with Smedley.

Simon realizes, of course, that telling Smedley could be disastrous. In his experience, straight men detest the idea that the lovely female avatar they're with might actually be another man. This knowledge can unhinge them. Simon, as Simone, has disclosed this unwelcome fact to a couple of his online lovers, and both of them took angry swings at his virtual face before storming away. Their surprise is idiotic, really, since it's widely known that loads of men prowl sex sites as females. Many straight men hunt for lesbian sex, and they often end up making love to female avatars operated by other men. Smedley has to know this, Simon thinks, if he really owns these sites.

Simon is so lost in his thoughts that he barely hears what Smedley is saying.

"So, as I said, we're willing to pay Ralf and Suzy richly for returning with us to Washington and going through this small and safe surgical procedure," Smedley says.

"Suzy?"

"Suzy Claiborne."

"I told you," Espinoza butts in, "that the domed Artemis—"

"Quiet," Smedley says with a single hatchetlike gesture of his right hand.

Simon changes the subject. He pulls the latest *Tribune* out of his shoulder sack and drops it on the table. "You might want to take a look at this," he says.

"I'd heard about this newspaper," Smedley says, picking it up. "But I'd never seen it."

"Try reading the story," Simon says.

He watches Smedley's eyes racing back and forth across the text. Espinoza, behind him, moves his eyes more deliberately. "Hey wait!" Espinoza says, as Smedley turns to the continuation of the story. Smedley pays him no attention. When he finishes the story, he puts down the paper and looks straight at Simon, right into the eyes that have hovered before his own during moments of the most intense passion. In virtual idylls, from Cuernavaca, Mexico, to Istanbul, Smedley has swum in those eyes. Simon doesn't flinch. He stares back, inviting whatever may come from it.

But Smedley pursues a different tack. "What's your circulation?" he asks.

"Huh?"

Smedley waves the newspaper. "How many of these things do you sell?"

"Well, that information—"

"It can't be too many," Smedley says.

"It has an influential readership."

"Who publishes this?"

Simon doesn't answer. The interview with his lover isn't going as he imagined.

# THIRTY-SIX

In the sunlit La Luciernaga Café, just beyond the anti-drone barriers, a special booth is reserved for Don Paquito and his friends. It has an antique oblong table with faded red Formica coating, and is surrounded by brown leather seating. The location may appear unusual for the press lord of Juárez—right across the narrow corridor from the men's room. But as Francisco sits down for breakfast with Ralf and Ellen, he explains that it's useful to be near the back door. That, he says with a smile, came in useful one time many years ago.

He's practically inviting the question, but Ralf doesn't oblige. "So," he says, "you were telling me about the boost processing facility near Fort Bliss. . . ."

"Shhhh," Francisco whispers. "Keep your voice down." He tells Ralf and Ellen about a machine in a building on Paisano Drive, near Bowie High School, which can operate the boost "just like a head." The army, he says, uses it "to interrogate the deceased."

"I find that hard to believe," Ralf says.

Francisco shrugs. "We've written a story about it." He signals to the waitress, who pours coffee and ice water and drops a basket of steaming tortillas on the table. Francisco orders huevos rancheros for the three of them before asking Ellen, "You like eggs, don't you princess?"

Ellen nods and smiles as Ralf rolls his eyes.

"Hot sauce?" Francisco asks. "*¿Salsa picante?*"

After Ellen nods again, he says, "Good," and returns to the chip discussion. "So you find it hard to believe," he says to Ralf.

Ralf avoids his father's eyes, this time by studying his own finger as he draws letters with it on the side of his water glass. He explains, a bit too thoroughly for the other two, that the chip works only with commands established over time in its host brain. Each interface is unique, he says, just like each brain. "You might take a bite of this tortilla," he says, reaching for one, "and the flavor and texture will create a pattern of behavior in the neurons in your brain. It might have to do with what's going on with your teeth, the smells, the memories. It might be connected to your language, how the word 'tortilla' sounds, where you were when you first heard the word, what other words and sounds you connect it to.

"My 'tortilla' signals," he continues, tracing a "T" on the glass, "are going to be entirely different. Now over time, my boost has learned to trigger certain patterns in my neurons that respond to my understandings of words and concepts. It has also learned to interpret them. It understands me, and I understand it. But if you or Ellen were to put my boost in your head, it would take you time to retrain it."

He looks up from the glass to his father. "So I guess I could see how they could download data from a boost in this machine you're talking about. But I don't understand how it can behave like a boost—since it will be missing the human brain."

"But if you're sitting at the machine," Ellen says, "and you're giving it commands, then the brain is yours."

"I . . . guess," Ralf says. "But I'm not at all clear on how the interface would work."

"We will traverse that bridge when we reach it," Francisco says cheerfully as the eggs arrive. "The key question," he says, dropping to a whisper as the waitress departs, "is how to get you and your chip over to El Paso, and at the controls of that machine."

# THIRTY-SEVEN

**3/11/72 10:49 a.m. Juárez Standard Time**

Deep in thought, Simon steps out of Trastos and stubs his toe on the cinder block steps. The pain is intense and Simon flies into a rage. He swears loudly in English and reaches down toward his toe. He can't do much for it, since it's throbbing inside his shoe. So he grabs a fistful of loose dirt from the road, bunches it in his fist, and hurls it onto the ground. The drone, nearly as wide as the street itself, looks on impassively, no doubt recording the scene and transmitting it to its overlords in the American Department of Homeland Security.

The woman who runs the store pokes her head out the door. *"¿Todo bien, Señor Simón?"*

Simon composes himself and nods. He sees Smedley's face, marked with obligatory concern, peering behind her. He hurries off, away from the drone, embarrassed.

Simon is angry, and feels hurt. As he walks back toward the bus to take him downtown, he finds himself berating George Smedley. Even if Smedley failed to identify his virtual lover by his eyes, he had to know that Simon held a critical position in the enterprise. More than a simple courier for Don Paquito, he runs the finances. Simon told him as much. But Smedley, sitting there in his exercise suit, seemed to look right past Simon. As far as Smedley was concerned, it was clear, Simon fell into the same ranks as the omnivorous Oscar Espinoza: the servant class. Smedley entrusted him with a message for Don Paquito and practically dismissed him.

Maybe it's his ponytail, Simon thinks, running his hand to the back of his head. Did he look like a less than fully serious adult?

But as Simon waits alone at the open air bus stop, his toe throbbing and *The Tribune* still folded under his arm, he understands that George Smedley isn't his problem. The Smedleys of the world will come and go, in virtual and physical worlds, some of them paying more attention to him than others. No, the enduring issue for Simon, the one that looms above his entire life, is his father. Francisco is proud, proud of his power in Juárez and his place in the world. He's proud of *The Tribune*'s sterling reputation—at least among a tiny elite—as perhaps the only source of trustworthy news in the world. Francisco seems to have pushed to one side the nasty details of his climb to power, the double-dealing and occasional brutality, and has come to associate himself with the ideal of press freedom, even truth.

This might not bother Simon so much if Francisco didn't take him for granted. But he does. Simon efficiently handles his job, taking the billions that pour in and parking them as investments all over the world. Working with Chui, he distributes money, often secretly, to suppliers who skirt the economic embargo of Juárez, shipping vital paper, ink, and machine parts into the wild city. He sprinkles payments—or bribes—among the police and military on both sides of the border to keep Francisco's industrial machinery humming. Without Simon's work, *The Tribune* wouldn't last a month. Yet from Francisco's perspective, the work simply happens—perhaps because it's supposed to, or thanks to his inspired leadership. He has engineered a marvelous system. The journalists, the delivery boys, the cleaning and maintenance teams—they're all interchangeable components, as are Simon and Chui.

Now, Simon thinks, baby brother comes onto the scene, with Ellen. Simon can see his father light up when Ralf enters the room—and even more when he sees Ellen. Francisco lavishes attention on the two. He plies them with food and tequila and teaches them Spanish words. He tells them his tired old stories, with all of the nastiness carefully clipped out. Yesterday he called them into his office, saying, *"Vengan para aca, mis joyas,"* or "Come in here, my jewels." Simon felt like gagging. He can almost sense Francisco's relief to be united with a son who loves women, and might produce his grandchildren. It doesn't hurt that Ralf brought along a woman who might have stepped out of a Botticelli canvas. These new elements of his family make Francisco giddy with pride and feed his hormones. Simon can imagine him, after a few tequilas, hugging Ralf, telling him with teary eyes how much he loves him, and then slipping around the corner to seduce Ellen. It could happen.

In Ralf, the father seems to believe he has found a soul mate. He respects Ralf's mathematical genius. He is unperturbed by Ralf's shyness. It doesn't even seem to bother Francisco that Ralf has not yet figured out what to call him, simply addressing him as "you."

What thrills Francisco about Ralf—and deepens the wedge between himself and Simon—is Ralf's new status as wild. Simon, by contrast, is the son with the boost. Francisco doesn't dwell on the irony that Simon is clumsy with his boost, and often wishes he didn't have to trouble with it, while Ralf practically lived in his. What matters to Francisco is now. Ralf is as wild and free in his head as a cave-painting Cro-Magnon—the Juárez ideal. Simon not only has a boost, but he uses it to carry on a virtual sex life with avatars that, as far as Francisco is concerned, are of the wrong gender. He and his father would never discuss such things. But Simon can sense contempt. It has been on the rise since Ralf and Ellen arrived.

The bus doesn't come. It's chilly out, though not as cold as yesterday, and Simon, to keep warm, walks along a trail of shanties toward the downtown. He's still stewing about his father. It bothers him that Francisco remains so proud of his outlaw status. He keeps the big poster of Emiliano Zapata on his office wall and has a smaller framed photo of Che Guevara on his desk.

Both those men, Simon has learned, were gunned down by the governments they fought. The Mexican army ambushed Zapata. The CIA hunted down Che. Yet Francisco works for the very government he claims to oppose. The United States quietly uses Francisco, and has benefited from his help since his service in Paraguay during the chip wars. Francisco has always been careful to keep the relationship in its place. He was probably working for the gringos even while running drugs out of Bolivia.

Francisco never told Simon about his rise to power in Juárez. "Let sleeping dogs snore," he laughed one time when Simon brought it up. But in his three years working for his father, Simon has put together pieces of the narrative.

In his early years in Juárez, as Francisco said at lunch, two drug lords, Greñas and Mortífero, ran the declining narcotics business in Juárez. Francisco, an outsider with a South American accent and a pronounced limp, was careful to make himself useful to both ringleaders. Using his growing network of reporters, he dug up intelligence that he provided for free. Each lord got his share. With time, each one began to suspect that the other was getting the more valuable tips. This suspicion cast a shadow over Francisco's business. He was convinced that one of the two would mount a takeover. It would be just a matter of abducting Francisco—who couldn't even run away on his bum leg—and threatening to kill him if he didn't work exclusively for one side or the other. Sometime in 2045 or '46, old-timers decades later told Simon, Francisco was getting word through his intelligence network that both sides were targeting him. The abduction might come in a matter of days. So one morning he secretly delivered himself and his business to the more brutal of the two, Greñas. In return, he asked only for protection from Mortífero. Then he told Greñas his plan.

A couple days later, one of Francisco's couriers delivered an intelligence packet to Mortífero, whose headquarters were on the east side of Juárez, a neighborhood of modest houses where people parked their cars on their tiny lawns. It was near the Bridge of the Americas, the main trucking route to the U.S. The packet told of a warehouse in Fabens, just fifteen miles down the river, that was full of meds and pleasure drugs—antidepressants, muscle relaxers, sleeping pills, heroin tabs, and the so-called buzz-rushers that were the rage when Francisco and Stella were in college. An entire container had been abandoned, and it would be sitting there, with only one guard defending it, until the Long Beach cartel—one of the last drug mafias in the U.S.—could free up a truck from San Antonio. It was an enormous supply, and free. But there was so much that Mortífero would have to send dozens of mounted traffickers across a narrow river crossing to pick it up.

That very night, Mortífero dispatched eighteen men on horseback to Fabens. Just as they reached the warehouse, they were ambushed by U.S. Drug Enforcement Agency forces, and fourteen of them were killed. The survivors were forced to escort a disguised SWAT team back to headquarters. They entered the building with a hail of flash grenades and then shot the dazed drug runners, including Mortífero, before racing back across the Bridge of the Americas to El Paso.

That night at the Greñas headquarters, not far from *The Tribune* offices, the celebration lasted till dawn. It seemed all of professional Juárez was there—narcos, merchants, even journalists from *The Tribune* and, of course, an entire brothel. Toward the end of the party, a drunk Greñas embraced a cold sober Francisco and whispered slurred promises to build an empire together.

That was when Francisco delivered the line he'd been honing for weeks. "Sixteen of the men in your army," he said, "work for the DEA. They have chips in their heads and are in constant communication—and with me. If you attempt to kill them, or me, you'll be dead within minutes." This was an especially bold lie, since any DEA agents in the dead zone of Juárez would be unable to message with each other. Also, Francisco himself was every bit as wild as Greñas. But he wore a beret that night that evoked the image of the original capped workers in Shanghai. The Paraguayan publisher seemed to wield powers and alliances that Greñas only vaguely understood. He seemed formidable, all the more so for having dispatched Mortífero and his army in a single day.

Francisco told the morose drug lord that he had arranged a safe exit for him. A plane waiting at an airstrip just a mile away would carry him to Costa Rica, where he would be fitted with a boost and employed at a casino hotel.

Greñas left that morning, without even packing a bag, and was never heard from again. He probably didn't

even make it to the airport. Francisco assigned his partner, Sibo, to the job of shutting down the dying drug
business. He accomplished this within months, but died
in one of its last battles. That left Francisco alone at the
top. In the week following Greñas's departure, Francisco
had hired dozens of the narco's troops. Some formed a
new police department, which answered to the leader
now known as Don Paquito. Others were using their
trafficking skills to build a distribution for Ciudad
Juárez's new and fast-growing export: newspapers.

Simon wonders if his father has had anyone killed
since those early days. He walks along the dirt road near
the river, lost in his thoughts, when he feels a familiar
spark in his head. His boost has found a network connection, a rare hot spot in Juárez. Simon watches hundreds of messages pour in. He promptly sends a message
to Chui, asking about news. He hears back almost instantly that Vallinger is looking for Smedley. "Anything
else?" He hears the minibus bumping along behind him.
According to Chui's source, he learns, the lobbyist is
"steaming mad about today's story."

Simon is thrilled to hear that. Proud again to be working for the paper, he signs off from Chui and climbs in
to the crowded bus. It's not until he's seated that he begins to sift through his trove of messages. Among hundreds of come-ons for sex sites, he sees one message
from his mother, dated Thursday. "Cover's blown. John
Vallinger is after us. Leaving Montclair and heading
with Suzy to El Paso."

Stella's coming to El Paso? Simon immediately tries
to respond, before even thinking about what to tell her.

But the network connection, alive for an instant, is dead. He wonders who Suzy is and why his mother is coming down. Why would John Vallinger be chasing her? Simon knew she was involved in opposition politics, but was she important enough to anger John Vallinger? Does she know that Don Paquito, the reputed drug lord, is actually Francisco, and is running the newspaper here? Simon has no idea. But he cannot imagine any other reason that would lead his mother to come down.

# THIRTY-EIGHT

After breakfast, Francisco directs Ralf and Ellen down a spiral metal staircase into the print shop. He follows them, leading with his right foot, step by step, and dragging his left leg behind. He shows them the hulking stainless steel machinery, a throwback to the twentieth century. The paper, stretched like connecting tissue from one module to the next, carries the same front-page story about the Respect function in the coming cognitive update. Francisco explains how photography, more than a century ago, replaced the original system of typesetting, where men specially trained to write backward and upside down would arrange the metal letters one by one. This, he says, was a direct descendant of Gutenberg's original movable type.

Ralf has little time for the history lesson. He wants to know how he can get his boost to the chip reader in El Paso. He has to see if the code on his chip includes the Respect function, and if he can eliminate it, or rewrite it, and then hack his revisions into the national system in Washington. It's a daunting job, and the update is only five days away. He has no interest in hearing about Johannes Gutenberg. That type of information he can look up—if he ever gets a boost back in his head.

Ellen, though, encourages Francisco with more questions. She asks him why the American government permits the circulation of *The Tribune* in the U.S. "There's no way they don't know about it," she says.

"Know about it?" Francisco laughs. "They're my biggest subscribers!" He explains how the government sends a truck from Fort Bliss every morning to pick up bundles of the latest edition at Simon's tavern, the Cavalry Club. They fly them out to offices on both coasts, and to Chicago, Dallas, and Atlanta. Another van passes by daily and picks up a bundle for the bank offices on Wall Street. "We could shut down our entire distribution network and make plenty of money just selling to the U.S. government and Wall Street alone," he says, adding that the Chinese also airship several hundred copies per day.

"If a subscription costs so much," Ellen asks, "why don't people just send images of the pages back and forth in their boosts? No offense. But that's what I'd probably do."

"The government helps us there, too," Francisco says. The last thing the Americans want is for *The Tribune*'s news to reach 430 million people. "There might be an uprising," he says. So an official in the Department of Homeland Security actually came down to El Paso, to

Simon's tavern, to deliver "watermarking" technology. With this, *The Tribune* embeds background patterns on every sheet. Francisco picks up a copy of the paper and holds it up to the light. "See there, that gray circle with the line through it?" he says, tracing his finger around the page.

Ralf squints at the paper and shakes his head.

Ellen backs up, to get a fuller look at the page. "Oh, I think I see it," she says.

"Once you see it, it's hard to ignore," Francisco says. "Anyway, Homeland Security monitors the traffic between the chips. When they see people exchanging images carrying that watermark, they automatically delete it. People get back a message warning them that they've been violating international copyrights, and that if they persist they face big fines, or even limits on their boosts. It's as if the American government works for me."

"I thought you were on the most-wanted list," Ralf says.

Francisco laughs. "That's just for show. If they wanted to arrest me, they could drop a SWAT team in here and have me, dead or alive, in about six minutes."

"What about the drones," Ellen asks, "and all the defenses you have up around here?"

"Those drones are part of the same show, so that Americans will think their government is at war with the narco traffickers who are supposedly running Juárez," Francisco says. "It's all lies. If the drones are targeted at anyone, it's at people like you. They don't want you going back and telling people that life over here is . . . well, I wouldn't call it 'normal,' but—it isn't anything like the hell they describe. The last thing they want is for you to go back with a copy of *The Tribune*. That could be destabilizing. The way they see it, *The Tribune* is classified intelligence, only to be read by the political and business elite."

He hushes as footsteps come down the metal stairs. Simon appears, just back from his meeting with George Smedley. His cheeks are pink from the cold, and his hair, usually tied back in the ponytail, falls across his forehead. "You telling them about the watermark?" he asks.

Francisco nods.

"Yeah, it's as if the Americans work for us," Simon mocks. "Thank God for that watermark. Wouldn't want the wrong people to be reading the news."

Francisco avoids the confrontation with Simon by taking a step to the machine and scrutinizing one of its long steel arms. He says nothing.

"So," Simon continues, "I got word from El Paso this morning that John Vallinger read this story"—he points to the paper in the machine—"and he's steaming mad." He turns to Ralf and Ellen. "You know all about John Vallinger, right?"

They both nod.

"He's one of our subscribers," Simon says. "He actually pays a premium to get snippets of the news delivered through the boost. These are just summaries of the stories, you see. So he doesn't have issues with the watermark. Other people do. But not John Vallinger."

Francisco lowers his head closer to the steel arm, as

if studying each of the rivets attaching it to the body of the machine.

Ellen, trying to ignore the tension between Simon and his father, focuses on the key issue: spreading word about the Respect function. She asks Simon if it would be possible to publish a copy of the paper without the watermark, so that people can learn details about the update, and start protesting. "Otherwise, this might turn into a dictatorship."

"I'm betting that most of our subscribers are pretty thrilled with the Respect function," Simon says. "These are powerful people, and having a more obedient population sounds ideal to them."

"It's not ideal for me," Ellen says.

"Well, you're not supposed to know about this," Simon says. "You only know because . . . well, because of all the events that led you to cross into Juárez. You're not the target reader of *The Tribune*. People like you, you live your life, spend a lot of time in virtual worlds, you might not even notice that one day it just feels better to buy the leading brands of one thing or another, and to support the America First! party. Nothing's really changed that much. Are you really worse off for not knowing the details about the software in the boost?"

"You don't need to insult me!" Ellen says, fighting to hold back tears. She runs to the staircase, hops up the stairs two at a time, enters the deserted newsroom, and slams the door behind her.

"Nice job," Ralf says to his brother.

"She needed to hear it. You needed to hear it," Simon says.

They both look at Francisco, who has dropped the guise of inspecting machinery and is now simply staring at the floor.

"So," Ralf says to his father. "How about getting this story onto the boost?"

Francisco bats his eyes and looks up the staircase. Then he responds meekly. "It would destroy my business model."

"That's what this is about?" Ralf says, spreading his arms toward the massive machinery. "A business model?"

"We employ lots of people," Francisco says, looking up at Ralf. "We're the economic engine of an entire city, a city that's under embargo. We need this to survive."

"Papá," Simon says. "We have Chui over there in El Paso. He just placed a few billion Renminbi into a Singapore fixed-asset fund, and he's looking into a hedge fund out of Montevideo that returns 23% a year. This business model you talk about is making you rich. But let's not pretend you're investing it all into Juárez."

# THIRTY-NINE

**3/12/72 9:13 a.m. Eastern Standard Time**

"When he was little, I wondered if Ralf had some form of autism," Stella says. "He was spending all of his time—I mean *all* of it—on his chip. So I'm a thirty-year-old widow, I've lost my job, I've got one kid in open rebellion and the other simply won't talk to me. He barely comes into my world."

"He does get quiet," Suzy says, looking out the window at the New Jersey Turnpike. "I think he's a genius, though. At least that's what everyone at the office always says."

"Yes, we heard those things," Stella answers.

They're driving a southern route to El Paso, heading down toward Washington before turning west into the Shenandoah mountains of Virginia and beyond. Suzy begged for this longer route, saying that she couldn't stand another drive through Pennsylvania. "It goes on forever."

Stella's only objection was that they'd be putting themselves closer to Vallinger and his henchmen.

"You think he'll lay off if we happen to be in Ohio instead of Virginia?" Suzy said. "He won't be chasing us on horses."

"I guess you're right," Stella said, as she loaded the two bags into Suzy's cobalt blue Shar-pei.

Now, as they speed past the exits for Philadelphia, she cranes her neck and looks toward the sky. Suzy, sitting to her left, swivels in her seat and looks out the back window. "There are two guys in that green car back there that have been looking at us since we left the Parkway," she says. "If you're hunting for something to worry about, that might not be a bad place to start."

They continue south through Delaware and Maryland, and then angle west toward Virginia. Stella takes her grandfather's book, *Donkey Show,* from her black purse and starts to reread it. "Getting ready for El Paso," she says.

"Don't you find it distracting to turn the pages?" Suzy asks.

"You get used to it."

"I don't think I ever would."

As the blue Shar-pei drives through Washington's Virginia suburbs, a tiny blue drone, no bigger than a hornet, hovers a constant two feet over the roof. The drone records the messaging and conversation occurring within the Shar-pei. It transmits the streams to the green Sheng-li following them and to Tyler Dahl, who monitors the conversation in his boost while exercising on his treadmill.

The Flynn brothers, both in their twenties, ride in the Sheng-li. The older of the two, Al, is slumped in his chair, sleeping. He's tall and dark. His sloped chin is nested on his chest. His little brother Gerry, twice as thick and a head shorter, is hunting in a virtual Serengeti. He sits erect in his seat, his eyes open, like someone who is waiting breathlessly for a fearsome black mamba to slither past. Neither man listens to the conversation coming from Suzy and Stella. But both the men are hoping that the order to apprehend them comes sooner rather than later. Early on, when they picked up Suzy's car near Newark, they heard the two women arguing about whether to go through Pennsylvania. That was when they saw that this assignment could stretch far beyond Saturday morning. When they heard Stella mention El Paso, both groaned. "There goes my golf game," Gerry said.

Dahl, listening in his Dupont Circle apartment, was alarmed as well. If the two women were headed to El Paso, something was up in Juárez. It was going to be a long weekend. He messaged Vallinger that he had news on Stella, but received no response.

It isn't until nearly lunchtime when Vallinger's angry voice erupts in Dahl's head. He has just read yesterday's *Tribune* story, about the Respect function in the boost, and is livid. "How did she know?" he asks.

"Know what?" Dahl asks.

"About Respect!"

"They must have good sources in the DM," Dahl says. Then he informs Vallinger that Stella and Suzy are headed to El Paso.

"Well stop them, for Christ's sake!"

"And do what?"

Vallinger tells him to bring the women in for interrogation. Dahl passes on the order to the Flynns in the green Sheng-li. For Gerry, the order pops up as a bubble of text above a herd of wildebeests in Tanzania. He sighs and returns from virtual Africa to the Sheng-li racing through the Shenandoah mountains of Virginia. He hears the women talking. The older one is saying something about the husband who left her a million years ago.

He wakes up Al. "Gotta stop them," he says.

He sends a command to the bumblebee drone, which promptly transmits a signal to Suzy's car.

Suzy notices it first. She interrupts Stella, who is now going on about Ralf. "We're slowing down," she says, pointing to the speedometer. They sit, speechless, as their car signals a turn to the right. It exits the highway, followed by the green Sheng-li, and turns up a small rural road. After passing a farm, it pulls off near a grove of pine trees and stops with a wheeze of its hydrogen engine. The Sheng-li parks behind it.

"You stay here, in the car," Stella says to Suzy. "I'll handle this." She has no plan, but feels that the situation calls for leadership, even if it's blind.

She gets out of the car thinking: This is where I'm going to die. She doesn't feel sad about it, at least not yet. She looks past the pine trees, toward a small brook, which gurgles noisily and disappears around a bend. That's where they'll throw my body, she thinks. She wonders if and when anyone will find it. Maybe not until nothing remains but her bones. She realizes that she's analyzing the scenario with the coldness, and finality, of a physical anthropologist. She nearly failed that course in college.

The two doors of the green Sheng-li open in unison, the one on the right banging against a pine tree. Stella sees two men emerge from the vehicle. These are my executioners, she says to herself. One is tall with a weak chin; the other one, much stockier, is placing a gray hood over his head, and fiddling with the string to tie it under his chin. His sweatshirt says St. Joseph's, and Stella finds herself wondering if he's from Philadelphia, and if he might be Catholic, and what bearing that might have on her chances. They say nothing, but the tall one, heading toward Stella, walks with a slight stoop and wears an embarrassed look on his face.

These men don't look like killers, she thinks. This is just a situation that must be managed. She opens her mouth to speak to them, when the car door opens behind her, slamming into the back of her thigh. "Sorry," Suzy says, wedging out of the car.

The Flynns stop, transfixed by the beauty of the domed Artemis.

Before Stella can say anything, Suzy hurtles toward the shorter man with the St. Joseph's sweatshirt. She yells a single word—"asshole!"—and tackles him. Using the power of her tall body and the leg strength gained through years of running, she drives him onto his back. He falls onto rocky soil still hard from winter and covered with yellowed pine needles. Suzy begins to pummel him with her fists and elbows. Stella and the tall man watch, their mouths agape. Then the tall man, as if remembering that he has a job to do, fishes what looks like a wooden pellet from his pocket, steps toward Suzy, and raises his weapon above her.

Stella screams. Suzy stops her attack and looks up, and the man cracks down on her forehead. Suzy collapses.

Stella reaches into her own coat pocket and the Chinese-made tool of curved plastic that the messenger delivered. He included instructions, she knows, but she doesn't remember them. The tall man is still staring at Suzy. Her arms frame her head, which looks like a painting of a sleeping goddess. He pays no attention to Stella. She points the zapper at his head just as he turns toward her, and presses the button. His expression changes from angry to confused, and then goes blank as his knees buckle. He sits back on the ground and then lies down and closes his eyes. For a moment his body shakes and is then as peaceful as death. The younger man is now climbing to his feet and rushing toward Stella, yelling. She points the zapper at his face and again pulls the button. He goes quiet, tumbles to the ground, and repeats the movements of his partner. In a matter of seconds, he too appears dead.

Stella looks down at the three bodies. She is reminded of the last scene in Hamlet, and it occurs to her that the actors in the theater climb back to their feet as soon as the curtain closes. Are these three dead or just stunned? She returns the zapper to her pocket, but keeps her hand on it. Bending down over Suzy, she reaches with her left hand to Suzy's face. It's warm and seems alive. She puts a finger under Suzy's nose and feels breathing. For her own safety, she knows, she should check on the two men, but she doesn't have the stomach for it. If they're dead, she killed them, and if they're alive, they could jump up and kill her. For the moment, she'd rather not know.

Instead, she concentrates on Suzy. She slaps her face gently and then a little harder, whispering, "Hey. Hey." Suzy doesn't respond. Stella lifts her right eyelid and sees only the white orb of the eye threaded with spidery red veins. This isn't going to work, she thinks. She lifts Suzy's right leg and tries to drag her toward the car. With a big heave she moves the body about a half inch, maybe less. The space between the body and Suzy's car, she judges, is about the length of her Montclair living room. It would be near impossible to drag the body that distance even if it were carpeted. Over stony soil, it's out of the question.

She hurries to the blue Shar-pei, thinking that she'll back it up right beside Suzy, and then try to hoist her into the backseat. But when she presses the Start button, nothing happens. It's locked, and it won't start unless it reads Suzy's irises.

Stella slumps in the car and considers her options. She could take off on foot. But the nearest house or business is likely to be miles away. Why would anyone help her?

She sees movement among the fallen. It's the tall man. His hand is inching its way toward his face. Stella gasps. Should she zap them again? The first time, it was self-defense. But if she goes over to the bodies and re-zaps them, it will feel like an execution—assuming that it kills them.

She grabs her purse and climbs out of the car. She starts to jog toward the woods. Then, on a whim, she stops and turns around, back to the green Sheng-li. She climbs in. She pushes the Start button. The engine starts with a whir. Must be a rental, she thinks. She looks toward the bodies. Only two are lying there. The tall man is up. He is lurching toward her. He has a child-like smile on his face, as if he has just learned how to walk. He reaches the car and pounds on its hood. He's yelling. Stella, looking up, can see the white topography of his molars.

"Take me to Washington, DC," she tells the car. The car processes the command and calls up its mapping application. The man is at her window now, and his expression has changed from amusement to betrayal. He opens the door and grabs at Stella's arm. As he does, the car pulls away, its tires sending up a cloud of dust and pebbles. Stella slams shut the door. The Sheng-li executes a neat U-turn, missing a pine tree with its left front fender by inches. Then it spins left on the road and accelerates in the direction of the highway. Stella looks back and sees the man standing in the middle of the road. However worried he is about losing the car or botching his assignment, Stella imagines, he has to be wondering about his zapped boost—if he's as wild as he feels, and if he'll be that way forever.

# FORTY

John Vallinger reclines in his zero-gravity chair and gazes sadly at a hologram that hangs above him like a thunder cloud. It's tuned to the highway traffic in the Washington area. The lobbyist looks every bit his age. The wrinkles in his face, from his forehead to his mouth, all tilt downward. He wears his black woolen tunic like a shroud. Vallinger could easily be running the surveillance video and intelligence from his own boost, and even watching it from his own home. But out of pure spite he has summoned his assistant, Tyler Dahl, to the K Street offices. It's as if he blames Dahl for the disastrous news story that appeared in yesterday's *Tribune,* the one exposing the Respect function. It could be worse, of course. *The Tribune* reaches only a tiny minority of Americans. A fair number of them are already in the know about the coming update and positioned to profit from it. But *The Tribune* article ties the Respect software to Vallinger's business, providing privileged and embarrassing details. It also gives the clear impression that despite his rhetoric, Vallinger is moved less by patriotism than profits. In fact, readers of the article might assume that he works for the Chinese government.

Earlier in the day, as Vallinger stepped into the office, he did not even bother to say hello to his assistant. "I don't know what I'll do if I learn that someone in my organization has been feeding her news," he sputtered as he took off his overcoat. "That person will not enjoy anything worth calling a life." He hung up his coat and walked toward his assistant.

"Feeding news to who?" Dahl asked.

"To whom."

"To whom, then?"

"To Stella Kellogg, you dope!" Vallinger snapped his fingers in front of Dahl's startled face. "Have you feasted your eyes on yesterday's Mexican paper yet? Do you understand why we're here?" Since that moment, he has berated the young man sometimes at high decibels, other times in muttered asides. When Dahl fails to hear his boss and asks him to repeat his instructions, Vallinger rants at him. Perhaps in protest, Dahl has turned his pants and shirt to the same bright green as the Sheng-li that appears to be carrying Stella Kellogg from the scene of the ambush, in the woody Virginia suburbs, toward Washington. The two men watch the image of the car as it inches its way across the suburban countryside.

"Where the hell is she going?" Vallinger asks. Ever since he had Dahl prepare the headache signal for her boost, she has sped up to the maximum of 90 miles per hour. She's passing lazy Sunday traffic, winding her way through Hay Market and past Bull Run.

"Anybody's guess," says Dahl.

Vallinger orders Dahl to study the log of the boosts involved in the incident in Northern Virginia. Within seconds, the young man provides the details. The Flynn brothers in their green Sheng-li overtook the blue Sharpei carrying Stella Kellogg and Suzy Claiborne at 1:56 p.m. outside the town of Stephens City, in Virginia. The two cars stopped at 1:58. Three minutes later, the boosts of the two brothers appeared to go dead, one within seconds of the other. They might still be alive, he says, adding that boosts inside the body of the dead continue to function for weeks, even months.

"What's your point!" Vallinger snaps.

"Just that you can be alive with a dead boost, or dead with a live boost. There's no correlation."

"So, dead or alive, we know they've been zapped," Vallinger says.

"Either that or abducted by extra-terrestrials," Dahl says.

This leads Vallinger to conclude that the revolutionary DM, in addition to planting a source deep inside his own business, has gotten its hands on one of the limited supply of Chinese-made zappers. In a quiet, regretful tone, he instructs Dahl to communicate this breach to "our Chinese friends."

"Excuse me?"

"LET THE CHINESE KNOW THAT WE MIGHT HAVE A GODDAMNED MOLE IN OUR HOUSE,"

Vallinger says. After wiping the spittle from around his mouth with the back of his hand, he adds in a grim monotone: "For all I know, it might be you."

As Dahl obediently composes a message in his boost, Vallinger turns his attention to Suzy Claiborne, who is apparently heading in her own Shar-pei to Washington. He can track her boost, but can't tell from boost scans or satellite shots if she's accompanied by his two goons. They may be with her, or with Kellogg—or as Dahl suggests, with Martians. In the end, it makes no difference. Those wild men are as lost to him as they are to themselves.

"Follow Claiborne's car," he tells Dahl. "She may lead us to the rest of her network. You never know. Maybe those beasts will bring her in. You should go over to Virginia," he says, referring to his Detention Center, "in case they do."

# PART IV

———

# washington

# FORTY-ONE

Stella looks blankly out the window as the green Sheng-li winds its way through Washington's Virginia suburbs. She has to come up quickly with a plan. John Vallinger, she knows, has the means to track her boost, minute by minute. He can send someone or something to kill her, or more likely, deliver death or crippling injury through a short-circuiting software app. She has heard about such things. Vallinger, with his tight connections to the Chinese, is bound to have the full arsenal.

As she passes Leesburg, Stella thinks about Suzy. She doubts they killed her, and she knows that at least one of the men is alive. So all three are probably awake by now, coming to grips with their new circumstances: Suzy a captive, the men newly wild. She wonders if they'll take Suzy to Vallinger, or perhaps to an interrogation center. For all she knows, they might be a mile or two behind her.

She looks at her messages. There's one from a colleague at the DM. It's written in code that Vallinger's team could probably untangle in a matter of seconds, she thinks. It asks her to confirm that John Vallinger actually paid a visit to her safe house in Montclair. Old news, she thinks, not bothering to respond. She flips to her outbox and is surprised to see that a message she sent to Simon appears to have been received. Could he be back in El Paso? She sends him another one, telling him that she's taking a detour, and might not be in El Paso quite as soon as she had hoped. The message bounces back. A new message pops in. It's from John Vallinger. "Are you coming alone?" he asks.

Stella doesn't know how to respond, or if she should.

"I see you," a new message says. "Answer me."

Stella's heart races. She works to breathe deeply and evenly. She passes a sign pointing to Washington and Alexandria. Then the pain starts. It begins as a tingle in her mouth, near a molar, and then it creeps up the side of her face, intensifying until her cheek feels like it's roasting from the inside. She moans as a new message comes in. "Answer me."

Stella does not answer. Through the blinding pain, she ransacks her messages for an address and then gives it to the car. The Sheng-li promptly crosses three lanes of traffic and angles toward Alexandria.

# FORTY-TWO

**3/13/72 8:56 a.m. Eastern Standard Time**

Stella Kellogg looks around. She's in a white room with smudges on the walls, the windows covered with tattered curtains. It takes a moment to recall where she is. Her head hurts, but the pain is on the skin, not inside. She reaches up to her temple and touches a bandage. Then she remembers. She consults her boost and gets no response. On a table next to her bed, she sees a small clear plastic case with her name printed on it. Inside is cellulose packaging, and inside that, she's sure, is her boost.

For the first time in nearly three decades she is alone with her mind. Unlike Ralf, she never liked her boost, blaming it for the sadness of her life, her dead husband, the two distant children, her solitary existence in Montclair, the tragedy of the United States. She spent days on end ignoring her boost, living the thoughts and feelings of the wet brain she was born with. Yet it was always there—a presence, a tool, a powerful link to the rest of humanity. Without it, she feels vulnerable and out of touch.

She turns sideways on the bed and looks at her boost's plastic sarcophagus. Whoever holds that box, she knows, is in danger. She considers throwing it out the window, onto the cobblestone street of old-town Alexandria. But that would be irresponsible. Someone might pick it up and find himself arrested by private security guards, like the two that she and Suzy confronted yesterday. She catches her breath at the memory of that scene. She remembers zapping those two men, the looks on their faces as they crumpled to the ground, and then the one who ran after her and reached through the open door for her arm. She thinks of Suzy. Where could she be now? She composes a quick message for her—"You okay?"—and then remembers that she has nothing to send it with. This is the limitation of her new wild life.

Stella hears a knock on the door. It opens a crack and a familiar Asian face peers in. Bao-Zhi. He wears a gentle smile. He pushes open the door and walks in wearing white surgeon scrubs.

"How did you know I was here?" Stella asks, before remembering that Bao-Zhi doesn't speak a word of English. She doesn't even have her boost to guide her in writing the Chinese characters for him.

"We traced your boost," he says in clear, if accented, English.

"You speak English!"

"When I choose to," he says, smiling.

Over the next few minutes, Bao-Zhi prepares Stella

for the transition to wild life. He gives her two bags of food, one protein, one vegetable. "It will taste vile," he says, strutting his vocabulary. "But you won't starve." Then he hands her a small box with a simulated boost signal, which she puts in her black purse. "You can't do anything with it," he says, "but when they scan the highway, at least your car doesn't look wild. I would have given one to Ralf," he adds, "but the shipment just came in day before yesterday."

"You said 'my car'?" Stella asks.

"The green one that brought you here," he says.

They continue their conversation, in hushed tones, on the way out of the clinic. Stella carries her black purse over her right shoulder and the two bags of food in her left hand. She notices that Bao-Zhi greets the doctors and medical personnel with familiar smiles and waves. He tells her that he does jobs for them.

"Did you take out Ralf's chip?" she asks.

"No, that was an intruder," he says. "An amateur."

"And did you"—she lowers her voice to a whisper—"kill him?"

Bao-Zhi smiles. "Do you believe everything John Vallinger says about me?"

Minutes later, the green Sheng-li, following directions to a Mesa Street address in El Paso, pulls out of the driveway. Stella, newly wild and emotionally drained, starts off the trip stretched out in the backseat. She carries the black box with the simulated boost. But the plastic case with her own boost, the one carrying decades of memories, remains behind, in the pocket of Bao-Zhi's white smock.

# FORTY-THREE

The March winds blow in from the west. They pick up balls of tumbleweed and bits of garbage and send them dancing through the dusty outskirts of Ciudad Juárez. The winds also seem to lift a big part of the Chihuahua Desert into the air and carry it toward downtown and beyond—maybe, thinks Oscar Espinoza, as far as the Big Bend. Espinoza feels the desert grit in his teeth, which makes him wish he could wash them one more time in Juárez, preferably with a plate of chimichangas, or a bowl of steaming *menudo*. He's had his fill of goat.

A meal doesn't look likely. Several paces ahead of him, a determined George Smedley marches into the west wind. He leans forward to keep his balance. In one hand, he clenches his Panama hat, still sporting its battered brown feather. Placing the hat on his head in this wind would be something like a ritual sacrifice, Espinoza thinks. This leads him to wonder if the ancient Indians in Juárez ever ripped out people's hearts. He knows the narcos did.

Before breakfast this morning, he and Smedley were relaxing in their cots, waiting for the expected invitation to Don Paquito's headquarters, when they heard a knock on the back door. Smedley thought it was just windblown debris. But the *señora* opened the door to two visitors. It turned out to be Don Paquito, a trim man who walked with a cane. He smiled a lot and did most of the talking. He was with his son Simon, who nervously twirled his ponytail around a finger. He seemed grouchier than his father. "We came through the back way to avoid that big ugly machine out front," Don Paquito said, referring to the drone.

Once the four sat down around the metal card table at Trastos, Espinoza expected Smedley to push for Ralf Alvare, and his boost, to return to Washington. He knew Smedley had no intention of paying any money, and it was no sure thing that John Vallinger, once he had Alvare in custody, would make good on any promises. But still, Espinoza wanted to see how much Smedley offered, and how the bargaining went.

But Smedley immediately talked to Don Paquito as a fellow publisher. As the *señora* poured them more coffee and placed a basket of pastries on the table, Smedley talked about the big story in the newspaper. "I don't like this development one bit," Smedley said. With the Respect function in their boosts, he said, people would bow down to their bosses. This might turn him into "a slave to John Vallinger." Espinoza was startled to hear

Smedley denounce Vallinger, especially to a Mexican drug lord, of all people. Smedley said that the Respect function would favor large businesses over small. As an entrepreneur, he said, this was worrisome.

"An entrepreneur?" Don Paquito said.

"I'm a publisher, sort of like you," Smedley said, looking proud for the first time. "Except my business is more modern. It's in the boost." When Don Paquito asked for details, Smedley walked him through it. "When you sell your newspaper," he said, "you sell an experience. I'm just guessing here, but I would bet that when your ideal reader picks up *The Tribune,* he steps into the newspaper, in a sense. He lives the stories."

"In a sense," Don Paquito said with a shrug.

"Well, in my businesses, my customers get to live in the worlds my team and I build. You could say that they not only consume the editorial content, but also, by interacting with each other there, they create it."

"You mean that you sell virtual worlds."

"Exactly."

"I know all about them," Don Paquito said as he dipped the corner of a croissant into his coffee and bit it off. "I participate in the modern world, even as a wild man who sells a product printed on paper." He smiled as Smedley tried to excuse himself. "So I would imagine," he went on, "that most of your content on these sites is sexual. That's where the market is, if I understand it."

Smedley coughed. "We do a bit of that," he said.

"What's your circulation?"

"We're midsized," Smedley said. He paused to elevate

the number, and ended up multiplying it by ten. "About 30 million unique visitors a month," he said.

At this point, Simon surprised the two by breaking into the conversation. "I think I've been on your sites," he said to Smedley. "I was in one in Istanbul. It was quite a beautiful experience. A bedroom overlooking the Bosporus." Smedley nodded uncomfortably. "Then there was another place, in a Cuernavaca hotel called Las Mañanitas. Is that your site, too?"

Smedley, his face bright red, nodded and reached for his coffee. Don Paquito watched his son with a perplexed smile.

"I absolutely loved it there," Simon said. "Congratulations. I mean, really. Had a fantastic time. So what I was telling my dad," he went on, "is that there might be some sort of way to collaborate, bringing together the digital and the molecular, sort of like we did in Cuernavaca." He smiled at Smedley. "Maybe some kind of synergy."

Espinoza looked across the table at Don Paquito and shrugged his massive shoulders. Then, battling his instinct to pick up a pastry, he stood up from the table and walked out into the street where the drone, like a faithful pet, was still waiting. He stood out in the cold for another half hour, feeling the west wind grow stronger. Finally, the three other men came out. A black car appeared. Simon and Don Paquito stepped into it and took off for downtown. As Smedley approached Espinoza, he pointed to the north. "Tunnel," he said.

Espinoza started to say something about lunch, and Smedley interrupted him. "No time for food."

**3/13/72 12:01 p.m. Eastern Standard Time**

John Vallinger is regaling his aide about his days in Mountain View with the founders of Google, Larry and Sergei. They were on a first-name basis, he says. "They had this huge airplane that they parked over at the Moffett Field—"

Tyler Dahl puts his hand up. He sees a new message in his boost.

"What is it?" Vallinger asks.

"It's just—"

"Just what!"

"Smedley's back from Juárez."

"With Alvare?"

"No."

"Then with Alvare's boost?"

Dahl shakes his head. "No, he's just asking us to turn off his headache."

"Tell him to get some results, and I'll consider it," Vallinger says. "Otherwise, he can crawl back to Juárez with that big friend of his."

"He says we have one minute to turn it off."

"Or what?"

"He's not saying."

"Amp it up then," Vallinger says.

"Do you think that's smart?"

"AMP IT UP!"

Dahl has the controls in his boost, and tells Vallinger that he's made the adjustment. Then the two men wait. Dahl can hear Vallinger's labored breathing. Dahl walks to the window and looks out at the sparse Sunday traffic on K Street. He envies the people circulating in the early spring drizzle. Some might be heading to a hockey game or even spending real time in real space with their families. They don't know about the coming update, much less the Respect function. They have never given anyone a digital headache. Only a few of them have suffered one, and they probably thought it had something to do with the sinuses, or perhaps an impacted molar. None of them have to deal with John Vallinger. Those people, he thinks, lead happy lives.

His reverie is interrupted by another message from Smedley. "Oh my," he says.

"What now?" Vallinger asks.

"Smedley says he's at war with us."

### 3/13/72 10:09 a.m. Mountain Standard Time

George Smedley, his aching head in his hand, sits on the hood of Oscar Espinoza's KIFF. It's still parked on the abandoned Santa Teresa golf club, within a nine-iron shot of the sand trap tunnel to Juárez. He has his Panama hat wedged between his thighs to keep it from blowing away. The feather is now gone, probably somewhere in the tunnel. Espinoza sits inside the truck. He has the seat reclined and is sleeping loudly.

The boost reception here is spotty, but strong enough for the suffering Smedley to carry out his business. After his exchange with Dahl, he calls his Pentagon connections and cancels the drone escort in Juárez. It just gets in his way over there.

Then he turns to the more pressing business. Smedley

has brought back a special copy of yesterday's *Tribune,* one without watermarked pages. This, Simon told him, will allow him to distribute images of the pages.

It still feels odd to be doing business with a man who, as a female avatar, has had his way with Smedley's body. But when it comes to sex, Smedley prides himself on his open mind, and he is content to accept Simon as his lover—especially now that he's at war with John Vallinger. He and Simon share a common cause. Smedley finds it ennobling to be so open-minded. To be fighting against John Vallinger places him for the first time among the defenders of freedom. Smedley would entertain nothing but wonderful feelings about himself and his life, he reflects, if he didn't have a splitting headache.

Holding the paper flat against the hood of the KIFF, he captures images of the first page, and then he turns to the inside page with the rest of the lead story. He captures the image, and then sends both of them to his tech team in Singapore with explicit instructions.

When he receives confirmation that the pages have arrived, he pounds on the windshield and gestures toward the sand trap. Oscar Espinoza descends from his KIFF with a wistful air. He pauses to take in the mammoth brown vehicle one more time and then trots after Smedley, who is already digging through the white sand, and reaching for the trap door to the tunnel.

**3/13/72 5:00 p.m. Eastern Standard Time**
On their Sunday afternoon rambles, thousands of visitors to the virtual world *Hard to Miss an Artemis* come across something unusual. Their avatars pass through

the usual gateway to the site, but posted to one side, right next to the bulletin board, is a sign with a simple command: "Read This!" Most of the visitors barely pause to take it in. But a few stop, and what they see is *The Tribune*'s lead story on the Respect function in the coming chip update. Smedley's tech team in Asia designed the sign as a peel-away pad of paper. Visitors who want copies of the article can tear off a sheet, fold it, and place it in their pockets. Then, when they mingle with others on the site, they can hand out copies. Once off the site, the papers vanish and turn into links to Smedley's virtual world. One of the ideas, after all, is to drive new traffic to *Hard to Miss an Artemis*.

In the first hours, the results are discouraging. Of the 14,643 people who visit the site, only 420 stop to read the article. Of those, only 84 tear off a copy and place it in their virtual pockets. Seeing these numbers, the Singapore team turns to more pressing business: the long overdue upgrade of the *Tasty Twins* site, which is losing market share to a host of competitors, some of them featuring quintuplets. Sex sites, it seems, are no place to break political and tech news.

But the story picks up through the course of the night. Although only a small minority stop to read the news, each person who takes away a copy of the story passes it on to an average of four people, and those people share it at about the same rate, inside and outside of the site. *The Tribune* article is going viral. By Monday morning, traffic at the Artemis site is up to more than 96,000 every hour—14 times the usual number. Most of the new visitors are barely looking into the virtual world. They skip the hook-ups with cheerleaders, the Second Empire boudoirs, and the new weekly feature—topless Artemi dressed as Pocahontas, paddling canoes. Most simply read the news and grab copies for their friends. A few stop to leave comments on the bulletin board. Some complain about the Artemis site, calling it "tasteless" and "disgusting," even when compared to other sex sites. But some of the notes on the board are of a different flavor. "If you don't like this news, come to the Liberty Bell in Philadelphia, Monday at 5," one said. "Bring your friends." Others call for protests in San Francisco, New York, Washington, and Dallas.

# FORTY-FOUR

**3/14/72 9:16 a.m. Eastern Standard Time**

In the woods near Vienna, Virginia, stands a large cube made of black glass. This three-story building, with ten thousand square feet of office space, is Varagon Inc.'s interrogation center. In addition to the professional rooms, provided with cutting-edge surveillance technology and cabinets packed with various medications, the center features luxury bedrooms, an exercise gym, and a sauna, with a pool and basketball court outside. On Monday morning, Tyler Dahl pads down to the kitchen in search of breakfast protein. Dahl spent all day Sunday at the facility, in the company of an anesthesiologist and an armed guard, on the off chance that the newly wild Flynn brothers would bring in Suzy Claiborne with a story to tell. They never did. Dahl assumes they're lost forever, even dead.

As he forages for food, he sees that seventeen messages are waiting for him. Three of them discuss the

Washington Capitals hockey game Sunday night. The Flyers wasted the home team, 9-0. One is from Vallinger, asking for news of Suzy Claiborne. The other thirteen are all links to a message board in the *Hard to Miss an Artemis* virtual world. Dahl visits the site and reads the article, which by this point he knows verbatim. Then he scans some of the calls for protests on the bulletin board.

Fortunately, it's only reaching a few people on this site, Dahl thinks, and it's not one of the popular ones. If this is the extent of Smedley's mischief, Vallinger will be relieved. Standing at the entrance gate of the virtual world, Dahl tears off a copy. Then, on a whim, he dons an off-the-shelf male avatar and takes a free introductory stroll around the site. Dahl wasn't planning to have a sexual encounter. In fact, he knows he should hurry to send a copy of the article to his boss. But he soon finds himself sitting on the floor of a canoe crafted from bark and looking into the eyes of the loveliest Pocahontas imaginable. Naked above the waist, she paddles up the virtual James River, past herons and egrets perched on a single leg. Her paddle strokes leave a series of perfect whirlpools on the glassy surface of the water. A bald eagle swoops down in front of the canoe, crosses the river, snaps up a gray hare in its talons, and flies off. The Indian princess regards Dahl's avatar with soft green eyes and says, "Can you believe this shit?"

Dahl is dismayed to hear Pocahontas stray so far from character. "Believe what?" he asks.

"The news about the Respect function in the update," she says. "I had no idea."

Dahl says he agrees with her.

"Where do you live?" the Indian princess asks as she continues to paddle.

"Washington, DC," Dahl says, immediately regretting telling her the truth.

"Me too. There's a rally this afternoon outside the American History Museum, on the Mall. You going?"

"I don't know," Dahl says. "I'll be at work."

"Oh." The Indian keeps paddling. Her coppery skin glistens. The animals in the woods make their morning sounds. "Listen," she says, "are we going to do it or what?"

"Actually, I'm kind of busy," Dahl says. He holds up the visitor's pass he wears around his virtual neck. "I think they'd cut me off after, like, ten minutes." Without waiting for Pocahontas's disappointed response, he hits the jump function, which vaults him from the canoe to the exit. In another moment, he's returned to the physical world—sitting on the bunk bed in the Virginia apartment. He has carried back a link to *The Tribune* story. Like thousands of other visitors to the *Hard to Miss an Artemis* site, he intends to share the article, but with only one interested party.

# FORTY-FIVE

**3/14/72 9:16 a.m. Eastern Standard Time**

Suzy Claiborne opens her eyes. It's morning, and she's curled up in the backseat of her Shar-pei.

"About time!" says the shorter of her two captors.

Suzy is famished and her head aches. She touches a painful bump on her forehead. She notices that her blouse is misbuttoned, and the strap of her bra is tangled. But she's pretty sure—and relieved—that they left her leggings in place. Her bladder is so full it hurts.

"We need to borrow your irises to get this car moving," says the short one. He introduces himself as Gerry and says his brother, much taller, is Al. He says she has slept for thirty-six hours.

Still feeling groggy, Suzy walks into the woods to pee. They must have given her a dose of something to make her sleep long. She returns to the car and sits in the front seat. She presses the Start button and the motor hums. Then she returns to the backseat and lies down.

The three of them take off heading east toward Vienna, Virginia. Suzy sees that the Flynns have eaten most of the provisions she and Stella packed for their trip. But one bag of vegetables remains. She devours it, turning it with her boost into a Caesar salad. Then she soothes her headache with a painkiller app.

Once the car gets them to Vienna, Gerry says, it will have to switch from auto pilot, since they don't know the exact address of their destination. "We're missing some signals," he says with a chuckle, pointing to his boost-dead head. Without working boosts and with no maps, they soon get hopelessly lost. For more than an hour and a half, they circle a shopping district of Tyson's Corner. Suzy's Shar-pei is little help. It has no data on the secret facility.

Nonetheless, the brothers seem to enjoy themselves. They yell at each other and laugh endlessly at each other's silly jokes. What Suzy cannot understand, from her position in the backseat, is how two brothers who have lost their boosts could be having so much fun. If this is how they act after an failed mission with disastrous long-term consequences, she thinks, they must be the life of the party when things go right.

Finally, Gerry, the more talkative of the two, turns around in his seat. "Okay," he says, looking directly at her breasts. "This is a little embarrassing, but you're going to have to help us a little. We have to take you to a place where you'll undergo . . . a bit of interrogation. Nothing serious. Just a few questions. But we can't find it. Could you do us a big favor and look for it in your boost?"

Suzy understands that resistance on her part might

mean endless loops around Tyson's Corner, so she agrees to help them. They tell her that the facility has a basketball court and a kidney-shaped pool in the back. She locates the shapes in her boost, and within minutes they're pulling up in front of the black cube on a leafy cul-de-sac in Vienna.

Al knocks, and a short young man holding a bowl of breakfast protein opens the door. His hair stands up on one side, as if he went to bed after a shower and is missing a comb. Al tells Tyler Dahl that they picked up Suzy Claiborne, as instructed—he points to the fuzzy-headed Artemis standing between them. But in the course of the arrest, "her partner, now a fugitive, turned off our boosts. So," he says with a smile, "we're going to have to get those turned on again."

Dahl shakes his head sadly. "I'm afraid that won't be possible," he says. He explains that the Chinese-made tool Stella apparently used did not turn off the boosts, but instead wiped them clean.

The two brothers gape at each other. "So," says Gerry, "we have to learn everything over again, load a lot of data onto the boost, that sort of thing?"

Dahl shakes his head again and breaks the news that their boosts are dead: useless collections of carbon nanotubes lodged in their heads for the rest of their lives. He leaves them with a scrap of hope. In some places, he's heard, people can get dead people's boosts. "You might look into that." He closes the door gently on the two brothers and guides Suzy inside. Suzy hears their keening high-pitched cries as she is led into the heart of John Vallinger's private detention facility.

```
FORTY-SIX
```

Stella wakes up and sees palms pass by. She opens the window and sultry air fills the Sheng-li. Do palms like this grow in Arkansas? Oklahoma? Texas? She has no idea where she is. When she was a child, in the pre-boost era, towns and roads had signs. Some still remain, but they're relics. She doesn't see any.

The sun looks high in the southern sky, which means it's close to noon. If she left at five in the afternoon and it's noon, the car has been traveling at 95 miles per hour for nineteen hours. She calculates that she's about eighteen hundred miles from Washington. This has to be New Mexico, she thinks, or West Texas.

She stares out the window and thinks about her two sons in Ciudad Juárez. She wonders if Ralf will ever get used to being wild, and if Simon can make a living by running a tavern. She tries to picture Simon. Will he be fat now? He always had that tendency. Bald? At least he'd lose that ponytail. She wonders if Simon will ever forgive her for shooing away his father and then sending him to that horrid military academy. It occurs to her that Simon might have a boyfriend in El Paso. Maybe that's why he moved there. It amazes her that this idea, so logical, has never entered her mind before. She considers the possibility that her boost may have stifled her curiosity.

What else did it stifle? It's been decades since Stella tried to speak the Spanish she learned with her wet brain. The Spanish reminded her of Francisco, and of what she had lost. It also bothered her that so many people got by in life with advanced Spanish-language apps, without so much as learning the difference between *ser* and *estar,* not to mention the endless complexity of the subjunctive case.

As the green Sheng-li races through whichever state she's in, Stella practices her Spanish subjunctive with sentences about her sons. *Ojalá que mis hijos me reconozcan. Ojalá que me quieran. Ojalá que los encuentre, Ojalá que mi marido estuviera vivo.* . . . What started out as a grammar exercise, she realizes, is turning into a wish list for her life. She hopes she can find her sons and that they will love her, and she wishes her husband were still alive.

She wipes tears from her eyes and pulls the cracked copy of *Donkey Show* from her purse. Soon she is with her grandfather, Tom Harley, roaming both sides of the Mexican border on bicycle. He's making a silly mess out of his reporting. His love life with the woman who would become Stella's grandmother is a comedy of misunderstandings. The story makes her laugh. When she looks up, she sees that the car is moving along a commercial street. People are riding on horseback. Brown mountains, the same ones her grandfather described, loom to her left. The car turns into a parking lot and stops.

Stella walks into the dark and nearly deserted Cavalry Club and says hello to the man behind the bar. He looks at her closely and says, "Don't tell me: you're Simon's mother."

"How did you know?"

"I'm not getting anything from you," Chui says, "I'm beginning to think it runs in the family." He tells her that if all goes according to plan, Ralf should be coming by in the next day or so, maybe with Simon and Ellen. He's not sure. "Want a beer while you wait?" he asks.

"I could use one," Stella says, plopping onto a bar stool.

# FORTY-SEVEN

**3/13/72 1:47 p.m. Eastern Standard Time**

Tyler Dahl, who considers himself scrupulously correct in his dealings with women, would never admit to anyone his disappointment when studying the stored memories of Suzy Claiborne. Dahl had secretly looked forward to experiencing life snippets featuring the domed Artemis, one of the most marvelous specimens he had ever seen. He had the anesthesiologist put Suzy to sleep and he placed her lovely head in the new boost-reading cradle. But once he fitted the experiential helmet onto his own head, he found himself disappointed. As he flipped through the stored scenes of her life, he realized that they featured everyone Suzy saw—but almost nothing of Suzy herself.

The second complication, far more serious for his intelligence-gathering mission, is the vastness of Suzy Claiborne's database. She has her entire life recorded on that chip. It would take at least twenty-six years to in-

spect it all. So how can Dahl, operating on a tight deadline, unearth the crucial five or ten minutes when she is
talking to her superiors at the DM, or conspiring with
Stella Kellogg to disrupt the national software update?
One conversation in a life is like a single grain of sand
on a long beach. "I can't find anything," he mutters to
himself. The new cradle is useless, he concludes, without better search.

Deep down, Dahl is fairly certain that these two
women—the Artemis with her fuzzy head in the cradle
and the older one who has disappeared from the Alexandria clinic—are not the sources for *The Tribune*
articles. Dahl knows this because he suspects that he
himself, with only the best intentions, provided the information.

He never meant to. However, as he called down to
El Paso every day for *The Tribune* headlines, he developed quite a rapport with Chui, the source in El Paso.
They conversed, boost to boost. Dahl had a feeling that
they saw things the same way. In the course of these discussions, some of them lasting an hour or two, Chui
apparently learned quite a bit about the coming update.
Dahl has enough self-awareness to detect the absurdity
in the current situation. The leaker is plundering the
memories of another person looking for evidence of
leaks.

He isn't going to find any. So instead he surfs Suzy
Claiborne's chip looking for interesting scenes in her life.
He first sees a man who must be her father, his angry
face right up to hers, barking at her to eat her protein.
With the helmet providing stored data from all the

senses, Dahl smells alcohol on the man's breath and feels the warm heavy air of the South in summer. He gets a glimpse in the mirror and sees a lovely young face, with green eyes and freckles, red hair spilling down her forehead. Why did she become an Artemis? he wonders. He flips forward. He's in a lecture hall at a university, listening to a professor talk about Proust's madeleine, and how memory was different in the era before the boost. Dahl is interested in the subject, but Suzy Claiborne apparently nodded off. The memory goes dark. He flips far ahead. He's in a coffee shop. A young man is sitting across the table blowing onto his cold fingers. Suzy is telling him to look at a gate, 318 Blue.

Ralf Alvare, Dahl thinks. He recognizes him from images he's seen. He watches the rest of the conversation. At one point, Suzy looks to the right, at an Asian man drinking tea at the next table. It's Bao-Zhi, looking just like the image Vallinger showed him. He must have been following either Ralf or Suzy. Dahl wonders where he might be now. Could he be in El Paso? Or Juárez? He'll raise that question with Vallinger. The Bao-Zhi spotting is the closest Dahl has come to a discovery in the Claiborne memory cache. Other than that, it's been a waste of time.

He flips forward once more. That same Asian face, twisted with passion, is rocking an inch above Suzy Claiborne's. At first, Dahl feels physically invaded and then, once he gets used to it, he experiences waves of intense pleasure. Breathing heavily, he yanks the helmet from his head.

He looks into the cradle and sees Suzy Claiborne

making writhing motions. Could she be experiencing the same scenes he has been living? It stands to reason, he thinks.

A message pops into his boost. It's from Vallinger and is typically succinct: "?"

He messages back that without a decent search function, boost hunting is a waste of time. He adds that he saw a key Claiborne scene with Ralf Alvare, and that Bao-Zhi was following them.

"Who is the leaker?" Vallinger asks. "Who is her boss at the DM? Details, please."

Dahl tells him that he's missing this information, and Vallinger messages that they'll have to move to the next step: an analysis of the connections among the billions of neurons—the connectome—in Suzy Claiborne's brain. This will provide the memories from the wet side of her cognition, what Vallinger calls "the missing piece."

Dahl, who understands both the science behind the connectome and the logistics involved, responds: "Won't work. The wet brain is long on emotions, short on data. Plus, you cannot analyze the connectome of a live person."

"Correct," Vallinger responds. "Prepare to euthanize."

# FORTY-EIGHT

**3/14/72 1:53 p.m. Mountain Standard Time**

Ellen walks from the kitchen through the *playa* to her bedroom with a glass of brown fruit juice—*agua de tamarindo*—when she glances into the newsroom and sees her pursuer, the hulking man with the flattened nose. The sight startles her, and she spills some of the juice on the floor. Francisco seems to be showing the news operation to two newcomers, the big man and a much smaller, slighter one who's wearing a beige exercise suit and a dirty Panama hat.

Oscar Espinoza spots Ellen and waves. Ellen ducks into the bedroom, leaving the puddle of juice untouched, and shuts the door.

She sees Ralf still pacing in front of the bed, and whispers, "The guy who chased me through El Paso?" She points toward the door. "He's out there with your dad, getting a tour."

Ralf nods. He explains that the other man, Smedley,

used to work for John Vallinger and is now publishing *Tribune* articles on his sex site.

Ellen laughs. "You think they spice up the articles for the site? I can't imagine their horny customers taking time to read the newspaper."

Ralf doesn't bother to argue the point. He shrugs and sits down on the bed. He has dark bags under his eyes, and he has run his fingers back through his hair so much that it's standing on end.

For hours, Ralf has been waiting for word about an appointment in El Paso. Francisco, working with Simon, is arranging with military sources there to give Ralf limited access to the chip-reading technology in a facility just across the road from Bowie High School. It would be a half hour walk away—if the border didn't get in the way. Letting an outsider into the building, of course, is a sensitive matter. The people providing the access are demanding rich payments and security guarantees for themselves and their families. Simon, working from a hot spot he located on the west side of Juárez, is arranging the logistics, and Chui, from his office at the tavern, is lining up the financing. Ralf knows that when the word comes, he might have only an hour to cross the border and make his way to the facility, on East Paisano Drive. Once there, he'll have a maximum of two hours to work on the code on his chip.

Every detail seems daunting. At first, Ralf assumed that he would return to El Paso through the Santa Teresa tunnel, and take Ellen's Sheng-li—presumably still parked there—straight to East Paisano Drive. But Simon has told him that that route is far too slow. "It would be a thirty-mile circle, and the place we're going is only about a mile and a half east of here." So Francisco's allies in El Paso will plant their own people on the border patrol. They'll look the other way when Ralf and Simon squeeze through the same hole in the fence that Ellen used, and then race up on horseback to the facility.

"Horses again?" Ralf said.

"Much safer. They don't track them," Simon said.

Ralf also faces family issues. On Saturday he was shocked to hear that his mother and Suzy Claiborne were driving down to El Paso. At first, Ralf focused on the intense awkwardness of the visit. The meeting between his parents, twenty-nine years after Francisco's disappearance, was bound to be an ordeal. He imagined them screaming at each other, or crying, or maybe falling into each other's arms and starting over again. He didn't know which would be worst.

Ralf also dreaded dealing with his mother without the escape hatch of the boost. It would just be the two of them, looking at each other and talking, maybe for the first time ever. He shared this worry with Simon, who had little patience for it.

"Hey Ralf," he said. "It's not that hard. You look at her. You talk. You listen. You talk some more. Your problem is that you think way too much about this stuff. You obsess."

Ralf spent most of Sunday walking back and forth between the newspaper offices and the Kentucky Club. He called Chui every half hour or so to ask if his mother and Suzy had arrived. The answer, invariably, was no.

Ralf sits on a corner of the bed, looking sick. It was bad enough that John Vallinger was after the two women. The fact that they're still not here forty-eight hours later spells likely disaster.

"You're worried about your mom," Ellen says.

He nods as he runs his fingers again through his hair.

"Let's go over to the Kentucky Club," she says, opening the bedroom door. She gestures toward the visitors in the newsroom. "I've got to get away from them, and you can have a drink."

Ralf nods. He grabs the chip, housed in the blue snuff bottle, and jams it into his jacket pocket. On the way out, he slips on a puddle, rights himself, and trots after her. "No drinking for me until I do the work on the chip," Ralf says.

"Oh yeah," Ellen says as he catches up to her. "Forgot about that."

# FORTY-NINE

**3/14/72 4:00 p.m. Eastern Standard Time**

The demonstrators begin to gather Monday afternoon, near the Museum of Natural History on the Mall. It's just a few dozen at first, several of them carrying signs. One says: "RESPECT OUR FREEDOM!" They mill about, exchanging their outrage and fears. Some laugh that the news-breaking story about the Respect function in the software update came on a sex site; others seem embarrassed by that fact. No one can remember attending a political demonstration before, though they have heard of them in the pre-boost era. Didn't Martin Luther King deliver his "I have a dream" speech near here?

It starts to drizzle, and umbrellas pop up. The crowd grows to one hundred, and then to several hundred, and late in the afternoon they start to march. A long trail of umbrellas snakes its way north on 12th Street. Instead of turning left toward the White House on Pennsylvania Avenue, they proceed north. More fall into their ranks as the demonstrators pass. When they reach G Street, streams of people emerge from the Metro Center station and join the crowd. At K Street they turn left. By five o'clock, thousands are jammed into Franklin Square. Protesters stand on benches and hang on to low branches of trees. A few are draped on the statue of Commodore John Barry, a Revolutionary War hero. They shout up toward the top floor of the Tongyi Tower. "Stop the chip! Sell out! Don't play with our minds!" Then a chant begins, and it grows louder as more protesters join. "Vallinger, traitor! Vallinger, traitor! Vallinger, traitor!"

John Vallinger, standing in his office on the twentieth floor, looks down on the crowd. He cannot hear through the soundproof windows, but he can read the signs. Two of his assistants mingling below are sending him updates.

"I heard one guy say he wants to kill you," one of his aides reports.

"Get an image of him!" Vallinger responds. "The police should know about this."

Earlier in the afternoon, one corporate client canceled its contract with Vallinger. "One of the provisos," the CEO told him in a boost-to-boost talk, "was that this would stay quiet. You haven't held up your side of the bargain." Two others—a food giant and the nation's largest insurer—have left messages that they want meetings right away. Someone also called from the White House.

Vallinger's team is busy creating news stories and videos blaming the demonstrations around the country on "wild exaggerations and lies" spread by terrorist organizations and "drug traffickers based in the wild outpost of Ciudad Juárez, the murder capital of the world." The objectives of these groups, according to Varagon Inc., is to stymie the economic advance of the United States, to foment chaos in the country, and eventually, to return the country to its wild state. "This would result in economic collapse and mass starvation and—for all intents and purposes—the end of the United States of America."

"We just need time," Vallinger says to no one in particular. He steps away from the window and sits at his desk. When the software is updated, in two days, people will fall into line. Protests will evaporate. Clients who are nervous now will clamor to bid for high Respect rankings in the boost, which will guarantee them rich profits. Yes, it's difficult now, Vallinger thinks. But who said that building the richest business in the history of the world would be easy?

He just has to make sure that no more damaging news seeps out in the coming hours. For this, he calls his source at the Joint Chiefs and sics the military on two terrorists conspiring to bring down the country. Stella Kellogg of Montclair, New Jersey, and "a Chinaman named Bao-Zhi."

"We have thousands of Bao-Zhi's around here," his source complains. "It would be like looking for a terrorist named Fred, or John."

Vallinger provides images and background material on the two, and instructs his source to take "the most energetic measures against them."

"What do you mean by that?"

"I'll let you interpret that as you may."

Vallinger turns back to the window. Someone in Franklin Square beams a search light on his window, turning the centenarian into a silhouette presiding high above the demonstration.

"There he is!" People shout, pointing up. The chants resume. The ancient lobbyist places an ear to the glass but still hears nothing.

"Two more days," he murmurs to himself as he puts on his raincoat and prepares to leave for the day.

# FIFTY

Ralf walks into the Kentucky Club, followed by Ellen. He waves to the bartender and immediately picks up the phone on the bar. A moment later he is talking to his mother. She's sobbing. "Ralf, you have to save her," she says. Over the next few minutes, between sobs and hiccups, Stella explains to him that Suzy is imprisoned in one of John Vallinger's hideaways, somewhere in northern Virginia, and that "the monster" has given orders to "euthanize her." One of Vallinger's assistants, he says, talks regularly to Chui, and he just got the word from Vallinger. "You have to save her," she repeats. "You cannot let this happen."

Ralf is dumbstruck by the news. He has no clue how to save Suzy from John Vallinger. And his mother seems highly emotional.

"Mother," he says, "have you been drinking?"

"What's that have to do with anything!" Stella says.

She then tells him a disjointed story, something about leaving Suzy with wild men in Virginia and then going to Alexandria and becoming wild herself and running into a Chinese guy who, a few days earlier, had bound Vallinger like a stuck pig in her living room in Montclair. As it turned out, he knows how to speak English. "I gave him my boost," Stella says.

Ralf makes little sense of it.

"You have to save her," his mother repeats, sounding sober. "You just have to."

"Okay," Ralf says, "I will."

"Good."

Since the conversation is already careening wildly, Ralf decides to drop the bombshell. "Mother," he says, "do you have any idea who Don Paquito is?"

"Yes," she says quietly. "I figured that out." She explains that she was working on her Spanish on the way down, and at one point she started to review nicknames. "Some of them are strange," she says. "Pepe comes from Jose, Kike comes from Enrique. Then I get to this bar, and the bartender's name is Chui, and I think, 'That comes from Jesus.' And he starts to tell me about this Don Paquito, and I immediately think, Paquito comes from Francisco. Well," she goes on, "Chui's a very nice man, and very discreet. But eventually he tells me that Don Paquito runs the newspaper, and that both of my sons are in touch with him. Or for all I know you work for him. And I think: that son of a bitch ducked out thirty years ago, and now he's grabbing back my family."

Ralf doesn't know what to say. "Well, it's not quite that simple . . . ," he stammers.

"Listen, Ralfie," Stella says. "Maybe he's a nice man. Maybe he's a good father. I don't care. It seems like he's become powerful and rich. Tell him to save Suzy."

### 3/14/72 9:56 p.m. Juárez Standard Time

Simon bursts through the newsroom and into the *playa*. His cheeks are red from the wind and his eyes bug out. He rushes up to Smedley, who's sitting at a Corona table with a bowl of soup. Oscar Espinoza is at the next table, working his way through a plate of *chilaquiles* with green sauce.

"Your site is going nuts," Simon says to Smedley. "Thirty-three million visitors in the last twenty-four hours."

"You can't be counting the zeros right," Smedley says.

"Oh I am. I checked and double-checked. More than a million messages are on the bulletin board. It's out of control. People are setting up demonstrations all over the place."

Smedley asks him if he has news on the demonstrations. "No," Simon says. "There's nothing worth looking at in the boost. But I see all kinds of statements denouncing erroneous reports coming from drug traffickers and terrorists. So I think somebody must be worried."

Francisco emerges from his office. He's limping more than usual and looks weary. "We're following the story," he tells Simon. "Big demonstrations all over the country. Your mother, who's at your tavern and apparently drinking heavily, just appeared on the FBI's Most Wanted list, along with a Chinese friend of hers. John Vallinger has arrested the woman she was traveling with. He has issued an order to kill her."

Simon sits down heavily, all of his excitement gone. "What are we going to do?"

"Just you watch," Francisco says. He motions to Smedley, who follows him into his office.

# FIFTY-ONE

**3/15/72 7:58 a.m. Eastern Standard Time**

A fisherman wearing dark glasses and a blue Yankees cap crosses Connecticut Avenue from the zoo into Washington's Woodley Park neighborhood. He hurries up Cathedral Avenue and then breaks into a jog.

There's little time to waste, Bao-Zhi knows. Ever since last night, when he and Stella appeared on the Most Wanted list, her boost has been attracting loads of attention. Bao-Zhi isn't too worried about himself. He has no boost for them to hunt, and the chip he carries in his backpack emits a commodity boost signal. He can blend into crowds, and police no longer know how to find people the old-fashioned way—by scanning their faces, scooping up DNA, or asking friends to identify them.

The danger comes from Stella's boost. Last night, police stopped his Metro at McPherson Square and checked every person in the train. He got through. But he knows that a closer hunt, with handheld detectors, will zero in on her chip, exposing him. He wandered the city all night, hiding the packet with her chip behind trees and between cars, and then snatching it when he saw surveillance starting to mount and moving it to another spot. It was exhausting. He's tempted simply to destroy it. But he knows the chip has value.

Early this morning he spotted a fishing rod leaning against a porch in Mount Pleasant, near the zoo. He stole it and tied the plastic container with the boost to the line. Then he dropped it in Rock Creek. He let it drift far downstream and then reeled it in. If someone came, he thought, he would cut the line. But when he heard the brakes of a police car screech in the parking lot behind him, he abandoned his own plan. He reeled in the chip and took off through the zoo.

On an empty section of 28th Street NW, Bao-Zhi kneels down by a storm drain. It's shaded by a towering sycamore tree. He looks around. No one seems to be watching him. He reaches into the drain with Stella's chip and flips it past the concrete shelf, into the water below. He hears a tiny splash. He lets out some line, and then some more. Eventually, he releases hundreds of yards of line. Then he detaches the reel from the rod, and jams it into a squirrel hole in the sycamore. He hides it with wet and rotting leaves.

When Bao-Zhi reaches busy Connecticut Avenue, he hears a buzz. Three tiny drones fly over his head, missing him by only inches. He watches them fly to the middle of the avenue, where they circle over a man-hole. He hears an air patrol approaching.

Bao-Zhi turns around and again walks up Cathedral Avenue. He needs a better plan.

# FIFTY-TWO

Spring in Virginia, Suzy Claiborne sees, is at least a couple of weeks ahead of Montclair. A magnolia tree out the window is flowering, and the forest's new lime green leaves shimmer in the morning sun. Suzy heaps two piles on her breakfast plate, one of protein, the other of fruit, and she sits down at the kitchen table with Tyler Dahl. Suzy is wearing her blue running clothes. She was hoping to take a morning jog before breakfast. But Dahl steered her instead to the treadmill in the exercise room. "I could get in trouble if you go out," he explained.

"Wouldn't want that to happen," Suzy said, flashing a brilliant smile.

She takes her breakfast as eggs benedict and slices of mango, and immediately regrets it. The mango app makes it taste like candy. She pushes the fruit to one side and moves to the eggs. She's surprised to see that Dahl has prepared an old-fashioned pot of coffee. Its aroma fills the kitchen.

"So," she says, "yesterday you were taking a little look-around in my boost. See anything interesting?"

Dahl, startled by the question, pauses. "Did you grow up in the South?" he asks.

"Little Rock," she says.

"I saw one scene, I think with your dad. Did he have a drinking problem?"

"I don't think he'd call it a problem," she says. "He drank all the time and beat my mother and scared my brother out of the house at age sixteen. But if you asked him, I don't think he'd say he had a problem with his drinking. We did."

Her father, she says, dominated their lives. One day her mother woke her up and told her she had a doctor's appointment. "That was when I found out they were going to turn me into an Artemis," she says, adding, "I used to have red hair and freckles. Most people thought I was pretty cute."

Dahl nods, but holds back from telling her that he saw that in her boost.

It wasn't until years later, long after the procedure, that she heard from her mother that before their marriage, her father had had an Artemis girlfriend. "She dumped him, probably because he was a drunk. Then he wanted me to look like her. Of course, I was disgusted," she says. "I shaved my head, which really pissed him off. We had a few . . . disagreements. Then I left home."

Dahl asks her how she landed her job with the DM.

"I'm not very political," Suzy says. "But it was a job.

A professor at college told me about it. The pay's not great, but you meet interesting people." She smiles at him, which highlights her dimples.

"What I want to know," she goes on, "is how you got tied up with that slimy boss of yours."

"He's very powerful, you know," Dahl starts out. "Of course the pay is good. Or actually, great." He goes on to tell her that he mapped out his career in mathematical terms. If he wanted to exert his influence on global affairs, it made "more sense to have moderate influence over a powerful force than large influence over a weak one."

Suzy scrunches her nose. "Why don't you just say the money's good, and leave it at that?"

"No, seriously," he says. "I have clout there." He boasts that he is the "sole intermediary" between Vallinger and *The Tribune*. And he also has the power to soften some of Vallinger's punishing dictates. The other day, he says, Vallinger told him to "amp up" a punitive headache on one of his employees. "And I ignored the order," he says proudly. "Blew it off."

Suzy doesn't have to say one word for Dahl to realize how foolish he sounds. "Well, it wasn't that big a deal," he says, taking a sip of coffee. Then he asks if she'd "mind answering a few questions about Stella Kellogg."

"Sure," she says, pouring herself more coffee. "You'll get a lot more by talking to me than digging around in my boost."

Over the next hour, Suzy gives Dahl what she calls "a worm's eye view of the DM." She tells him how someone got her a job in the Update Division at HHS and gave her instructions to befriend Ralf Alvare. "He's sort of a genius," she says. "Nice guy, but has some social issues." Then she got word, probably from DM sources in China, that her segment had an open surveillance gate, and that she should show it to Alvare. Next thing she knew, she was whisked away to a big depressing house in New Jersey. "It felt like a jail." She looks around the kitchen of the Detention Center. "A little like this," she says. "But this one is actually more cheerful." She smiles at Dahl, leading him to believe that perhaps it's his presence that helps to lighten the mood.

In the Montclair safe house, she found herself "mossing out" with Stella Kellogg, "a real sweetheart, but very sad. She's basically lost her family." The other occupant of the house was a wild Chinese guy named Bao-Zhi. "I think I would have died of boredom if it hadn't been for him."

"He's on the FBI's Most Wanted list," Dahl says.

"Bao-Zhi?"

Dahl nods. "So is Stella Kellogg."

Suzy almost drops her cup, and a few drops of the coffee splash onto the kitchen table. "You've got to be kidding me!"

"Seriously."

"She doesn't know *anything*! We'd see that paper, *The Tribune,* and it was all news to us." Suzy places a hand on Dahl's. "Tyler," she says. "Remember how you were saying that you were a moderate force in a powerful organization?"

He nods and swallows.

"Listen to me now," she says, looking deeply into his

eyes. "You've got to use that power to help Stella. They're going to kill her, and I'm telling you, she's not even close to the decisions."

At that moment, a message from John Vallinger pops into Dahl's boost. He leans back, freeing his hand from Suzy's, and reads it: "Status please."

# FIFTY-THREE

Traffic is backed up on Connecticut Avenue. Police cars are gathered at the center of the street. A navy flier hovers above. As his Houyi inches along, John Vallinger leans back in his recliner. Frustrated that Tyler Dahl is not answering his messages, he tries something new: He visits a sex site: *Hard to Miss an Artemis*.

A crowd of avatars is gathered at the gate. Vallinger figures they're reading yesterday's story about the Respect function. He moves up and sees that the article is still posted on the wall, and the bulletin board next to it is overflowing with notices and comments. But the people at the gate aren't reading that material. They're lined up to select avatars.

Vallinger quickly learns that *The Tribune* has published other articles on the site. But to read them, people have to pick an avatar and pass through the gate. That's

Smedley, trying to expand his filthy business, Vallinger thinks. He looks up from his boost, sees the traffic is still stalled, and decides to try out the site. He selects the avatar that looks like a Roman centurion and makes his way inside.

The scene is a mess. An angry minority of the customers have come for the sex. And yet most of the splendid Artemi, sculpted centurions, and Indian princesses turn out to be newspaper readers who rebuff their advances. Some call them perverts. Pushing and fighting breaks out.

Vallinger angles his avatar to one side and studies a large billboard covered with newspaper articles. One of them, the profile he was so pleased with five days ago, features a large image of him. He sees other articles that discuss the open surveillance gate, the tight relations between China and the U.S. Chamber of Commerce, and the censoring of news in the boost. Vallinger tears off copies of them all, stuffs them into his virtual pocket, and exits the site.

When he next looks up, his Houyi is making its way through an angry crowd of protesters. They're overflowing from Franklin Square onto K Street. One young woman recognizes him and yells, "It's Vallinger!" A horde rushes to the car and beats at the windows with their hands and kicks at the fenders as the car descends into the underground parking garage.

When John Vallinger steps out of the car and walks toward the elevator, he is alone and unharmed, but shaken.

But when he gets upstairs, one of his technicians runs up to him with news. "Ralf Alvare has popped up."

"Where is he?" Vallinger asks as he ambles to his office.

"Somewhere in the Southwest."

# FIFTY-FOUR

Ralf pushes a button. A small hatch in the machine opens, exposing a titanium shelf.

"That's where you put it," Simon whispers.

"I know." With a custom-built tool, which looks like a miniature spatula—the size a chipmunk might use—he removes his boost from the blue snuff bottle and places it gingerly on the shelf. He blows gently to coax it the last millimeter or two, and then pushes the button again. The shelf retracts.

"You can wear this," Simon says, holding up a helmet, "if you want to experience it."

"I think it might be depressing," Ralf says. "You know . . . seeing what I lost."

"The interface should be a whole lot better."

"Okay," Ralf says.

"And you don't have much time."

"I said okay!"

It was just after dawn that a messenger arrived at headquarters with word that the chip facility in El Paso would be available at nine. Simon, working with Chui by phone from the Kentucky Club, had an hour to set up a security opening at the border and arrange for horses. A little after seven, the two brothers weaved their way through the anti-drone barriers, past the merchants setting up their taco and *barbacoa* stands, and to the plank that Ellen had crossed. Simon walked across first and wriggled his body through a gap in the chain fence. Ralf followed. The two horses were supposed to be tied to a lamp post on South Ochoa Street. They weren't around.

Simon messaged Chui and heard that they'd be there by eight.

"Call them off," Simon responded. "We'll walk." So the two brothers headed north to Paisano Drive and then east. As they approached, they could see the venerable Bowie High School on the right side of the street. But on the left, where the chip facility was supposed to be, they saw what looked like a vacant lot piled high with festering garbage. A homeless man came up to them pushing a shopping cart full of empty cans.

"Simon?" he said.

Simon nodded, and the man led them into the lot, leaving his cart to one side. He pulled a remote from his pocket and touched a button. A trap door opened. Ralf and Simon followed him into a bright illuminated space, its walls plastered with posters from early in the century. Simon pointed out a yellow-faced creature to

Ralf and started to explain who Homer Simpson was, but Ralf, focused on the job ahead, wasn't listening.

"I think this was an old bomb shelter," Simon said.

"Uh-huh." Ralf, scanning from left to right, spotted a stainless steel machine with an expansive bright screen. "That's what we're here for," he said.

As the machine reads his chip, Ralf puts on the helmet. No bigger than a yarmulke, it's designed to cover just the crown of the head. "When I put this on," he asks, "will they be able to locate me?"

"No." Simon shakes his head. "This place gets the same signal camouflage as the other national security sites, like the White House and the Pentagon. They'll probably be able to tell that you're somewhere in the Southwest, but that's about all."

"Good," Ralf says. As the helmet establishes contact, it's as if he has his boost back. Ten days of messages are streaming in. His virtual worlds deliver reminders of pending sex vacations and basketball games. He doesn't need the big screen. He sees everything in his head— just the way it should be. The demands on his attention leave him dizzy. But he concentrates and focuses on two segments of the update, his and Suzy's.

While Simon watches, Ralf picks apart the code. Except for his darting eyes, the activity is invisible. For Simon, who feels foreign to this technology, it's as if his brother is composing a symphony in his head.

Then a message from Chui pops into Simon's boost. "Your mom wants to come join you. What do I tell her?"

"Tell her no," Simon answers. "Too dangerous. She should be over in Juárez now."

"I told her that. She won't take a no."

Simon doesn't dare interrupt Ralf. For twenty-five minutes the computer scientist works feverishly. "This is a lot of work," he says, clearly enjoying himself.

"Get it done in a hurry," Simon tells him, "because Mom's coming over."

# FIFTY-FIVE

"She was pregnant and had a ten-year-old, who was extremely difficult, and she had a big job. I cheated on her, then I left her. Made out that I was dead. So no, to answer your question, I'm not going to pretend I'm 'excited' that she's here. I know I deserve it. I do. But the timing's very bad. Couldn't be worse."

Francisco is sitting with Ellen at a Corona table in the *playa*. He's pushing fried plantains with cream back and forth on his plate. He has drained three cups of coffee but barely eaten a bite of his breakfast.

Ellen is wearing a red cotton dress printed with flowers. She bought it for one yellow coin at the outdoor market. These dresses are the uniform in Juárez for thousands of women, in all shapes and sizes. When Ellen wears her new dress, tying the sash high around her waist, she looks like a 1940s-era movie star.

She doesn't have much time for Francisco's self-pity.

"You say you have timing issues?" she says, sounding skeptical.

"The chip update is tomorrow night," he says. "We're the only paper covering it. For the first time since the '40s, people are taking to the streets in the United States. This man," he points to Smedley, who's sitting across the room, "wants me to put the entire newspaper on one of his sites, even though there's a chance no one will pay me for it. So I'm facing urgent business decisions." He pauses to think of more complications. "My two sons are over in El Paso, taking great risks to break into a government installation, and this lobbyist in Washington has arrested a woman—my wife's friend—and is threatening to dissect her brain looking for secrets. So no, it's not the ideal day to work out thirty years of personal history with my wife." He shrugs. "Or ex-wife."

"Can I be frank with you?" Ellen says, leaning toward Francisco.

He looks up from his plate and nods.

"All those years ago, you used what was going on in the world as an excuse not to deal with your family. You left them to have your revolution, or whatever you had in Uruguay."

"Paraguay," he says softly.

"Paraguay. So now you feel guilty about what you did, and you're using what's going on in the world as an excuse again to avoid your wife. Or ex-wife."

"You may be right, but it would still be easier if she came next week."

"What's she going to do?" Ellen says. "Make you feel

guilty? You already do. I think you're being a bit of a chicken, here."

"I have regrets," he says matter-of-factly.

"You want everything. You want money and power you've built here and the family you left behind."

"Am I so different from anybody else?" he asks. "So different from you?"

Ellen, surprised at the turn in the conversation, says nothing.

"You benefit from your beauty," he explains. "But you don't want to give up the honesty—*lo auténtico*—of the face you gave up for it. There's two of you, and you want them both. That's your problem."

Ellen sits up with a jolt. "Have you been talking to Ralf about me?"

"Believe me, *guapa*, if I can get Ralf to talk to me about anything, it certainly isn't you." He recalls their lunch together, when he asked to see the photo of the pre-Artemis Ellen, and she showed him one of Julia Roberts. "That's when I saw that you had issues. But then again, how can you have two different faces in life and *not* have issues?"

"You recognized her?"

"Of course I did. She was once a famous movie star." He laughs. "You could have picked someone a little more obscure."

They're interrupted by George Smedley, who walks up to their table. He too has gone shopping in Juárez. He's wearing a pair of khakis with a razor crease, and somewhere he unearthed a yellow golf shirt with a logo resembling his trademark feather on its chest. "Don Paquito," he says, "if we're going to get the paper in the boost by tomorrow, we have to start loading it now."

"Give me more time," Francisco says, waving him away. "I haven't made up my mind."

# FIFTY-SIX

Simon gets a message and hurries to the door while Ralf, wearing the helmet, continues his work. A minute later, Simon returns with Stella in tow. Her jeans and white shirt are coated with dust from her horse ride; her gray hair is a tangled mess. And Ralf has never seen her anywhere close to this happy. She rushes toward him, her shoes clattering on the polished tiles, and throws her arms around him, taking care not to disturb his helmet. She kisses him on the chin, the cheek, anywhere she can reach, and finally on the wound above his temple where his boost was removed.

Ralf finds himself hoping she gave Simon an equally warm hello.

She pulls back from him to see his eyes, and he notices the bandage over her own temple. Anticipating his question, she says, "Oh yes. I'm just like you."

Ralf is about to ask her why when a message arrives from John Vallinger. "We need to talk."

Ralf puts up his hand for silence and then tells his mother and brother that Vallinger is messaging with him. "What do I say to him?"

Stella puts the tip of her thumb in her mouth for a moment, composing, and then says: "Tell him that if he so much as touches Suzy Claiborne, you'll fry his brain."

Ralf considers it. "Probably not the best approach," he says.

"Let's think strategically," Simon says. "Why don't you tell him that you'll fly to Washington and would like to work to fix the software update? Make like you're cooperating, and buy time."

"And what about Suzy?" Stella says.

"Well, Ralf's not going to work with him if he goes around euthanizing his coworkers." Simon turns to Ralf. "You'd have to make that clear."

"Right," Ralf says. Then his face contorts with pain and he lets loose a howl. He rips off the helmet and buries his head in his hands.

"Headache?" Simon asks.

He nods without looking up.

# FIFTY-SEVEN

**3/15/72 11:41 a.m. Eastern Standard Time**

Bao-Zhi can see that time is running out. For three hours, he has been sneaking to the storm drain on 28th Street, reeling in Stella's boost and then, minutes later, letting out the line. The police have followed these underground movements, yo-yoing their squad cars and drones up and back, between Connecticut and Cathedral Avenues. Any minute now they'll send agents into the sewage system with orders to fish out Stella's dead body. Instead, they'll find the plastic container holding her boost bobbing on the water. No doubt they'll follow the fish line straight to the sycamore tree that the exhausted Bao-Zhi is leaning against. It's just a matter of time.

What Bao-Zhi needs is to find a digital refuge for the chip—a place to lay low until he's ready to put it to use. He considers making a run to Stella's radio-free house in Montclair. But it's far, and now that she's on the Most Wanted list, it's bound to be under surveillance. Also, Bao-Zhi cannot afford to forget that he too is on the list. It is true that as a wild man with a commodity chip he's much harder to track. But people still recognize a face from time to time.

He thinks of other dead zones. Defense targets like the Pentagon, of course, are shielded. But that place will be crawling with security. Then there's the White House. . . .

Bao-Zhi hatches a plan.

# FIFTY-EIGHT

The headache from Vallinger came into Ralf's boost at 9:48 a.m., which means that he still has more than an hour to keep working at the machine. He must either replace the helmet, and endure the crippling pain, or learn how to navigate his chip the old-fashioned way, with hand gestures on the big screen. This is hard, because the elements of the boost that he knew as thoughts and memories are represented on the screen as files and folders, most of them with machine tags that Ralf struggles to recognize. As Stella and Simon look on, he scrutinizes the screen. Then he begins to touch it. He tries opening memories by separating his thumb and forefinger. It works. They watch a few seconds of a little league game in which a bored Ralf lies down in right field and looks up at the wind blowing in a towering elm. He skips ahead and opens another. On the screen they watch a hand gently stroking the neck and bare shoulder of a dazzling Artemis. With a pinch of his fingers, Ralf quickly closes the file.

"How sweet," Stella says, unaware that the Artemis Ralf was caressing was an avatar. Simon knows better.

After a half hour, Ralf appears to have mastered the system. He has located both segments of the software update. Simon and Stella watch wordlessly as he tinkers with the code. They hear him talking to himself as he untangles long algorithms. "Okay, let's try this here . . . uh-huh . . . and then we'll put that little bugger up there . . . and then . . . Shit!" As this continues, his tone grows angrier and more frustrated.

Finally he looks up. "It's not going to work," he says. "It just isn't. I could rewrite the code, but I'd have to test it extensively. And then I'd have to either hack into the system—tomorrow—or convince one of my colleagues there to let me do it. It just isn't realistic. There's no time."

"So what do we do?" Stella asks.

"We can't change the code by tomorrow," Ralf says. "But we can force the people in Washington to—or at least to postpone the update."

"You mean with the paper?" Simon says.

"That's your tool," Ralf says. "I'm going to be waging the battle in the boost. I think I'm off to a good start. But I'll need to be back here tomorrow."

He moves to close down the system and Stella stops him, putting a hand on his. "What about Suzy?" she asks.

"Oh shit," Ralf says. "Forgot." He looks at the time on the screen. 10:49 a.m. "Do we have any slack?" he asks Simon.

"None. It's a hard stop at eleven."

"Okay. Here goes." He bends forward, and his fingers dance across the screen. He starts talking to himself again, but in happier tones. At 10:56, he leans back. "Got it."

"What?" Simon asks.

"You know that headache Vallinger sent me? I've isolated the algorithm, and now that he's messaged me, I have his address." Ralf places a long string of code into a field on the screen and then dictates a message: "This is a ten-second sample. But if you or your people lay a finger on Suzy Claiborne, you will live with this pain until you die." Then he touches the screen, sending the message and a dose of pain into the head of a centenarian on K Street.

The three of them sit for a moment, contemplating Ralf's work. Then Stella asks, "Shouldn't we warn Suzy?"

"Yes, of course," Ralf says. "I forgot about that." He looks at the clock. 10:58. "What should we tell her?"

"How about this?" Simon says. "John Vallinger has sent orders to kill you so that he can study your brain."

"I don't want to scare her too much," Stella says.

"Mom," Simon says. "She has to know."

"We only have a minute," Ralf says. He dictates the gruesome message.

"Tell her I say hi," Stella says.

"Stella says hi," he adds, and sends it just as the screen goes black and the machine spits out the tiny shelf holding his boost.

# FIFTY-NINE

**3/15/72 12:54 p.m. Eastern Standard Time**

One unexpected bonus at the Detention Center, Suzy Claiborne notes, are the silk sheets. She's also pleasantly surprised to be enjoying the company of her keeper, Tyler Dahl. He's cute, she thinks, if a bit full of himself. It's true that he can be a bit tiresome as a lover, certainly compared to the dexterous Bao-Zhi. Still, things could be worse.

She rolls across the black silk sheets and snuggles against Dahl, who's lost in a post-coital slumber. She gives him a kiss on the eye. He opens it slowly.

"Hey," she says.

"Hey."

"What are we doing the rest of the day?"

Before he can answer, she receives Ralf's message from El Paso. With a gasp, she jumps out of bed and begins throwing on her clothes.

"What's wrong?" he asks.

"You prick."

"What is it?"

"Have you been given orders . . . to kill me?"

"Who says that?" He sits up in the bed.

"Have you?"

"I can explain."

She rushes toward him and punches him hard in the side of the face.

"Stop it!" he shouts. "I can explain!"

She reaches down into the sheets, grabs his scrotum, and gives it a terrific squeeze.

"Stop it!" he moans.

She relaxes her grip. "Okay. Explain."

He tells her that he got a message from Vallinger that he was supposed to "euthanize" her for an analysis of her connectome. "But of course, I didn't plan to do it."

"He's waiting for you to kill me?"

"Well, not me. Ted."

"Who's Ted?"

"The anesthesiologist. The guy downstairs."

"The bald guy with the stun gun?"

"No, that's the guard."

Suzy listens and hears the faint clinking of silverware and two voices talking in the kitchen. "So you just figured you'd screw me, tell Ted to blow off his orders, and tell John Vallinger tough luck. Is that it?"

"Well, I hadn't really thought it through to that level of detail."

She squeezes her fist again.

"Ouch!"

# SIXTY

By lunchtime on Tuesday, *The Tribune*'s news coverage of the coming software update is convulsing the nation. Software hackers have devised a work-around so that people can share the folded copies of the articles without bothering to visit the *Hard to Miss an Artemis* site. More than half a billion copies circulate in the boost-sphere—more than one per citizen. Demonstrations have erupted in two hundred cities and towns. And worried Americans are contacting everyone with power, from multinational companies to politicians, to voice their concerns about the coming update—and especially the Respect function.

In the K Street offices of Varagon Inc., twenty stories above a sea of protesters in Franklin Square, John Vallinger is feeling shaken. Minutes ago, he received a threatening message from Ralf Alvare and suffered ten seconds of excruciating pain. When he fell to the floor and moaned, several staffers hurried into his office, fearing he was suffering a stroke. Since then, Vallinger has recovered his strength and revamped his strategy. He now sees that it's far too late for a connectome analysis. The potential value of the information, he understands, is dubious at best. It was more the scientist in him, or the voyeur, than the pragmatic businessman who came up with that idea. He'll shelve it. At this critical juncture, icy pragmatism must rule. If Suzy Claiborne is already "euthanized," he'll simply have Dahl dispose of the body.

Vallinger is more concerned about business. In the last hour, several more customers have canceled contracts, and he's hearing from senators and congressmen—the same ones who have been following his orders for decades—that they might call for investigative hearings and postpone the update.

Meantime, Vallinger has learned from security sources that Stella Kellogg is still circulating in Washington. Her signal was picked up on the Metro yesterday. Then she spent time this morning in the Woodley Park neighborhood before moving east, "at jogging speed," to the Red Line Metro stop at the zoo. Attempts to apprehend her "have so far been unsuccessful." Vallinger has urged his contacts to "interdict her sooner rather than later, dead or alive." Walking toward an emergency staff meeting, he adds that she's a "highly dangerous agent in the pay of foreigners who wish to bring us down."

His staff awaits him patiently. Entering the conference room, Vallinger lowers himself haltingly into the chair at the head of the long oak table. Glowering from one side to the other, he tells his employees that they have to "brave this storm just one more day." Once the nation's boosts are updated, the outrage will subside, he predicts.

His staffers nod. They exchange uneasy glances and trade messages across the table, but no one utters a word. Many of them, Vallinger knows, have to be wondering if the Respect function could possibly render them even more sheeplike than they already are. Vallinger misses Tyler Dahl, his only employee capable of independent thought—that is, if he doesn't include Smedley. Vallinger shudders at the thought of the porn entrepreneur who is now "at war" with him.

As his staffers message back and forth, comparing status notes on their clients and no doubt wondering about the future of the firm, Vallinger messages Dahl: "Losing clients, but just have to make it one more day." Then he adds, in a postscript: "What's the status of SC?"

He hears back immediately. "Hang in there. Some changes in status of SC."

Vallinger switches to voice and hears from Dahl that Suzy Claiborne somehow found out what was up and managed to take control of the Detention Center. She has locked the anesthesiologist and the guard outside, Dahl says. "I can hear them pounding on the kitchen door. They probably need to use the bathroom."

Vallinger is mystified by this news. "Why don't you just let them in?" he asks.

"She has me locked in the supply closet. And if I manage to get out, she has it rigged so that all this crap will fall on my head, including one of those antique clocks from the living room."

Vallinger leans back and sighs. "Get control of the situation," he orders. "If you come up short, I'm coming out there myself."

# SIXTY-ONE

The leading DM protesters in Washington get word in early afternoon to move their troops from Franklin Square down to the White House. This doesn't seem to make sense. The opposition should stay focused on Vallinger, who stands to make a fortune from the Respect function. This is business. The president is a bit player in the drama, if she's involved at all. But the DM organizers obediently round up a couple hundred of their grumbling forces and march them over to 16th Street.

As they pass McPherson Square, Bao-Zhi, still wearing his Yankees cap and dark glasses, bounds out of the Metro and joins them. When they reach the White House, the group resumes its chants. Shielded by protesters, Bao-Zhi reaches through the black iron fence and hides Stella's chip behind a boxwood shrub. He tosses some dirt on it and then jumps to his feet and joins the protesters. After a few minutes, he slips away in search of a place to sleep.

# SIXTY-TWO

Stella walks into the newsroom, looks out at a room full of café tables and potted palms, and sees her husband sitting alone. He is drinking a cup of coffee and reading a newspaper. He's thinner than he once was, with gray hair at his temples. The way his head is tilted, she can't see the bottom half of his face. But as he turns the page of the newspaper, she sees his hands and remembers how small they were.

Francisco looks up. He sees her and smiles as he gets to his feet.

Stella dreamed of this moment for decades, time and again through all of those years that she thought he was dead. And she has been anticipating this meeting, nervously, ever since she figured out that Francisco was Don Paquito, and that she would be seeing him in Juárez. For the last day, she has been awash in emotions. Being without her chip has added to the intensity since the wet brain, unlike the boost, wraps feelings into every thought or calculation.

Yet now that the moment has come and Francisco is limping toward her, Stella feels nothing. Why is he limping? she wonders. And why do I feel so blasé?

Francisco, an inch shorter, reaches with his small hands and places them on her cheeks. He looks into her eyes and tells her that she is still beautiful and that he's sorry.

All Stella can think is that he has practiced this line. Emotionally, she is not engaged. She looks into his eyes and inspects them not as windows into a soul, but as shiny tools. She studies the yellow specks in the brown of his irises. At the bottom of each one she sees the reflection of her own white blouse. The image reminds her of an art history class she took with Francisco. Dutch painters in the fifteenth century, she recalls, used to capture such details. She remembers the name Jan van Eyck.

Francisco has stopped talking. He pulls back from her face and waits for her to say something. In her anticipation of this moment, Stella realizes, she failed to prepare any lines of her own. Finally, feeling the pressure to deliver a line, she says, "Why didn't you tell me you weren't dead?"

Francisco starts to answer. He repeats that he's sorry and starts talking about the chip wars and Paraguay. Stella can tell, even half listening, that he has practiced these lines, too. She doesn't want to hear them. Maybe later, but not now.

She's aware that people are looking at them. Ralf and Simon are to her left. Two other men are on the other side, one of them enormous with something dreadfully wrong with his nose. Francisco keeps talking, something about people he met in Bolivia.

She interrupts him: "What can you do to save Suzy?"

# SIXTY-THREE

**3/15/72 7:02 p.m. Eastern Standard Time**

Rush hour is winding down in Washington and evening has fallen. For the last hour, the demonstrators in Franklin Square have blocked traffic on K Street for a "vigil." They're holding candles and chanting. John Vallinger cannot hear them through his window, which is a small relief. He sees that some of the people blocked in traffic are stepping out of their cars—abandoning them—to join the protest.

He returns to his desk and continues to read *Tribune* articles in his boost. He's interrupted by a message from a security source. Stella Kellogg was tracked riding on the Metro from the zoo to Metro Center, he learns, and from there to McPherson Square, where she apparently joined a parade of demonstrators to the White House. "She's there now?" Vallinger asks.

"Her signal has vanished. But that tends to happen around the White House."

"So then she's there. Go arrest her."

"We went. Couldn't find her."

Vallinger feels enraged. This woman's son has delivered a dose of the greatest pain he has ever suffered, and is threatening to turn the rest of his life into a living hell. Her husband is running a newspaper whose sole aim, it appears, is to destroy him. The woman who appears to be orchestrating this all stands five blocks away—and they can't find her.

"Have you considered that she may be engaged in a plot against the president?" Vallinger asks.

"Well, no . . ."

"I would call it a reasonable assumption," the lobbyist says. "If she is spotted again, I would urge that she be dealt with preemptively."

"Understood," his source says.

Vallinger returns to his reading. Even though he gets *The Tribune* every day, he must have missed a few of these stories. One of them describes his "brilliant" strategy of planting the leak about the open surveillance gate to divert the attention of his enemies, including the DM, from the much more controversial Respect function in the update. A source close to Vallinger quotes him describing the maneuver as a "head fake." The article explains the obscure basketball term "from early in the century" and how it relates to the case.

Vallinger stops and rereads the paragraph. He remembers discussing the head fake, but with whom? He goes into his boost and surfs back to Thursday. Even before watching the scene, he remembers it. Then he sees the video. Tyler Dahl stands before him as Vallinger describes—a bit laboriously, in retrospect—a basket-ball term from his childhood. He hears his own proud voice: "They took the story we wanted them to run with, and not the one we wanted to hide." The image of Dahl stands before him, nodding.

Vallinger remembers the rest of the conversation. That was when he told Dahl, in absolute confidence, about the Respect function. Within minutes, he thinks, the young aide who appeared so much more intelligent than the others, and infinitely more trustworthy than Smedley, was off blabbing to a reporter at *The Tribune*.

Dahl is the leak. This means that Stella Kellogg, whose death he has just ordered, may be innocent—or at least not as guilty as he thought. Vallinger briefly considers messaging his security source and calling off the kill order. But that would make him look weak and inde-cisive, which is the last thing he can afford at this juncture.

Plus, he's busy. He has to figure out how to deal with the mole currently locked in the bedroom of his deten-tion facility. For a half hour, Vallinger sits at his desk and thinks. Then he comes up with an idea. At the end of a long and harrowing day, John Vallinger breaks into a smile.

# SIXTY-FOUR

It isn't until the cocktail hour, when Stella sips her first margarita in decades and tries out her Spanish, that she feels herself warming ever so slightly to Francisco. They're standing in the *playa*, next to the tallest palm, and Stella recalls, in her halting and rusty Spanish, that afternoon at Middlebury, when the professors discussed the startling news about the "capped" workers in China.

"Do you remember what you said?" she asks him.

"It was something about a dictatorship," he says.

"Yes, but you said that those of us without chips were going to be Neanderthals, while everyone else became Cro-Magnon," she says. "Do you still believe that?"

"No," he says. "I had stopped believing that even before we moved to Washington. I became convinced that people were confusing tools with intelligence. They still do."

"That's a relief," Stella says, "because we're Neanderthals now, you and I."

Francisco smiles and offers her another drink.

"This one will do," she says with a cool smile. She heads off to talk to Ellen.

Later, at dinner, Stella finds herself sitting between Simon and an enormous man named Oscar Espinoza, a colleague of Smedley's. He seems very pleasant and tells her that he was once a boxer—a conclusion anyone could easily have drawn, Stella thinks, from one look at his face. Her conversation with him draws to a close as the food arrives.

Stella feels uneasy talking to Simon, who worked with his father for more than three years without telling her that Francisco was alive. They'll discuss that later, she decides, and instead asks him where he lives in El Paso.

"A neighborhood called Sunset Heights," he says. "A historic district. If you climb up on the roof here, you can actually see it. It's less than a mile away." He pauses and unwraps the corn husk from a tamale. "Listen, Mom," he says, turning to her. "I'm sorry I didn't tell you about Papa. I should have."

"We weren't talking much about anything, you and I," she says. "Or any of us, for that matter."

"We will be now."

A voice interrupts them, saying, "Don Paquito!" It's Smedley, still wearing his yellow golf shirt. "Don Paquito," he repeats, "I think we should revisit the idea of printing your entire newspaper on one of my sites, every day."

"I told you I'd think about it," Francisco says.

"The time is now," Smedley says. "The update is tomorrow night. Just the release of the articles on the Artemis site . . ." He stops, evidently embarrassed by his reference to his sex site. He looks at Ellen and says, "Excuse me."

Then he continues, "Just the articles on that one site have stirred up the whole country. People are in the streets for the first time in decades. As one publisher to another, you've got to get the news out. If you publish the paper tonight in the boost, you'll have 200 million readers tomorrow. It could change history."

Francisco shakes his head. "How many of those people will pay?"

"Ask for donations and you'll probably get a mint."

"Sacrifice my whole business model, the economics of this entire city, for the promise of donations?" Francisco says. "I don't think that's wise."

No one says anything. The only noises are the clinking of silverware and the sounds of chewing and swallowing, which are especially pronounced, Stella notices, to her right.

Then Ellen speaks up. She recently heard, she says, about the day when students at Middlebury learned about the Chinese experiments with enhanced workers in Shanghai. "Of all the students," she says, turning to Francisco, "you were the only one who stood up against it. Isn't that right?"

"There might have been somebody else," Francisco mumbles.

"And you warned about dictators using chips to control people, right?"

"I think my argument was essentially Darwinian," Francisco says. "But I probably made a point about dictators. That was on my mind back then."

"Right. So now what you predicted has come true. You've helped me to see this. And tomorrow they're going to turn us into something like slaves . . ." Ellen's voice starts to break, and she takes a sip of her margarita. It makes her cough. She stops, dabs at her eyes with her handkerchief and takes a sip of ice water, and then starts again. "Look," she says, changing her tack, "we all screw up. We cheat, we lie, we do all kinds of things we're ashamed of. And then sometimes, if we're lucky, we have a chance to do something good, to make up for things, or at least to try to." She looks up the table at Francisco. "You have a chance to give the world something so . . . wonderful. . . ." She breaks into tears again, as Ralf puts his arm around her shoulders and kisses the top of her head.

"All right, all right," Francisco says. He looks at Smedley. "She's right. Go ahead with it."

# SIXTY-FIVE

A technician at the Department of Health and Human Services in Washington presses a button to deliver the software update twenty-four hours ahead of schedule. Issued by special request, it goes to a single citizen identified only by a hash tag.

Sleeping on the floor of a supply closet in Virginia, his head propped on a box of detergent and a spare mop head, Tyler Dahl dreams he is riding in a fast car. Something flashes in his boost and the car screeches to a halt, runs backward, and then takes off again. Dahl rolls over, wraps his arms around the mop head, and keeps dreaming.

The technician in Washington receives a message: "Update successful?"

He checks. For this he calls up Tyler Dahl's boost on the large screen and enters through the new surveillance gate, 318 Blue. Stretching before him are seemingly endless aisles of memories and images. It looks like an entire life. The calculating division rises like a factory to his left.

"Update appears successful," he replies.

"And the Respect function?"

"Testing will be possible only when the subject is awake."

# SIXTY-SIX

**3/16/72 6:02 a.m. Eastern Standard Time**

Bao-Zhi strolls up Pennsylvania Avenue at dawn, still wearing his Yankees cap and sunglasses. He's surprised to find a handful of protesters still carrying on their vigil. One is hunched over a poster stretched out on the sidewalk, writing: "March 16: The last day of American freedom." Bao-Zhi walks past them and stops by the black iron fence to tie his sneaker. He looks through it, past the boxwood shrub, and sees a glint of plastic.

Still there, he thinks. He'll be back later, when there's a larger crowd to blend into. He makes his way six blocks east, to Chinatown, where he knows a place that makes a tasty breakfast soup for a small and secretive wild clientele.

# SIXTY-SEVEN

**3/16/72 6:14 a.m. Eastern Standard Time**

John Vallinger knows he should focus all of his energy on the job at hand: beating back growing opposition to the software update. It's the defining event of his career. Pushing it through today will require smart and ceaseless diplomacy with his clients, politicians, and his national security contacts, maybe even the public. He has no time to waste.

And yet, as the first morning light streams through his window of his lonely house in Cleveland Park, Vallinger sits in an armchair by his bed working intently on an experiment. It involves testing the Respect function in Tyler Dahl's newly updated boost. For this, he needs to compose an effective message. In a sense, he thinks, the message is an algorithm—a set of commands. And yet the commands will not be processed by a machine, but by a discerning and intelligent person. Even with the Respect update in his boost, Dahl is not likely to follow orders that sound insane, or even unreasonable. Vallinger cannot tell him to lop off Suzy Claiborne's head or to stab her in the heart with a kitchen knife. If Vallinger understands the software well—and he has sat through endless discussions about it, in English and Chinese—people with this program will still have their wits about them. But they'll find themselves inclined to heed authorities, simply because it feels better. (Vallinger, prudently, has opted to skip the update himself.)

So he must compose a reasonable note that nonetheless will lead Dahl to commit a crime, one serious enough to land him in deep trouble. This will be John Vallinger's revenge on a once trusted aide who has betrayed him. In a day of unrelenting work, this will be his one bit of fun.

He writes: "Subdue Suzy Claiborne when she brings you breakfast. Tie her up and punish her until she details the leadership structure of the DM. I expect you to have it by ten a.m. Don't play soft. No holds barred. Leave the guard and doctor outside. They'll only get in the way. Good luck. Your Boss."

Vallinger reads it through twice, admiring the restraint and the balanced tone. It's worth a shot, he thinks. He sends it to Tyler Dahl's updated boost. Then he rises to get dressed for what promises to be a long day.

# SIXTY-EIGHT

Tyler Dahl wakes up after a dream-filled sleep on the floor of the supply closet with his arm around a mop head. He has a crick in his neck. As he stands up and rubs it, he sees a new message from Vallinger. He reads it. The message reads like an order Dr. Frankenstein would give to his hunchbacked assistant, Igor. Better to ignore it, Dahl thinks, and he wonders for the first time if the pressure is unhinging his boss. Dahl is convinced that Suzy Claiborne knows almost nothing about the senior leadership of the DM. Beating her won't do any good. Yet the idea behind the first part of the order—subduing her when she brings breakfast—makes sense.

He calls out from the closet. "Suzy, I'm starving! Can you bring some breakfast? I promise I won't try anything."

Suzy hears him and pays no attention. She cleans her teeth by putting toothpaste on a finger and rubbing them. Then she works out for forty-five minutes on a rowing machine in the exercise room, lifts weights for a half hour, and sits in the sauna. After showering, she gets dressed and sends a message to Ralf: "I have Dahl locked up and am alone in the house. Don't know what to do. Ideas?" She sends it, but receives no confirmation of delivery.

Hungry for breakfast, she goes downstairs, where Dahl's pleas are louder and more bothersome. "Pleeeeese Suzy," he yells, pounding on the door. "Just something to eat."

"Quiet," she yells. She looks outside. The guard and the doctor are nowhere to be seen, and a red car that was parked in the driveway is gone. She figures that they went home, or maybe to a hotel.

"Pleeese Suzy!"

He won't shut up. Suzy grabs a box of protein and walks toward the closet. She'll open the door six inches, she figures, and jam it in. But when she opens the door, it hits a piece of twine which pulls out the leg from a shelf she mounted yesterday. The booby trap releases a cascade of canned food and knick-knacks onto her. An antique Swiss cuckoo clock, made of brass and dark wood, strikes the side of her head. She crumples to the ground, bleeding.

Tyler Dahl steps out of the closet feeling a sense of great satisfaction. "She's subdued," he thinks. "I'm following his orders without even doing anything."

Suzy lies unconscious on the living-room floor. Dahl finds a towel and presses it to her wound. It doesn't seem to be bleeding much. In the same supply closet he slept in, he finds a ball of twine and scissors. He puts his arms under Suzy and tries to lift her onto a coffee table. She's big—taller than he is, and built like an Amazon. He remembers her tossing him around like a plaything in bed. He can barely budge her body. So he binds her wrists and ties them to the leg of a heavy couch. He does the same to her ankles and hitches them to the stairway banister.

When she comes to, he figures, he'll interrogate her. Maybe she knows more than he thinks. Dahl walks into the kitchen for breakfast. He's smiling. And feels better about himself than he has in months. Could it have something to do with last night's dreams?

When he returns to the stairway landing, Dahl sees that Suzy has managed to roll over to her right side. Her bound arms are twisted, which makes her look even more like a prisoner, and more lovely. He's tempted to kiss her, despite the beating she gave him yesterday and the miserable night she subjected him to in the closet. He kneels down and bends his face to hers. But instead of kissing her, he cuffs her cheek with his fist. He does it again, this time a little harder.

She groans.

Funny, Dahl thinks. He has never punched anyone in his life. Yet it seems to come as naturally as breathing. He gives her another punch, this time near the eye. It's about the same place she punched him yesterday. Remembering that, he hits her again.

She's awake now, and tries to sit up. But the bindings hold her down. Her eyes flash at him. "Getting your kicks, Tyler?"

He doesn't say anything, but punches her again. Then he reaches down to her neck and tries to grab her wind pipe between his thumb and forefinger. With a frantic movement of her head, she slips out of his grasp.

She's panting now, her head back on the floor.

"You know," Dahl says, "this is the first time I've ever hit anyone. I actually object to violence."

"Then why are you doing this?" Suzy asks in a quiet voice.

"I don't know. It just feels like the right thing to do." He pauses. "I'd like to ask you a few questions. Okay?"

She doesn't answer and he slaps her face. Then he does it again.

Suzy writhes, pulling at the bindings on her wrists and ankles. They're tight. She sends a message to Ralf, telling him that Tyler Dahl has her tied on the floor and is beating her. The message doesn't go through. "What do you want to know?" she asks Dahl. Maybe talking with him will buy some time.

## SIXTY-NINE

**3/16/72 8:32 a.m. Mountain Standard Time**

Ralf, Simon, and Stella drive up in Ellen's Sheng-li to the garbage-strewn lot. They're fifteen minutes late for their session. Originally they planned to cross again through the downtown fence. But Simon couldn't arrange the security for it, and they had to ride fifteen miles west in Francisco's gas-chugging Buick, crawl through the Santa Teresa tunnel, and endure the rush hour traffic back to El Paso on I-10.

The software update is scheduled for midnight on the East Coast, only thirteen and a half hours from now. Ralf will have only forty-five minutes at the machine to derail it.

He loads his chip onto the tray and inserts it, and the contents of his boost pop up on the screen. He sees two new messages from Suzy. With his mother and brother looking over his shoulder, he opens and reads them.

They exchange glances but say nothing as Ralf responds. "I'm here. Is he torturing you?"

She responds right away. "I think he's doing it for fun."

Ralf asks her if he can ride shotgun in her boost, and she gives him the go-ahead. Ralf's hands flit across the large screen, and a moment later the three of them are looking at a bright living room furnished like a hotel. The floor is strewn with cans of food and what look like pieces of a clock. As Suzy turns her head they see a young man with short blond hair and piercing blue eyes staring down at her. He's smiling. Then a fist comes toward them and the image jolts to the right and shakes for a second or two. Then it returns to Dahl, who looks content.

"Holy God," Stella says.

"Ask him why he's doing this," Ralf says.

"Why are you doing this, Tyler?" she says.

"I'm just asking you some questions," he says.

"But why are you hitting me?"

"I told you," he said. "It feels like the right thing to do. The right approach."

"Ask him if he got orders this morning from his boss," Ralf says.

Suzy relays the question.

"Uh-huh," he says. "He wants me to interrogate you." He hits her on the shoulder, causing the image in El Paso to shake.

"That prick," Ralf mutters.

He touches the screen and delivers a message to John Vallinger. "Did you tell your man to torture Suzy?"

Vallinger is standing at his window, looking at the demonstration below when the message arrives. A handful of congressmen have joined the protesters' ranks. He can see one who has benefited from Vallinger's largess for decades. He's shaking his fist toward Vallinger's window. And there are reports that senators are pushing for emergency hearings. But to Vallinger's relief, analysts doubt they can get them started before the end of the week.

He reads the message from Alvare, and his heart skips a beat. It's working—better than he could have imagined. Dahl interpreted his order for a "rough" interrogation just the way he hoped. Could the software be sophisticated enough to interpret the goals of the authority figure, and to look past the vague wording of a command? Vallinger wonders about that.

It's only then that he remembers Alvare's threat from yesterday. The genius hacked and now controls the headache code. His shoulders sag. How stupid to have forgotten. This leads him to wonder if he might be losing his edge. Or maybe he's simply overworked. In any case, he now regrets his early-morning experiment with the new technology. He cannot afford complications today.

"I know nothing about it," he answers.

The response pops up immediately. "Liar."

A moment later, John Vallinger collapses to the floor with a crippling headache. Aides rush into his office and prop him back onto his chair.

# SEVENTY

Ralf has only twenty-three minutes left on the machine. The screen is still showing what Suzy sees. For now, it's an empty room. The picture rises and falls gently with her breath. Tyler Dahl has apparently stepped away.

Ralf tells Simon and Stella that he's given Vallinger a nasty headache. "What do I do now?" he asks.

"Tell him to call off Suzy's torture," Stella says.

"Okay, Mom. But we've only got twenty-two minutes to get Vallinger to cancel the update. We have to prioritize here."

"You will not arrange your priorities to abandon Suzy," Stella says.

"Okay, okay," Ralf says. "But I'm going to break into this guy's head." His fingers fly over the screen. Nothing changes. Ralf stops, closes his eyes, and concentrates. Then he puts his fingers back to work. The scene on the screen changes. It shows the view out a window in

Washington. Teeming protesters are gathered below. For as far as Vallinger and his copilots can see, from east to west, K Street is packed with angry people.

"Get a load of that!" Simon says.

Stella's not impressed. "What about Suzy?" she asks.

"Right," Ralf says. He issues more commands, and the screen divides into two windows, one showing Vallinger's point of view, the other Suzy's.

Ralf, his voice now active inside Vallinger's boost, tells the lobbyist that he has twenty minutes to postpone the update. "Or you'll have this headache for the rest of your days."

"Not going to happen," Vallinger says. He turns around. On the left side of the screen, Ralf, Stella, and Simon watch as he moves. The image seems to lurch through his office, out into the lobby where concerned employees ask him if he's okay. He ignores them and continues out the door. His finger presses the Down button on the elevator.

"He's not paying any attention to you," Simon says.

Stella, her eyes fixed on the right side of the screen, grabs Simon's hand. "That guy's coming back into Suzy's room," she says. The three of them look to the right. Tyler Dahl is looming above her, still smiling. A glint of metal shines in the corner of the screen. It looks like he's holding scissors. Suzy looks away from him and closes her eyes. That side of the screen goes dark.

On the other side, Vallinger is coming into a parking garage. Standing by the wall of the garage is a man wearing dark glasses and a blue baseball cap.

"I could swear that's Bao-Zhi," Stella says.

"The guy who was in your third floor, with the drums?" Simon says.

"Uh-huh."

Vallinger looks away from Bao-Zhi and makes his way toward an immense black Houyi. He opens the door and enters. In pained and halting words he gives the car an address in Alexandria. The car moves forward toward the exit.

"He's going to the clinic I went to," Stella says. She touches Ralf's shoulder. "The one we both went to. He's getting his boost taken out."

Suzy's eyes open and the picture appears on the screen. The scissors are out of her vision, but the image swings back and forth as she writhes. "Suzy," Ralf says. "Listen to me. Tell him that we are recording absolutely everything he is doing. He's committing a crime, and we're watching."

Suzy tells Tyler Dahl that he's being watched. He disappears from the room and comes back with a big roll of gray masking tape. They hear a ripping noise, and then the screen goes black. They hear Suzy scream.

John Vallinger's Houyi inches through the sea of protesters on K Street. Angry faces press up against the glass, yelling at him. People holding signs pound on the windows with their fists. Two young men climb onto the hood of the car and beat against the windshield. But he continues forward and finally breaks free. The car turns left on 14th Street. As Vallinger puts his aching head in his hands, the image on the screen shows only blurred fingers.

"We only have eleven minutes," Simon says.

Ralf touches the screen to talk to Vallinger. "You don't have to get your boost taken out," he says. "Just tell them to postpone the update by two weeks and get your man to stop torturing."

"You, young man," Vallinger says, "can go to hell."

Another voice speaks into Vallinger's boost. "We've spotted the target."

"Good," he says. "Proceed with interdiction. Keep the messages vague," he adds. "We have an interested party riding shotgun here."

"Roger."

"Who are you after?" Ralf asks.

"Someone you might know very well," Vallinger says. "Maybe you might consider taking off the headache."

The voice returns. "Target heading south on 14th Street."

"Northwest?" Vallinger says. "Which cross street?"

"Pennsylvania."

"She must be following me!" Vallinger turns around in his seat and looks out his back window. He sees a stream of protesters heading west, toward the White House. He looks at the vehicles following him.

"We can't take action this close to the White House," his source says.

"Okay," Vallinger says. "As soon as you can." His car heads south toward the Mall. Again, he twists to look out the back window. "What kind of vehicle is she in?" he asks. "I can probably see her."

"It looks . . ."

His Houyi crosses the Mall and approaches the Tidal Basin on the right.

Vallinger sits back in his seat and addresses Ralf. "Alvare. You tuned in at just the right time. It looks like you might get to see through my eyes as your mother gets blown to smithereens. You might take a moment to tell her good-bye."

Simon, fearing that Vallinger has somehow rigged Stella to explode, hugs his mother fiercely. He runs his hand up and down her back, searching for wires. But Ralf, who has a clearer idea of what's happening, makes a calming gesture with his hands and points to the screen.

"Okay. We have clearance now. It's a Houyi, sir. A big black one."

"What?" Vallinger says. Than he starts to yell, "No, no!" But his communication is cut short when a missile strikes his car, pulverizing the Houyi, the lobbyist inside it, and a chip, no bigger than a bee's wing, that operated for twenty-nine years inside Stella Kellogg's head.

The image on the left side of the screen goes black.

Suzy screams, as if responding to the missile strike that obliterated John Vallinger. Ralf expands her vision to fill the screen. She can now see through a gap in the taped blindfold, enough to show a bit of her arm. It's covered with blood.

"Four minutes left," Simon says.

"Suzy," Ralf tells her. "Tell him that John Vallinger is dead. I ordered him killed. I have replaced Vallinger. His employees now report to me."

Suzy, whimpering, says, "What?"

"Tell him John Vallinger is dead. If he opens his boost to me, I can show him the video."

"Vallinger's dead," Suzy says to Dahl. He's standing above her with the scissors in his right hand. One of the blades is covered with blood.

"Huh?"

"He's dead," Suzy says. "My friend Ralf had him killed."

"Fat chance."

"Want to see the video?"

Two minutes later, an apologetic Tyler Dahl is unbinding Suzy Claiborne, and pressing a warm towel on her wounded elbow. "I feel terrible about this, but it feels so great to be doing the right thing now," he says.

Suzy startles him by reaching up with her powerful arms and grabbing him at the level of his ribs. She hoists him above her. Shaking him angrily, she says, "I'm so tired of hearing about your stupid feelings." Then she rolls sideways, drops Tyler Dahl on the floor, and climbs to her feet.

The time on the machine in El Paso runs out. Its screen goes dark and Ralf's boost pops out.

# EPILOGUE

**3/16/72 12:13 p.m. Juárez Standard Time**

When Stella, Simon, and Ralf finally make it through the Santa Teresa tunnel and back to headquarters, a celebration erupts. Francisco pops open a magnum of French champagne and rushes through the crowded *playa*, filling glasses for Smedley and Espinoza, Ellen and his two sons. Stella, covered with dirt from her tunnel crawl, cannot find a champagne glass and holds out a beer mug instead. "Fill it about halfway," she says to Francisco, giving him a hint of a smile.

Reporters rush in from the newsroom with paper coffee cups. Francisco dispenses a few drops into each, but tells them that they have huge stories to report and write. What's more, now that they're writing for the boost, they no longer have a full day to develop their articles. "I want them out there by this afternoon," he tells them in Spanish. Groans fill the newsroom.

The champagne quickly runs dry, and the party moves

down the street to the Kentucky Club. A few of the reporters insist on tagging along. They'll need to call Chui on the phone there, they say, to get the latest from the boost-sphere. Francisco is in no mood to say no.

Upon arriving at the Kentucky Club, Francisco promptly declares an open bar. Within minutes, much of the crowd on Avenida Juárez—the wild Swedes and Africans and Mexican candy vendors—has moved inside, hoisting beers and margaritas.

Oscar Espinoza, holding a Bohemia beer in each hand, sidles up to Francisco and tells him he wants to relocate to Juárez. "Is there a job for someone like me at the newspaper?" he asks.

Francisco asks if he has any writing or editing experience.

Espinoza says his strengths would be more in the security arena, or perhaps distribution—"assuming I could get my KIFF over here."

Ellen and Ralf make their way past the bar and into one of the leather-upholstered booths near the dart board. After they sit down, Ralf reaches across the table and holds Ellen's hand. "I missed you," he says.

Ellen smiles. "You didn't miss me for a minute while you were working at that machine, with your boost running."

"True," he admits, "but that was only forty-seven minutes of the time. I missed you crawling through the tunnel, and riding down I-10 in our Sheng-li, which by the way is filthier than you can imagine."

He pauses for a moment to deliver his prepared remarks. "Do you know how wonderful you were last night at dinner, speaking up to my father the way you did?" He looks directly into her eyes, which doesn't come naturally to him. "The beauty isn't just your face. It's inside of you," he says. "That's where you're the most beautiful."

Tears well in Ellen's eyes, but before she can say anything, George Smedley slides onto the bench next to her and places a sloshing pitcher of margaritas on the table. "I'm telling Don Paquito over there," he says, pointing with a wavering hand in the direction of the bar, "how he needs to shift this whole operation from subscriptions to advertising." Smedley adds that he has offered to run the digital side of the business from New York or Washington. "But he wants me to move down here."

"Three hundred and ten sunny days a year," Ellen says. "You'd probably have to team up with Simon," she adds with a mischievous smile.

"Well, as I say," Smedley says, "I might be able to do it from New York or Washington."

Francisco, fresh from a talk with one his reporters, approaches the table. He squeezes in next to Ralf and delivers the latest news. Some fifteen minutes after Vallinger's car blew up, Vienna police descended on the interrogation center. Like millions of others, they'd read the new virtual edition of *The Tribune*. Its lead story—that Vallinger's people were holding a woman captive and threatening to euthanize her—led them to the black cube at the end of the cul-de-sac. "Suzy refused to press charges," he says with a puzzled shrug. He reaches for Smedley's pitcher and fills everyone's glasses, including his own. "Now that *pendejo* who was cutting and punching her is going to be running Varagon."

"Tyler Dahl?" Smedley asks.

"The board voted on it a half hour after the explosion. Virtual meeting, I guess. They also asked the government to postpone the chip update for a month. I imagine they're going to have hearings about it in Congress."

"We'll need to send a reporter there, Don Paquito," Smedley says, sounding already like one of the team. "Has to be someone with a boost. You can't cover Washington without one."

Francisco nods. "If we're going to work together," he says to Smedley, "you're going to have to figure out something else to call me." He tells them that he's planning to run a big series of articles on the real Ciudad Juárez. "We're going to strip the myths from the place, and that is going to put an end to this Don Paquito business."

Ralf excuses himself and moves toward the bar, where he sees Stella and Simon. Stella has the phone pressed up to one ear and is plugging the other with a finger. She's shouting to be heard above the din. "TELL HER THE KEY'S UNDER THE USUAL ROCK," she yells. "HE CAN PLAY HIS DRUM IN THE BEDROOM, BUT NO COOKING UP THERE. I DON'T WANT THE HOUSE TO BURN DOWN BEFORE I SELL IT." She hangs up, smiling, and says that Suzy and Bao-Zhi will be moving into the Montclair house. She tells them that she's thinking of moving, either to Washington or El Paso. "Silly to be alone," she says.

As Ellen joins the family huddle, Ralf brings up the ethical conundrum he's facing. He has video evidence in his boost that Tyler Dahl tortured Suzy Claiborne. "Do I show it to the police?"

Ellen and Stella both nod eagerly.

Simon, rubbing his chin with one hand, shakes his head. "I'm not so sure," he says. "Suzy herself has the very same evidence in her boost, but she decided not to press charges. So why should you?"

"Because the man's a torturer," Ellen says.

"That's the ethical dilemma I'm talking about," Ralf says. He explains that Tyler Dahl, the new president of Varagon, will have a crucial voice on future updates of the boost. He's also one of the few people in the country, perhaps the only one, to carry the new Respect function in his chip. "If I've established myself as an authority in his world, and he gets an addictive high from following my commands, don't you think he could be useful to us?"

"Just for the record," Stella says, "it is not okay in my book to take advantage of someone who's been given the miserable software that the rest of us are so eager to avoid."

"Not even if the orders we're giving him benefit 430 million people?" Ralf asks.

"What's the benefit?" Ellen asks. "Just avoiding the update?"

"No," Ralf says. "I want to develop a new app for the boost." He explains that people should have "all the great stuff" in the boost, but also the freedom to disconnect from the grid "and go wild. If the president of Varagon supports it, I bet I can make the change."

"What are you thinking of?" says Simon. "Some sort of boost-ejector button?"

"No," Ralf says. "Just a simple on-off switch. It could change the way things work. If Tyler Dahl had one," he adds as an example, "he could turn it off and deal rationally with at least two authority figures in his life."

"You and who else?" Stella asks.

"Judging from the manhandling she gave him when he untied her, I'd say Suzy," Ralf says. "And if Tyler Dahl's her puppet, he'll be a lot more useful to her running Varagon than sitting in jail."